MONEY GRIP 2
A Novel by Divine G

I0654500

Also by Divine G

Novels:

Baby Doll (Published by Q-Boro Books)

Money-Grip (Published by Divine G Entertainment)

Enigma of Love (Published by Divine G Entertainment)

The Canarsie Connection (Published by Divine G Entertainment)

No Other Love (Published by Divine G Entertainment)

TGONG (Published by Divine G Entertainment)

Time Jack (Published by Divine G Entertainment)

Short Stories:

Averted Hearts (appearing in *The Game*, published by Triple Crown Publications)

Stage Plays:

Peak-Zone (appearing in *Exiled Voices, Portals of Discovery*, published by New England College Press)

Films:

Sing Sing (Co-writer of the A24 movie *Sing Sing*)

Dedication

This novel is dedicated to the numerous family members, friends, and associates who were instrumental in helping me to get this sequel written, edited, and published. This list of supporters is so huge I am apprehensive about attempting to mention names. Based on past experience, if someone is left out, and feels he or she should have been mentioned, it creates bad feelings. This time, I'm playing it safe, and sending out a universal dedication to all those who played a part in the success of this novel. If you were there, by my side, had my back, then you are that person I am dedicating this novel to. Once again, thanks for all the love, support, patience and understanding.

CHAPTER # 1

"Gently take his arms," Doctor Kenneth Myers said to Willie as he held onto Rasheen's legs. "And help me lift him on this table."

The two heaved Rasheen upwards by his extremities and delicately laid his inert body on an Aluminum table covered with a sparkling white sheet that resembled a standard operating table.

With frantic urgency, Doctor Myers, with his face full of sandy brown hair, a pasty white complexion, and genuine scruffy like features, began to cut away Rasheen clothing in order to get a visual of the apparent bullet wound somewhere to the lower area of his mid-section. The blood was everywhere, he was unconscious, and it deeply alarmed Doctor Myers, because he had no extra blood on the premises, and Rasheen's unconsciousness was a signal that he was in very grave danger.

Meanwhile, Willie stood by, watching while in a very nervous state. The smell of antiseptics and alcohol increased his agitation, because he equated these scents with pain and suffering, and hospitals; a place he hated. His fingers and toes were crossed, and the urge to scream at the Doctor to hurry up and tell him if Rasheen was still alive was very compelling, but he could see that the Doctor was already moving at a pace that announced he was doing as best as he could. As though the Doctor was reading his mind, Willie saw Doctor Myers began hastily checking Rasheen's pulse.

"He's hanging on," Doctor Myers said out loud. "But his pulse is very weak one." He rushed over to the other side of the room to the oxygen tank and zipped it over towards Rasheen. Within seconds, the oxygen mask was clamped on Rasheen's face and the Doctor resumed his business. As he located the bullet wound, Doctor Myers told himself once again that he was going to stop gambling; if he could control that monkey on his back he could stop these illicit medical relationships. Thanks to his addiction to Sin City (Las

Vegas), he was forced to agree to this arrangement, which enabled him to kill two birds with one stone (make some extra cash and clear up a gambling debt owed to Cee-more, a black gangster with strong ties to a South-Central Los Angeles gang called the Rangers).

Willie nervously rocked his weight back and forth from one foot to the other, while his mixed ancestral features grew more terror-stricken with each tumbling moment; one second his Mexican attributes were pushing forth through his Irish traits, while his African American characteristics remained the most dominant of the others. The three ethic elements formed a conglomeration of a warped network of complete dread and despair and as the thought of not finding out where Rasheen stashed all that money took center stage in his mind, he couldn't help uttering a silent prayer.

Doctor Myers' gray eyes swiftly scrolled across Rasheen's naked body, searching for any additional bullet wounds as his latex gloved hands wiped away the blood from the wound at the base of his stomach; he saw this was going to be a very difficult procedure, because there was no doubt the bullet may have traveled and could now be anywhere in his body. Plus, with the loss of so much blood there were landmines at every turn of every corner.

Suddenly, a medium built black woman with golden brown skin and pretty huge eyes rushed into the makeshift operating room talking excitedly, "Kenneth, I thought we agreed to put a limit on how many of these—"

"Not now, Felicia, please."

As Felicia came up alongside of her husband, examining Rasheen's wound, Willie had his hand ready to pull the 9-mm. The way she rudely and abruptly barraged into the room almost unhinged him, and the first thing that came to his mind was danger; he had immediately relaxed when he saw it was Doctor Myers' wife. She was dressed in a sky-blue terry cloth robe, and matching night slippers. Willie instantly noticed the sister was carrying some serious junk in her trunk, and he admired the doctor's good taste in a woman with a big booming backside. He smiled inwardly because he could never fully understand racially mixed marriages, even though he was the epitome of a racially mixed individual. He guessed it was because he had an unquenchable appetite for black women with big bodacious butts.

"My, God, Kenneth," Felicia beamed after drawing her own medical conclusions after examining the apparent bullet injury, and this man's comatose state. She was a pediatric doctor and was currently going to medical school to become a surgical specialist, but bullet wounds were basic medical injuries that she'd long since been privy to. "Maybe, me—-why don't we get this man to a hospital, or maybe even call the police. He's been shot!"

Doctor Myers nervously glanced over at Willie. "Easy, Willie," He saw Willie was already becoming very nervous and was about to reach for his weapon. "We're not calling any police around here. I promised no hospitals, and no police." He gave Felicia a stare down that could've killed a herd of buffalo. "Felicia, I made a commitment to this client, and instead of you distracting me, why don't you help out. Put those years of schooling to work. I need your help here."

Felicia drew closer to Rasheen's lifeless body and began checking his pulse. "This man is going to need a very lot of blood," The thought of this man dying in her home terrified her immensely. "Without a transfusion he's gonna die, Kenneth."

Doctor Myers felt his anger about to boil up like a pressure cooker at full blast. His wife had this remarkable way of saying and doing things that irritated his last nerve. Couldn't she see these men were dangerous and a part of the underworld? Why can't she see that mentioning death could get this guy riled up? Jesus! "Please, Felicia, I need you to—"

"Kenneth, I thought we agreed to talk about these freelance, off-the-books medical procedures." She said rhetorically as she allowed her professionally trained eyes to fall upon Rasheen's unconscious grill. Damn, that face looked very familiar, she realized as she leaned in closer as Doctor Myers worked expertly on the gut wound. Oh, my God! She suddenly remembered that face. She saw it on a bulletin board in the Post Office, on the Federal Wanted List. She remembered this man was wanted for a series of very serious crimes. Oh, my god, this is crazy, she thought as she pulled away from the observation, and forced herself not to begin pacing.

Felicia casually cut her eyes at Willie and for the first time she truly noticed this man's presence. It took moments for her expert eyes to conclude that he was in possession of a gun. In that instance it was as if a floodgate of hundreds of varying scenarios was slammed wide open and swamped her mind; none of these mental images depicted anything good, and her survival instincts kicked in instinctually. Her heart pounded as she decided she had to do something, but she had to make certain it was done in a way that wouldn't put her and Doctor Myers in harm's way.

Felicia began adjusting the oxygen apparatus. "Looks like we're going to need some more sterilized utensils, local anesthesia and gauzes." She headed for the door. "I'll go get them. I'll be right back."

"Bring an IV kit as well," Doctor Myers said without looking up.

"Yeah, I gotcha." She said as she was about to step through the threshold and looked back and saw Willie staring her down with a vicious screw face. Felicia pulled away from the staring match and slid out of the room. When she was down the hall, she made a quick dip into the dining room, and headed straight for the phone.

CHAPTER # 2

A shot rang out from the other side of the huge dance hall like room within Killer Kato's mansion; the bullet struck the wall several feet from Aaron Wilson just as he and his men entered, which caused them to frantically scramble and take cover while returning fire. The bombardment of bullets gnawed and chipped away at the expensive picture covered walls, gold trimmed furniture, and other exotic objects.

"Move that way!" Aaron shouted to Raul, a Colombian man dressed in a sleek brown suit, while pointing towards a spiral staircase. He turned and shouted to his partner, a fellow FBI agent. "Norman, that way!" He pointed in the other direction as he watched him, Eugene Lee and several Colombians follow his instructions moving in a crouched, low stepping fashion. The current plan was to box in this lone gunner, with the intention of capturing him alive.

About an hour ago, Aaron and his hit team had stormed this Lakeside ten-million-dollar compound owned by Colin Gibson, AKA Killer Kato and had literally mowed down anyone in their path. After noticing Killer Kato wasn't amongst the dead, and realizing his team that were supposed to enter from the back of the mansion had not responded to his attempts to contact them through their communication devices, Aaron revised his instructions to his team as he said, "Don't kill 'em all! Capture at least one alive!" The thought of not knowing where to track Killer Kato, if he happened to slip pass his wrath, was unthinkable.

Aaron shouted over the sporadic gunfire, while crouching behind a wooden gold trimmed desk, "Cease fire! Stop shooting!" When the last of the gunfire ceased completely, Aaron shouted to the man hiding behind a statute of an American Eagle positioned in the middle of a pond sprinkling water from its wings down into an expensive marble pool, "Yo' check this out my man. You're out gunned, and you ain't got enough bullets to last much longer. I'll make you a deal. Come out with your hands up, we talk. You tell us what we wanna know, and you live to see another day. Believe me Homie, Killer Kato ain't worth dying for, no matter how much that chump is paying."

Harry O cowered behind the marble water statue, trembling with his two 9 millimeters ready to continue spitting flames. He couldn't believe these cats vamped the mansion, bodying shit like maniac storm troopers. Killer Kato had told them to be on point if anyone tried to step to them, but he didn't say it would be Aaron and his mob of dirty federal agents and that they had come here with full intentions of killing every god damn thing moving. On two occasions two of his homies, GQ and Farlow, tried to give up, and came out with their hands up, and Aaron straight out murdered them in cold blood. Now he was trying to play him!? Fuck that shit! In that moment he decided to go out with a bang. Harry O patted the back pockets of his baggy Guess jeans to make sure the two extra clips were still there, psyched himself into believing the extra 32 bullets would miraculously get him out of this jam, and sprung to his feet with both biscuits blazing, answering Aaron's proposition with the most effective universal language known to the human race.

Twenty minutes later, after a massive exchange of gunfire, Harry O fired his last shot, while clutching his side from the stray bullet that struck him. Moments later when he saw Aaron easing towards him with his weapon trained in standard law enforcement fashion, he continued pulling the trigger of his empty weapon, dreading what was coming next.

Aaron kicked the gun out of Harry O's hand as the others converged on the defeated lone gunner like army ants swarming towards an intruder that entered their nest.

Aaron looked at his watch and realized he'd wasted far too much time on this one individual. He yelled to Capone, a medium built Colombian man with chinky eyes and an evil looking scar on his right cheek, "Finish checking every inch of this place."

As Capone rushed towards the entrance with eight other Colombians following him, Aaron said to Norman Qing, Donald Mooney, and Eugene Lee (the remainder of what was left of his precious Rainbow squad). "I guess we can start searching for any cash on hands, jewels or anything else of value; ain't no sense is walking away from this empty handed."

"That sounds like music to my ears," Norman said and rushed towards the spiral staircase as Donald and Eugene followed in his footsteps.

Aaron stared down at the lone gunner and said with a devious smirk, "My man, you better hope like hell we find your boss, or you better be able to tell us how to find him. Cause shit is gonna get real ugly up in here, if you suffering from a case of the mums."

Aaron glanced at his watch again, realizing Bob was doing a dam good job at holding back the local police this long. He was expecting a call on his cell phone at least a half hour ago. Aaron pulled up a chair and rested his exhaustion-ridden body. As he waited for his men to return, while Harry O laid sighing in pain and looking scared, all the drama of this one crazy, vicious, and hectic night crashed down upon him. He lost three close friends, fellow federal agents, all because Killer Kato thought he could bite off more than he could chew and get away with it. But the true root of this entire goddamn calamity was that son of a bitch, Rasheen Smith! The noxious blend of various emotions engulfing his mind was making him tremble with something even he didn't understand. The hell he now had to go through to explain how this catastrophe happened brought on an icy cold wave of sheer horror that was already immobilizing him. He quickly shook loose of these crippling thoughts, since right now he had to handle the business at hand with an uninhibited mindset.

As Aaron shifted in his seat and stared down at Harry O, Raul returned and said breathing hard, "Capone said it looks like he got away, out the back. Our whole crew was cut down back there. We snatched up a woman, but she says she don't know nothin' cause she's the maid."

Aaron stared into the eyes of Harry O and spoke as he rose from the chair. "Here's the part where you can save yourself a whole—"

"I don't know where that motherfucker's at!" Harry O's venomous response was unadulterated and clear. "I ain't that nigga's baby-sitter! And for the record, motherfucker!" His voice became even more venomous. "I ain't no rat bastard, chief!"

Aaron allowed the wicked grin to slowly crawl across his face as he took aim and fired a shot into Harry O's left kneecap.

"AHHHHH . . . ."

Harry O's scream nearly shattered the glass ornaments dangling from the chandelier hanging overhead.

Aaron spoke in a genuinely sadistic manner. "Oh, don't start crying like a little bitch now! You's thug ass nigga ain't yah!" He fired another shot; this time the fiery hot lead ripped into Harry O's right ankle.

"AHHHHH . . . ."

Harry O screamed even louder this time.

Suddenly, Aaron's cell phone buzzed, and he reached for it as he moved swiftly towards the other side of the room away from the screaming man. He flipped open the wireless phone built to military specs and said, "What's up." It was Bob and he was speaking excitedly. As the conversation progressed so did Aaron's excitement. When Bob finished explaining the new developments, a smile had successfully wiggled its way onto Aaron's grill, and he was now anxious to get out of this mansion and to the place where Bob guaranteed him there would be a brilliant surprise.

Aaron disconnected the call and began barking off commands with military seriousness and precision. "Pack it up! We out! We outta here right now!" He said to Raul, the man in the brown suit. "Go tell everybody to meet out front, pronto!"

CHAPTER # 3

Willie sat scrutinizing Doctor Myers as he worked diligently on Rasheen while his wife handed him utensils when he asked for them. She was dressed in a light green, real doctor's outfit now, and that gorgeous ass of her was still the center of attraction. However, Willie's nervousness and anxiety was so revved up he had to take a seat and try to come up with a way to handle this situation. Something was definitely wrong with the Doctor's wife.

About five minutes ago, after she returned, Willie noticed she was acting very strangely. Every time she thought she heard the door or the phone she nearly jumped out of her skin as if she was waiting for something big to happen. Normally, he knew he had to keep his habitual paranoia in check, because he had an uncanny knack for always allowing his mind to make things much bigger than they really were, and on several occasions, he had embarrassed himself by overreacting hastily. But, this time, Willie was certain this was different. The way Felicia was acting it was clear that this bitch went out there and did something she wasn't supposed to do, and his survival instincts were telling him he had better hurry up and do something before it was too late.

Meanwhile, Felicia kept nervously cutting her eyes at Willie. He was making her very nervous; she was deeply terrified by the way he angrily snarled at her. After she wiped up the blood that sprinkled on the table containing the surgical tools, she glanced at her watch for the hundredth time, wondering what the hell was taking so long! She hated when people dragged their damn feet at times like this, and it completely infuriated her because she had made it very clear that this was a life and death situation. She had literally drilled the fact that this was an emergency, so that it was clearly understood that swift action was absolutely warranted.

Doctor Myers looked up, saw his wife's worried facial expression and wondered what she was up to? Then, he refocused his attention back to the surgical wound. He was grateful he was able to find the bullet and had to do a limited amount of cutting in order to remove it. By the way the bullet entered it appeared that it had nipped the bulletproof vest, which considerably slowed down the bullet's trajectory upon entry. This was just a theory, of course, but it was the only one he could think of to explain how the bullet managed to get tangled up in Rasheen's large intestines and stopped in this section of his body, instead traveling about while ricocheting off bones. Indeed, he saw Rasheen was very lucky, and now if he could convince Felicia into talking Regina into smuggling some blood from the hospital, he would be even luckier. He'd been constructing imaginary scenarios of what he could say to convince Felicia to assist with this endeavor, but each time he would scratch out the newly conceived approach and construct another interior speech. Looking at Rasheen's sluggish heartbeat, and therefore his gradually weakening blood pressure, it was evident that this speech regarding the retrieval of transfusion blood could no longer be put off.

Just as Doctor Myers was about to activate a dialogue with his wife, Willie went completely ballistics.

"I want y'all to put Rasheen's cloths on!" Willie shouted while brandishing his 9-mm. "Whatever you up to Mrs. Myers that shit ain't going down!"

Felicia stammered, "W—what—what are you—"

"You heard what I said!" Willie continued shouting.

Doctor Myers was sincerely galvanized with shock as his eyes grew wide and crazy looking; he held up his trembling hands and spoke with a soft, shaky voice. "W—Willie please p—put that g—gun away."

"I said put his clothes on! We gettin' the fuck out of here—"

There was a frantic knock on the front door, which nearly spun the room into total chaos as Willie recoiled, and the reaction became contagious as Doctor Myers and Felicia embraced each other in terror.

* *** *

Aaron Wilson saw the Lakeside police vehicles scattered about the highway as he sat in the passenger seat of the slowly approaching four-door Ford Escort. Norman Qing was behind the wheel navigating the vehicle towards the apparent murder scene, and Eugene and Donald were in a blue Malibu trailing up the rear. Their Colombian assistants were instructed to remain at the mansion and to finish retrieving all the valuables, and once finished to meet them at the rendezvous location.

When the Escort came to a stop next to the Lakeside patrol vehicle flanking a strip of yellow crime scene tape, Aaron eased out the car, hoping Bob had his facts right. Norman walked along side of him while Eugene and Donald remained in the Malibu. Aaron and Norman eased under the waist high yellow tape and approached a white policeman who had three other uniformed officers buzzing around him like he was the man in charge. Despite the fact it was the crack of dawn and all four of these federal agents had been up all night long, engaged in a mission that was military in nature in view of the fact they had fired among them well over 2 thousand rounds of ammunition, they still looked sharp, clean, focused and ready for action.

Aaron's eyes were pulled to the three bodies lying sprawled out with white sheets covering them and long streams of blood that formulated into coagulated pools of partially dried liquid. He looked further to his right and saw the two county homicide detectives looking down at a group of expended bullet casings, who were dressed in the same fashion as him and his fellow FBI agents. Aaron pulled his badge as he approached the boss man in uniform, since he was the closest, and displayed his badge while announcing. "FBI. I'm special agent Wilson. This is special agent, Qing."

"I'm Sgt. Kaplan," He looked the two up and down with a mixture of disdain and perplexity. "And what can I do for you G-men?"

Aaron smiled; he liked to be identified as a G-man, like Eliot Ness. "We have reason to believe the subject of a federal investigation may be one of these individuals within your crime scene."

"Yeah, the infamous Killer Kato has apparently been put to rest," Sgt Kaplan gestured towards the body furthest from the shoulder of the highway. "If you wanna see for yourself, you can be my guest." As he watched Aaron and Norman conduct their identification, he continued speaking. "With him all in the newspapers and on TV, with all that gangster rap madness, we ain't surprised you G-men been keeping an eye on this here fella. But I must say it was unfortunate Ms. Crystal Walker had to join him," He gestured to the body a few feet from Killer Kato's. "And Lameek Smith was another surprise . . . . "

Aaron stared at Killer Kato's virtually missing face as the Sergeant continued proffering his unsolicited views; he then scanned the numerous body shots. If it weren't for the shape and contorts of his forehead, and body features, he would've had difficulty making a positive ID, in light of the fact the head wound was really quite gruesome. As the surge of relief heightened, so did the confusion regarding who did the deed. The ten-million-dollar question was who not only killed the infamous Killer Kato, but also snuffed out his top rapper, and a close aid, all in one sweep. He rose to his feet and saw Norman was conducting a crime scene breakdown. He moved over to Lameek's body and his rage percolated to life when he laid eyes on his corpse. He was now second-guessing his decision to kidnap this little fuck, because this one course of action caused so much bullshit! He sighed angrily as the dreaded realization that his three friends and fellow agents were lying dead in an empty lot in Victorville as a result of this faulty decision, and he might be out of a job or might even end up in prison once the smoke cleared. He still couldn't believe Killer Kato had stepped to him over this clown ass motherfucker, and it was apparent he'd misread Killer. Even though he knew nothing of Killer Kato's being Lameek's father, he was certain there was something he obviously was not privy to, and whatever the issue was, it was something strong enough to make Killer Kato put himself and his career on the line.

"There was apparently another shooter," Norman said to no one in particular as he closely scrutinized all the evidence in the immediate vicinity.

Aaron looked about the area and said, "And whoever it was," He saw the droplets of blood next to the eight empty shell casings, "was shot and drove away in a vehicle." He had followed the blood droplets and saw them suddenly stopped, which meant the bleeder got in a vehicle and drove away. In any event, it was apparent they didn't walk to this secluded area.

"That's right," Sgt. Kaplan confirmed. "Based on the layout, it was a shootout, but the odd thing is it looks like Lameek either shot himself, or was tussling with someone in an attempt to either get hold of or to get away from the weapon right there." He pointed at the gun near Killer Kato. "But it appears he was shot somehow during the struggle."

Aaron saw the automatic weapon lying in between Killer Kato and Lameek, and the acid in his stomach, and that little voice in his head was telling him this fiasco was probably the work of Rasheen Smith. He'd recently found out through Bob that Killer Kato was believed to have killed Barbara Smith (Rasheen and Lameek's mother), and Rasheen also had a bone to pick with Killer because he was the root of the prison sentence he caught, and not only abandoned him, but had also stole his childhood sweetheart, Crystal Walker, who he saw was also among the dead. But, how did he let his baby brother get killed in this incident? This particular puzzle really disturbed him most, because Rasheen had went through great lengths to rescue Lameek when he and his men had kidnapped him, and it made no sense for Rasheen to allow him to end up dead. He looked around at the crime scene again with hopes that it would proffer a clear answer to this current inquiry, but no answers materialized.

Aaron shook his head with a lethal blend of fury, confusion, and impatience converging into a gigantic ball of negatively charged emotions. And how did he slip in and get to Killer before he did? It wasn't that he gave a shit who killed Colin Gibson, it was just the mere fact this slick ass nigga was able to do it right under his nose was what disturbed him. He turned, locked eyes with the boss cop and said, "I'm certain you gentlemen have all the hospitals on alert for anyone entering with a bullet wound?"

"Of course," Sgt. Kaplan's tone resonated with clear indignation. "It's standard procedure under the circumstance."

There was a brief moment of intense silence.

Aaron gave Sgt. Kaplan a facial gesture, which announced he was waiting to hear the rest. When nothing else followed, he said, "So you're saying none of the local hospitals received any such admittance?"

"They haven't informed us of anything yet, but it's still too early to lock into anything. According to the coroner these bodies haven't been dead more than three hours."

As Aaron allowed his eyes to continue absorbing the crime scene, he heard Sgt. Kaplan's communication device come to life and saw him pull it from his utility belt.

"Yeah, talk to me," Sgt Kaplan said into the walkie-talkie.

A static-laced male voice crackled through the device. "This is dispatcher calling to inform you of a transmission regarding a sighting of an injured man, exiting a limousine. Requesting permission on how to proceed."

"Send Charlie over in sector six; tell him go check it out and report directly to me." Sgt. Kaplan said as he noticed the federal agents eavesdropping on his conversation.

"Roger that." The voice said. "Over and out."

Sgt. Kaplan placed the walkie-talkie back in its slot and said, "If there's anything specific you need, I'll be over here." He gestured as he moved towards the coroner's van. "However, if you have any suggestions on how we should handle the mass media circus that's coming shortly, we'll be happy to hear your advice."

"Spin it however you please," Aaron said as he gave Norman a head gesture to stay put as he headed towards the car. He needed to contact Bob and see what was up with this sighting the sergeant just mentioned before he rushed off on a goose chase. After entering the car, and talking with Bob for two minutes, he realized this was more than worth pursuing; it was a sure shot jackpot, since he could now also get rid of Rasheen. He eased out of the car and waved to Norman, who strutted towards the car.

When Norman got behind the wheel and started the car, Aaron said, "I think we found Rasheen. Once we're a considerable distance away from here, I need you to get hot footed on that gas pedal; it would be real nice if we could intercept that patrol car they're sending to check out this lead . . ."

CHAPTER # 4

Willie was pointing his gun at Doctor Myers and his wife while in a clear panicked state. His hand with the pointed gun trembled as his convoluted mind struggled to come up with a solution to deal with the person knocking at the door. His eyes were wide with confusion as his stare bounced back and forth; from Doctor Myers clutching his wife to the hallway leading to the front door, where the pounding continued.

Felicia was shocked by Willie's erratic reaction, and had she known he would have overreacted in this fashion she would have went about it differently. She spoke softly. "Please, relax, Willie. That person at the door is here to help."

Doctor Myers was just as confused and shocked as Willie upon hearing this statement. "What are you talking about Feli—"

"I called Regina," Felicia exclaimed, and then said to Willie as Doctor Myers sighed angrily. "Come with me to the door and see for yourself." She headed towards the hallway, but stopped abruptly when Willie jabbed the gun at her.

Willie couldn't seem to find enough trust in his heart; this could be a trick. "Why you didn't say something earlier!? I think you lying. You tryin' to play me!" He was already wondering if he took them as hostages would it get him and Rasheen anywhere. "I think you called the police!"

"That's nonsense, Willie," Doctor Myers said with an offended tone. "She said it's Regina. She's the person who handles my transfusion blood. If you want to save Mr. Smith's life, please allow Regina to enter." He gave his wife an angry glance, which said he was not happy at all with these silly surprises of hers. He'd told her time and time again not to play these kinds of head games when there was a medical situation underway!

Willie instantly sensed he may have over-reacted once again, but he couldn't take any chances, since Mrs. Myers's behavior was just too suspicious. However, we would give her the chance to prove herself. "Okay, let's go! Both of you; move to the door. Slowly!"

Doctor Myers and Felicia rushed down the hallway as Willie followed. When they reached the front door Willie peeked out the peephole while keeping his gun pointed. He saw a white woman with blond curls, and red lipstick. His heart dropped to his feet because this woman definitely didn't look like the police; he lowered his weapon as his shoulders sagged, and he stepped out the way. "Go ahead, let her in."

As Felicia rushed to the door and unfastened the locks, Doctor Myers and Willie locked eyes. Willie's eyes were at first filled with defiance, but the energy slowly transformed into shame as Regina rushed inside with two suitcases, explaining that it was the transfusion blood and followed Regina as the two headed towards the makeshift operating room.

Willie tried to make his eyes say sorry, but he saw the angry sneer on the doctor's face, which compelled him to verbalize what was going on inside of him. "Hey, Doctor Myers I'm sorry about that, man. But let's keep it real; your wife should've said something earlier. I—I—Don't—" Rasheen's well-being skirted across his mind, and the thought of losing the doctor's help on account of him wigging out, deeply disturbed him. He spoke humbly and respectfully. "You know I ain't no mind reader, doc. But on the up and up, I'm sorry I fucked up like that, but your wife gotta take some of the blame here."

Doctor Myers sighed tiredly, "You're right." He certainly couldn't put all the blame on Willie. "My wife has this thing for surprising me, and she doesn't seem to realize that some surprises are not meant to be utilized at certain moments. Apology accepted Willie," he reached out his hand and Willie shook it. "And I hope you except my apology in return." He headed towards the operating room with Willie on his heels.

As the doctor entered the operating room and took charge, Willie instantly felt the compulsion to look out the window, and noticed this sensation was pulling him as though it had a magnetic attraction on his whole body. Willie gave into the temptation and eased over to the window. He slid the curtain aside ever so slightly, peeking out from behind the curtains. He began scanning the crack of dawn terrain.

When Willie saw a blue two-door car across the street with a white man inside of it, his heart jumped in his chest. He closely observed this man, who had dark, short hair, and for some odd reason, he noticed his demeanor and aura broadcasted law enforcement. After spending so many countless years of his life living on the wrong side of the law, he realized his very being had developed an innate radar for detecting the police.

When Willie entered the operation room, and asked Regina was the car out front with the man inside of it affiliated with her and she convincingly confirmed it was not, Willie knew for sure he had a major problem on his hands, especially since it looked like the man was checking out the van, he brought Rasheen here in.

* ** *

Aaron sat in the passenger seat with his tired eyes plastered on the empty highway as Norman was pushing the car to speeds fluctuating between 70 to 90 mph.

Suddenly, Aaron felt his cell phone buzzing and he retrieved it from his suit jacket pocket. When he saw Klingaman's caller ID number, he wanted to throw the damn phone to the floor, and stomp it to pieces. This could mean only one thing; the Victorville catastrophe was in full swing and about to bite him on the backside;

Carlos, Bruce and Ted's bodies were discovered along with the numerous other bodies, and since he was the crew chief, it was time to start explaining. He was hoping he could've completed this mission by knocking Rasheen out of the picture, which was the sole reason he was out here on the west coast in the first place, but that was apparently out the window! He was trying to find some relief in the fact that Killer Kato was dead, but upon analyzing his original mission objective it was obvious he had failed.

Before Aaron activated the phone he said to Norman, "It's Klingaman; looks like we ran out of time." He saw Norman angrily muttered the word "Shit!" Aaron spoke with a serious tone. "While I'm talking to Klingaman, call Capone and Raul and tell them to get over to that address and check out this lead." He drew a deep breath, activated his cell phone, and braced himself for the storm, hoping the story he and his team concocted would fly.

* *** *

Willie stood watching as Doctor Myers, Felicia, and Regina pumped blood into Rasheen's body. They had one of his arms hooked to a clear bag of solution that they called an IV, while the other arm was connected to a bag of blood.

As Willie watched them fix up Rasheen, his mind began wandering again, and the only thing that seemed to stay on in his immediate thoughts was all that money he saw Rasheen and Ja-King counting when they were at the house in Glendale. There were millions in straight, hard-core cash, and they had 16 pure gold bars that had to be worth millions. And then the jewels crossed his mind, and he felt an anxiety saturated with a deep yearning starting to grip his heart; the thought of not being able to get hold of that kind of money was truly frightening. To waste that much money was beyond a sin! It was even worse than a cardinal sin!

Immediately on the tail end of the mental images of all that money, Willie remembered the car parked out front; he'd been sneaking peeks out the window every couple of minutes or so, and all the man did during the four times Willie checked was just sit there. The thought crossed his mind to sneak out back, creep up on this cat, put a few slugs in him for safe keepings, and make a clean get away with Rasheen in the van, but he knew that was the same as courting with disaster, since that would also mean he would have to kill the doctor and his family since they saw his and Rasheen's faces. Since he wasn't sure whether they had rat in their blood, killing them would be the only logical way to guarantee a clean escape.

Then, suddenly, that inner voice told him to stop stuntin'! He knew damn well he was no gunman. Of course, he enjoyed hanging out with real hitters that stepped to shit with bullets flying, but he almost never got directly involved with front-line street work. Nevertheless, he enjoyed fantasizing stepping to his business like a real live thug and OT gangster. After sweeping all those crazy thoughts from his mind, it became clear that the only thing left to do was to play it by ear, and if this cat in the car tried to step to him, he would then have to do what he had to do, whatever that might be.

Willie slid the curtain aside. The car was gone!? The initial shock was a unique one because it contained a strong flair of fear instead of elatedness, because he had no idea what this sudden disappearance was really all about and couldn't help but feel that it was an omen telling him he had better get out of this house. Willie struggled to slow down his runaway mind, and again, he felt like he was being pulled in three different directions; there was no question he was scared of making another wrong decision. He didn't need Rasheen to remind him that a wrong move could cost them their lives . . . . and all that money!

Doctor Myers cleared his throat loudly, pulling Willie out of his reverie and said, "I got some bad news, Willie." He inspected him closely to get a feeling of how Willie might respond, and when he saw Willie's eyes about to become misty, he said, "I was under the impression that Rasheen was merely unconscious, but—" He sighed nervously. "But, after this transfusion, it seems evident that Rasheen is in a coma—I suspect the loss of so much blood caused this, but—"

"How long is he gonna be in this coma!?" Willie's tone was beyond deadly serious; it was well within the danger zone. "Is he gonna wake up from this shit, doc!?"

There was a moment of silence.

Doctor Myers gave Felicia and Regina the signal that everything was okay as they exited stage left, sensing the sparks were about to fly. When Doctor Myers saw Willie observing the two with suspicious eyes as they exited the room, he said, "They're okay. I told you before; no one is calling any police, Willie. Please relax. Now, the good thing as far as Rasheen is concerned is there is a chance he will come out of this coma. Let's give it a few days and see how it goes." He took a moment to collect his thoughts because what was coming next was the real issue that was getting him uptight. He needed all of his money, plus the money it would cost to house Rasheen here until he woke up, if he woke up. "Listen, Willie, I need payment as soon as possible, and I—"

"How much you want, Doc?" Willie asked while staring him straight in the eyes. This was always the best tactic to determine if a person was trying to pull a sham. "How much is this gonna cost?"

Doctor Myers felt the urge to jack up the price, but successfully fought back this crazy compulsion out of fear of the likely consequences if he got caught, and said, "Standard rates; thirty thousand for the surgery. And another ten for the housemaid to watch over him for the first two weeks. However, I believe if he's gonna awake, it'll be within the week."

Willie chewed on those numbers for a quick moment and felt they were fair enough, since Cee-more had already pulled his coat to the standard price. He started nodding his head to give the doctor the signal it was doable. But the only problem was, if he gave the doctor 40 grand, it would have to come out of his personal stash, and that scared him silly because if Rasheen didn't wake up from that coma, and ended up dying that would mean he would have to kiss all that cash goodbye. It scared him but he had to take the chance. "Listen, Doc, you take care of my partner, and I'll be back tonight with your money."

Willie slid out the house, looking over his shoulder every step of the way as he got in the van and breezed away, searching for any cars following him. Later that night, Willie returned with the 40 grand, and saw Rasheen was still sleeping like a baby.

As Willie sat staring at Rasheen, he reflected on the phone call he made to Lora, the woman he left in charge of his store in San Diego (Willie's Wares) and the bad news just never seemed to stop piling up. According to Lora, business was terrible, and she needed him to send her the rent, including this month and last month's rent, which added up to a little over $4,000. Since Willie's stash was dribbling away at a remarkably rapid rate, he was already scoping out a few places to hit, but his logical mind told him it would be safer and wiser to wait for Rasheen to wake up, so that he could get his girl Sharon to check out things before diving into such a huge job.

As the days evolved into a week, Willie was literally on the verge of losing control; his patience had disappeared two days ago, and he was now demanding that the Doctor find a way to get Rasheen "the fuck outta this coma!" Although Willie was subconsciously aware that Doctor Myers had no control over when Rasheen would awake, it just felt crucial to maintaining his sanity that he try to do something to stop this torturous wait. Even the sexual excursion he had with a hooker in a nearby hotel didn't do much to tame his overwhelming impatience that was about to spiral into all out emotional pandemonium.

CHAPTER # 5

During the weeks that progressed, Aaron Wilson's luck wasn't much different from Willie's. Although he successfully convinced his supervisor Klingaman that the deaths of Bruce, Carlos, and Ted occurred when they went to the Mojave Desert town Victorville in pursuit of a lead, and the conflict was an unfortunate mishap due to their unexplained altercation with the South Central Rangers, it didn't fly too well when Aaron asked to be allowed to personally continue pursuing Rasheen Smith in the west coast region of the country. Simply put, the case was now in the hands of that regional office, and there was absolutely nothing else to discuss.

This spell of bad luck seemed to be all inclusive because it reached into almost all areas of this clandestine west coast mission; one major instance occurred when Capone went to check out the lead Aaron instructed him to investigate regarding a man exiting a limousine, and not only did Capone find out that the Limo was connected to the Killer Kato shooting several miles away, but he also discovered that it was not wise to get too close to law enforcement officials while they were investigating a delicate matter; Capone walked into a confrontation with the Lakeside police when he drew too close to the evidence within this crime scene involving the limo, and upon being questioned he fled the area. After a twenty-mile car chase Capone and one of his assistants crashed into a moving truck on highway 78, bringing the high-speed chase to a very deadly and ghastly conclusion when Capone and his assistant were crushed into an unidentifiable mess of gore by the 18 wheeler that ran over their small foreign car.

However, there was some good news that came into existence when Keith and Aaron managed to get hold of one of Jack-Mack's safe deposit boxes located in Grant Central Station. The 210-thousand-dollar cash catch was split right down the middle and

Keith and Aaron added the 105 grand to their secured overseas bank accounts with their minds twirling with bliss. It also wasn't surprising they were oblivious of the fact that they both had more than enough money to quit the game while they were ahead. However, they were embraced by a huge surprise when they read the newspaper articles indicating Killer Kato was Lameek's biological father, which explained why Colin Gibson stepped to Aaron the way that he did.

With millions of stolen dollars to their names Aaron and Keith could've easily lived happily ever after, but because of the awesome grip that money had over their minds, bodies, and souls, it never even crossed their minds that they should move on to the next chapters of their lives; instead, they continued searching for new ways to gain more money, while working diligently to come up with a plan to track down and kill Rasheen Smith.

* ** *

Camila Nelson sat on the side of her bunk with her elbows propped on her knees, and her shoulders and spirit sagging like a wounded prize fighter refusing to go back out into the ring for another bout. Her dark, golden brown complexion was crisp, clean, and smooth with relief from the wear and tear that fast urban life was known to inflict upon those firmly caught up in that particular lifestyle. Even her body had filled out nicely, and seemed to age like fine wine in that it thickened in all the right places; her body was the subject of most of the envy directed at her from the other prisoners, but her knuckle game kept the jealousy from being too overtly displayed.

But her convoluted mind was nowhere in accord with her neat, refreshing outer appearance. Her son Rasheen Junior stayed on her mind more than anything else, and so did her son's father. Although the prison had a nursery where the kids were housed, and she spent time with little Rah once a day, cuddling his little one and a half year old body with her motherly hugs and kisses, she still felt deprived as though her inability to be with her child around the clock was a clear breach of some cardinal law, and her mind, body and soul ached with this irrefutable reality.

She'd been watching and reading all the news reports broadcasting the brutal murder of several Hoodaroma affiliates, including Killer Kato (Colin Gibson), Lameek Smith, Crystal Walker, and numerous others. Not surprisingly, most reports attributed the deaths to Killer Kato's underhanded dealings in the rap industry, theorizing that rival gangsters may have been responsible. They explicitly pointed out the yearlong war he waged against the Italian and Russian mobs. A particular piece of information that stirred Camila's curiosity was the fact they said they had found at the murder scene, the blood of an apprehended suspect, but didn't mention this person's name.

She didn't know why, but she didn't have to be told that it was Rasheen's blood; her boo said he was going to step to his fuckin' business and that's just what he did. *Yeah, baby, do you. I know it was you who laid that bitch ass foul ass nigga down!* But despite knowing Rasheen was responsible for putting Killer Kato's black ass where he belonged, she was scared that he got shot and didn't make it. The thought of little Rasheen never seeing his father scared her immensely, but not being able to ride with Rasheen again frightened her even more.

She rose to her feet as the thought of Rasheen's possible death consumed her once again, and the annoying feeling compelled her to pace, back and forth in her 5 x 9 foot cell. She couldn't bear to face the reality that Rasheen wouldn't be by her side when she stepped to the two C.O.s who'd been trying to rape her for the last year, and forcing her to sell their weed. She refused to allow herself to be abused by Officer Richards and Rodriguez, and on a dozen occasions, she fought them tooth and nail when they tried to basically rape her. They would first physically beat her mercilessly with rubber Billy clubs, and then would set her up by planting a knife in her cell, throw her in SHU, and then they would keep coming; even though it became clear if she didn't bend her bid would be an extremely hard one, she fought and fought and fought back some more until finally they realized she couldn't be broken. That's when they settled for simply convincing her to sell their drugs, and she went with the program since hustling was something she was used to doing anyway. She sighed loudly.

"Hey, girl," Camila's next cell neighbor, Big Margo, said with her husking voice, "you a'ight over there?" Her voice matched her big burly body. "I can feel all that drama coming right through these walls." She laughed.

"You know me, Margo, just thinking out loud, that all."

"I got some chips over here if you want some," Margo pulled the big bag from underneath her bunk, "I can't eat all this stuff by myself," she said jokingly.

Camila laughed, "Girl, you know you lying. That little ass bag ain't gone do nothing but get you all upset."

"Amen to take, girl," Margo said as she crammed her mouth with the chips. "Make sure you hold onto yo' stuff, cause I'll be jugglin' your junk in a minute or two."

"One for two, and we can do the do," She sat back down on her bunk and the silence returned as Big Margo went back to listening to her cassette player. Camila tried to think about other things; she picked up a street novel by Amar Cohen and attempted to force herself to read; after completing one page, and upon realizing she couldn't remember anything she'd just read, she tossed the book aside, and resumed the position (elbows on knees with sagging shoulders coupled with a moping facial expression).

Camila guessed no matter what she did it would all boil down to the fact that her stress was here to stay, and there was more than enough of it to go around. But a real stressful upcoming event was she was going to be released in another month and her mind repeatedly returned to this issue with almost as much frequency as Little Rasheen did.

She was being released to her aunt's crib in Crown Heights Brooklyn, and it was going to be hell living with Aunt Fatima. She was a church fanatic with bible totting quotes for any and every occasion and had no problem making church involvement a prerequisite to living under her roof, and most of all, Aunt Fatima didn't discriminate when it came time to enforce her church fanatic rules; it was clear, no church no stay here.

Despite her difficult relationship with her Aunt Fatima, Camila was grateful she had finally came around and stopped accusing her of being the cause of Amar's untimely death like the rest of the family was still doing. She'd often wondered if Aunt Fatima and the rest of the family had known Amar was the cause of her predicament, and had stolen all of her hard-earned money (even though it was the proceeds from Dominican drug stash house robberies), would they still view him as some kind of innocent victim?

The sound of jiggling keys was heard at the end of the gallery, and she looked at the cheap watch she'd purchased from J.L Marcus and saw it was time for the change of shift. She made a quick calculation and remembered it was about that time of the month when Richards and Rodriguez worked the night tour.

Camila's anxiety lit up like a red alert alarm on a bank vault about to be opened in an unauthorized fashion. As the keys drew closer her hatred increased with every footstep that was heard clearly. Although they never got the pussy, the mere thought that these foul bastards kept trying to break her down was enough to make her vow she was going to step to her business when her feet hit the bricks.

When Camila saw the face of C.O. Richards, a black man with a low haircut, and crossed eyes, staring at her through the bars, she locked eyes with this scum-bag, promising that she would have her way real soon.

CHAPTER # 6

The cloudy mental images of the group of little kids playing in the park were almost as distorted as their cheering voices of glee. At the seat of this restricted consciousness were many other images that were so discombobulated that there was no logical cohesion to any of these mental pictures, other than the fact they were images from a distant past. But those little children in the park apparently held some intense importance, because they kept coming back, and didn't stay hidden within the subconscious realm for very long.

Then, there were the smells, tastes, sounds, and most of all, the exquisite sensations of pain.

Everything seemed to compliment these sporadic episodes of insidious pain, even down to the coppery taste of oxygen depraved blood, down to the pungent odor of a gangrened wound that simply refused to succumb to the body's remarkable healing mechanisms, on up to the sound of ringing ears initiated after being bludgeoned to a bloody pulp by a sadistic cop's steel plated Billy-club. Indeed, this pain was all encompassing and just as debilitating.

But those cheering small voices were helping Rasheen Smith re-gain his place in the world of the living, because he'd saw himself among these groups of mental images, but was certain it wasn't him per se, but was sure it was someone from him, of him, like him, made from him, and therefore it was him.

From this dream world he'd concluded it had to be his newborn son.

Thanks to these potent images, and the innate wisdom of knowing he had a child that needed him, Rasheen felt a powerful spiritual like force pulling him. Despite his dream world suffering, he summoned his mind to awaken, and to his utter surprise, he awoke. He opened his matter-laden eyelids to a world that was almost as dreamingly cloudy as the one he'd just retreated from. Before his mind completely registered that he was in a neatly kept room, the throbbing agony transmitting from his gut saturated his entire body with a new pain far more furious than the afflictions his mind dreamed about moments ago.

When the tears of realization grabbed hold of his mind, he cried hard and long.

That night that brought him to this place consumed his memory bank, and Lameek's status materialized. His baby brother was dead! He killed his little brother because he wanted to run his fuckin' mouth instead of steppin' to his business! If he had started shooting the minute they stepped foot out of the Limo, Lameek would still be alive! The tears that rolled from his eyes were as genuine as racial profiling in America. The pain of this loss was even more overwhelming than the stomach pain, and nothing else seemed to hurt more than knowing if he had took care of the situation correctly, Lameek would still be on this planet blessing folks with inspiring rap lyrics.

Then, the status of his other loved ones appeared; his mother (forever gone), Jack Mack (dead and stinking), Dirty Ricky (pushing up daisies), Ja-King (on lock down), Candy (prison bound), and Camila (locked up). Misfortune seemed to be everywhere.

It took only seconds to realize he might have been luckier if he hadn't awakened to all this crippling anguish. There was no question he could already feel his inner mental workings rearranging themselves in many new, and unanticipated ways.

As Rasheen continued examining his surroundings, he saw that the hook up with Cee-more was the real deal if ever there were such a thing. This had to be Doctor Myers's crib, he concluded as he instantly realized the pain in his gut was so ferocious it was causing his head to feel like a little madman was inside his cranium going berserk with a sledgehammer on anything in his path. It was obvious he needed some painkillers immediately and began looking for one of those nurse calling remote control devices like the one he had when he was inside Woodhall hospital that time he was shot before.

Moving his head ever so slightly, it took seconds to determine there was no such device. Then he wondered could he talk. His throat was dry, and the saliva he was trying to generate wasn't helping a bit. The minute he tried to activate his voice box a fire exploded in his throat, and he received his answer when the "ahhh" sound slid from his mouth, but the razor-cutting pain that came with it confirmed it wasn't worth it.

The sudden, overwhelming sensation of thirst appeared almost as if the mere act of trying to speak flicked on the thirst component in his mind. Oh, no, not this shit again! He brooded in agony, because it was just like before; that thirsty feeling was no motherfuckin' joke, he said inwardly as soothing images of ice-cold drinks swirled inside his mind. Then the thought of having another shit bag made him swear up and down that he was going to find a definite way to avoid getting hit like this ever again.

As he settled back down, an instance of glee grasped his heart for the first time when the image of the bullets he pumped into Killer Kato's ass appeared. It felt good but the pain of losing Lameek made this victory bittersweet. When he felt the tears about to start back up again, he moved his mind to another topic; his money.

As Rasheen tried to count all the huge sums of money, he had stashed all over the place, and realizing he had enough of it to find a nice little hiding place, snatch up his son and Camila, and chill the fuck out, he heard someone enter the house. The sound of rattling brown paper bags came from down the hallway outside the room and announced to Rasheen that someone had done some shopping, and he was praying whoever it was had some god damn pain killers in those bags of goodies.

Rasheen swallowed hard and realized that the reason his voice box was on fire was because he hadn't used it in such a long time and probably because it had to be slowly awakened. Despite the pain he experienced moments ago, he took a deep breath and tried to speak again.

Through the scratchy pain, a hoarse whisper oozed from his mouth, "Yo' who's that out there!?"

He could tell whoever it was had heard him by the sudden stopping motion. This person was now approaching. When he saw the dark-skinned, heavy-set woman that looked like the epitome of a Jamaican nurse aide, he gave her a hard stare.

"Mr. Smith, I see you've finally decided to join us," she said with a heavy Jamaican accent as she came right up to the bedside, and began checking his IV and other tubings connected to him. "My name is Chairman Dillon. You can call me Big D like everybody else. I've been takin' care of you for the past two weeks, and chile, you are a hand full, I might add."

Rasheen saw she gave him that knowing expression laced with an omnipotent grin that said she knew some private things about him. He didn't have to conclude that they were personal since upon reading between the lines of her statement that he was a "handful" said it all. "Where's Doctor Myers?" Rasheen's voice felt like it was getting better with each word he spoke. "And what's up with Willie?"

"Doctor Myers will be home soon, soon," Big D grabbed Rasheen's wrist and checked his pulse. "Your Willie friend, I haven't seen him in a few days, but he did leave a number with the doctor." She gently laid his arm down, pulled the white sheet off Rasheen and began inspecting his stomach wound.

The cool air that caressed Rasheen's body was truly stimulating to all of his nerve ends, and despite its soothing sensation it surprisingly made the pain flare up even more, as if the pain was competing with the good sensations, making perfectly clear that it was the head honcho in this show. Rasheen spoke through the gray cloud of suffering. "You got any strong pain killers? I can't take the pain Big D."

"Oh, yes, Chile," Big D flipped the sheet back to its original position. "Me sorry 'bout that. That shoulda been the first thing I asked yah. Be right back." She switched out the room.

When she returned with the glass of water and a hand full of pills, and after Rasheen greedily gulped down the pills, he said to Big D, "You said I been asleep for two weeks?"

"That's right chile, the doctor said you were in a mild coma,"

"I need to look at the news reports on TV, and some two-week-old newspapers. Can you help me out?"

Big D smiled broadly as her big biscuit cheeks turned into big buns, "Mr. Smith, if you're trying to find out what's going on you can talk to old Big D and I'll give you the whole run down."

Rasheen sighed frustratedly, "I just need to check out a few—"

"They said in the papers that they're still looking for a suspect who left some blood at the crime scene, but they still haven't mentioned your name, Mr. Smith. I've been keeping a close eye on this, and so has the doctor."

Rasheen felt a terror gripping him. The thought of her knowing he was at that grisly murder scene didn't sit right with him at all. When he saw Big D's fake smile, he hoped and prayed this woman didn't spazz out and try to turn him in before he was able to get out of this bed-ridden state he was currently locked in.

* ** *

About several hundred miles away in a Brooklyn three family private house in the Flatbush section of the borough, Bam Bam sat with a cigar in his mouth, looking at the stack of money on the polished red wood coffee table directly in front of him, while Big Gains AKA

Gold Tooth Born, had his back to Bam Bam as he stared out the second-floor window.

In the background, a Wu Tang Clan tune whispered through the radio padlocked on Power 105 radio station.

The unfortunate news of Killer Kato's death still had these two Lieutenants grappling with the very disheartening news. They both were dressed in typical urban attire consisting of baggy clothes, Timberland construction boots, expensive Cuban link gold necklaces with matching rings and bracelets and had angry black man sneers plastered on their goatee-laden mugs.

Bam Bam was contemplating his answer to Big Gains' enthusiastic suggestion and spoke as he started dumping huge stacks of money in a green duffle bag. "The only shit that got my mind all fucked up right now is, Killer Kato ain't even hook us up with the connect." Although he had already found another connect, it was wise to see how Big Gains felt about the matter. "And since Crazy B done went and got himself murdered too, now we gotta find a brand new motherfuckin' connect!"

Big Gains spun around and stared at Bam Bam with a locked jawed expression, "I didn't ask you about no motherfuckin' product connect!" he sat in the chair across from Bam Bam, "I ask what you wanna do about this nigga Rasheen. The peeps said this cat had his hands in Killer Kato's and Crazy B's deaths; now that we know this fo' sho' what we gonna do!?"

"Whatever, whatever," Bam Bam tossed the duffle bag to the side, and tapped ashes into the ashtray, feeling good homie could care less about the connect. "What you wanna do?"

"I say we rally up them troops of yours out there slinging them things and get this shit here crackin!"

Bam Bam smiled at his homie of about two decades, but he really wanted to tell Big Gains what was really on his mind; fuck Killer Kato! Fuck Crazy B! And fuck you too if you too stupid not to let go of that silly ass loyalty bullshit! As he shifted in his seat, Bam Bam dreaded the thought of pulling good workers off the street, and start losing money in order to go chasing a dude that actually did him a favor when he smoked Killer Kato and Crazy B. This was exceptionally good fortune for him, since he was getting control of a lucrative drug empire, and no longer had to give up a huge percentage of the cash he brought in.

But, instead of sharing what was on his mind, Bam Bam put on his new mask, and played his hand accordingly, since Big Gains was Killer's man to the bitter end, and there was no way of flippin' him against Killer. "Yeah, we gonna step to this cat. Killer and Crazy was Fam, sun. Yeah, I'll pull Frukwan's coat, and we'll work on gettin' this thing poppin'. What I need you to do, is get more info on Rasheen. From what I heard that nigga got hit up. Who's to say this chump ain't laid out somewhere dead and sinking? Before we go wiggin' out and start chasin' a ghost or some crazy shit, we need to make sure this dude is still alive."

Big Gains rose to his feet, since Bam Bam was right, and spoke as he headed for the door. "I'ma hit Kazoe up on the cell and let you know what time it is later tonight." He stopped with his hand on the doorknob, turned and faced Bam Bam, "If I find out for sure he's alive, I hope you got them troops ready to hit the bricks on a second's notice. That means we gonna need you too." Big Gains disappeared out the door.

Bam Bam leaned back in his chair, savoring the cigar smoke. When he blew the smoke out slowly, he wondered would Kazoe and his peeps suspect him of being the cause of Big Gains' untimely demise, if drive-by shooters suddenly wet his ass up?

The more Bam Bam pondered the idea, the more it became evident this wasn't a good time for those sorts of extreme actions; it would probably be much wiser to simply help him step to Rasheen, if he was still alive, especially considering the fact all the love Killer

Kato had been showing all these ballers, hustlers and players all across the country. With that much hood love floating around, the natural response would be to avenge his death, since it might be too risky to start making waves too fast.

But, once all this episodic loyalty bullshit ran its course (which wouldn't last too long since folks in the hood had memory capacity that lasted as long as palms were being greased, or the big bad wolf was looking over their shoulders), and if Big Gains didn't understand that he was the new boss man of this operation, then he was going to knock that gold tooth smile off his face; permanently.

CHAPTER # 7

Four days later Rasheen sat in the light green soft cushioned chair across from the bed he couldn't wait to get the hell out of; the bed sores that had formulated on his backside, the upper part of his back, and the heels of his feet made him think he'd contracted some kind of dreaded disease that could only be cured by getting the hell away from that damn bed.

Rasheen was peering out the window at the empty residential streets, waiting for Willie to come pick him up, so that he could get the hell out of Doctor Myers's life. It was a little after 8 o'clock in the evening and he could hear Doctor Myers and Felicia still arguing in the living room about Doctor Myers's gambling problems, despite the fact they'd been at it for about an hour straight. He must've fucked up some kinda terrible in view of the way the Mrs's temper was bursting at the seams.

Rasheen sighed, realizing it was sad to say that it was a beautiful thing the Doc had this little problem of his or else he wouldn't have been able to receive such quality medical treatment under the circumstances. Thank God for the ole mighty games of chance, he heard himself cheered inwardly as Felicia sounded like she was on the verge of crying.

There was also no doubt he had worn out his welcome about a week ago, and if it weren't for the money Willie had hit the Doc off with, he suspected that Felicia would've had him removed from their home immediately, probably the minute they discovered he was in a coma. He could tell she wasn't a mean-spirited woman; he had put himself in her shoe and could empathize; she was feed up with her husband's precarious activities, and he couldn't blame her.

The other day he had eavesdropped on one of their arguments and discovered that Doctor Myers had done the same covert medical procedure with a mob guy who was shot three times and ended up

41

not paying him all the money he owed, and almost caused further problems when the guy started talking about their arrangement around the wrong people. Rasheen saw this was the reason the Doc required a ten-thousand-dollar deposit, just for his agreeing to assist, even if in the event, no such accident ever occurred, and this deposit was non-refundable. The Doc's prices were very expensive, but they were worth every dime, since surviving a serious bullet injury without legitimate medical attention was mathematically impossible, and as they say, no amount of money in the world was worth playing games with your life. Any fool would give up any amount of money to save his life, and Rasheen was no fool.

Suddenly, Rasheen saw Willie's blue van pull up in front of the house, and he struggled to his feet. He grabbed the walking cane, and then the small brown paper bag filled with several bottles of pills. Rasheen crept towards the front of the house like an old, eighty-year-old senior citizen. The stitches in his stomach were removed yesterday, but the colostic (shit) bag had to stay for a couple of more weeks.

He caught a final glimpse of his reflection in the mirror hanging over the dresser, and was amazed by all the weight he had lost, and the amount of facial hair that grew on his face; he looked like Robinson Crusoe's brother, but much more skinner. Although the sickly grayish tone of his skin was gradually clearing up, the big black bags under his eyes gave him that truly madman look that embarrassed him at the thought of others seeing him in this wretched state. But he had to admit the way he looked was a superb disguise, because even he didn't believe it was him when he first got hold of a mirror. By the time Rasheen was about halfway down the hall, Willie was just knocking on the door, and Felicia was still arguing as she approached the door.

Felicia stopped talking as she looked out the peephole, saw it was Willie and opened the door; sighing with relief since they were finally getting rid of Rasheen. "Hello, Willie, come on in."

"How yah doin', Mrs. Myers," Willie smiled, and couldn't help stealing a peek at them juicy thighs and hips of hers as he slid pass her.

When Rasheen wobbled into the living room, he saw Doctor Myers sitting with his head bowed and his hands massaging his temples. "Well, Doc, I guess this is it."

Doctor Myers shook off the stress like an expert, and sprung to his feet with a smile, "It was a pleasure doing business with you, Mr. Smith." He reached out his hand and the two shook. "I guess it would be highly inappropriate to say I hope to see you again, but believe it or not, out of all my previous clients, I must say you were one of the best. But, I do believe we need one last check up to make sure that wound is healing—"

"Sorry, Doc, I'm serious, I can't do that. Don't worry; I'll be all right from here."

Doctor Myers sighed, realizing Rasheen's mind was made up on the matter, "Well, make sure you take those pills as prescribed. Anytime I can be of service, you know how to reach me."

Rasheen was glad to hear those words as he gave the doctor a nodding gesture but was sure this was the last time he would see him; he then gave Willie a head nod as he approached. "Doctor Myers, I'm feelin' your services so much, I'm giving you a bonus."

Willie reached in his pocket, retrieved an envelope containing five thousand dollars and handed it to Doctor Myers.

Once the envelope was in the doctor's hands, Rasheen began limping towards the door as the doctor's elated facial expression grew into a restrained smile as he appreciated the weight of the envelope. Upon reaching the door, Rasheen turned and said, "Once again, Doctor Myers, Mrs. Myers, thank you very much." He turned, exited the house, and that was the last he ever saw of Doctor Myers, his gorgeous wife Felicia, and the nurse aide, Big D.

During the ride in the van, while heading for Rasheen's last place of residence in Westwood, Rasheen and Willie talked strictly about business.

From behind the wheel, Willie said, "I checked out that Hoodaroma lawyer. I got his address, and everything. You were right; his name is Phillip Henderson, and I was surprised to also find out he's the new owner of the company."

The owner!? Rasheen was definitely surprised by this piece of information. "You sure that ain't a rumor or some shit? How the hell he get to be the owner just like that!?"

"This shit ain't no rumor, bet that. Phillip Henderson is the new CEO of Hoodaroma. I saw it on the website with my own eyes. When we settle down, I'll let you check it out for yourself."

Rasheen had to shake his head to that one; he didn't know if this was good or bad. After looking at his plan from this new vantage point, Rasheen realized it really didn't matter what Phillip was up to. The bottom line was that he was going to find a way to get possession of Lameek's millions of dollars, since by law he was the rightful and only heir to that money, at least that's what the copy of the contract he got from Lameek had said. The mere mental mentioning of Lameek stirred his emotions instantly, and he started reflecting on his situation. He felt odd; he felt unmotivated, and most of all, he felt like he wanted to get away from everything. But, he also knew he had to get access to his brother's money. "Can we get to this chump without having to bang out with an army?"

"No doubt about it. He got some peeps working with him that know a few of my peeps. I can get next to him."

"Good," Rasheen continued nodding. "After we get this stash over here in Westwood, we step to that immediately."

There was a long moment of silence.

"Listen, Rah," Willie couldn't hold this thought until later. "I know you got some things in the fire, but I've been checking out this mansion over in Summers County. Man, this shit gotta be holdin' a couple mills. I was wondering—"

"That's dead," Rasheen said point blank. He hated to be the bearer of bad news, but all that crib hitting shit was a thing of the past; he also wondered if the time was right to let Willie know his stay in Cali was over once he got his money together. As the silence increased, he realized it might be wise to lead Willie along until he got everything he needed out of him. "Come on, Willie, look at me. I'm fucked up. Imagine me trying to pull off a job like that with a mufuckin' shit bag on? The smell of this stinkin' shit alone, will get us busted."

Willie laughed, assuming Rasheen was telling him everything was on standby until he was 100%. "Yeah, you right. I guess my money is getting so low I'm ready to run up in something with the quickness. But I don't think it'll hurt to get in touch with your girl, Sharon, and get her started on this piece. Word, Rah, this place is crazy huge, man, and . . ."

As Willie went on and on about this mansion he'd scoped out, Rasheen realized the name Sharon brought on a litany of reminders. Willie was right about one thing; he definitely had to get in touch with Sharon Walker. The last time he spoke to her she had informed him that the feds were hunting him. For some strange reason, he now felt there was more to this situation involving the feds than she was telling him, and he couldn't fix his mind to believe that merely because he had kidnapped a Colombian cartel turned snitch that this was the cause for the FBI to start searching for and stealing his money stashed in safe deposit boxes in Atlanta.

There was something foul and funky smelling about this whole set up, and it was obvious Sharon might be able to provide him with the answers he needed to put his bewildered mind at ease. Now, he hoped his crib over in Westwood was still intact, so he could get to his specially made laptop he had buried along with the money, gold, and jewels in the backyard. Despite his severely weak condition, he decided he was going to dig up that money and other items the minute he stepped foot in his crib.

Three hours later, the blue van pulled up in front of the Westwood house, and Rasheen was surprised when he saw a night-light on in the living room area of what apparently used to be the house he was renting. There was no question there was a new occupant.

Willie peered across Rasheen at the crib and knew this couldn't be it. "This is yo' place, Rah?" The terror in his voice was stronger than the dread resonating from inside of Rasheen at this moment. "Look like somebody up in your piece, man."

Rasheen felt the urge to curse and scream, "Ain't this about a mufuckin' bitch! That cock suckin' mufucka canceled my lease and brought in a new customer." He instantly started wondering was this due to the police snooping around, and the thought made him start looking around the area for any police.

After a moment Rasheen swept that thought to the side because that was unlikely since he'd used a fictitious name, this county was many miles away from Lakeside, and he was certain he'd covered his tracks. This was simply a case of a greedy ass landlord, who was overreaching in an attempt to squeeze every dollar out of a situation.

"You think they found your stash?" Willie's concern was genuine. "Looks they done got real comfy up in yo' piece, man."

Rasheen was certain they hadn't found the stash, unless they were into hunting for buried treasures. He ignored Willie's inquiry as he sat staring at the house, trying to come up with a plan. He looked at his watch and saw it was a little after eleven o'clock. The star lit sky announced to him that it was a perfect night for a breaking and entering adventure, but his body told him that even if he got inside, he wouldn't have enough energy to dig up the stash anyway. Then, suddenly, something else hit his mind, and he decided to go for it. Even though he knew where Willie stood, one's loyalty could never be over-tested. Reluctantly, he decided to inform Willie that tonight was out of the question, "How much cheddar you got left?"

Willie sighed angrily as he checked his pockets with an attitude, "I'm damn near on E, Rah. If we don't do something soon—"

"How much money you got!?" Rasheen was getting pissed off now, because Willie knew damn well he was holding major cash, and for him to even question him on some petty shit like this was making him see the real side of Willie. "I can and plan to pay you fifteen times over the shit you kicked out, so be easy, man." He wanted to go in hard on him, but common sense told him not to even try it, cause Willie did save his life, and he still needed him in order to get the fuck out of this frying pan.

Willie counted his cash, and said, "Pocket change comes up to about four grand. I got about ten gees in my Western Union account."

Rasheen nodded as he gazed at the house; it was time to hit him with the coup de grace. "That's more than enough to hold us over at a hotel until tomorrow—"

"Naw, Rah, no hotels, man. You too hot for that shit and you know it. You left blood at that murder scene, and you can bet your ass by now they know it was you. Without a better disguise than that hair on your face, you gonna done off! If you show your face in any commercial district with surveillance cameras, they'll be dead on you, man. Before 9/11 shit would've been different."

Rasheen smiled inwardly, because Willie passed the test. It was good he wouldn't let him walk into a death trap. Plus, he wanted Willie to say what he'd just said from his own mouth, because he had just laid the foundation for what was coming next. Nevertheless, he wondered would this same energy prevail once they got this money in their hands tonight. "You got them pieces on you?"

Willie smiled, "Never leave home without 'em. We going in or what?"

Rasheen maintained a straight face, "Like you said, in so many words; if I don't get out of this part of the State, I'm bound to catch a bad decision. That don't leave us too many options, do it?" Red Man's rap song, Time 4 Sum Acksion, came alive inside his mind, and surprisingly it wasn't as hard hitting as it used to be when he was running the Streets of Brooklyn.

Willie nodded as he scooted out of the driver's seat and went to the back of the van to retrieve the two 9-mms he had stashed in a sophisticated hiding place.

Three minutes later, Rasheen was ringing the doorbell of the house that used to be his; Willie stood on the side out of view. When the chubby Latino man answered the door, Rasheen mentioned the landlord's name (Mr. Mark Ramirez), and explained that he was sent over to briefly inspect an electrical box in the basement, and when the door was opened, Rasheen and Willie rushed inside with their guns drawn. Five minutes later, the Latino man with glasses, a baldhead, and a beer belly, along with his young girlfriend, and another much younger male were tied up, blindfolded and gagged.

Rasheen found the two shovels of his still in the tool shack, and Willie started digging in the location Rasheen directed him to.

Rasheen sat exhaustedly on a lounge chair, watching Willie dig as his mind was jumping around like a grasshopper trying to get away from the hot surface of a toasty hot frying pan. He didn't know why, but he felt internally awkward almost as if he was in the body of a complete stranger. It was crazy because he didn't feel that familiar rush; the thrill that tickled his tummy when he stepped to his business in this fashion. He didn't know why, but he actually felt a strong sense of disgust, almost as if something inside of him was telling him this was wrong and was nothing to be proud about. It wasn't like he didn't know this; it was just that now it had suddenly dawned on him in such a way that it was touching his inner being in an unusual manner.

Suddenly, that voice from within shouted, you losing your edge, sun! You slippin'! He shook loose of the voice and then his son jumped into the spotlight of his mental perception. Damn, he couldn't wait to see, embrace, and spend time with his little man, especially since Camila said in her letter to Candy that he looked just like him. The thrill of him being a father made him extremely happy, but it also terrified him deeply.

For the twentieth time since awakening from the coma, Rasheen asked himself, what kind of father could he be to a child living this kind of crazy ass life? The answer slapped him hard in the face each time his mind toyed with this topic, since its obviousness was truly ridiculously clear, and he was certain this was the cause of all this sudden apprehensive energy that was flowing from him. Images of those kids playing in the park that helped pull him back to the world of the living danced in his mind as he saw Willie paused for a moment to catch his breath.

There was no doubt he wanted to be a father to little Rasheen; and not just any old father either, but he wanted to be a good dad. Not like that motherfucker who conceived him and had never saw this lowlife motherfucker! He hated this imaginary dad so immensely that the aversion propelled him into a mindset where he vowed to never do what that good for nothing nigga had done to him! Just to spite him, whoever the hell he was, Rasheen decided many years ago that when he became a dad, he would be a good father to any child he'd brought into this world.

Then, as if the pessimistic component of his mind was itching to be heard, that voice returned, and reminded him that all that was too late. The law wanted him; Connecticut wanted him; the feds were hunting him, and now there was no doubt that the Lakeside Police Department were looking for him in connection with Killer Kato's death. Simply put, he was facing natural life imprisonment, or maybe even the death penalty. The mere thought of this reality plunged his spirit into a crippling depression.

Just when he felt himself about to fold up, give up, roll over and scream "uncle", an inner force slapped him back to his senses. Things were definitely fucked up. He'd created so much confusion, chaos, and utter hell in his life, but the one thing that was for certain, he was still alive, and as long as he was breathing air, walking, talking and thinking, he could change whatever it was that had gotten him into this twisted ass place he was currently wallowing in.

First, it seemed obvious that he would have to change the way he was currently living. That was going to be hard, because he'd been ripping and running, and robbing and stealing so long, his mind couldn't fathom doing anything else. Also, because he'd been chasing Killer Kato for a considerable portion of his life, he felt empty just realizing that part of his personality was no longer present.

Before the pessimistic component of his mind took hold, a portion of a famous quote he had committed to memory many years ago while in prison faded into the front of his mind. '. . . Believing in yourself when others do not. This is the only way you will reach your goals and objectives.' He interpreted this as saying that if you don't believe in yourself, yo ass is dead and stinking before you even get in the game! He savored this quote as he struggled to pull up more of these powerful words of inspiration and then, suddenly, a surprise-ridden smile inched its way onto his face as he noticed he was remembering the many other empowering quotes he was so fond of memorizing back then; these sayings, quotes and adages were very deep and thought provoking. They were the type of jewels that could fit almost any positive situation, and when he reiterated them, they seemed to have a magical effect on him and now—

"I just hit something," Willie said with glee in his voice, pulling Rasheen from his reverie.

Rasheen struggled to his feet and approached. He arrived at the four foot by five foot hole and peered down inside as Willie began sweeping away the dirt with his hands.

Suddenly, the headlights of a car cascaded across the objects inside the backyard.

Rasheen and Willie were galvanized into an instant state of attention, because the car had pulled into the driveway of this house. They both gave each other that look as their hearts began pounding in their chests because it was evident major drama was amidst.

Rasheen began limping hastily towards the house with Willie close on his back. They both had their weapons in the ready position.

Just as Rasheen entered the house the doorbell was activated, which brought Rasheen and Willie to a full stop as they gave each other thoughtful stares that asked, what next!?

Rasheen told himself to be easy; it was probably nothing, and with that thought circulating inside his mind, he tiptoed to the door and peeked out the peephole.

When he saw the two white men dressed in dark business suits, and they each had that unmistakable look of law enforcement written all over their demeanor, Rasheen's heart dropped to his feet. Although he wanted badly to get away from his old ways, he realized he would have to put that particular promise on hold, and would have to start living it out after he addressed this issue . . . which would likely be addressed with the use of smoking guns.

CHAPTER # 8

Aaron had on a white chief's hat as he stood in front of the flaming hot barbeque grill, repositioning the four T-bone steaks. His white cotton short outfit had splattered grease stains all over it, and the first thing anyone with eyes would be compelled to ask upon seeing him would be, why don't he put on an apron for Christ sake!?

A few feet away, Keith Ramsey sat on a beach-like lounge chair with a bottle of Budweiser in his hand; his sky-blue cotton short set outfit was as spotless as the flaws on a Michelangelo painting. Sitting in lounge chairs next to him in a circular fashion were Eugene Lee and Norman Qing, and clothing wise they were similarly dressed as Keith and Aaron; the only difference was they both had on dark sunglasses.

There were happy clusters of kids playing in the huge backyard area of Aaron's half a million-dollar mansion, while the scattered groups of women were either lounging under shady trees, huddled around card tables, or sitting on benches gossiping. Aaron's wife, Geraldine, a slim high yellow, black woman with chinky eyes, was playing cards with Keith and Eugene's wives (Wanda and Nancy, respectively) along with two of her neighborhood girlfriends. The sun was beaming its fiery hot rays on the Atlanta landscape as though it was endeavoring to bake the surface into a golden, crispy, crust similar to the outer layer of an oven-baked French Croissant.

In the background, Harold Melvin and the Blue Notes' "Wake Up Everybody" could be heard coming from the stereo component near the patio a few dozen yards away from the picnic area.

Aaron Wilson sat his steak fork down on the nearby Aluminum table, took a few steps towards his comrades, and said, "Man, ain't this paradise? We haven't had one of these get-togethers since last year." He retrieved his bottle of beer from the lounge table in the middle of their circle and sipped on the icy cold drink. "We need to do this shit more often."

"Can't have it both ways," Eugene said, with his retreating hairline, natural bulging eyes, and light brown complexion. "We either work or play."

"Talking about work and play," Keith said. "Y'all gotta come up with a way to get Klingaman to ease up on that west coast assignment. Those DNA tests confirmed it was Rasheen Smith, and I'm not buying that bullshit that he's probably dead." The thought of having an enemy of the likes of Rasheen lurking in the shadows, who had no problem putting some slugs in people he deemed a foe, didn't set well with him.

Aaron went back to the grill and flipped the steaks as Norman said, "Keith, you worked with Klingaman; he's not gonna bend unless we can produce new evidence showing the Cali office may undermine this investigation." His slanted eyes widened as though he was challenging him to refutable this piece of information.

"The California team found nothing," Keith said. "I would say that's grounds to demand you guys be re-assigned—"

"It don't mean that," Aaron said as he sat in his lounge chair and impatiently locked eyes with Keith. "It could mean anything, but the last thing it can mean is that the agents from that office are ineffective. We take that position, solely because they didn't find this guy, we'll be digging ourselves deeper into shit. It's totally unreasonable to question those agents' ineffectiveness, because this guy is good with evading the long arm of the law." He wanted to point out to him that he was once again grabbing at straws, but instead, he decided to go at him at a difference angle. "We gotta play this one by ear. Ride slow and easy and keep our eyes open and ears to the ground."

"And let's not forget," Norman said. "We just got around that fiasco with the lost of Ted, Carlos, and Bruce by the skin of our teeth.

We start re-stirring up attention on this Rasheen Smith issue before the issue dies down, we'll be playing ourselves. It'll look too personal, and we may cause ourselves to become the subjects of an internal investigation."

Aaron said with a conclusive tone, "I know it's not wise to sleep on a guy like Rasheen, Keith, but until we get a sighting on him, it would be insanity to keep searching and making all types of waves when he might not even be alive."

"I gotta agree with Aaron," Eugene chimed in. "And mind you now, those blood tests indicated the source of that particular blood came from a gut wound. A lot of vital organs are in that area of the body, and without immediate medical attention, death would be right around the corner."

Norman added, "Every hospital within a hundred miles of that murder scene said no one entered with gunshot wounds fitting that description. In fact, regional agents were sent to interview every person shot in all those hospitals and none of them was Rasheen."

"Yeah," Keith said with an attitude. "You right about that; y'all right about it all. He was shot, and he apparently didn't check into any of those hospitals. When we calculate the amount of time it would take for the average person to bleed to death, it would confirm that he couldn't have traveled beyond those hospitals and lived. Yeah, we know all that." He paused for dramatic emphasis. "But, where's the body?"

There was no response.

Keith continued, "In my book, where there is no body, there is no death. Since this chump knows me, and I'm the one who put myself on front street with this job, I'm not gonna sleep on this issue, so don't expect me to. This clown was supposed to been dead a long time ago like all the others."

"Hold up, bro," Aaron said, feeling slightly offended. "We're not asking you to sleep on this guy; we're just asking you not to over-react. You're asking us to step to Klingaman again and basically try to force or manipulate him into re-assigning us to this case. You worked in the agency, Keith, and you know it don't work like that. We talked about this in detail, and I told you, we got a plan, but I see this is so deeply under your skin, you refuse to believe what I'm telling you. I told you, we got Fred Messer out there who promised he's gonna take this case very serious. He's a bulldog; he don't play when it comes to stuff like this. Believe me, if Rasheen shows up anywhere in California, we'll know."

"I'm serious about what I told you earlier," Norman said as he sat his empty bottle of bud on the table. "If he's still alive, you and I can personally fly out there in our spare time and put in some clandestine work if you like."

Keith again pondered the sincerity of their speeches, and it still wasn't reassuring enough for him to calm his nerves. He figured he'd throw out his firm reminder one last time for safe keeping. "Okay, I hear what y'all saying. I guess we gotta hang tight. But you guys better know that this Security firm of ours was built with money taken from this cat Rasheen. We're bringing in accounts so huge, in another two or three years we'll all have enough money to retire as very rich men with lucrative bank accounts that are completely legal. Unfortunately, we chose to step to those living on the wrong side of the law to gain our funds to make our dreams a reality, and because of that, you better remember these guys can't go running to the law when they get jacked for their shit. I obviously don't have to keep repeating it because I've said it a thousand times, if I said it ten times. They can settle their beefs in only one way. That's why we agreed that we'd prevent that by getting them before they get us . . . ."

As Keith babbled on about getting the guys they robbed before they got to them, Aaron realized he was growing very weary with his friend of more than two decades; they were buddies ever since Junior High School. After a moment, he figured it was time to clear his mind, and the only way to do that was to talk about more easy money. "Check this out," he cut into Keith comments. "Pardon me for interrupting, but this almost slipped my mind and I gotta get it out before I forget. I checked out that guy with the clubs in Texas. He's sitting on 5 mills in cash and he's looking for a way to clean that money up. He's willing to give up a mill to do it."

"What's there to talk about?" Eugene was grinning broadly. "Set it up."

The others collectively muttered comments in agreement.

"The question we should be asking," Keith said as he sat his empty bottle on the table, feeling happy by the news but also apprehensive because he was the main player that engaged in money washing missions, "is who's going to be the lead—"

"Daddy, daddy," A pretty caramel colored girl with pigtails in her head, who was no more than six years old, shouted at Aaron as she ran with her arms extended. She leaped into his embrace. "They keep taking the ball from us, daddy." Three other little girls that followed her ran to their respective dads.

Aaron held his daughter, Armenia up in his arms as Eugene cuddled his two daughters, and Keith embraced his daughter, Kimberly.

The group of four little boys had taken their ball and were now tossing it back and forth amongst themselves teasingly.

Norman shouted to his son, "Nelson, give them back the ball."

Nelson was clearly a carbon copy of his father, even down to the unusually large hands in comparison to his other body proportions. He tossed the ball to his dad and said, "We was only trying to get them to play with us."

With smiles on their faces Aaron, Keith, Norman, and Eugene got up and began spending some quality time with their children, chasing, tickling and toying with them, as the kids screamed and cheered with glee.

As Aaron enjoyed this priceless moment, his subconscious mind was in a place that was making him very dangerous. He gazed at his daughter and son Aaron junior, and then his eyes slid over to his wife, Geraldine. His mind savored the level of love he had for his family, and realized there were no limits to the things he would do to keep them happy, content, and most of all, safe. As all the wonderful years of good times coursed through his mind, something deep down inside was warning him that if he didn't tighten up all those loose ends currently floating around, all of this could end in an instant.

CHAPTER # 9

"Yo Rasheen!" The dream world shout was commingled with the cheering voices of children screaming and playing in a park on monkey bars, sliding boards, and seesaws. The images were vivid with a strong touch of surrealness. Then, that same adult voice chiseled its way into the picture again, "Yo' Rah, wake up, man."

This time the rude outside interference shattered the dream completely and Rasheen felt his perception shifted from the dream world to the here and now in the same way as a high-powered water hose spraying away a wet wall painting, sweeping away the colorful substances in a matter of seconds.

Rasheen opened his eyes lethargically and saw Willie staring down at him with Lora, a big boned brown skinned sister with a strikingly small waist, standing next to him with a silver food tray in her hands. She had a thing for breakfast or lunch in bed, and the way she stood smiling and handling the tray proved it.

"Man," Willie said smiling. "You been sleep for 12 straight hours, man, and I figured you should at least put some food in your system. It ain't good to go all them hours without food, man."

Lora sat her hefty rump on the side of the bed, since the tray was getting a bit heavy. The scrambled eggs, toast, pancakes, maple syrup, meatless sausages, chicken patties, and fresh squeezed orange juice weighed a bit once they were merged on a single tray.

Rasheen eased up into a sitting position with his back propped on the headboard of the bed, allowing the heavy sheet of grogginess to vanish. The first thing that struck him was the throbbing pain in his gut, and noticed the same thing happened yesterday morning when he awoke. He'd been here in this San Diego apartment Willie claimed was more secured than Fort Knox for two days so far.

Suddenly, that night in Westwood re-entered Rasheen's mind once again, and he was truly thankful that the two men that knocked on the door while they were digging up the stash turned out to be Real Estate agents, who were engaged in a late night interview. When Rasheen had opened the door with his 9-mm hidden behind his back, they introduced themselves as associates of Mark Ramirez, and further indicated that they were there to speak to the new occupant about "a few unresolved matters involving the lease." Rasheen brandished his 9-mm, pulled them inside, and Willie tied them up alongside of the other three.

After digging up the three duffle bags of treasurers, he and Willie fled the house, and headed for San Diego. Once they were safe and sound in Willie's stomping grounds, they called the Westwood police and informed them of the five people that were gagged and bound inside the house.

Rasheen unleashed a bone slapping stretch and was irritated by the fact Willie apparently ignored what he told him yesterday; that he couldn't eat anything until he slayed the dragon in his mouth. "I gotta hit the bathroom first." Rasheen flipped his legs out of the bed, forcing Lora to move out of his way. He shuffled towards the bathroom like he was on the movie set of a zombie flick.

As Rasheen entered the bathroom, he reflected on the way Willie and Lora were treating him, which confirmed the awesome power that money had on the human mind. He had counted almost two million dollars in cash before his fingers started getting tired; there were 16 pure gold bars, and almost two-dozen priceless jewels that Rasheen noticed was the main source of Willie's saliva dribbling antics. The way Willie and Lora were drooling over all these goodies was making him very nervous, but under the circumstances, he had no choice but to trust them since he had no one else. He was relying on the fact that they knew he was a cold-blooded killer, went everywhere with the 9-mm tucked away in the shoulder holster strapped to him at all times, even when he slept, and if they sneezed wrong, he would splatter their melons all over this apartment.

Although Rasheen was still grappling with trust issues when it came to matters of money, the one thing he had to admit was undeniable was the fact Willie was loyal and wasn't a grimy dude. Ja-King assured him that Willie was the real deal, and he was glad he was blessed to have him on his team and watching his back.

As Rasheen took care of his bathroom business, he reflected on the piece of paper he found in one of the duffel bags. The small handwritten note from Lameek contained information on how to get in contact with a person named The Judge whom Lameek assured him could "make anything happen". Upon finding this handwritten note, Rasheen felt a vicious wave of flashbacks skating across his mind, and this piece of paper instantly became a priceless object. He didn't even contemplate contacting this person until now. By the way Lameek spoke about this person, it was clear this person could help even though Rasheen was on the run, and he was now looking at this contact information much more seriously. Once he got himself situated, he made a mental note to reach out to this person called The Judge.

Another priceless object he found in one of the duffel bags was Lameek's first and third CDs. To his utter surprise, he was able to play them during the ride to San Diego without getting too emotional, and noticed he still felt the same level of enthusiastic stimulation he used to feel when he listened to his baby brother's rap lyrics when he was alive.

After Rasheen made a leak, dumped his shit bag, brushed his teeth, popped two pain killers, and ravaged the meal Lora prepared for him, he told Willie it was time to take another crack at contacting Sharon. Yesterday, her signal kept coming up as an invalid number, but Rasheen knew this only meant she was either busy with other matters, and couldn't respond now, or she had discarded her secured contact numbers all together. Rasheen couldn't seem to make his mind believe the latter was even possible, because it would spell disaster, so the only thing that registered in his mind at the moment was that she was preoccupied.

A few hours later, Rasheen sat at the kitchen table with the small compact laptop computer in front of him. He typed in the codes again and the same statement indicating an invalid number popped on the screen. Willie was sitting across from him reading a newspaper and Lora was somewhere in the back of the apartment.

Rasheen tried not to show his anger; he sighed and tried the number again. That same message appeared. Rasheen decided to log onto another website and try Sharon again in a few more minutes. He opened the Hoodaroma website again, and still couldn't believe Phillip Henderson was indeed the CEO of Hoodaroma. He read as many of the advertisements on the site as he could before his rage began to consume him. They were exploiting the deaths of Killer Kato and Lameek as if this was the best thing that ever happened to Hoodaroma. He could care less what they were doing as far as Colin Gibson was concerned, but what infuriated him was the fact they were painting Lameek into a monster.

Then, suddenly, Rasheen came across the fact that Killer Kato was Lameek's father, and they had the audacity to have the DNA documents on the web to prove it!

Rasheen's anger forced him to leave the website, and to try Sharon's number again. His heart leaped in his chest when he saw the affirmative response. "Yeah! There you go, baby boo!"

Willie rushed over to the laptop, feeling a ton of stress instantly dissipating from his shoulders.

Rasheen wondered should he activate the audio speakerphone component, so that he could hear everything without having to type. He trusted Willie, but he didn't know what delicate info she might have for him, and Rasheen learned many years ago that his business was only his business unless he deemed in advance the information was of a public nature.

After a moment of contemplation, Rasheen decided to utilize the headphones and the microphone. He assumed the issues up in the air wouldn't violate his rule of thumb regarding his business but made a mental note to ask Willie to give him his privacy if the situation called for it.

"Sharon, it's me, Rasheen," He made no effort to conceal the relief mixed with happiness in his voice.

"My God, Rasheen!?" She also didn't hide the shock that consumed her. She had just entered the house she had leased in Florida as a part time get away hide out and was just getting ready to have a few drinks with Robert McCall, her date, who was nothing more than a temporary bed buddy. He was currently in the living room waiting for her to return. "I thought you were dead, honey!"

"I'm good, boo," He leaned back in the chair with the microphone close to his mouth, as Willie sat back down across from him. "I got hit up pretty bad, but it's all good. I stepped to my business, took care of things on this side of town, but I slipped." His voice crackled with grief as Lameek entered his mind. "My baby bro got caught in the cross."

"Yeah, I know, Rasheen." She said softly upon hearing the pain in his voice and it forced her to find a seat on the nearby waterbed. "I heard the news reports. I'm sorry for you, Rah. I know what you're going through. I also heard what happened to Ja-King."

"Yeah, it's fucked up. I damn near lost my whole team." He had told her what happened to Jack Mack after it happened, so she was already aware of that lost. "I just heard they laced Candy up with murder charges for those cops. Shit ain't looking good for her at all. As far as I know she's holding it down; she staying firm, and ain't getting cheesy. She wasn't a rat when she was moving with us, but when they start talking the death penalty, ain't no telling what's gonna happen." He sighed because the loss of his brother was eating him up more than any other issue.

"Try to hold your head, cause you're gonna need it." She paused, wondering should she hit him up with some more bad news. After a moment, she got up and closed the bedroom door to make sure Robert couldn't hear anything she was about to say, even though she was already certain her voice was low enough not to reach his ears. "Listen, Rasheen, I hope you sitting down because I got a whole lot of other crazy things to share with you."

As the silence echoed from the other end of the line, Rasheen's heart pivoted in the opposite direction. He really wasn't in the mood for more bad news but knew there was no sense in trying to run from it. A moment later, he felt compelled to shatter the silence, since this was her way of telling him it was of a devastating nature, and he couldn't take the suspense any longer. "I see it's serious. I hear you loud and clear, Sharon. Let it ride, baby-doll."

Sharon sighed for further emphasis. "Keith played you, Rasheen. All that money you and Jack Mack invested in Supremetech Security Services was a scam. That chump took you and Jack's money, and got his man, Aaron Wilson, a FBI agent to go out there to kill you in order to cover up his tracks. That's why the feds are looking for you; it was Aaron Wilson behind that. He's the one who clipped your safe deposit boxes in Atlanta, and they even got hold of Jack's boxes. Just recently they snatched up one of Jack's boxes in New York, over in Grand Central Station."

There was a penetrating silence.

Rasheen stared at the laptop computer screen in a mesmerized daze. His mind felt like it was undergoing an information intake overload similar to a 10-ounce bottle being forced to hold 12 ounces of liquid. He felt a foreboding anger forming, but he held it in check with a great struggle, because he needed answers to a series of questions before venting his emotions. "Did this security company fold, or is it still in business?"

"It's still up. It's a legit setup, actually. The scam involves how the company was built on money Keith, Aaron, and their FBI friends took from ballers, hustlers, dealers, or anyone on the wrong side of the law."

Rasheen calmly shifted in his seat as he stared into Willie's thirsty eyes. "How many boxes of mine did they clip?"

"Three of yours in Atlanta, and two of Jack's. In New York they caught one of Jack's, and from what I can tell they're still combing through as many boxes as they can get authorization to crack open; they're trying to find all the boxes y'all got hidden."

Rasheen sighed with partial relief, since there were two boxes of his remaining and three of Jack's left. His anxiety flared up because he had to hurry up and get them before they got them. "How much cash did they catch in my Atlanta boxes?"

"From you they caught about 5 hundred gees, I heard. Jack, it was about 3 hundred grand."

Rasheen made a quick calculation, and the facts indicated it wasn't as bad as he expected. He sighed because they caught the three small stashes. In total that meant they missed 1.5 million of his hard-earned cash. "How much of Jack's money they got from the New York box?"

"That was a big one; it was about an 8 hundred-thousand-dollar pop."

Rasheen calculated what was left of Jack's stash and decided 6 hundred gees was worth fighting for. He was grateful Jack had given him the name and numbers to his boxes, and he had done the same with two out of his five boxes. His mind instantly made another connection, "Did you know those fed dudes kidnapped Lameek?"

"No, I had no idea!"

"Did you hear them making plans to kidnap anybody?"

Sharon thought about the question, and realized she did recall hearing one of Keith's phone conversations, where he had mentioned something about "snatching him up", but she couldn't believe they would throw Lameek in the mix because he was an innocent citizen that had nothing to do with Rasheen's illicit activities. "You saying they kidnapped Lameek to get to you!?"

"Motherfuckin' right they kidnapped him to get to me!" Rasheen was about to start huffing and puffing. "That's how he got caught up in all this shit. These dirty FBI dudes made me meet them in Victorville in order to get Lameek back, but Killer Kato stepped in. He got Lameek from them, and then, I went to Killer's mansion, and that's where I stepped to the business. The bottom line is, if they had left Lameek out of this bullshit. . ." His voice was strained with extreme hate. "He would still be alive today." His heart yearned for retributive justice.

"As a matter of fact, I did hear Keith mention something about snatching up someone, but at the time I had no idea he was talking about your brother, or anything connected to you." Sharon shook her head pitifully as she imagined the emotional pain Rasheen was experiencing.

The silence returned.

Rasheen snapped his mind back into a proactive state. "I got one more beef to step to before I head east, and I'm gonna need you, boo." He saw Willie lit up like an exploding star. "It might be stupid to ask you this, but I need to know . . . . You still down for me, baby-doll?"

Sharon smiled as she said, "Yeah, you still like asking stupid questions. Now, I'ma up the ante, and get ghetto funky with you, since you shootin' dumb shit at me. Plus, I'm ready to get off the merry-go-round."

Rasheen rode the brief moment of silence until it reached a ridiculous level and said, "A'ight, I see whatever it is ain't no joke. Let's hear it."

"Now that all this major drama is cleared up out there, I'm sending for you; we gonna do us, and I ain't acceptin' no more excuses about handling beefs, since all that is a thing of the past."

The silence returned, but this time it wasn't due to Sharon trying to make a subtle and subliminal statement; this time it was Rasheen engaged in the non-verbal communication tactic. She was basically telling him that she was cashing in on the checks Rasheen had been selling her in an effort to get her on his team; he had told her that he would settle down with her once he cleared up all the impending beefs cluttering up his life, but what he never got around to telling her was that he had a new born son and was planning to be with his little Shorty. Since Sharon wanted children of her own, had very jealous tendencies, took rejection relatively hard, and Rasheen couldn't survive without her computer expertise, he did the only logical thing any sane man in his position would have done, even though he had just laid the foundation to a new hornet's nest of drama that promised to haunt him for the rest of his life.

CHAPTER # 10

About two weeks after Rasheen contacted Sharon, Phillip Henderson sat in a cushioned chair in the VIP balcony of the World-class dance hall in Hollywood Hills staring down at the partygoers. The blaring rap song by Clay Ripper, the current man of the hour, had a hard-hitting type of bass that would propel anyone into a head rocking, body bobbing mood, and Phillip was no exception.

Taping his foot to the funky beat, Phillip had a drink in his hand as his two bodyguards, Derek Ramos and Troy Thomas, stood near the door watching his other close staff members sniffing blow, heroin, ecstasy, and all sorts of other mind shattering substances. Phillip could never understand what possessed people to put that poison in their bodies, and wanted to ban it completely from around him, but knew the havoc such a policy would cause. In fact, it wasn't hard to believe he wouldn't have a staff if he enforced such a policy. *Ole backward hustling ass idiots!* he fumed inwardly as he pulled his attention from them and put it back to where it belonged.

They were celebrating Clay Ripper's new CD release entitled Blue Dog Blues; despite the arduous road this project took to get to release status it was receiving rave reviews from just about every hip hop magazine, record industry critics, and all the other hip-hop institutions across the globe. This was Clay Ripper's second CD release, but his first with Hoodaroma, and was Phillip's first major project since he took the reins of the Hoodaroma Entertainment machine.

In spite of the heavy jovial atmosphere, Phillip was overwhelmed with stress, fear, and anxiety. There was simply too much shit happening too fast, and keeping up was enviably an ordeal in and of itself. But he was very happy inwardly, since he'd gotten total control of Killer Kato's empire with a series of maneuvers he'd started putting in place the minute Killer started warring with the Guineas and Russians, assuming he couldn't possibly survive a knock-down, toe to toe match with the two combined. When Killer had upset the Gangster world by forcing a truce from both heavy hitters, Phillip was on the verge of scrapping his covert scheme that involved the creation of a fictitious Will that gave him total control over the company, but then came Rasheen who finished the job. Not only did he finish the job, but Rasheen had gone the extra mile and put a big beautiful cherry right on top of that wonderful cake of fame, fortune and riches when he got Lameek killed, and himself in the process!

He instantly stopped his mental apparatus as he critiqued the thought involving Rasheen being dead, because he still hadn't received confirmation that Rasheen's body was found. Although the Lakeside Police were adamantly claiming the assailant couldn't have made it out of the area, he knew how arrogant folks in a position of authority had a way of twisting things around to put themselves in a positive light. But he subconsciously knew his conclusion that Rasheen was dead was merely his way of trying to force a situation into reality by engaging in the art of wishful thinking. They say if you think positively you can will it into existence, and vice versa, which was a maxim Phillip believed in whole-heartedly.

Phillip gulped down the remainder of his Veuve Cliquet champagne and sat the empty glass on the nearby table. The smash hit rap song ended and the second song that was destined to be a hit faded right into action. He was riding high on delight; he had total control of Hoodaroma and had cashed in all of Killer Kato's personal property, making a whopping 20 million dollars that went straight into his pocket, tax-free. For the first time in his life, he was able to shower his wife (Natalie) and two children (Frederick & Nina) with gifts, cars, promises of extravagant vacations, and anything their hearts desired. Even after he paid 20% to the Italians (he was now under their protection, since he didn't have the heart or the muscle to do what Killer Kato did), there was still more than enough money to make his mind spiral with bliss.

Everything about this was just too fucking good to be true, Phillip concluded resoundingly; he sighed with that usual pessimistic energy that seemed to master all his mental faculties, and decided for the tenth time, he had to prepare himself for some kind of monkey wrench being thrown into the picture. Good luck and fortune of this great magnitude always had a remarkable way of slipping from his grasp, and his instincts were telling him this would be no difference from the countless times shit blew up in his face when he was within reaching distance of gaining true wealth and supreme financial greatness.

The time when he was about to become a partner at the law firm he invested a small fortune of time and energy, and how the scandal involving old Mrs. Miller's pension had dropped out of the sky and crushed his dreams suddenly came to mind. Then, there was that time when Triacom Entertainment Inc. was about to make him the head of the entire company's Legal Department, or army for a better term, but he was beat out of that position at the very last minute because someone revealed that he was involved in the Miller scandal. Although he was never formally charged in that scandal, the mere suspicion of being involved in such a diabolical fraud was enough to cripple his career. But then Killer Kato came along, picked him up, tucked him under the wing, and put in motion this ultimate break he'd been waiting patiently for.

Derek approached with a muscle-bound strut and a big baby-faced smirk, and said to Phillip, "Clay just hit me on the cell; he told me to tell you the reporter from Vibe Magazine just got here. He wants you to sit in on the interview."

Phillip rose to his feet, and felt woozy from the two drinks, "Hey, listen y'all," He got the attention of his staff. "Cassandra is here." His announcement stopped them in mid-sniff. "If y'all leave out before

I get back, clean up behind yourself." He headed for the door and could see the confused expressions on their faces that indicated they thought he was losing his mind, since they were renting this place to have fun, not to clean up behind themselves. Denise Wallace gave Phillip an additional smirk that clearly said, they had workers who were paid to do that, for Christ Sakes!

As Phillip eased down the thick gold-carpeted stairs, his mind returned to the most stressful issue of all the others; was Rasheen Smith dead or not. This issue stayed on his mind for the simple reason, if he was still alive, he could possibly become the sole heir to this whole goddamn company. Since he saw the contract that Barbara Smith signed, giving her and Rasheen complete control over all of Lameek's assets, and since Killer Kato was officially Lameek's biological father, Rasheen was technically one of the heirs to his wealth. Although there was a lot of gray areas, and the complexity of the laws surrounding this matter could tie up this whole company in a vicious, lengthy court battle, there was very little debate that if Rasheen was alive, it would spell disaster, any way it went.

As Phillip reached the bottom of the stairs about to enter the dance floor, he had to commend himself on how he was able to get Killer Kato's four daughters out of the way by giving them 10% of the company's total worth. Despite the devastating hit the company took when those hackers transferred damn near 7 million dollars of the company's operational funds to various phony, non-for-profit organizations that folded immediately after they got hold of these allegedly donated funds, Hoodaroma was still in the game. With all the media hype circulating over Killer and Lameek's death, along with their sudden irrefutable familial relationship, record sells were literally ripping off the company's roof.

Phillip dipped and weaved past the partygoers, heading for the elegant room on the other side of this huge dancehall. He was still praying that Lameek had not given Rasheen a copy of that contract.

There was no doubt Lameek had access to the contract, and probably photocopied it. *That little snooping son of a bitch was always sneaking around in the official file room*, he realized, and now he regretted he hadn't come up with a contingency plan for something like this. But, then again, who would've known both Lameek and Killer would be murdered in one single incident, and everything regarding the fake Will he constructed would unfold in such a remarkably prefect fashion.

Suddenly, Phillip could hear that nagging voice of virtue and morality reminding him that if that contract got into the wrong hands it wouldn't merely create problems as far as him maintaining control of Hoodaroma, but it also might even open doors to a criminal probe into the company's business dealings, at which time he would likely be staring at a stiff prison sentence for fraud, falsifying official documents, perjury, and god only knows what other federal and state criminal charges. As he gave Sharlene (a female gangster rapper he recently signed) a warm greeting, he concluded that he had to find a way to give his stress-laden mind a rest, and the only way to do that was to find out whether Rasheen Smith was dead.

When Phillip saw Clay talking to a brown skin woman with dread-lots and two simple looking men that had a camcorder and a still camera in their hands, something tugged at his gut as he sauntered towards the group. He assumed this unexplained tension was due to the fact Cassandra wasn't amongst the Vibe team; he immediately stopped his runaway mind from turning an ant hill into a mountain and told himself this wasn't a basis for getting crazy with his over-precautious, borderline paranoid antics, since it wasn't odd for the regulars to get replaced at a moment's notice to tend to more pressing matters.

Clay spoke with his whinny voice when Phillip arrived, "Hey, Phil, this is the Vibe peeps. Cassandra couldn't make it."

"It's a pleasure to meet you, Mr. Henderson," Lora said professionally, hoping the dread-lot wig she wore and the make-up wasn't too fake looking. "My name is Darlene Washington." She shook his hand. "You're the next rap mogul and I'm hoping to be a part of that awesome rise to pure stardom."

Phillip smiled as he shook Willie's hand and then Rasheen's, who introduced themselves as "Henry" (Willie) and "Harry" (Rasheen). Phillip felt an alarming vibration when he touched Harry's hand and stared into the man's eyes. It felt almost as if he somehow knew this man; he immediately shot down this premonition, realizing he needed a break bad. "It's a pleasure your magazine is interested in our endeavors. We're respectfully humbled by your actions."

Rasheen and Willie were dressed in nerdy attire and had on stage make-up that convincingly altered their skin complexions. Rasheen had gone all out with his disguise by changing the color of his hair to a reddish brown, and had added green contact lenses to the get up. He even altered his walk, hoping his effeminate gestures weren't too contrived to the point that they were giving him away. When Phillip gave him that weird look, he thought the jig was up, but then he conveyed a facial gesture, which demonstrated that he had shoved off whatever suspicion had tried to formulate.

"Do you have a room in the back somewhere?" Lora said to Phillip and Clay, her eyes bouncing back and forth between the two. "I would like two types of shots of you, Clay; one in a cool, tranquil atmosphere, and the other in the party area. But let's get the cool out of the way first."

"That's fair enough," Phillip said as he led the way towards a corridor; Derek and Troy were dead on Phillip's heels.

As Rasheen followed, he gave Willie the eye signal to get the heaters ready.

Earlier, once the three of them got pass security with the two 9-mms by hiding them inside the video camera, Willie went to the bathroom, and placed the weapons in reaching distance (in his waist), and so far he was unable to slide Rasheen his 9-mm, since too many eyes were on them.

As they followed Phillip, the bodyguards, and Clay Ripper, down the elegant corridor that was carpeted and had extravagant lamps on the walls, Rasheen was still closely examining the two bodyguards to determine what type of weapons they were handling. There was no question they were holding heat, since the bulges underneath their Miami Vice like suits were quite vivid. The thought of disarming them without getting the draw on them first crossed his mind, and since he'd finally gotten rid of that awful smelling shit bag about three days ago, and mainly because his stomach surgery scars had totally healed, he felt in the mood to get physical in a real thuggish kind of way. It took only a fraction of a second to kill that thought, since he'd lost his brother with a similar game-playing tactic. This time it was about strictly stepping to the business in the most effective manner with the least amount of words and risks.

As they entered an office that looked like a millionaire's living room, Rasheen immediately began taking note of how they could secure this situation. Certain military maneuvers he'd read about in various books started tumbling around inside his mind, and he was surprised to see some of that stuff could be utilized in a simple mission such as this one. Looking around in all directions, Rasheen surprisingly noticed there were no video cameras, or at least it didn't appear to have any, he corrected himself.

As Clay and Phillip took seats on the brown crush velvet sofa, while the bodyguards had split up, Rasheen nodded to Willie, signaling him that he would dee up on the bodyguard that stood near the door, and he should step to the one standing near Phillip. When he saw Willie understood clearly, he gave him the signal to go for it.

In a flash, Willie pulled both weapons, handed one to Rasheen as he took aim at Phillip while shouting, "Hands in the air!"

Rasheen took aim at Derek, the bodyguard by the door who was about to reach for his weapon. "Don't turn it into a homicide, big homie!" He eased over towards Derek as Willie did the same to Troy. "Hands up! All the way up like you wanna touch the fuckin' ceiling!"

Within minutes, the bodyguards were disarmed, gagged, and bound.

Rasheen decided to pull Phillip away from the others. He walked over and stared down into Phillip's eyes. "You's a real slick mufucka, ain't yah!?" He saw Phillip was about to say something, but Rasheen cut him off when he grabbed him violently by the collar and yanked him to his feet. He marched with Phillip flailing his arms in terror as he headed for the other side of the huge room and shoved him down in a chair near a fake, but very convincing looking fireplace.

"What's wrong!?" Phillip shrieked explosively. "What have I done!? Who sent you!? I'm under Sammy Galucci's protection. If you have any discrepancies—"

"Shut the fuck up and listen carefully." Rasheen saw he had Phillip's full attention. It was amazing how effective a little roughing up could completely discombobulate a spineless thief, he realized as he enjoyed the terror emitting from Phillip's eyes. "Me and your business ain't got shit to do with that grease ball mufucka." Rasheen reached into his pocket and pulled out the contract he had gotten from Lameek and slammed it into Phillip's lap, making sure the blow had a hard impact on his right leg.

Phillip picked up the several sheets of paper that were stapled together, and before his eyes registered that this was a contract his mind had told him he was sitting across from the man he'd been brooding over ever since he'd experienced true wealth for the first time in his life. He started reading the contract he was all too familiar with; his hands trembled of their own volition, and he tried to appear strong and unmoved, but it was impossible. "Okay, okay, let's deal with this sensibly."

"The only thing I'm trying to hear right now is how the fuck am I gonna get my brother's money out of your mufuckin' hands, and into the hands it rightfully belong. If you ain't talking that kind of business, I'm forewarning you, you cruisin' for the ass whipping of yo' mufuckin' life!"

Phillip instantly felt a strong sense of hope, since if Rasheen was only here for money, he was sure he could give him an offer he couldn't refuse. As long as he got out of this alive, he was certain he could fix anything that had gotten out of hand, especially with Sammy backing him. The goal was to get out of this in one piece and without losing his life. "I understand clearly"

Rasheen saw the glimmer of hope resonating across Phillip's face, but he also noticed it was emitting something else; it was difficult to tell exactly what it was, nevertheless, he saw Phillip was ripe for the next phase of this plan.

Rasheen reached in his back pocket, relieved the envelope full of pictures, and tossed them into Phillip's lap. The envelope ricocheted and fell to the floor. As Phillip reached for the envelope Rasheen said, "These are a few little reminders to keep you focused on the bigger picture."

When Phillip saw the reflections of his wife, daughter and son, while they were each involved in their mundane daily activities, he felt his bowels become weak. The picture of his wife inside of a clothing store holding up a blouse, and the one of her getting inside her cream-colored Mercedes Benz told him that someone was following his family around; this was apparently the case despite the fact he had thought he had hidden them extremely well. But the photos that nearly caused him to shit in his pants were the ones of his children exiting and entering their home. "W—What do you want fr—from me, Rasheen?" He stammered with terror. "And why are you dragging my family—"

"Nigga, don't play that innocent victim bullshit with me, man." Rasheen leaned back in the chair as his 9-mm was in a relaxed position. "Now that you understand I'm not playin' no fuckin' games with you, now we can talk about how you get me out of your life permanently." He saw Phillip's nervousness slowly whining down. "I'm not a greedy man, Phillip." He partially lied, since if he could take all this nigga's money solely for the sake of just having it he would. "My research tells me Hoodaroma is worth tens of millions of dollars. My research also tells me Lameek was easily worth 20 million."

There was a moment of silence as Rasheen searched for a reaction but saw nothing.

Rasheen continued, "And if we liquidated everything my baby brother owned it might be 30 mill or more. Like I said, I ain't greedy, so if you put 10 million in my hands, I'm gone, outta here. All Lameek's rights to a piece of Killer Kato's Estate, and everything else will disappear when I'm gone. Pay me, and that contract will vanish into thin air; you'll never see me again." He was really lying now. "And you can keep it moving with your throat-cut scams and schemes."

Phillip tried to lock eyes with Rasheen, but he couldn't do it. It took only seconds to conclude that this was an offer he couldn't refuse, even if he subconsciously sensed that Rasheen was lying when he said after he paid the 10 million everything would go away. But he realized there was something he could do to provide himself a small margin of protection. He cleared his voice, and said, "Rasheen, if I agree to this arrangement, how are you going to guarantee me that all of these issues will be cleared up? Are you willing to sign a contract, agreeing to the circumstances of this agreement?"

Rasheen smiled inwardly because Sharon had told him Phillip would do something like this. In an effort not to expose his ace in the hole, Rasheen went into his actor's mode. "Like I said, man, you give me that 10 mill, I'll do what's needed to bring some closure to this situation. If signing a contract seals the deal, so you and I can get on with our lives, then go on and draw up that contract. In the meantime, I need you to transfer half that doe to this bank account." He reached in his pocket, found the piece of paper and handed it to Phillip. "When I get conformation that this money has touched down, then we—"

"Hold up, Rasheen," Phillip said without looking at the piece of paper. "If we're going to resolve this like businessmen, in a traditional business fashion, then I suggest we stop the threats, and waving these guns around—"

Rasheen violently pointed the 9-mm at Phillip's head, making sure the barrel was a mere inch from his forehead. "Whoever said this was a traditional business transaction!? And who the fuck is you to start demanding shit!?"

Phillip recoiled and saw there was no way of taking control of this situation.

"All I wanna know is, are you gonna send the 5 mills right now to the account number on that paper?"

"Yeah, yes, I told you I'll play ball, but I need a moment to construct the contract."

"Okay, but that ain't got shit to do with you conveying that money." Rasheen waved to Lora, who approached as she pulled from her back pocket her cellular phone that was a combination of so many other computerized appliances it was useless to even attempt to itemize these sophisticated accessories.

Phillip hesitantly took the phone, and instantly saw it had the capacity to transfer money from one account to another. As Phillip sat with the phone in his hand, while the room was ringing with heavy silence, his mind was working well beyond over-time. It irked him that he was unable to measure Rasheen's degree of contractual faithfulness.

Then, suddenly, an idea hit Phillip like a swift snap kick to the backside; the excitement galvanized his fingers into a state of urgency as they began to activate the dials. He looked up into Rasheen's eyes, and realized this particular plan would not only work, but would work so well he might even be able to watch Rasheen breathe his last breath.

CHAPTER # 11

Bam Bam felt the sheet burns on his knees growing more irritating as he pounded in and out of Rebecca doggy style. With his hands clasped firmly around the base of her small waist, he couldn't take his eyes off the sight of her picture-perfect puddin' that was surrounded by a smooth, creamy caramel colored backside with a enough meat on it to satisfy three studs; the sensation of her warm silky smooth insides embracing his condom-covered manhood was simulating enough to make the knee burns almost transparent. Her pillow talk in the form of sensuous "ohs" and "ahs" along with her synchronized body rhythm and the flapping sound of his hips tapping off her jingling rump only served to make the moment that much more engaging, especially since she made him wait three weeks to hit the skins, cost him six dates of wining and dining, and a few stressful arguments with his babies' momma, Shanequa (who wasn't buying his excuse that he was out trying to find another connect).

After several minutes locked in this sex position, Bam Bam felt ready to unleash, but his ego was telling him it would be suicide if he gave into this temptation. The rap song about minutemen tickled at the base of his memory bank, causing his groin muscles to activate and locked down the nut with padlocking efficiency. Since he had full intentions of coming back for seconds, thirds, and so on, of Rebecca's luscious lips between her legs, he was determined to make an excellent first impression, and there was obviously no better way to do that than to stroke this thing long and strong and do it bold with a whole lot of soul!

Just as he slowed it down to a turtle's pace, he heard his cell phone buzzing and rumbling on the nightstand, causing Rebecca to sigh with frustration on cue. *Yeah! Saved by the buzzer!* He sighed inwardly as he pulled out from her bumper and snatched up the phone.

"What's happenin'?" Bam Bam shouted exhaustibly as he wiped away the runaway beads of sweat that were threatening to drip into his eyes.

On the other end Big Gains said, "Good news, homie," He was smiling as he sat behind the wheel of his black Hummer parked at the red light on the corner of Saratoga and Blake Avenue. "Rasheen's alive. He stepped to Phil and tried to press him for some cheddar."

Bam Bam tried to hold back the boiling rage, but some of it was so blinding that drops of it inadvertently slipped from the cracks. "You callin' me about that shit at this time of night!? Man, I'm with my mufuckin' girl—"

"Fuck them stink bitches!" Big Gains snapped back. "Nigga, we got a mufucka on the loose that murder fam! What kinda bullshit you on!? You ain't with the program!?"

Bam Bam rose to his feet, headed for the bathroom, gave Rebecca the nod that he'd be right back as he entered, and closed the door behind him. "Yo' listen, Gains, come by tomorrow afternoon; I'll have the team here and we'll figure out how we gonna track this chump down. Right now, son, I'm tapping that broad Rebecca, and you know I been working on that piece for a minute, son. I'm up in it, and man that pussy good as all outdoors! I was about to blast off, and here you come callin' me, son. You gotta do something about your timing—"

"A'ight, a'ight, I'm digging you, man." Big Gains hit the gas pedal when the light turned green. "You know how I do shit. Business before bullshit is the rule. When you talk to yo' team, let 'em know we going out west on the first thing smokin'." He paused, waiting to hear Bam Bam start bitching and complaining. When it didn't come, he continued. "Poison Red told me he got some people out in Cali who said they saw Rasheen somewhere in San Diego. I told him to turn it up, and to have something for us in a couple hours. From the way it looks, I think scam Jones is gonna come through. Basically, Bam, when the shit drop, we pop!"

Bam Bam wanted to blow up on Big Gains; he honestly didn't feel like flinging his troops into a precarious and non-money-making situation, in order to put in work for a straight up creep ass nigga. Now that he just found out that Killer Kato and Crazy B were playing him when they paid him way below standard lieutenant rates, and they lied about just about everything regarding prices for keys, and the wages for street workers, it was becoming nearly impossible to bust his gun with confidence in the name of this foul dude who was fucking him around on every level.

When Bam Bam noticed he was caught in a daze, and his silence was broadcasting his apprehension, he told Big Gains what he wanted to hear while already concocting an excuse to get out of traveling to the west coast. "Okay, son, I'm feelin' you!" He sounded hyped up, and enthusiastic. "Now that's how you supposed to handle shit, Gains." He said cheerfully. "Get your facts and info in order before calling the team into play. I'm on it, son. After I get my skeet on, I'll call Frukwan immediately!"

Big Gains was nodding his head as Bam Bam spoke; he wasn't convinced. He was about to hit him with one of his "what if" scenarios as a subtle way to remind him that his britches weren't too big to get burnt but decided to let Bam Bam go back to his business. "I'll see you at about 10 o'clock. Talk to you then; peace."

He disconnected the cellular phone and tucked it into his jacket pocket. As he was cruising down the deserted streets of Brownsville Brooklyn, Big Gains saw there was no way around doing what he was hoping he didn't have to do.

Big Gains sighed indecisively, because Frukwan was going to take this shit hard! Frukwan was a good dude, and was real tight with Bam Bam, but Bam Bam was getting real loose. Too loose for a bitch ass dude that ain't never bodied a mufuckin' thing in his life, and was allowed to live like a Don solely because he had the backing of Killer Kato and Crazy B; now that those two were out of the way it was amazing how this weak ass clown was stupid enough to think he could continue beating his chest like he was a true blue gorilla, and that the real gorillas wouldn't step to that ass. This shit was truly sickening! Then, to top it off, he was giving off a vibe that showed clearly, he was gettin' on some serious foot dragging shit when it came time to avenge the death of the peeps that made it possible for his bitch ass to live the way he was living. He was committing a violation of the utmost degree, and as far as Big Gains was concerned, it was totally unacceptable and would not be tolerated.

Big Gains made a right turn onto Eastern Parkway, and noticed the only issue he was grappling with at the moment was how was he going to kill Bam Bam's bitch ass and do it in such a way that it didn't fuck up the business? After a moment he decided to sleep on it for a few hours, knowing something would appear once he cleared and rested his mind.

On the other side of town, Bam Bam was doing the same thing Big Gains was doing . . . trying to figure out how to get rid of a so-called comrade, without causing his own demise.

* ** *

Several hours later, Aaron Wilson disconnected his cell phone as he sat in the passenger seat of the agency vehicle as Donald Mooney was navigating the car down the Atlanta freeway, heading towards Dewitt Food Conglomerate Company to put the finishing touches on a six-month investigation into the company's unlawful business activities, consisting of telecommunication's fraud, price gouging and money laundering.

Aaron sat the phone down on his leg in slow motion, as he fought back the several different emotional surges exploding through his central nervous system. His silence was indicative of the sudden turmoil that clutched his being, and he could sense Donald was almost as infuriated as he was. He couldn't and didn't want to believe what Phillip had just told him!

"Well, I guess we're gonna have a whole lot of moonlighting on our hands." Donald actually wasn't surprised Rasheen was still alive but knew he couldn't express that opinion. Although he merely heard bits and pieces of Aaron's phone conversation with the Hoodaroma lawyer in California, there was enough tension transmitting from him to figure out Rasheen was still alive and was making some serious noise out there on the west coast, which meant he could be coming to see them. "This might not be as bad as we're making it out to be, Aaron. This guy is like the walking dead, anyway. They confirmed that he's the main suspect for those murders. A triple homicide is something that will get him on our top ten most wanted list, and you know the success rate of capture once a perpetrator appears on that list. Hell, I'll make the request; it'll be just a matter of time before he's apprehended."

Aaron wanted to scream and yell at Donald for not realizing the obvious implications. With great struggle he spoke calmly, "Yeah, we could get him on that most wanted list without much trouble." He turned, and locked eyes with his partner as his crazy screw face became screwier by the seconds. "But what do you think is gonna happen if by chance he starts talking, and starts saying things that might make another agent, or a state or city law enforcement official, wonder. And what if that agent, or cop, whoever it might be, starts snooping around and stumbles onto something? I don't want to sound paranoid or anything, but let's be realists here. If a new, hungry agent hears about some of the things this guy Rasheen knows, and this cop is trying to become a super cop over-night,

83

there is no telling what could happen. The safest way to handle this problem is to tie all loose ends, with the least amount of official contact as possible."

Donald felt a jolt of realization. "I see what you mean." Then, he felt a ping of embarrassment when it dawned on him that he failed to put that simple analogy into its proper context. All the illicit activities they'd been successfully engaged in for the past several years required that they prevent anyone with even an inkling of information about anything they did to be wiped away from the equation. "I agree; this guy has gotta go."

About six hours later, Aaron, Keith, Norman, Eugene, and even Donald Mooney sat around a small coffee table inside of Keith's Peachtree Condo with tension in their bodily gestures, and tight-lipped expressions that were about as serious as the end results of Hurricane Katrina.

Keith leaned forward while talking with animated hand gestures, "I mean, how the hell did we miss this!? If we knew this guy was Rasheen's brother's lawyer, basic one oh one intelligence gathering, and criminal capturing procedures say we should've immediately put a tag and a tail on him."

Aaron sighed almost impatiently, "It ain't that open and shut, Keith." He felt very self-conscious about this discussion, because he never told Keith he knew Phillip Henderson personally. Actually, he had several dealings with that scary ass handkerchief head Negro on the strength of Killer Kato, but honestly believed Rasheen was dead and that it was a waste of time putting a tail on Phillip. "Without official authorization to continue our investigation, we couldn't stay out there! Unless we had our own private jet where we could slide back and forth from California to Georgia, I don't know how the hell we could've reported to work and go steppin' to this lawyer and pursuing any leads he may have been able to provide us."

Keith angrily laid back on the sofa, while struggling not to start ranting and raving.

Eugene said reassuringly, "Man, we gonna clip this fool." He'd been trying to figure out exactly how they would do it, but nothing came to mind. "And if you stressing out about him confronting you, you need to stop it, Keith. Imagine this guy coming down here in our territory thinking he could do something to anyone of us? Fuck, we're federal agents for crying out loud, and this cat ain't no idiot."

Aaron wanted to tell Eugene to shut the fuck up; his remarks were only stirring up more anxiety. It was obvious there was a chance that Rasheen would step to them, despite the fact they were federal agents. He came to this conclusion because if someone had stolen that much money from him, he would have hunted the guilty party down with unrelenting viciousness. "Eugene, do us all a favor and let's assume the worst, please. That's why we called this meeting. He's alive, we fucked him around royally, and he's a threat to us in the worse kind of way."

"He knows absolutely too fuckin' much," Norman had one leg folded over the other. "As it stands, he's an uncontrolled eyewitness to that Victorville ordeal." He shook his head disbelievingly at the consequences of what would happen to them if he started running off his mouth, describing things that only an eyewitness would know. "The bottom line is that we gotta work over-time and find him quick."

"I can't believe we let this guy live this long," Donald said in an almost condescending tone, "He knows where our company is located, and even worked in this establishment." He had warned against this, and just had to get his I told you so lick in. "I'm not trying to rub salt in anyone's wounds; I'm just reminding us all that these over-confident strategies can't happen again. I mean, let's face it, had we disposed of him and his friends while they were here in Atlanta—"

"Killing them in another state was the wisest approach," Keith lashed out, furious by all this Monday morning quarterbacking bullshit. "Yeah, you said otherwise, but we voted, and the majority won." He sighed as he cupped his hands to his head, drew in several deep breathes, and re-focused his mind; now wasn't the time to start losing it, and creating dissension amongst their ranks, and since he was the mastermind of this elaborate endeavor to make sure they all retired as extremely wealthy people, it was his obligation to keep things in order. "Okay y'all, all right. Let's not rehash all that stuff from the past. We learned from it, now let's move forward. We came here to brainstorm and find a solution. From henceforth, everything we put on the table should be a possible solution."

Norman spoke nonchalantly. "I think we should take another crack at that bank account number Rasheen gave Phillip. A $5 million transfer is too god dam big to not leave some kind of tracks."

"We already hit it from all angles," Donald said. "Unless we add some new information to our wire search, I can't see beating a dead horse to death getting us anywhere."

Eugene said, "Phil said that $5 million was the first installment. Keeping our eyes on that next transaction is where it's at."

"That's already in motion," Keith confirmed. "I got four sets of eyes on it."

Eugene spoke, "Maybe we should talk to Phil again . . .

Aaron sat in a trance as the others went back and forth with a series of suggestions that were starting to get ridiculous with each new proposition. There was a suggestion surfing across the surface of his mind that he sensed could work, but knew Keith wouldn't agree to it. He didn't want to throw it out there, but the harsh reality was that there weren't many other options left, and even though this proposition would unveil an emotionally charged topic, it had to at least be considered, he told himself. There was also another long-range maneuver that stood the chance of producing results, but this current idea circulating through his mind would have to be put on the table first.

After a moment of pondering how to present it, Aaron stomped all over Norman's comments, "Wow, wait a minute, what about this." He locked eyes with Keith, and once the room became quiet, and said. "Why don't we see if we could get Sharon Walker to try to draw this chump out of hiding? From what I noticed, when he was here, he had the hots for her. If we could get her to—"

"No fuckin' way!" Keith spat with a disgusted tone. "Sharon don't give a shit about that clown. She told me from her own mouth she despised him!" His tone threatened to evolve into a boiling hot rant. "And why would we drag her into this anyway!?" His heart and the raw emotions took control, and even he didn't realize what he was doing. "And what you think'll happen to her if Rasheen finds out she's trying to set him up!?" He locked eyes with Aaron, because he knew he always had a hatred for Sharon, and this was probably his way of trying to get her killed. "I'll tell you what the fuck will happen! He'll smoke her black ass!" He was about to turn up his anger another notch, but realized his intimate memories of the good times he shared with Sharon were causing him to tell on himself (he wasn't over the relationship). He spoke softly, "Let's not involve people outside of our circle."

Aaron always suspected Keith hadn't fully gotten over that affair he had with Sharon, and now it was confirmed as far as he was concerned. Since they had thrown two other women who worked for Supremetech into an unfortunate situation to gain a huge monetary advantage and had even caused the untimely death of one of them when things got too hot in the kitchen, it was clear Keith couldn't let go. He'd personally never trusted Sharon; she had this sneaky, conniving way of manipulating things, and most of all, she was very smart, shroud, and relentless; she was too smart for him, but what scared him the most, she was an ex-government agent, who knew the business, knew the dirt, and knew how to evade fellow agents. As far as he was concerned she was a threat to them, since she wasn't fully onboard with their program, but they allowed her to work at Supremetech in view of her superb computer expertise. He wondered for the ten thousandth time was she privy to their underhanded dealings? He wanted desperately to believe she wasn't, but there was no telling what Keith had said to her while they were locked in those intimate moments.

As the group continued tossing out suggestions of how to neutralize this threat to their very existence, Aaron rewind his mind back to the times he saw Rasheen pushing up on Sharon. Although she reacted towards him in such a way that conveyed her disinterest, there was something in her eyes that said something else. That look said there was something going on there, and it often looked as if she was putting on some kind of public act.

Nodding his head as the revelation proliferated into a stolid lead that was well worth pursuing, Aaron vowed he would get on this one without the others knowing; his instincts and gut feelings were telling him there was something there, and if he looked behind the scenes long enough he was destined to find something.

"Pardon me," Aaron interjected again while holding up his right hand, deciding it was time to get the ball rolling, and to bring this meeting to a close, because this plan of last resort was too irresistible to pass up. "I was holding back this idea until the bitter end. It's a bit extreme, but I believe it'll work. Like anything else that has the potential to work, there's some chances we'll be taking, but the main thing is that it's doable. I'll put it on the table and let y'all decide." It took him five minutes to explain the plan.

When he saw the collective smiles on his comrades' faces, while their heads started moving bobbingly to a silent, imaginary beat, Aaron knew there was no need to ask whether they were with it, because their actions spoke far louder than their words could have ever done.

CHAPTER # 12

Rasheen sat in the window seat of the private jet, gaping at the specks on the ground below that were supposed to be cars, trucks and other moving objects, but looked like tiny, microscopic viruses moving across a specimen plate glass.

As Rasheen pulled away from the view, while breathing in and out several lung fills of air to stifle his anxiety, he was grateful the liquor was finally warming up his insides. He was surprised he wasn't sick to his stomach, since this was his first time ever flying in a plane. He was impressed by the way Sharon was working her magic wand once again; she had miraculously hooked up this daring escape from the west coast with the use of this jet, and had jokingly claimed, "I'm making arrangements to have you delivered to me first class air mail." Although Sharon gave hints suggesting this was her personal jet, his mind couldn't conceive the possibility of Sharon stepping to her business on such a grand scale, which would mean she had surpassed him by leaps and bounds; he made it his business to probe her in depth on this issue the minute he got the chance.

Rasheen was dressed in an ash gray Armani suit, black Gucci gator shoes, a black spandex mock neck shirt, had ice on his wrist and ring fingers that sparked an expensive glow throughout the entire interior of the aircraft, and was clean shaved with a meticulously neat goatee, and a Caesar haircut minus the waves. He took another swig of the Hennessey, realizing he could easily become addicted to this way of living. He'd been ripping and running, robbing and stealing, killing and scrapping and pursuing a vendetta so long, he'd almost forgotten how it felt to enjoy these finer things in life.

He reflected on the pass three weeks since his little visit with Phillip Henderson, and noticed things had been going so sweet he wondered if this spree of good luck would transform into the usual type of bad luck that always had a way of surpassing the good luck in ways that made the good luck actually bad luck. Despite his pessimism, he was convinced this good luck wouldn't change, at least not for a moment.

He peeked over the seat at the waitress, Sebrina, who was dressed in a tight-fitting skirt; she had a set of gorgeous legs and baby blues encased in an olive complexioned baby-face that made him contemplate coming down with a chronic case of jungle fever, and the lyrics of the Envogue song drizzled to the forefront of his thoughts, "Free your mind and the rest will follow, be color blind, don't be so shallow." Yes, sir, he could definitely get colorblind with this shortie here!

The sight reminded him that even if there was some bad luck peeping around corners, it still wouldn't change the success of the $5 million touch down; the bank account Sharon constructed solely for this transaction registered a successful transfer less than an hour after Phillip sent it and everybody was elated with a happiness that only a $5 million come off could stir up. Even Willie and Lora were delirious with delight, and rightfully so, since before bidding them a temporary farewell Rasheen blessed Willie with 3 hundred grand, 2 gold bars, and 2 of the priceless jewels for his services; Willie was speechless because he didn't expect to be rewarded in such a lucrative fashion.

Another major success occurred when he contacted Lameek's hook up. He had reached out to the Judge and from what he could tell so far, this was going to be one hell of an ace in the hole if this individual passed the test Rasheen was constructing. After the burnt marks he received during his dealings with Keith Ramsey, no one would ever lay a finger on his cheddar until they passed a test of the likes of a trial by ordeal.

Now that Rasheen finally had a moment to enjoy some good, positive energy, under a new identity thanks to Sharon (his new name was Daniel Groven), he patted himself on the back for spreading love across the board. With help from Lora, he reached out to Rashango, wired him a few thousand dollars along with instructions to write back, and when he responded, Rasheen discovered Rashango was scheduled for release in three months. When he sent Camila some more money, along with the same message to write back, he was surprised he hadn't received an immediate kite from her like the time she had quickly responded when she responded to Candy's letter. In his previous letter she claimed she was moving in with her aunt in Crown Heights when she was released, and he hoped that hadn't changed, because he had full intentions of paying her a surprise visit, with full intentions of rescuing her and his son, once he got all the long-range foundations laid out.

However, when he wrote Candy and blessed her with a few dollars, things weren't as gravy as he thought they were. He had sent Candy five thousand dollars under a fictitious name, and a bogus P.O. Box, and she wrote back with her ride-or-die attitude still intact but was already letting the time get under her skin and inside her mind in the wrong way. When she answered Rasheen's inquiry involving whether or not she needed him to get her a private attorney, Candy had written, "nobody can help me out of this fuckin' trick bag, not even Houdini could turn a trick for me . . .The best thing you can do is keep your little cheesy ass cheddar. If things change, I'll let you know."

Then, later on in this same letter Candy had apparently started letting her emotions guide his fingers when she wrote, "But, on the up and up, Rah, I ain't feelin' the way y'all niggas left me for dead. If we would've stayed true to form, we all could've got up out of that fucked up shit! If my man didn't get popped, I wouldn't be up in here! What the fuck happen!? I thought we was fam!? And I thought you said we would never abandon fam!! Oh, I know what time it is,

I guess you like all them other fake ass niggas, who talk the talk, but when it comes time to walk the fuckin' walk you get happy feets!"

After reading this Rasheen had sat the letter down with his stress levels about to run amuck. Candy was disgruntled, felt betrayed, and was furious. Since there was nothing more dangerous than a woman in prison in that state of mind, who was convinced she had caught a bad one because she was double-crossed, he didn't have to be reminded that this was a recipe for the turning of state's evidence. By the time he ripped up the letter, he was already looking for ways to reach out and touch Candy; he couldn't understand how she wasn't able to correctly assess that night, because if she did, she would've known that it was impossible for him and Ja-King to save her. As he tried to sweep the issue under the thick rug inside his memory bank, a screaming inner voice made him second guess whether they really could've saved her, if they had tried harder.

His clandestine communications with Ja-King produced the best news of them all. Things were looking up for his homie; his bodyguards stepped up and were ready to take the weight, insisting that they were the ones who fired the shots that killed those by-standers and that Ja-King never fired a single shot, nor was he even in possession of a weapon; according to Ja-King if everything stayed at its current pace, he might be walking out the front gate real soon. Since he had major money of his own, he returned the five thousand dollars Rasheen had sent him.

"Rasheen, baby," Sebrina purred as she sashayed towards him. "You need another drink, honey?"

Rasheen couldn't control the smile that fizzled onto his face, "Why not, Sebrina." She was apparently his personal waitress for the duration of this trip, and it was only right he allowed her to do her job. Since he was the only passenger on the jet, the temptation to start flirting with hopes of tapping those pink skins was strong. *Damn! The smell of that jasmine like perfume aint no joke!* He felt his manhood acting like it was about to stand at attention. The urge to push up on Sebrina was very strong. The only thing stopped him cold in his tracks was the fact this could be a setup or a test on Sharon's part and right now the last thing he needed was the creation of any tension that would interfere with this relationship of theirs solely because he couldn't keep his dick in his pants.

He watched Sebrina glide towards the small compartment near the cockpit, and his mind went back on its mission as she disappeared inside the small room. His future plans were heavy on his mind. Images of him with his little Shorty, however, were the strongest mental pictures dancing inside his third eye.

Then, his thoughts suddenly came to a skidding halt; reality nudged its way into the mental picture and Keith Ramsey and Aaron Wilson's faces appeared. They were gunning for him. They wanted him dead, had made an attempt to kill him already, and caused the death of Lameek in the process. All of this because they had swindled him and Jack-Mack out of millions, robbed their safe deposit boxes, and wanted him dead to cover up their tracks. This was drama at its most unadulterated level.

According to Sharon, Keith and Aaron had no intentions of stopping their efforts to kill him until he was six feet under, which meant if he intended to live to enjoy seeing his son grow up, he'd have to either kill them first, or go underground into deep hiding, looking over his shoulder for the rest of his life, while hoping and praying they never found him. This was a reality he simply could not ignore; it was one that stayed on his mind constantly; it was also a reality that would hinder all other future dreams from becoming a reality, and most of all, it was a reality that called for action, even if doing nothing was the approach he decided to take, but something most definitely had to happen.

He pushed his thoughts onto another issue, and Lameek returned. The pain in his heart caused him to cringe instantly.

Months had gone by since the death of his baby brother and yet the pain was just as hurtful as it was when he saw Lameek's body recoil when the gun went off as he and Killer Kato wrestled for control of it. Every time he thought about his inability to even attend Lameek's funeral services, in the same way he was denied the opportunity to attend his mother's funeral, he felt a revengeful spark of blinding rage boiling up inside of him.

Only after he tamed his emotions with a mind trembling struggle was he able to listen to that voice in the subterranean regions of his mind. It was telling him all of this tit for tat, fighting hate with hate, and addressing death with more death was taking him nowhere, but around and around in a circle of destruction, misery, and the senseless affliction of pain and suffering. So many people he loved had died, and he could connect these tragedies to his own actions in some way; his mother, Dirty Ricky, Lameek, Crystal, and Jack-Mack were the ones that hurt the most.

The others such as Black Bob, Randy Doylson, Dario Montero, unknown shop owners, rich mansion owners, security guards, prison-house rapists, wanna be gangstas and simpleminded fools too stupid to follow instructions such as "nothing move but the money", and the countless Colombian, Dominican, and other drug dealers still didn't touch his heart as much since they were causalities of an urban war, and had, in any event, put themselves in a situation to become a victim of the game. This treacherous merry-go-round was one filled with guaranteed episodes of bloodshed and shattered dreams on all spectrums of the scale, under circumstances where there were very few winners.

It was a merry-go-round he wanted to get off; notwithstanding his new aspirations he understood clearly that he had made a bed that he was destine to sleep in, but he could also feel the awesome power of the universal was giving him one last chance to get off this treadmill of mayhem and melancholy, and if he blew this opportunity, it would be his last chance to make right all of these wrongs. Why he felt this way he couldn't explain it in words, but it was so clear to him that he couldn't dispute it. On top of that, he had enough money to live very good for the rest of his life, and the thought of staying in the game now that he was rich seemed so irrational, reckless and utterly stupid, even though at one time in his not so distant past he'd never thought there would ever come a time he would be sitting here thinking like this.

Rasheen pitifully shook his head in deep thought as the wave of depression proliferated. This new way of thinking frightened him because he was turning into something considered the unforgivable in most hoods across the country; he was getting soft, he was turning into a bitch; a heartless baller with no balls, and a boss nigga who was demoted to a buster. For some odd reason, he no longer even felt a burning desire to unleash the violent rage inside of him, nor did he detect that familiar unquenchable thirst for unlimited amounts of money.

When he assessed the source of this sudden shift and apprehensiveness, his search led him to the most recent gunshot wound. That last shooting did something crazy to him, and he didn't want to believe there was some kind of mystical force behind this traumatic ordeal, but it did something to his mind, body, soul, and conscience; those wounds changed him in ways that he didn't understand, and it scared him.

"Here's your drink, Rasheen," Sebrina broke into his deep thought process as she handed him the drink with clanking ice cubes, and returned to her seat near the cockpit while throwing her black girl ass like she was trying to break something.

When he resumed his mental aerobics, his future plans with Sharon entered his mind; this was another chapter in his life that would test him in many drama filled ways. He smiled since he'd recently found out that Sharon wasn't the sweet little goody two shoe who was a brainy act with impeccable computer skills he had thought she was. In many ways it didn't totally amaze him that she had a lot of illicit side businesses that she controlled as a silent partner, but what did surprise him was the fact she was an ex-government agent; she didn't say what federal agency she once worked for, but she promised to talk with him about that in the future.

About two hours later, the pilot said, "Please fasten your seat belts, we're landing very shortly."

When the jet came to a stop on the private landing strip in Tallahassee Florida, Rasheen gathered his carry along bag, and headed for the door. As he stepped through the small door and began stepping down the portable steps of the jet, he was looking for Sharon's familiar face, but what he suddenly saw shook the pillars of his soul.

* ** *

Big Gains pulled his black Hummer into the parking space on the corner of Rutland Road and East 98th Street and threw the gear in park.

Sitting next to him in the passenger seat was Frukwan, a top lieutenant of Killer Kato's drug enterprise under Bam Bam's command, who had a high yellow complexion, a slim physique, and a set of evil looking eyes that gave off a very scary aura. They both were dressed in standard hood attire; baggy jeans, Tims, and hoodie style jackets designed for the current spring weather.

The late-night streets were dark, deserted and consistent with the time: 3:02 am. Whispering through the radio was a new Hot 97 rap song by Money-Man; it was obvious the title of this track was "Paper Maker" by the way the hook pounded this fact into the minds of the listeners.

Frukwan spoke with clear impatience in his voice, "Yo', son, what's this shit about? I ain't with all these waitin' games."

Big Gains was gazing at the rearview mirror as he watched the black Thunderbird, about several cars behind him, whipped into the parking space; he then saw Jackhammer Jones get out the car and headed towards him. Jackhammer was dressed like a construction worker; he had on worn Levi denim jeans, beige timberland boots, and an old lumberjack looking flannel shirt. The only thing missing was his hard hat; he did have on a tool belt concealed under his olive-green army field-jacket, but it didn't contain screwdrivers, hammers, and other standard construction worker tools; it possessed other utensils applicable to his part time trade.

Big Gains waited until Jackhammer walked pass the Hummer, sighed and said, "How long we known each other, Fruit?"

Frukwan didn't know where this was going, but all the mystery surrounding the moment told him it would be best to answer the question without a whole lot of back talk. "About 10 or 12 years, somethin' like that."

Big Gains saw Jackhammer position himself inside the vestibule of an apartment building about several establishments from the building he was watching. He was glad Frukwan saw what was taking place, since this was what it was intended to do. "Who you knew longer, me or Bam Bam?"

Frukwan thought about the inquiry, and then said, "I think we all started gettin' paper around the same time. Back in the 90s when we was hustlin' for Killer, doing hand to hand slingin' and workin' in steel gate spots, I think." He saw Big Gains was staring at a familiar tenement building about a half a block away, and the strange dude who was posted up a few buildings away. "Come on Gains, what's happenin', son? You bring me out here and got me all in the dark. You got this car following us around; now the dude inside the car is chillin' near Bam Bam's baby momma's crib and you hittin' me in the head with all these crazy questions, and shit." He caressed his 9-mm nonchalantly, since in this game no sane baller would ever go on a trip like this one without holding hardware; by the way things were unfolding he was starting to assume this might be a run directed at him.

"What's the penalty for disloyalty?"

Frukwan smiled nervously, "According to my definition, or Killer's?"

"Is there a difference?"

"Not with the penalty part; it's death. But disloyalty for some might not be seen as disloyalty for others. Some cats been doing grimy shit so long, they don't know how to do nothing else but grimy shit. Disloyalty and grime go hand in hand."

Big Gains saw this was a perfect opportunity to share one of his what if scenarios. He reached over and turned off Hot 97, cutting off the new NAS song just as it started. "What if we was all on a ship sailing on the high seas, and a motherfucker, all of a sudden, tried to punch holes in the bottom of the ship. Let's say, he was mad about somethin' for whatever reason it might be, or it could be he was just buggin' the fuck out. Wouldn't it be common sense to say, because we all on this ship, if this mufucka shinks, we all fucked up in the game? Now, I wanna ask you, what should we do to this fool for trying to kill us all? Should we standby and ignore him, or should we stop him?"

Frukwan was staring at the dude posted up down the block and was becoming slightly irritated by Big Gain's what if games, but knew it was never wise not to play along, "I say we should split his mufuckin' helmet wide open and throw his dumb ass overboard."

"That's right!" Big Gains cheered as if Frukwan had just answered the $10 million dollar question. "Now let's bring it into focus a little, bring it more closer to home." He turned and locked eyes with Frukwan this time. "What if a nigga turned his back on fellow homies that was murdered, and these homies that caught a bad one was showing dudes mad love; made sure all his homies was eaten love love. How would you deal with a disloyal homie like that, Frukwan?"

He knew it! Frukwan now saw exactly what this was all about. "Yo' Gains, this got something to do with Bam not pullin' my coat about getting the team ready to roll out there to Cali?" When he received no answer, he felt the butterflies in his gut growing in numbers. Reflecting on his discussion with Bam Bam, when he was trying to get him to flip on Big Gains, he now wondered if Big Gains had found out about that internal conspiracy. His hand went for his weapon of its own volition, and the gesture provided some degree of comfort; if he was going to die, he promised he was going to take Big Gains with him.

The headlights of a car appeared up ahead, causing Big Gains and then Frukwan to crouch down in their seats until it passed.

"For the record," Frukwan said. "You know where I stand with Rasheen; if you ain't heard, me and him got lifetime beef. He hit up my cousin Snoop back in the day, and put him in a wheelchair for life, so you know where I stand with this beef." When the silence persisted, a terror-stricken nervousness coursing through his veins, and he wanted to try to talk Big Gains out of this apparent hit on Bam Bam, but by the looks of all the logistical circumstances, it was apparently way too late for that. Plus, he didn't want to appear to be soft.

Big Gains felt compel to break the long, uncomfortable silence, "Did Crazy B ever give you the run-down on how the chain of command works with this fam?"

"Yeah, no doubt. He said you and Bam Bam was the generals. He said you was top dog with the clubs, and Bam Bam was the man with the drugs." He couldn't curtail his urge to play stupid. "Where we going with this?"

Big Gains glanced at his watch, wondering what the fuck was taking this fool so long to come out. "I like to keep things real, and the only way to do that as far as I'm concerned is to deal straight up with those considered fam. You know it ain't about a lot talkin', it's about showing and proving—"

Big Gains saw the door of the apartment building he was watching open, and out stepped Bam Bam. He cut his eyes at Frukwan, saw him maintain his composure, and then glanced down the block as Jackhammer was already in motion.

Frukwan felt his heart pounding in his ears as he saw it was definitely a hit on Bam Bam. He wanted to call to him, intervene and save him, but he couldn't. He glanced over and saw Big Gain's hand propped on his leg within reaching distance of the weapon tucked in his waist, apparently waiting for him to try something stupid.

Big Gains spoke softly, "You know shit don't change, cause a few folks at the top take a fall. They say we don't die we multiply." He knew he didn't have to pull his heater because Frukwan wasn't suicidal, even if he and Bam Bam were real tight.

Jackhammer Jones caught up to Bam Bam just as he was almost upon his green Cherokee jeep and opened fire on him with a silencer-equipped weapon. Based Bam Bam's violent head jerking response, it was evident Jackhammer was in the head-hunting mode tonight. As Bam Bam collapsed to the pavement, Jackhammer Jones casually instituted his trademark contract-killing maneuver. He straddled over Bam Bam's body, pulled another 9-mm, took aim with both weapons, and pumped two shots from each gun into Bam Bam's chest while maintaining a stance as though he was operating a jackhammer.

As Jackhammer Jones calmly headed back towards the black Hummer, Big Gains said in a businesslike manner, "I wanted you to see this, cause I didn't want you gettin' the twisted version." He turned the ignition and the Hummer's engine rumbled to life. "Bam

Bam committed the ultimate violation. He turned his back on his duty to avenge the death of a fellow team player, he was plotting to kill me, he all of a sudden started stealing paper from us, he didn't even show up at Killer and Crazy's funerals and he was forewarned." He gave Jackhammer acknowledging head nods as he walked past the vehicle, heading for his Thunderbird. "Now that I'm the general of both divisions, you wanna take Bam Bam's position?"

"Hey, son, you know how I get down," Frukwan was smiling from ear to ear. "I'm about stackin' paper and keeping it funky, son. How Crazy B used to say it, give me my marching orders and let me march."

As Big Gains pulled the Hummer onto the street, and cruised away, he said, "Tomorrow, I need you to rally up a few top hitters and get at me by noon time. I hope you like Cali, cause its gonna be like home until we smoke this dude, and the faster we get rid of Rasheen, the faster we can get back here to these stomping grounds, so we can start back fattenin' up our pockets."

CHAPTER # 13

"Hold it right there!" Sharon groaned through the ecstasy-laden sensations racing through her body. "Right there, right there," her voice cooed in a sensuous manner as she threw her hips in an upward manner. "Yes! Don't stop!"

Rasheen had both of Sharon's voluptuous, chocolate-colored legs cocked on his shoulders as his manhood slithered in and out of her juicy tunnel of joy and pleasure palace. Every so often he would peek down at his and her sex organs tussling with each other, and the sight would increase the excitement in a wonderful kind of way. Even though he wore a condom, he could still feel the luscious warmth of Sharon's watery insides caressing against the latex. The softness of her body commingled with her rhythmic hip movements, and the smell of her exotic perfume fumigating the room, only served to make this one of the most memorable sexual moments of his life.

Not surprisingly, everything about this moment reminded him that he'd never gotten around to eating pussy. He was 29 years old, made millions, been to hell and back, but he still didn't know how pussy tasted! The strong curiosity was egging him to go down on Sharon, and if he had known for certain he was the main one hitting these lovely skins he was currently inside of, he might've went for it. But, the truth of the matter was, he knew somebody else had to be hitting these skins, since he wasn't. Before his tongue touched a woman's love tunnel, he had to be certain he was the main man driving up in that tunnel.

He'd been working feverishly on Sharon for about twenty minutes so far and was dripping sweat as if his bodily fluids were pouring from him by the bucket loads, even though they had the air conditioner on full blast.

As he maintained the dance like rhythm, Rasheen reflected on the moment he exited the jet when he saw the two burly black men dressed in black suits with earpiece communicators dangling from the side of their faces, and he thought he had walked into a deathtrap. His first mental response was that the two men were Keith and Aaron, and after the initial shock subsided and his mind started operating on a sensible level, his eyes registered the images correctly. None of the men were Keith or Aaron. They approached him, introduced themselves as assistants of Sharon and escorted him to the Lexus waiting out front of the private landing strip, where Sharon sat in the back smiling.

Rasheen felt the fire in his groin growing rapidly towards the point of no return and he attempted to slow down his pace, but Sharon wasn't having any of it, since she'd already came twice. She latched onto his butt cheeks and took charge by accelerating her pumping motion while making sure Rasheen couldn't stop her endeavor to make him come.

"Ohhh!" Rasheen moaned with pleasure as the hot juices exploded from his body. "Ahhh!" When Sharon started making orgasmic noises along with him, he felt the nut becoming more monstrous with each spasmodic extraction of his semen sack and his lady lovin' log.

When the mind-numbing moment of sensual gratification ended, Rasheen rolled onto his back exhaustedly. A euphoric sense of sheer satisfaction was sweeping across his entire being. "Damn, Sharon! What you tryin' to go to me, girl!"

Breathing hard Sharon said through her pleasing exhaustion. "Something I should've done a long time ago." She cuddled closer to Rasheen and started brushing her fingers across the grotesque surgery scars on his stomach.

Rasheen felt self-conscious about the scars, and attempted to roll away, but Sharon held him in place.

"Come on, man, cut it out. Not my super thug getting all sensitive over a few battle scars." She scooted closer to him and kissed him on the cheek. "The bad boy thing has been in style since before the both of us was even heard of."

They both laughed.

"Naw, it ain't like that, Sharon," Rasheen embraced her in his arms. "It's just these damn things look so nasty I don't want these ugly ass scars souring the mood. Oh yeah, girl, I'm good for about four more rounds before the night's over."

He sprung up, took off the condom, tossed it in the trash can, and washed off the bodily fluids with a wet cloth they had soaking in a pan of warm water mixed with disinfectant and spermicide just for this purpose. When he was through, he slid back into his position next to Sharon. It was time to get inside of her head. There were so many issues they needed to talk about he didn't know where the hell to start. It took a second to decide to get the biggest issues out of the way first.

"This drama I got with Keith and Aaron," Rasheen stared at the ceiling. "You said it's gotta be stepped to in a delicate way. Actually, it may sound crazy for me to say what I'm about to say, but I'm thinking about taking all the doe I got, get me a nice mansion somewhere in a secluded place overseas on one of those Caribbean Islands, and try to enjoy what's left of this thing called life."

Sharon felt a shock wave rumble through her body. This was certainly not what she was expecting to hear, and it was in total conflict with what she was planning. "You can't be serious, boo. It ain't that simple. Just cause you feel like closing the book on all these issues from your pass don't mean all these folks trying to take you out are gonna stop. Those Colombians will never stop hunting you. Phillip Henderson is already rallying up the troops and got those Italian boys already asking questions. Aaron and Keith are definitely going to keep coming until you're dead. Aaron's still with the Bureau, and Keith still has crazy connections with the Bureau even though he left—"

"Keith was a FBI agent!?"

"Was he a FBI agent!? He almost made it to a supervisor before he got caught up in a series of scandals. They found him guilty of taking bribes, manipulating criminal prosecutions, tampering with evidence, and affiliating with well-known underworld figures. Instead of arresting him, they forced him to resign. Basically, he got some influential people to pull some strings and got him off without doing a day in prison. He was what folks from the hood would call 'the man'. In fact, Aaron is still under Keith's spell, and the others are under Aaron's spell." She wanted to mention her extensive and very intimate relationship with Keith but figured that was too personal to share with just anyone. Then, it dawned on her that revealing this sort of information would only interfere with what she was trying to accomplish with Rasheen. "Believe me, Rasheen, these are the type of people you can't run from. There's only one way to handle a situation of this magnitude."

Rasheen sighed because he knew she was technically correct. He was hoping she would support his change of attitude, even though it wasn't reality based when looking at it under a microscope. The only way to handle this was to kill them first, but he was weary with all this high-octane drama. "Yeah, I guess there's no running away from these beefs." He changed his voice to sound like that famous movie announcer. "My life is gonna be one, big, crazy rollercoaster ride, filled with bloodthirsty pursuits of vendettas, and mad gunplay." His attempt to lighten up the moment fell flat on its face, since Sharon apparently didn't catch it. "Then again, when I look at how Aaron and Keith caused my brother's death, I know if I don't step to my business, my conscience will never let me rest."

Rasheen felt the piercing pain in his chest and welcomed the sensation because it always had a way of stirring to life that hate-filled energy that always made things happen, and since hate mixed with the need for revenge was something that had kept him going strong this long, he allowed this negative but healthy energy to push this other new energy aside.

There was a moment of silence and they both rode it with a unique comfort.

Rasheen decided now was the time to lay the cards on the table regarding his numerous personal aspirations. "Listen Sharon, I got some issues I need to put out there. I know me and you been talkin' about vibin' on a much more serious level, and obviously I'm with that. You understand my situation and you still ready to roll with me, and I'm feelin' that. But, there's something I never told you."

Sharon's heart fluttered because this was sounding like the introduction to some bad news.

Rasheen continued, "I don't think it'll fuck up what we tryin' to establish, but I could be wrong." He went into a heavy silence to give Sharon a taste of her own medicine.

Sharon smiled as she sighed, "Alright, alright, it's serious. Let's hear it."

"I got a little Shorty by this chick I had on my team when we was makin' money in New York. She was like my ride or die chick, and you know how shit happens. It ain't no love bird shit between us, you know." He was instantly reminded of the fact he never really saw Camila as wifey material; it also dawned on him that he really wasn't thrilled about her, per se, having his seed. With a slight struggle, Rasheen calmed this rapidly escalating agitation by reflecting on the lyrics from the Isley Brother's song, 'if you can't be with the one you love, you gotta love the one you're with'. He then said, point blank. "I tapped those skins, and she ended up pregnant."

"What's her name? Where is she now?"

"Her name's Camila. She on lock down in Connecticut. She'll be out in another month."

"What is it, a boy or a girl?"

"It's a boy."

"Where's the kid?

"She had him while in prison. I ain't even see my little man yet."
He beamed with pride just thinking about his son.

"Do you love her?" Sharon actually didn't care about that, but
it was the logical thing to ask under the circumstances. "Are you
planning to be with her?"

"On the real, I don't love her on some wifey shit or anything like
that, but Camila is a sho'nuff trooper, she held me down when I did
all that time, and as far as love on a friendship level, she's definitely
peeps. When we got together on some sex shit it was just one of
those things. She was there, and one thing led to another."

"Are you planning to be with her when she gets out?"

This was a tricky question, and it made him think; he had
contemplated this issue when he was on the west coast; he concluded
it was probably safer to give her the partial truth. "Since she's the
mother of my kid, I ain't got much of a choice but to make sure she's
a'ight. With all these niggas gunning—"

"I thought we agreed to lighten up on the use of the "N" word?"

"Yeah, you right, my bad. I've been trying to get that foul word
out of my vocab for the longest, but it's harder than I thought."

He catch an instant flashback of the time when he was in
Clinton State Prison and of this old timer named Abdullah, who
wouldn't allow anyone within feet of his surroundings to use that
word without receiving a stern fatherly talk. One time he slipped up,
called his homie a nigga as they walked the yard, and it cost him
a half an hour lecture on the historical use of the word nigger. To
his surprise, Rasheen had actually found the little talk to be very
inspiring, especially since at the time he was really into reading black
history books.

Rasheen pulled his thoughts from the reverie and continued,
"Like I was saying, with all this beef in the air, I gotta make sure my

son is safe; he's the only person I got left who I love more than I love myself, and let's face it, he's my weakness."

Sharon wondered was this situation with the kid going to interfere with her plan; after tossing around a few good/bad scenarios in her head, she decided it would be safe not to rock the boat. "Well, Rasheen; all I can say is, I'm for you. I'll try to keep my girly emotions in cheek, but I can't promise you anything." She decided to throw out a hint, in order to start softening him up; she had to get him onboard with the first phase of her plan. "But, Rasheen, when you really get down to it, the bigger issue between us is I got your back and I hope you got mine."

The silence returned.

"All the shit you've done for me, Sharon, you know you ain't gotta ever wonder if I got your back, boo." He wanted to remind her that he'd still be sitting in Willie's San Diego apartment with riches stacked damn near to the ceiling, trying to figure out his next move if it wasn't for her, but decided he had thanked her more than enough and didn't want to sound desperate or weak. "Talkin' about having each other's back, I might need you to help me find a place to hide Camila and little Rasheen." He was about to mention the Judge, but he was still checking him out to see if everything was on the straight and narrow.

"That's no problem."

"Good, I'm feelin' that. We talkin' money now, so what we gonna do about getting that other $5 million from Phillip Henderson? You said we'd talk about it later. I hope this is later enough?"

This was a difficult topic; she tried to conceal the tension growing through her body, because he wasn't going to like what she had to say. "My investigation says that money is dead for right now." She waited a moment to hear his disappointment, but it didn't follow. "Phillip is trying to set up a wire trap. He basically found a way to trace any kind of money transfer within seconds of the money being transmitted. In layperson's terms, this money can't be touched until I figure out a way to get around this little trick Phillip and I guess those Guineas are trying to spring on us."

"Yeah, I guess that really don't surprise me at all. But the good thing is that $5 million is in our hands." He was still flying high on what he saw on Sharon's computer. She had set up several bank accounts under several names that he had immediate access to. After he gave her a straight million for her time and efforts he'd had access to four million dollars at the mere touch of a few buttons. The only issue was correctly memorizing all these names, passwords, and numbers, so he could get access to the money whenever he needed it. "So, what's up with the contract situation? Is it still gonna be a touchdown with Phil making all these new moves?"

"That money's in the bag. Now that you're telling me you got a son," She nodded her head approvingly. "We're now in a far better position to get access to the company's entire wealth." She sighed animatedly. "But don't forget, this is a long range jhooks, but it's about as solid as they come."

Rasheen smiled broadly; he couldn't wait to see this long range run when it came to fruition. His mind started wandering, flashbacking to all sorts of things, and suddenly, for some odd reason Crystal Walker came to his mind; his hand unconsciously massaged the bullet wound she had inflicted on him, realizing he would never forget her, because whenever he saw or touched this ugly wound it would always remind him of her. Thinking of her also reminded him of the ironic fact that she was his childhood sweetheart, and of the fact that she had saved his life the first time he was shot when he robbed that Colombian drug spot in East New York.

Then, that coincidental issue skirted across his memory bank, and he started dissecting it once again. Crystal and Sharon had the same last name. Walker. He again wondered if they were related, and again concluded that Walker was a very common name, and there could be thousands, or maybe even tens of thousands of people in this country with that name, and not be related. There couldn't possibly be a blood relation between the two. Crystal lived in New York, while Sharon lived in Atlanta. He was about to put this issue to rest by simply asking Sharon if she had a family member named Crystal, but realized he was about to let his mind run wild, and he realized asking her would only complicate matters and stir up more questions that would have to be answered. In any event, he closed the issue after concluding that if Crystal was related to her, she would have attended Crystal's funeral, and since she never mentioned attending any funerals, he shoved the issue out of his mind permanently.

Rasheen felt Sharon toying with his scar again and was surprised he felt his Johnson responding to the touch. Before his nature was fully raised, he needed to ask her a few more things, "I need to jump back a little. When I was working at Supremetech, I noticed you had funny work hours; basically, you used to come in as you pleased, or whenever they needed you for special jobs, is it still this way?"

"Just about, yeah. Why you ask?"

"At some point I'm gonna need some help with getting my money out of my safe-deposit boxes; the ones they didn't clip yet. But I need you to find out how they clipped the ones they were able to catch?"

"That's a fair request," She suddenly realized this issue laid a good foundation to lead her into presenting her proposition. "Rasheen, I'm glad you wise enough to keep money scattered around; those little nest eggs can be a lifesaver. But, have you ever realize that money goes very quickly; it seems like the more you have of it the faster it disappears, and the more of it you need. Have you ever thought about that?"

"I think about that all the time. Money makes the world turn. Without it life can sure be bleak and filled with a lot of hardship."

"Amen to that." She purred preachingly. "And in your case Rasheen, you are absolutely going to need a very lot of money to keep yourself alive. The minute your money runs out, and as we both know, it will eventually run out if it's not being replenished, you probably will have to start counting your days on this planet."

Rasheen saw she was definitely going somewhere with this issue, and based on these little spurts of silence it was something big. "Yeah, I thought about that too."

"About how much money you got?" She laid fully on her back, staring up at the ceiling, feeling a chill coming over her, since the sexual heat had subsided. "A couple of mill I'm assuming. Maybe ten, twenty; maybe even thirty, huh?"

The silence was penetrating, since Rasheen was never into sharing with anyone the exact amount of his money.

Sharon continued. "What if I told you, even if you had forty million, you don't have enough to outrun the people on your ass?"

There was more silence.

"Now peep this." She inched closer to him until her shoulder touched him chest. "What if I can guarantee you that I got a plan that can get you access to enough money that'll set you up for life, you and your son? Let's face it, Rasheen, if you got the money, I got the hook ups to buy you the type of protection from almost anyone; if you can pay the price, you can literally disappear from the face of the planet without leaving a single trace."

Rasheen smiled because she was trying to sell him something and was doing a damn good job at it. "Listen, Sharon, you ain't gotta convince me that money goes fast like running water, and if you ain't got a constant supply of it coming in, even millions can dribble away at an amazing rate. You're obviously trying to say something. All you gotta do is say it."

Sharon propped her chin on his chest and gazed into his eyes. "There's some other things I'm into Rasheen that enable me to do what I do. It also enables me to buy all this expensive stuff you see. My access to various computer sciences are not merely connected to my personal skills, but it's also related to who I know and the other people I work with. Also, I'm part owner in a series of businesses; most illicit; some legit. But, for purposes of what I'm about to propose to you, we'll focus on the illicit ones. I have part ownership in a number of nightclubs, casinos, gambling establishments all across the country, in Las Vegas, Atlantic City, Upstate New York, all over. Most have illicit sections within these establishments that cater strictly to the illegal gambling market. Basically, I need you to assist me with those activities."

"What you need me to do, bodyguard you?" He felt the urge to play stupid once again. "Hold you down?"

"Yes, I needed you to hold me down, but not with guarding my body; that's what I have Bobby Curtis and Carlos Martinez for (the two men who met Rasheen at the airstrip). What I need you to do is going to require a crew; a well-organized team with experience in committing complex, and well thought out, robberies." She smiled and saw Rasheen's hesitant smile. "There's no doubt in my mind you're good at what you do, Rasheen, or else you wouldn't be laying here in my bed laying pipe to this good stuff, while in possession of millions of dollars of your own money."

Sharon wanted to inform him that she had four times what he owned but that would only complicate things. "I personally only fuck with the best. Believe me, Rasheen, I know a few people that would jump through my bra strap to get onboard with a job like this, but none of them in my opinion can touch you when it comes to organizing and making the right moves when under pressure. That's a gift that many don't possess, and will never possess, and in this game, if you don't have it naturally, it's very unlikely that you can learn it. That's why they call it a gift. And because you and I have developed a bond, both business and intimate, I wouldn't dare present something like this to anyone else."

Rasheen was surprised his initial response wasn't filled with excitement upon hearing this proposition. A couple of months ago, he would've jumped up with frantic happiness and would've done a whop dance. Then, Sharon's reality speech fizzled into his cerebral cortex, and his motivation moved not for the sake of greed, but for the sake of survival. Without money, big money, he would be a dead man walking. He was onboard with this money-making mission whether he liked it or not, and with a smile he realized he had a wicked team he could mobilize in no time, "Your speech was an award winning presentation. But it was a waste of your time." He became silent as he gazed into her eyes with a serious smirk. When he saw her disappointed frown, he felt good.

Sharon sighed as she laid flat on her back again. This shit didn't make any—

Rasheen grabbed her and started kissing her as she went with the flow. After a few seconds of deep kissing, Rasheen pulled away, and said, "Baby doll, I'm surprised I was able to push those buttons of yours so easily. As far as your proposition is concerned, I got your back, boo, and I got a team ready whenever you ready." He resumed kissing her, and noticed she was displaying her appreciation by making it clear she was now ready for another round.

Sharon whispered into his ear with her breathing accelerated, "Get that condom on, so we can take care of business."

After Rasheen put on the condom, and resumed his deep love making dance, it never crossed his mind that Sharon's proposition had a few obvious holes in it, and had he also known what this Casino robbing run was really all about, he not only would've said no, but he would've gotten far away from Sharon as fast as possible.

CHAPTER # 14

Ja-King steeped out of the front door of the Los Angeles County jail, expecting to find a slew of news reporters with flashing cameras, and microphones; he was surprised his dream team attorney, Bruce Stanton, had finally told him something that turned out to be accurate.

Dressed in casual attire, Ja-King headed for the blue SUV with Tania Singleton behind the wheel. He shook his head at the sight of Tania already bouncing happily in her seat with joyful gestures like an animated ten year old child about to go on a trip to Disneyland, and wondered what the hell was he getting himself into.

He snatched open the door and slid inside. The stimulating smell of the raspberry car refreshers dangling from the rearview mirror grabbed him instantly.

"Ja-King!" Tania leaped over and started kissing him in a true-blue groupie fashion. "You're out! You're out!" She was kissing while making smacking and humming sounds as though the kisses tasted good to her, and then spoke like she was talking to a small child. "I told you, you coming home to me, baby."

Ja-King saw Tania was getting carried away with all this lovie dovie shit. "Tania, get it together, girl." He unraveled her arms that were damn near straggling him. "Let's get outta here."

She happily put the car in gear, checked the side view mirror for any oncoming traffic, and whipped the ride onto the streets. She turned the volume back up on the CD player and the Mary J. Blige tune came back to life. She positioned the volume at a sensible level.

"First stop," Ja-King said as he reached for his pack of Newports. "The nearest ATM machine, then a hotel."

"I know the perfect hotel!" Tania beamed with airhead animation. "We gotta make this right, baby. It's gotta be special!"

As he lit his cigarette, Ja-King glanced over Tania's caramel complexion and saw it was spotlessly clean as always, and her Halle Berry features were making it hard to keep his dick from standing at attention. He blew out a cloud of cigarette smoke, and she screwed up her face, which causing him to buzz down the window.

"When you started smoking, boo?" Tania said almost as if the revelation shattered her whole world. "You didn't tell me you was a smoker. You never smoked when we was on those visits?"

He wanted to ask her did he see anyone else smoking on the jailhouse-visiting floor but decided to explain this sudden relapse instead. "Hey, Tania, shit was rough up in there. I stopped for years, but shit happens."

Tania twisted up her face, and after a moment she suddenly snapped back into her bubbly self. "So when we gonna start making moves, baby?"

"I see you ready for action already, huh, ma? That's good. Very good. Just know that this is a slow grind. My peeps plan things out thoroughly before we go diving into shit, and we don't fuck with nickel and dime shit, either." He glanced over at her again, reflecting back on how he met Tania. Her cousin T-Bone and him got cool while on lock down, eventually developing a strong friendship; T-bone was a professional bank robber, and Tania just happened to be his main sidekick. After T-Bone introduced him to her, she'd been coming to see him for months, and although Tania had serious hoochie momma ways, she was far from a common chicken head with low aspirations, and an amazing drive to simply layup, fuck, complain, and expect a dude to shower her in riches. To his surprise she was notorious for busting her gun, and sticking up all types of establishments, including banks and anything that contained money. She was the perfect partner for what he was planning.

"So is your charges gone for good!?" Tania said cheerfully. "Is your man holding down those charges or do you think he'll flip out at the last minute?"

"It's a done deal. Fred stepped up," Ja-king realized he was forever indebted to his most dedicated and reliable bodyguard, Fred Hamilton, who took all the weight for the accidental shooting of that innocent by-stander during the shootout at the Ecstasy Club, instigated by Killer Kato and Crazy B. Since the other men that were killed during that fiasco were considered co-actors, there wasn't much made out of the fact that others were murdered during that situation. "Yeah, Tania, I'm good to go for sho'!"

Tania locked eyes with Ja-King, smiling as she still couldn't believe he was her man. "I still can't believe you giving up the rap game, Ja-King. That's crazy! You was my favorite rapper!"

"Yeah, you told me that a hundred times, already. I was your favorite rapper." He said in a condescending tone and sighed as though being reminded of this fact had ignited a wave of depression. The mere mention of his rap career reminded him of that embarrassing moment he was caught in the hotel laying pipe to an undercover cop; the way all the other rappers were chewing into him, taking crazy shots at him while he was down, turning him into the laughingstock of the whole rap industry, it was clear the entertainment business was a thing of the pass for him. Since making big money was something he was addicted to, taking paper was the next best thing.

Ja-King flicked the ashes out the window and said, "I told you, I got a plan. My man Rasheen is the real deal when it comes to making money." The stash buried in the backyard of the Glendale house he and Rasheen rented came to mind; he hoped Rasheen wasn't going to start acting flaky over the money now that he was free. "We gonna team up but first I gotta reach out to my man Willie. Watch, girl, I'ma show you how this stick-up shit is done. The shit we step to'll make all that cheddar coming in from the rap game look like the paper those crumb snatchin' street corner cee-low gamblers be playin' with."

"Yeah, baby!" Tania's bubbly attitude was on full blast. "I can't wait to meet him and Willie. But what about the jobs I got lined up? I got plenty nice places ripe for the taking. They're scattered all over the place too. Before T-Bone got popped we were checking them out, and even when he was gone, I kept an eye on 'em."

"Don't worry about all that, ma. Let me handle that part of this relationship." He sucked on the cigarette and blew the smoke out the window. "First, let me get my nuts out of the god damn sand, then we talk some more about the work we gone get into." He glanced over at her juicy thighs bulging through the mini-skirt and felt his wood pulsating to life. Then, he noticed her easy, laid-back driving mannerisms. "Yo, Tania, what the hell wrong with your foot, girl? Put some lead in that thing!"

With an electrical smile, Tania took the gas pedal to the next level.

* ** *

Rashango, AKA Ronald Conyers, stepped out of the front gate of Comstock State prison, and unlike Ja-King, he had not a single soul waiting for him. He stood staring up at the dreary May skies and smiled triumphantly.

After spending thirteen years in prison for being in possession of marked money from a bank robbery that transpired over two thousand miles away from the location of his arrest, he noticed the air beyond the confines of one of New York State's notorious disciplinary institutions even smelled different.

Dressed in a cheap set of state issued blue jeans, reject Chuck Taylor sneakers, and a tight-fitting red sweatshirt, Rashango's clean cut facial features looked even more enraged, because he didn't have to convince any draconian parole board to release him; he opt to max out. Unlike most roaming around in this brutal system that prided itself on the level of revenge it was able to inflict on those who dared to get caught in this web of wickedness, Rashango with his blue-black complexion, refused to subject himself to the degrading charade of appearing before an inherently racist panel of oppressors, choosing instead to give them everything he owed them.

He reasoned that he was simply too black (both mentally and physically) to even delude himself into believing he stood even a far-fetched chance of receiving even an inkling of redress and giving them the satisfaction of stomping him in the face while he was down and trying to pull himself up was a no can't do.

Although he had an old plastic bag containing all of his worldly belongings flung over his shoulder, the only thing inside of it he considered worth any value was the contact information of how he could reach Rasheen Smith, and without question he had full intentions of putting this info to full use as he headed for the train station.

* ** *

Phillip Henderson sat across from Sammy Galucci as Sammy was wolfing down a huge plate of Fettuccine Alfredo with several side dishes surrounding this main dish. There were also bottles of wines on the small oval table that Phillip couldn't begin to name. In front of Phil was a small plate of a similar dish as the one Sammy was devouring but was much smaller, and he had barely touched it.

Several yards away Phil's bodyguards, Derek Ramos and Troy Thomas, sat at the bar, sipping weak alcohol beverages while trying to look just as dangerous as the mob connected men patronizing Sammy's establishment that been within the Galucci family since his grandfather came to America and set up shop here in Los Angeles California in 1902.

"Listen, Phil," Sammy said, after he swallowed. He raised his pudgy pointer finger that perfectly matched his heavy-set physique and aimed it at Phil. "What makes you think I give a shit about all this you're telling me? What do a bogus signature you got from this Rashi clown, got to do with you paying me my money?"

"It has a lot—"

"And what'd I give a shit about some gang bangers from Brooklyn that can't find this fuckin' guy? Ya tiptoe in my fuckin' place telling me if I don't help you clean up this shit the company's gonna go belly up, and I won't be able to get my money. That's not the kinda fuckin' news I like dropped in my lap while I'm enjoying a plate of Fettuccine Alfredo."

"I'm very sorry, Sammy, I didn't mean to come here and saturate you—"

"Hey! Don't come in here using those fuckin' sissy words! Speak fuckin' English will ya! Saturate? What kinda fuckin' word is that!?"

"Sorry, Sammy—"

"And stop being so fuckin' sorry!" He resumed consuming his dinner. "So what'd you suggest I do to help you straighten this out?"

"Ah, I was wondering if it's possible for you to handle this problem we got with Rasheen Smith."

"We!" Sammy said tauntingly with a mouthful of pasta. "This is our problem now, huh!?"

"Yes, I would say it is."

Sammy finished chewing, swallowed and said. "I see you're not a very good listener, or maybe your ears are fucked up or something. Lemme remind you, the way this thing works is like this; if you want my services, you pay me. The percentage you're paying is only for protection from other guys like me. What you're asking for is not protection. It's more of an offensive type a thing, ya know what I mean. It's gonna cost ya extra." He resumed stuffing his mouth.

Phil was about to blur out his willingness to pay whatever it would cost to get rid of Rasheen Smith, but he put on the brakes upon remembering all the horror stories he'd heard about how the mob was notorious for bloodsucking companies bone dry. He also slowed his role because he had to keep close tabs on his spending after he purchased two new homes. Immediately after Rasheen showed him those pictures of his family, he purchased two additional new places of residence, one in Santa Barbara and the other in Long Beach, both well away from all the Hollywood drama. With all these expenditures on his mind (money was good but wasting it was a cardinal sin), he had to play the game with Sammy as best he could. "I'm willing to pay you standard contract rates. I believe 75 thousand." He saw Sammy twist up his face. "I mean, I could've gone to the Russians and maybe gotten it a little cheaper but you told me—"

"Don't be a fuckin wise ass!" Sammy saw Phil was still testing the waters. "When you deal with us there's nobody else. And we're very jealous, as you can see." He added with breathtaking sarcasm. He also realized this moolie was begging him to teach him a lesson or two, which he had no problem obliging him in that department. "Send me half the money up front, a picture, and I'll get right on it. . ."

CHAPTER # 15

"All right! I heard you!" Camilla shouted to her aunt in the other room. *This crazy bitch is driving me crazy!* She sat at the kitchen table with Little Rasheen on her lap feeding him a container of garden pea baby food. Most of the food seemed to be all over her, the floor, the table, and him, since Rasheen was now fascinated with the laws of physics on how food responded when it was spit from his mouth. She heard her Aunt Fatima stomping towards her and braced herself for the imminent argument.

Aunt Fatima entered the dining area with her hands propped on her shapely hips. "Camila, you better take that bass outta your voice when you talk to me, girl." Fatima's youthful appearance was a clear representation of the power of the church once a person applied its principles properly, since in her heydays Fatima had been to hell and back (she was once addicted to dope, alcohol, and dick), her Christian transition was about as genuine as it could possibly get, especially since she decided to get Jesus in her life while lying in a hospital bed, dangling on to her life by a microscopic thread, under circumstances where her jealous boyfriend shot her in the chest because she accidentally knocked over his last bag of heron. She'd decided she was never going back to that life and would try to prevent any and everyone who crossed her path not to venture into that dangerous, destructive, depressive and inevitably deadly world, AKA the fast lane, the game. She came right up to Camila and said, "You ain't too grown for me to put you right over my leg and spank your behind."

Camila huffed and puffed inwardly. "Sorry, Auntie, I'm just saying, you told me that same thing yesterday, and I told you I'm going out looking next week."

"Stop procrastinating," Fatima retrieved a couple of napkins, and started cleaning up the mess. "A job is not going to come knocking on your door. I got the baby-sitter ready to watch Rasheen, so there's no excuse. You been here three weeks, and all you wanna do is sit around here talking about this child's father is coming to sweep you and him out of here, and into some fantasy dream land. That's not gonna cut it, Camila."

Camila continued feeding Rasheen as he talked his baby talk while pounding the palms of his little chubby hands on the table. She wanted to lash out at her aunt for talking that way to her, and for reminding her again that Rasheen wasn't coming to get them. After three weeks of sitting staring out the window, walking the streets while peering at the driver of every fancy car that passed, and still no Rasheen, she was finally starting to wonder if she was chasing a ghost. The only thing stopped her from giving up completely was the huge sum of money ($7,000) she received from some mysterious person with a California address, reminding her to be patient.

Camila decided to shut her auntie down with a reminder. "Auntie, I ain't free loadin', am I!? I pay my part of the rent, I buy all of Rasheen's food, so even if I ain't working, the bills is gettin' paid, ain't they? I ain't taking nothing from Faye—"

"This ain't about money!" Fatima tossed the napkins in the trashcan. "It's about getting you into the right type of activities that's going to keep you on the right track; keep you off those streets, out of prison, and alive! Working is a healthy way of doing that, Camila. An idle mind is the playground for the devil! That's a fact of life in this society in this day and time, and if you want my help, you have to prove that you're at least trying to help yourself. I don't want you to end up like Amar, child."

Camila wanted to sigh disrespectfully but chose instead to try again to quiet her auntie up. "At least I ain't hanging out or gettin' high and I'm going to church every Sunday. You can't tell me that's not a start."

There was a heavy silence and Camila saw she had succeeded in putting an end to the confrontation.

Four hours later, after Little Rasheen was sleep and Aunt Fatima was in her bedroom doing whatever she did at 11:35 in the evening, while her two younger cousins (Felicia 17 & Faye 16) were sound asleep, Camila sat looking out the living room window at the late-night streets. She'd developed this crazy habit during the last two weeks where she would sit in this chair with the TV on, while watching both the streets and her various cable television programs. Twice her auntie and cousins looked at her strangely as they moved about apartment, and she could tell they had thought she was on the verge of losing it.

She sighed as her mixed emotions amalgamated into a hoard of congestive indecisiveness that made her head hurt. It felt like her sense of hope was fading on all levels; an issue that really confused her was, she no longer had the desire to kill those C.O.s who abused her while in prison. After hearing various biblical sermons by Reverend Charles and Aunt Fatima, she realized she could soften her heart enough to forgive.

But, in truth, Camila knew the real root of this willingness to let go of her need to get them back had everything to do with the fact they never got the pussy and there were more important things she needed to focus on right now, like getting her pockets right. In any event, it was obvious an attempt to get at them would only waste value time trying to cater to issues of the ego, which was really nothing but a fake ass feel good moment that would disappear minutes after the deed was done. Plus, everybody on the inside knew C.O. Richards and Rodriguez were fucking with her, and if something suddenly happened to them, somebody was bound to make the connection and snitch her out; consequently, she would be on the run, fleeing from capital punishment or life without the possibility of parole. It simply wasn't worth all the headaches.

However, tonight she was really knocking on the door of giving up hope on Rasheen coming to her rescue. He had too much drama in his life to be bogging himself down with more drama. He was on the run; he had been shot up pretty bad, and most of all, she sensed that he had probably found him another bitch. In any event the law of averages told her that he would probably do like all these deadbeat niggas with hood mentalities (make a bunch of babies and then get gone when it came time to do the daddy thing).

She sighed angrily as she felt the tears swelling up in her eyes. Her hand mechanically went up to her face and began picking the acne bump that had formed. *I gotta slow up on all that chocolate!* Lately, when she consumed chocolate she found peace of mind, since it seemed to have a similar soothing effect as sex. She blinked away the rapidly forming tears. After all the years of trooping for Rasheen and this was how he was going to do her!? She could no longer stop her run away mind from embracing all the pessimistic vibrations that made more sense to her than all the other signals. Three weeks was way too long, and she had to stop playing this delusional head game with herself. Her auntie was right! That trifling ass nigga wasn't coming for her and little Rasheen . . .

She suddenly saw an old Buick pull up in front of the house and her heart pounded, while praying this wasn't going to be another false alarm. When she saw the nerdy looking dude with Malcolm X style glasses get out the car, Camila cursed inwardly because it was another god damn false alarm! She went back into her self-pitying and brooding mode while becoming furious with the silly looking dude as he approached the apartment building. Since this was a three family, three-story apartment building (she was on the first floor), she assumed the cornball cat was going to see Mrs. Garrett (on the third floor), since she was just as weird looking as this guy.

There was a knock on the door.

Camila was on fire now; she stomped towards the door assuming that not only was this dude stupid looking, but he obviously didn't follow instructions very well. Whoever he came to see had to have told this idiot where the fuck they lived, and he apparently had gotten it all wrong. She promised she was going to curse his ass out some type of crazy like.

Camila peeked through the peek hole to make sure, and then unfastened the locks, opened the door with the chain lock still in place, and spoke through the amply cracked door with a nasty attitude. "Can I help you?" Just as he was about to say something she stomped on his words. "If you looking for—"

"Easy, boo," Rasheen said smiling. "Where all that fire comin' from, ma?"

Camila nearly fainted when she heard the voice. The astonishment made her knees and bladder weak, and once the mind crippling shock faded to a reasonable level, she frantically unhooked the chain, snatched the door opened, and leaped into Rasheen's embrace. She couldn't stop the tears from pouring from her eyes.

Rasheen squeezed her just as hard as she was squeezing him to let her know he had her back. She started kissing him and he gave back the same energy she transmitted; he wanted to let her know it was time to turn up the volume on this thing like never before. He pulled from the kiss and whispered in her ear. "Where is he?" The excitement, commingled with a deeply rooted anxiousness in his voice was as unadulterated as uncut heron coming straight from an Afghanistan poppy field.

In a trance, Rasheen followed Camila into the apartment and over towards the cot in the far corner of the living room. Everything, except for his heart, was moving in slow motion as he glided towards the crib. He dreamed of this moment so many times he knew every intricate second would be ingrained in the network of his entire being for as long as he breathed air while on this planet.

When he arrived at the cot and saw his son lying on his stomach sleeping, Rasheen couldn't wait any longer. He had to hold him; touch him; embrace him, and let his little man know that his daddy was finally here and was going to make things right, even if he had to die trying. He awkwardly reached down to pick him up, stopped in mid-motion, and couldn't seem to figure out the correct way to hold his child. Plus, he noticed his son looked too delicate to handle just any old way and he was afraid he might hurt him if he didn't pick him up the right way. This was totally new territory for him.

Camila took charge when she sensed Rasheen needed some preliminary schooling on the art of handling a two-year-old child. She scooped him up with motherly expert precision, and gently placed him into Rasheen's wanting embrace.

Rasheen was beaming with something much stronger than pride as he stared down into the spitting image of himself. There was no questioning the fact this little guy was definitely his. He had his forehead, nose, lips, and cheekbones; this was a humbling moment that soothed his inner essence even though he never doubted this kid was his; but the universal saying, momma's baby, daddy's maybe, was a reality no sane person living in such a fast pace, sex-crazed society could ignore until the irrefutable facts were on the table.

"Relax, sit down, rest your legs," Camila whispered as she tugged on his arm and Rasheen sat on the unfolding sofa that was Camila's bed. She sat next to him unable to stop skinning and grinning with delight. "What took you so long!? I—-I was starting to get nervous; my mind was running crazy, thinking you got popped or—"

"I had to get things right before I came to get y'all. I had to clean out all those safe-deposit boxes and move that money to some safer places. Wasn't no sense in having y'all ripping and running by my side without a place to lay our heads." He saw his son was a hard sleeper, just like his dad. He only shifted a few times, since he'd picked him up. "You gonna love this place I got us. I went all out on this thing, got us all new identities, the whole shabang! The only fucked up thing is we gotta cut off all ties." He placed excessive emphasis on the word all. "If you ride with me, you ride all the way or not at all. There's no turning back once you take that step."

"Don't even try it, Rasheen." She wobbled her head on her shoulders in Shanana fashion. "You know where I stand with us! We in this together to end!"

Rasheen gently rose to his feet and placed his son back on the cot. He sat back down next to Camila and said exhaustedly. "We can bounce up outta here in the morning." He yawned explosively, drawing a stream of tears from his eyes. "I hope your aunt ain't gonna wild out when she find me sleepin'—"

"Fuck her! We out tomorrow; anything she gotta say don't mean shit no more."

Rasheen laid back comfortably and was already down slopping into a deep sleep.

Camila wanted to make him get up so she could unfold the sofa, but he looked so peaceful. A moment later she couldn't believe he was already sleeping. *Damn! He must've been putting in some crazy work!* She flipped his legs into a laying position, slid beside him, and allowed her tears of joy to flow once again as she propped her head on his chest, listening to the thumping of his heartbeat. She fell to sleep to his universal rhythm of life and slept good for a change.

The following morning, Aunt Fatima woke up the whole house and the entire neighborhood when she found Rasheen and Camila sleeping in a cuddling embrace. She assumed they had committed fornication and started raising the roof off the house. Within an hour of Rasheen, Camila and Little Rasheen opening their eyes, they were out of Aunt Fatima's life and on the road, heading for the ranch style mansion in Somerset New Jersey Rasheen purchased for almost a half million.

From behind the wheel Rasheen said, "A lot of shit has happened since that night you got touched, ma. A whole lot of shit."

Camila looked back at Little Rasheen fastened tightly in the child's safety chair, and saw he was having a ball with his rattle, while talking his toddler's talk. The Jadakiss rap song seeping softly from the car's speakers was barely loud enough to be heard. When Rasheen didn't follow up with the details, she decided to start probing, "A whole lot of shit like what? I know Lameek got murdered." She was about to mention her sheisty ass brother Amar and his sidekick Dapper D, but the incident regarding their deaths was one that earned the never talk about ever again status. "I'm assuming you did the deed to that bitch ass nigga Killer and his flunky, Crazy B."

"Yeah, that's business in the bag. But now there's some new shit in the air, and I basically gotta do these cats before they do me. Remember that dude Jack Mack was telling us about who was starting a security company?"

"Yeah, his name is Keith, or some shit."

"Keith Ramsey. That mufucka was playin' us all along. Clipped us for millions and then was planning to kill us to cover their tracks. After Jack-Mack died during a butchered burglary, I went out there to LA, and the next thing I know I got a gang of corrupt Feds hunting me down. Keith's man Aaron is a FBI agent and he got a crew; Keith is an ex-FBI agent."

"Wow," Camila said with raised eyebrows as she shook her head. "FBI!?"

"The mufuckas kidnapped Lameek, and I had to go get him. To make a long story short, they murdered Lameek when they got him involved in this beef I had with Killer, basically, and now they still trying to kill me."

"Damn!" Camila scanned the cars cruising rapidly down the New Jersey Turnpike, knowing what this meant. "Stepping to a federal agent, even if he's dirty or not ain't no small thing, boo."

"Yeah, I know. But you know how this shit go. It's kill or be killed. I ain't learned how to master the art of rubbing an H on my chest and handling shit. It ain't my style to put things in God's hands, on some coward ass cop out shit like a spineless bitch scared of his own fuckin' shadow. That ain't never been me, never was and never will be, especially when it involves a mufucka killing my blood and trying to kill me too."

"How you find all this out!?"

Rasheen was about to blurt out Sharon's name and her endeavors, but realized he never mentioned Sharon to her. After remembering Camila's highly possessive and envious tendencies, he decided to play it safe. "I got some peeps in a strategic place and they been pulling my coat to a lot things. This person is right under their noses, so shit is all good."

"So they killed Lameek?" She said with a mixture of disbelief and deep pain as her mind flashed back to how much she liked Lameek; a boiling rage began to percolate inside of her. "Fuck it! These chumps gotta get it. Ain't nothing to it but to do it."

The silence returned as Rasheen was bobbing his head to a rap song by Jay-Z.

Camila spoke as she bobbed her head to the beat. "I know you got some things lined up on the money tip, cause money don't grow on trees and bills gotta get paid regardless to whom or what."

Rasheen glanced over as he cracked a smile. "Yeah, I got a vicious team on standby." He knew she was going to be tight when he hit her with the rundown as it related to her, but he figured it was just an emotion she would eventually get over. "I even got Rashango on the team."

"He's out!?" She remembered the time she visited him at Sing Sing to get him to do that hit on that Dominican dude, Dario Montero, and how he was trying to press up on her. She had thought about telling Rasheen what happened, but her common sense told her Rashango was a key player in their money-making mission, and there was no need in creating any unnecessary tension, so she decided to let that incident bounce off of her, especially since she checked his ass real hard like. "When he got out!?

"A couple of weeks ago. I got him a bullshit crib for the moment; in New Jersey, and gave him some pocket change to hold him over for a minute. He's on deck, ready to step up when the whistle blows. The other part of the team you ain't met yet; my man Willie and his girl Lora is good peeps, and Ja-King and his chick Tania is ready to ride."

"Ja-King!?" Camila shook her head disbelievingly, still finding it hard to believe Ja-King was rolling with them. "I heard on the radio he beat that body and dropped out of the rap game all together. When Candy wrote me and told me he was movin' with y'all that shit bugged me the fuck out! He's a celebrity! I kept asking myself how the hell is Rah letting this dude step with the team with all the attention he's bringing with him!?"

"Well, he's with the program, and I can trust him." He held the moment of silence as he wondered should he share his ultimate goal with her as it stood right now. He sighed and said, "Listen, Camila, after I do a few more jobs, get about a 100 mill, we out of here for good. We gone find us a nice cozy spot on some Island somewhere and enjoy what little bit of life we got left. We gonna put Little Rah in some top-notch schools and shit, and let him be anything he wanna be, as long as it ain't no hustler, a thug, a stick up kid, or any occupation dealing with the unsavory side of the hood and the underworld—"

"What's wrong with being a hustler!?" Camila was dead serious.

Rasheen's head turned in slow motion as the fiery hot shock rippled through his body. "Cause I don't want him living the life we supposed to be trying to get the fuck out of! That's why he ain't gonna be no god damn hustler! I don't believe you even went there with me, Camila! You must be trippin' if you think this shit is something we gonna pass on to him."

Camila was about to debate the issue, but saw Rasheen was on fire. "I'm only messing with you, Rasheen," She tried to laugh it off.

"Don't fuck with me like that, Camila! Shit dealin' with Little Rasheen ain't to be taken lightly." He allowed his mind to relax as he made a mental note to watch her ass very closely from here on, because her inquiry was genuine. Before the heavy sheet of silence grew to an intense level, he said. "Now that we on the topic of Little Rah's wellbeing, I guess this leads us smoothly into me letting you know, you ain't rollin' with us on these runs coming up."

"But I'm—"

Rasheen violently held his pointer finger, inches from Camila's face. "These hits we about to get into are strictly bang-out missions. We got mad casinos, and heavily armed underground gambling operations lined up, and when we walk into these joints, we going in hard body! Now, if you think I'm gonna allow the mother of my son to be standing beside me with bullets flying, you gotta be crazy!"

"Please, Rasheen, don't do—"

"If shit don't go down right and both of us end up dead or in prison, then what the fuck do you think is gonna happen to our seed!?"

Camila was shattered; the tears were boiling to the surface, dripping from underneath her eyes lids. She was about to start cursing, while ranting and raving, until she saw the horrified expression on Rasheen's face as he stared at the rearview mirror.

"What the fuck!" Rasheen said as he analyzed the State Troopers tailing him. "These mufuckas are about to flag us!" His heart started pounding so hard he felt a nervous twitching surging throughout his entire central nervous system from head to toe. "Don't look back!" He stopped her from turning around and being nosy. "It'll make us look suspicious!"

With terror in her eyes Camila said, "You think we can stand a stop?"

Just as Rasheen was about to answer her inquiry, the sirens blurred.

Rasheen glanced back at his son, who was playing so happily with his little colorful toys that the sight was truly heart wrenching. Fuck! He sighed angrily as a silent prayer nervously coursed through his mind; he was hoping and praying what he was about to do was the best thing for the only other living organism on this planet he could genuinely say he loved more than himself.

CHAPTER # 16

At about the moment Rasheen was pushing the Buick down the New Jersey Turnpike, Aaron and Keith were inside a conference room locked in a real nasty argument.

"What the fuck you mean you can't tell me!?" Keith shot back with clenched teeth. He stood near a glass mobile cart used to serve drinks, while Aaron sat on the edge of the conference table with his arms folded. "I'm the top man of this operation."

"You see, that's why I didn't wanna say shit about this. You swore up and down that if I told you, you'd trust me and ride with this the way I'm calling it. What's the problem with you keeping your word?"

Keith was on the verge of exploding physically. "Keeping me in the dark about all the details of this plant you got inside Rasheen's crew is not the type of information you keep solely to yourself. Even if you believe you have some kind of logical reason for doing this, you never said you was going to keep the identity of this spy to yourself when you propose this to us—"

"So why did you agree to this? You swore if I gave you a heads up on the basics, you'd accept what I shared with you and what I would withhold. You agreed! Eugene, Norm, and even Donald agreed when I presented this to them. If you couldn't handle not knowing you shouldn't have agreed." He stared at Keith as he paced in a slight circle. There was no way he was revealing his spy, since Keith was weak when it came to Sharon. And little did he know he was feeding him this little tidbit of info to see if Rasheen and his crew would start acting strange, and if so, he could start flushing out the rat roaming the corridors of Supremetech. Although Sharon was the prime suspect, there were a few others that could fit the shoes of the culprit, and he had his eyes on them all. "I'm not giving up my CI, so let's move on to another topic."

Keith sighed with so much intense anger droplets of spittle sprayed from his mouth. "Alright, fuck it," He'd known Aaron long enough to know that by the tone of his current attitude, he wasn't going to bend, "So what's this shit about, they're about to go on some kind of robbing spree?"

"That's right, I'm sure it has something to do with gambling establishments, but unfortunately, my CI wasn't able to pinpoint exactly when, where, and how these robberies are going down."

Keith found himself a seat. His fingers began brushing across his low-cut goatee as though the gesture was provoking a deep thought process. "There's thousands of gambling establishments throughout the country! Did they mention where Rasheen is living? What state?"

"Nope, but the last I heard, he was planning a trip to Brooklyn; I told Big Gains to get his man Jackhammer Jones on point, and if he get a tab on him to contact me before doing anything."

"Finding out what state he was last seen should be a priority. That way we at least have a starting point. Did your CI indicate the State he was in when he found out Rasheen was making plans to go to Brooklyn?"

"No State, no location, no nothing. But I made it clear that this information is the most crucial of all. If we could find out where he's laying his head, we can end this shit without a whole lot of hustling and bustling." Aaron took a seat on the other side of the table, across from Keith. "I give him this much; he's smart enough to keep his team in the dark with everything."

Keith's mind was analyzing this plan of Rasheen's and wondered if they could use it to their advantage. Most gambling establishments handled major money. After contemplating a series of issues, he noticed the silence became heavy, and said, "What's the chance of us turning this into another payday? What if we let them get the money from at least one of those robberies and then we step in afterwards, kill them and take the money? One thing for sure, if Rasheen's hands are involved in this, it's definitely for some real money."

Aaron contained his frustration. "I thought about that, but after looking at all the circumstances, it might be safer to simply get this guy out of the way and focus on other less precarious projects."

"I say we put this on the floor and let the others vote on it." Keith shifted in his seat at the thought of throwing away good, easy money, solely because they were getting jittery over a few risky issues. "We in the business of doing what we do to make money, and if a little coordinating could result in us getting our hands on a large sum of cash, then we should at least seriously check it out to see if we can pull it off before scrapping it."

"I'm cool with that; we'll put it on the floor. If the majority agrees it's a viable endeavor, I'm on board. But for the record, I say we should get rid of this guy and keep it movin'."

There was a moment of silence.

"So how is he communicating with them? Are they meeting up face-to-face, cell phones, Internet? What?"

"Cell phones, and I think face-to-face a few times."

"And what happened at this face-to-face? This CI of yours couldn't pull your coat before this meeting of the minds?"

Aaron felt another explosion was coming. "My coat was pulled, but they met up in Chicago, and it wasn't enough time to mobilize anything. Plus, I wanted to see if this CI was serious, so I had him take pictures with his cell phone. I checked them out, and it's him, all the way. The next time around, we'll be ready to step to this, and end it."

Keith shook his head, feeling himself about to wig out on Aaron. "I see you really like this thing with not letting the right hand know what the left hand is doing." His sarcasm mixed with anger was explicit. "When the fuck were you going to tell me all this!?"

"Aren't we sitting in here now?" Aaron said calmly and unemotionally. "And didn't I call this meeting? And what the hell do it look like I'm doing?"

"Don't try to twist up what I'm saying. This is the kind of info I need to know."

Aaron firmly held his position. "What is it I'm doing right now? I'm sharing info."

Keith wondered how he was able to put up with Aaron's cockiness. "Okay, my bad, you right, this is what this meet was called for." He thought about their next move and said, "Let's lock into a few things before we close this meeting. I gotta get back to a few accounts. This is what I need you to do; talk to Phillip again and find out if any those mob guys he's in bed with got anyone who can get us unlimited access to a private jet. Unfortunately, McPhearson is showing his ass, and Sharon says she's unable to get Daniel to have one on standby."

Aaron screwed up his face at this approach, "I say we cut our losses from the starting line. Fuck those mob boys; they still got that grudge because we sided with Killer Kato against them. Yeah, they talking like it's a dead issue, but I got a few ears and eyes that say they're not gonna forget it. I'm not in the mood to start another war right now; the smartest thing right now is to pull back from them." He paused a moment, wondering how he was going to give Keith the bad news regarding Sharon. The mere mentioning of Sharon's name angered him in a way that was unhealthy to his sense of professionalism. "And as far as Sharon is concerned."

Keith locked eyes with Aaron; his expression conveyed a warning that said it better be good.

Aaron saw Keith's expression and decided to give him the watered-down version. "I asked around and found out that she used that jet a couple of weeks back. When I interviewed the pilot, he slipped up and told me she had someone flown from California to

Florida. I don't know if this person was Rasheen, since the pilot caught a case of the mums after he realized he said more than he was supposed to, but—"

"I see you're on this thing with Sharon like a pit bull. Why don't we call her in here and interrogate her!? She's here and we can both put our minds to rest—"

"Alright, easy man. We don't have to go to that extreme." He scolded himself for even mentioning this to Keith; if they were to put Sharon on point to the fact she was being watched it would kill his covert mission that entailed keeping a close eye on her. "You know me Keith, I check out every lead, no matter how off the mark it may appear. But, if you feel this is a dead end, then I'll pull back." He lied, since he'd not only found a solid lead, but this particular lead was so significant that it might lead him straight to Rasheen's doorstep, and when he pulled off this hit he decided that Keith would be the first to have the 'I told you so' thrown right in his face.

* ** *

"May I see your license and registration, please," The fat, red faced New Jersey Highway Patrolman said to Rasheen.

With his heart about to pound its way out of his chest, Rasheen said, "Yes, sir, officer," He politely reached over to the glove compartment, and retrieved the registration. After sitting upward, he dug in his back pocket for his wallet, acquired his license and handed the hard-nosed cop his papers.

Meanwhile, the cop was inspecting the interior of the car. Everything looked in order, he noticed, but the woman was acting unusually nervous. He continued sniffing for any smells of drug use or alcohol, or anything in plain view that would justify his facilitating his dislike for black folks, and still detected nothing. The urge to make up something was growing steadily. He wanted a bust real bad, he realized as he inspected Mr. Nathaniel Johnson's papers. "Okay, Mr. Johnson, please sit tight and I'll be right back." He headed for the patrol car and gave a head nod to his partner standing at the rear of the Buick watching for any hasty reactions from the passengers.

Rasheen watched both cops from the rearview, and when the cop who took the papers got inside the patrol car, he whispered to Camila. "If you into praying, you better start now, cause this is the first time I'm experimenting with those papers."

"These bastards are racial profiling us," Camila said. "We ain't do shit! They stopping us cause we DWB." She saw Rasheen's confused facial expression and clarified. "Driving while Black, DWB."

Rasheen inconspicuously retrieved the 9-mm from the special made compartment inside the door near the lever and sat on it. He wondered how he was going to shoot his way out of this one. Knocking one of them out of play wasn't going to be a problem, but the other cop standing at the rear of the car was going to be a major issue. He learned the hard way that all those Wild West gun-slinging antics were nothing but movie tricks. He sighed, and decided he'd let his iron will and desire to never return to prison to guide him through this situation.

A moment later, Rasheen saw the cop get out of the patrol car and approached. When he saw his hand go towards his weapon in his holster, he went for the 9-mm. Then, a second later, he saw it was a harmless gesture, and Rasheen relaxed his hand. His mind was going crazy, trying to decide should he get the draw on the cop first, and start shooting before it was too late, or should he wait to see how this would unfold. He forced himself to make a swift decision and went with his first instinct.

The cop stood at the driver side door and handed Rasheen his papers. He inspected the insides of the car again, and said, "Thank you for your time, Mr. Johnson. Have a nice day." He went back to his car, deliberately failed to inform Rasheen of the reason he was pulled over, and dared him to ask, because if Rasheen did, he had full intentions of turning the matter into something.

The relief that Rasheen and Camila sighed was one that they would never forget.

Two hours later, they pulled up in front of their ranch style home in a highly secluded, suburban region in Somerset County.

Camila was dumbfounded with utter disbelief; she got out of the car in a trance and literally stood mesmerized in the circular driveway staring at this mansion that looked like one of those houses from that TV program, Lifestyles of the Rich and Famous.

As Rasheen took Camila on a tour of this dream house, his pride grew with each soothing sound of amazement she made. Ever since his petty stickup kid days, he'd always dreamed of owning such a house like this one and was still on cloud nine. This ranch-style complex was complete with an in-ground swimming pool, full basketball court, a three car garage with a BMW and a Cadillac Escalade inside of it, four bedrooms, three bathrooms, walk in closets as big as a Sing Sing cell, and most crucial of all, it was surrounded by seclusion and a miniature woodland. The closest neighbor was about a half mile away.

After they were settled down, the first thing Rasheen did was get himself and Camila retested for any and all sexually transmitted diseases with HIV at the top of the list, and when they both received a relatively clean bill of health (Camila, however, had to be treated for HPV [Human papillomavirus] and a yeast infection), they celebrated their new home with their own private party, consisting of drinking to the point of drunkenness and fucking all night long like teenagers in heat.

Although in the past four years since his release from prison Rasheen had stacked Hollywood movie-star type paper, he immediately made it a rule that there would be no unnecessary splurging or squandering of money. After 29 years on this planet, Rasheen had thoroughly figured out that the only way to attain wealth was by saving money, and thanks to the countless books he'd been reading, he saw all those financial tips were much more than simply accurate; they were universal rules of thumb for anyone trying to become economically empowered.

Unfortunately, Camila had great difficulty grasping this money spending reality. She wanted to buy every designer style clothing she could lay her eyes and hands on, and wanted flashy cars, jewels and anything equated with being rich, since she'd saw these items as symbols of wealth and anyone who didn't have them couldn't say they had made it.

As the days turned into weeks, Rasheen's love for his son grew into something that didn't totally surprise him, but he was feeling that new mentality becoming more profound with each father and son moment he was blessed to have bestowed upon him. It didn't take long for his motives regarding his moneymaking and retribution-seeking missions to become unsteady. Looking into his son's eyes, listening to his "dadas" and "mamas", and watching him toddle around the house, while venturing into everything he could lay his little mitts on, Rasheen couldn't escape the reality that he had to get out of the game as fast as possible.

To make this matter more unbearable that recurring little voice of reason in the back of his mind kept telling him to pull out now, work with what he had, settle for investing the money he had in order to guarantee a consistent influx of that mean green, be content with enjoying life with his son, and by all means, don't go back out into the jungle! Give up the need for more money and revenge while you can!

This voice constantly battered Rasheen's brain cells daily. Then, at times, this same voice of logic would flip the script and start reminding him that he had no choice but to complete what he started; he had to stop the people who were bent on killing him by killing them first. But his plan for addressing Keith and Aaron was one of a long-range caliber, which called for patience, and unfortunately this was an attribute Rasheen was still learning to master.

By the time the first month's anniversary in the new home sweet home came and went, Camila had not only convinced Rasheen to go out with her to a club as a birthday gift to her, but she also got him to hire a baby-sitter, house attendant and maid all in one. Rosa Rodriguez was a Mexican immigrant thirsty for an off the books job, and after Rasheen got the Judge to thoroughly check her background, and saw she was trustworthy enough to allow her to work within the confines of his ultra-private household, he employed her at above standard pay rates ($8 an hour) with stipulations she had to be a live-in employee.

It didn't take long for Rasheen to realize Rosa was the best thing that happened to his family, because Camila was no housewife, and wasn't a very proficient mother either. There was no question that another month of the house looking like a project stairwell, Rasheen would've probably lost all patience with Camila's sloppy housekeeping antics, and their already rocky relationship would've went into a destructive downward spiral.

On the other side of Rasheen's two-sided life, he kept communications with Sharon Walker through the use of the Internet and a secured cellular phone. With the use of code names (Rasheen: Raw Dog – Sharon: Black Beauty), they communicated online and constructed a series of elaborate plans for their first of many gambling establishment robberies. Rasheen and Sharon transferred pictures of an underground Casino in Philadelphia, swapping them back and forth as they both expressed their tactical views on the best ways to pull off this robbery. There were even videotapes of consumers gambling and all the security personnel.

All the while Camila did everything in her powers to change Rasheen's mind about not allowing her to roll with him as his ride or die chick on these new money-making efforts. She worked on him virtually every day, came up with all sorts of reasons why he needed her, utilized several reverse psychology tactics and even outright resorted to tears of despair.

Finally, about two weeks before the first multi-million-dollar job was about to pop off, Rasheen gave in when Camila pointed out that on the battlefield, in the heat of combat, a wise general always surrounded himself with people who would never betray him, who proved already that they will roll with him to the bitter end. She placed great emphasis on the fact that he was going to need an extra set of eyes watching his back because big money of the likes they were about to touch could bring out the worse in some folks.

When Camila insisted that the FBI agents hunting him were notorious for flipping people and mentioned what happened to the Black Panthers when they were infiltrated back in the 1970s, Rasheen saw he had no choice but to let her roll with him, since she was the only one who's loyalty couldn't be unquestioned. Little did Camila know she had planted a gargantuan seed inside Rasheen's head, one that would prove to be the most life-sustaining jewel he had ever come in contact with.

With Camila now on deck with him in the field, he also was forced to make a series of arrangements designed to ensure Little Rasheen's safety and well-being was guaranteed if in the event something happened to the both of them. Whether or not these precautions would work was something Rasheen realized he would never know for certain, but what counted most was that he wasn't walking through the valley of death knowing there was a chance he would leave his son without some degree of security.

Rasheen and Camila exited the house while Little Rasheen was asleep.

Rasheen said to Rosa with a suitcase in both hands, "We'll call you twice a day every day. Only if there's an emergency are you to ever use that number I gave you." He headed for the green van as both women followed him. "Remember, no one besides you is allowed in the house." He wanted to tell her to stay out of the basement, but that would only serve as an invitation for her to be nosy, so he kept his mouth shut and hoped he had done a good job at concealing everything that could cause any controversy.

Rasheen and Camila got inside the van, and just before Rasheen pulled away, he said from behind the wheel, "We'll be back in a week. Take care of my little man. Peace, Rosa." He pulled off as Camila and Rosa waved good-bye.

As Rosa watched the van disappearing down the early evening horizon, the evil grin on her face broadcast a vibration that would've cost her this job if Rasheen or Camila had saw this twisted twinkle in her eyes.

Four hours later, Rasheen saw the highway sign that said Philadelphia was five miles away; it was time to activate the first phase; he pulled his cellular phone and hit the speed dial button that would connect him to Willie. When a voice answered, he said. "Yo' what's up, son!"

Willie was in a hotel room in Oklahoma with Lora lying on the bed watching TV. "Hey, Rasheen!" He said elatedly. "What's the deal, man?"

"You can let everybody know the job is in Philadelphia. Tell everybody to meet up at the Crowne Plaza Hotel Parking garage on Market Street and North 18th Street in Center City immediately. I'm a few hours away, so tell 'em to put a pep in their step. This ain't a test, so tell everybody to come ready to get their hands dirty." He hung up.

Willie disconnected the call and immediately informed the others.

After receiving the call, Ja-King and Rashango rushed out of their hotel rooms in various nearby States, heading for the destination.

* ** *

Twenty minutes later, about a few hundred miles away in Atlanta Georgia, Aaron also received a phone call as he sat cuddled up with his wife as they watched a home video starring Jack Nicholson. He snatched up the cell phone sitting on the nearby coffee table, flipped it open, and said. "Aaron here."

As the person on the other end of the line spoke, Aaron's excitement became evident to his wife as he inched away from her and headed for the kitchen. By the time he reached the kitchen, he said. "Whatever you do, stall as long as you can. I'm on my way, and bear in mind I'm in Atlanta, which means I got a long distance to travel. If you gotta move make sure you use your car. Don't disappoint me."

Aaron hung up the phone and took a minute for his mind to register what had just happened. A second later, he shook off the exhilaration and hastily began dialing numbers, informing his team that tonight was the night they would finally bring this long, drawn out mission to a nice, beautiful end.

CHAPTER # 17

"What if you had a dude spitting lies around you," Big Gains said as he sat in the seat nearest the window of the jet with a glass of Hennessey, while Frukwan sat in the row next to him with a similar glass, and Jackhammer Jones was sitting in the row in front of him, empty handed.

Big Gains continued, "And this dude is talking shit about the black man ain't create shit, he ain't did nothing to help build history, and that we is a disposal being because he did nothing, what would you do to shut this kinda fool down?"

Frukwan wasn't in the mode for this; they were about to get it on with some sho' nuff bangers, and he couldn't believe Big Gains wanted to do all of this sap raping, instead of talking about the hit they were about to do. "I don't know what I'd do, Big Gains; maybe Jackhammer could answer that."

Jackhammer Jones turned around with a vicious sneer on his face and locked eyes with Big Gains, almost as if he was daring him to ask the question; he had told him he didn't do any talking before work, and the thought of his explicit instructions being disobeyed was a sign that they thought he was a fuckin' joke. He was going to have to make himself clearly understood, he realized. If it wasn't for the huge sum of money they had gave him up front ($10,000), and the impending amount upon completion of the mission ($12,000), he would've reached over the seat and broken both Big Gains' and Frukwan's jaws, and would have even decapitated them just for the fuck of it.

Big Gains nearly lost his composure as he looked at Frukwan with the mad screw face, and then said nervously, "Naw—naw Jackhammer we got this, he didn't mean it; pardon us, man, he didn't mean to pull you in this discussion." He saw Jackhammer turn back around in slow motion and then he stared at Frukwan, sensing that

he had done this shit on purpose; he specifically told Frukwan not
to say anything, not to look at him wrong, and basically not to fuck
with Jackhammer under any circumstance! He was about to spazz
out on Frukwan, but decided he'd give him some verbal lashing at a
later time. "Basically, you trying to tell me, you ain't got an answer,
huh, Frukwan? I thought the Gods had answers to these types of
questions?"

"Being a part of the all eye seeing don't mean one person got the
answer to everything. A true wise man is one who knows he don't got
the answer to everything, and don't pretend he does."

"The answer is simple; you string this chump up by his fuckin'
heels, find a nice tall light pole, hang him high, and commence to
whippin' his monkey ass!" He frantically lashed out his hand as
though he was flicking a whip, with comedic fervor, causing Frukwan
to laugh. Then, he theatrically held up his hands as though to quiet
down his audience. "The reason we gotta lay down this level of
punishment is cause the damage those lies are causing is killing us!
One of our heavyweights, Amos Wilson once said, 'you are more a
victim of history when you do not know it'"

Frukwan thought about the connection between the
information presented and realized it didn't make sense; he was
about to challenge him to explain the connection, and then realized
this was probably another trick to get him involved in the discussion.
Instead, he decided to talk about something that was relevant to
the situation. "Where at in Philly are we supposed to reach out and
touch this cat, Rasheen?"

"When we get there, I told you, Cowboy'll be there waiting."
He reached in his waist and pulled out the two Dessert Eagles, and
said, "What difference does it make whether we know the game plan
now or later? As long as we moving heat like this across State lines
without obstacles that's all that matters."

DIVINE G

* *** *

Rasheen pulled the van into the Crowne Plaza Hotel Parking lot and headed for the third level. When Rasheen reached the level and made the right turn, he saw Willie's red Toyota, Ja-King's black Chevrolet, and Rashango's blue beat-up Oldsmobile parked in various scattered parking spaces. He was glad they knew to use simple, inexpensive rides, even though it didn't matter what they rode here in; it was just good to see they were using common-sense without him having to tell them how to handle every little detail.

As Rasheen brought the van to a stop, he saw both couples and Rashango get out of their cars and began approaching. He and Camila got out of the van, getting ready to spring the surprise on them.

"Rasheen, my mufuckin' ace boom bang!" Ja-King said with rap lyrical flair. Tania was walking along side of him with a huge, ridiculous looking smile on her face. She was bouncing up and down like an excited child about to be blessed with a treat.

After the group gave Rasheen a series of brotherly hugs and handshakes, Rasheen said. "There's been a slight change in plans. First, I need everybody to give me their cell phones, and any other electrical devices. They gotta go."

Willie's eyebrows crunched together, "What's up with this, Rah?"

"Yeah, man," Ja-King chimed in. "What's all this—"

"Either do it or you can bounce!" Rasheen said in such a straightforward fashion everybody knew there was no room for any debate.

They all started pulling out their cell phones, camera phones, and MP3 players as Camila stepped in front of each one with a opened green duffle bag in her hands for them to drop the phones inside.

Everyone complied.

"Camila's now gonna check y'all out with her metal detector, and when she's finished, we outta here."

Camila waved her wan across the bodies of first Lora, then Willie, Rashango, Tania and Ja-King. The only one who beeped was Tania, who was carrying a small 25 automatic, clearly violating Rasheen's instructions.

"Sorry y'all," Tania said smilingly, shrugging her shoulders. "I never go anywhere without my baby, and believe me, certain habits are very hard to break."

Rasheen cracked a smile and saw once again he was going to enjoy working with this crazy, fine lunatic bitch, since she seem to represent the epitome of a loyalistic psychopath. She was perfect for the type of situation they were about to walk into. "Small thing, Tania, but trust me; we gonna have plenty heaters at our disposal. Now, I need everybody in the van, and we'll drive to a location where we can bring everybody up to speed—"

"You want us to leave our wheels behind?" Lora inquired perplexingly.

"That's right." Rasheen climbed inside the passenger seat of the van. "Everybody in. We got a few hours before we open the curtains to this show, so let's go."

Everybody got in the van through the side door Camila had slid open; she then got behind the wheel and pulled off.

* ** *

Two hours later, Aaron Wilson was in the passenger seat as Eugene was behind the wheel of their blue rental car, cruising down the Streets of Philly. Four additional vehicles followed them; one contained Norman and Donald, another contained Big Gains, Frukwan, and Jackhammer Jones, and the last two contained several associates of Aaron and Keith's who lived in the area, including Cowboy.

Aaron had his cell phone in front of him, staring at the screen as the stationery signal indicated they were merely moments from the garage. His excitement wasn't as overwhelming as his confusion, which was not a good thing. The targets' vehicle had been in this location for an extended period, he realized, and that didn't make any sense at all, because they were supposed to be robbing a local gambling establishment, and it certainly didn't take hours to plan such a robbery.

Aaron was even more enraged by the fact his confidential informant still hadn't contacted him. His heart pounded when he saw the garage come into view and he activated the dial button on his cell phone. "This is it." His voice was steady. "Start splitting up as we planned. Everybody, make sure you stick with the plan."

Two minutes later, Aaron got out the car parked on the second level with his weapon in the ready as Eugene followed him.

They scurried silently up the ramp to the third level, listening for any noises.

Aaron knew the exact location of the car, since the cellular phone in his other hand was also a tracking mechanism that would guide him to the car with the homing device. When he saw the vehicle and no one was in it, he walked towards it with confusion and terror riveting his body as his eyes scanned the immediate area.

There was no question this place was empty, and since the plant had no idea where the job was going down, Aaron threw his infuriated hands up in the air while shouting, "Fuck!"

After forcing his mind into a state of calm, Aaron reactivated the dials on his cell phone in order to get a tracking signal on his plant's cell phone. When it came up, he saw the signal was a few miles away. Just as he was about to activate the cell phone's re-dial button, he saw his team rapidly converging towards him with their weapons ready.

He shouted to them. "Everybody, come on over." When they arrived, he continued, "The targets are not here. I got some new instructions . . ."

* ** *

Rasheen stood near the backgammon table watching the players happily playing the odds, while the croupiers were helping them with the process. Dressed in a black sleek business suit like most of the other males in attendance, Rasheen noticed the crowded subterranean room was filled with big wigs of all denominations. There were even a few Chinese cats running around the place, as well as some dudes with turbans wrapped around their heads, who must've been those Arab dudes with crazy cash from all that crude oil they sold. He could've sworn he saw that famous rapper Big Daddy Dane, and even upon a closer observation, he still couldn't tell if it was a look alike or not. In the background, elevator music played, creating a very soothing and peaceful atmosphere.

Rasheen scanned the huge gambling floor that had almost two-dozen tables with rich folks either hovering around them or sitting around them in circular fashion. The smell of money was wall to wall, and everybody was gambling up a storm. He'd already saw at least a million dollars exchanged hands just by approaching a few tables, watching the players making bets.

About twenty minutes ago, Rasheen and his team had entered Shooties on 52nd Street between Market and Arch. They had showed the heavily armed bouncers at the front door their special entry passes, and they entered. On the ground level was the legal gambling set ups, a dance floor, a strip club section, and an exotic bar where expensive drinks were served. During their planning session, they had decided that every penny moving in this joint was a target for the taking, and they intended to start from the basement and ascend to the ground floor.

Rasheen looked around again and saw Ja-King and Tania were in place. He turned around and saw Rashango was sitting at a card table on the other side of the room, pretending to be deeply involved in the game; he looked up and made eye contact with Rasheen, waiting for the signal. He saw Rashango's two diamond earrings sparkled in the reflection of the light; he still couldn't under this new style where men wore ear rings in both ears. According to Rashango, he was trying to "rock it like" his basketball idol Lebron James.

Rasheen pulled from the eye exchange, now checking out the several undercover security staff that thought they were unknown, but thanks to Sharon he had them all pegged, and basically marked for a swift take down. He just hoped he could knock them out of play without killing them, since homicides only complicated things. He'd gave clear instructions to the team to first try to disarm or immobilize them without use of deadly force, but the more he examined the situation the more he realized this might be virtually impossible.

As Rasheen moved to another table, he hoped Willie, Lora and Camila, who were upstairs on the ground floor, were in place; they're job was to secure the security control station up there the minute he gave the signal, and to seal off all the doors equipped with an automatic locking system that would shut down all escape routes once activated. Unlike most robberies, this was going to be one in which not one single penny would be allowed to slip through the cracks. Rasheen wasn't worried too much about the surveillance cameras, since Sharon had looped the cameras when Rasheen called her moments before they entered, and in any event, they had on costume make up that slightly altered their complexions and other facial features.

After they entered, they slid to the rest rooms, and just as Sharon promised, up inside the ceilings were an arsenal of the most sophisticated weaponry, ranging from 16 shot 9-mms with extended clips, .50 caliber handguns with armor-piercing rounds to compact Uzis and mini-machine guns. After the weapons were distributed to the entire team, and the thoroughly folded backpacks were stuffed into the waist of their pants, everyone took their places.

Rasheen wiped away the sweat from his brows; these hot as bulletproofed underclothing were suffocating him. After the last time he almost fell victim to a stray bullet, he made it a rule to use bulletproof clothing that covered the body from head to toe. The long John style bulletproof garments were nothing short of state of the arts, and Rasheen vowed to never go into the jungle without these underpants and shirts. In fact, his whole crew was bulletproofed down. The only reserve he had was that his head was on full blast; he had thought about utilizing bulletproofed hoodies but the thought of trying to wear such a garment under their current clothing wasn't making sense because it would've clearly attracted unnecessary attention.

He looked at his watch, and saw it was time. He pressed a button on his watch, sending out the go signal. With expert inconspicuousness, Rasheen pulled his silencer equipped 9-mm, concealed it behind his leg, and slid over to the covert security worker, who was looking the other way. Through the corner of his eye he saw Tania, Willie and Rashango deeing up on their designated security staff they were required to take down.

In almost perfect unison, all four of them shouted to the men to put their hands up, and just as they suspected the men tried to reach for their weapons, forcing Rasheen and his crew to fire silenced shots into the six men. Rasheen and Rashango had taken down two men each.

The movement within the whole room stopped on a dime as their minds registered the situation. With six bodies hitting the floor in an almost simultaneous manner, it didn't take a genius to figure out what was taking place.

"Listen up!" Rasheen announced as he pulled another silencer-equipped weapon (.50 caliber handgun). "If you co-operate, no one will get hurt or killed."

As Rasheen spoke, Ja-King and Tania bolted over to a hidden door at the far end of room where another man was behind a two-way mirror. Ja-King retrieved a small box from his front pocket, it was no bigger than a tic-tac container and he pressed the button. Just as Rasheen said it would, the door buzzed open.

Ja-King and Tania positioned themselves on either side of the door.

Ja-King kicked the door all the way open, and a wave of shots rang out.

The crowd inside the club went ballistic, screaming in terror while trying to get away from the gunfire.

Rasheen rushed backwards shouting. "Everybody down! Get on the ground face first!"

Suddenly, an Arab man with a turban on his head rushed towards Rasheen, and just as Rasheen turned, the man collided with him, knocking the wind clean out of him, while hurling him into an airborne collision with the hard marble floor.

The crowd was instantly galvanized into action upon seeing this daring act of heroism, and they all ran towards Rasheen about to pounce on him, but Rasheen squeezed off a shot that exploded one of the so-called superhero's head, spraying huge blood droplets and brain matter into the faces of the would be super-heroes. The others immediately hit the deck.

At the precise moment the hero charged towards Rasheen, Rashango fired an unsilenced shot into another suited man who also charged at him, the bullet cut the man down with blood splattering gruesomeness, since the armor-piercing bullet had cut straight through him, providing a gory exit wound the size of a hormone-laced grapefruit.

Rasheen tussled with the Arab guy as this hero tried desperately to disarm him; he couldn't believe this fool had forgotten about his other hand with the other gun. Rasheen turned the .50 caliber and pumped a bullet through the man's temple, literally decapitating the heroic maniac, while spraying blood everywhere. As the warm blood dripped from his face, Rasheen frantically sprung to his feet and saw everyone was face down on the floor. He then saw Ja-King and Tania had made it inside the hidden room.

Rasheen shouted. "Another trick like that and I'll kill everybody in this motherfucker!"

Meanwhile, upstairs, Willie, Lora, and Camila had received the signal, and went straight to the main security station that was in the back. Camila activated a similar box like the one Ja-King used to open the hidden door. When the door buzzed open, the three entered with their weapons trained and found the four men playing a game of cards.

Not surprisingly, one of the fools went for his gun, causing Lora and Camila to pump two silence shots into him, which took all the fight out of the others.

Camila rushed over to the remaining three men, grabbed the toughness looking one by the collar and snatched him to his feet with the gun clamped to his head. "Call all of your men to this station."

Lora slid near him and said, "And if we detect you're doing a terrible job, or playing some kinda head-game like your homie here," she gestured to the man on the floor, "this is what will happen to you." She stepped back one pace, took aim and fired a shot into one of the bouncer's head at pointblank range.

Willie was momentarily stunned by this over-the-top act of extreme violence as the man slithered from the seat and fell dead to the floor. Not only did she violate Rasheen's instructions not to kill if it could be avoided, but she made him realize he apparently didn't know the woman he'd been fucking for the last couple of years. He was grateful he wasn't into abusing women because it was clear he would've committed suicide.

The man rushed over to the control station, activated the universal communication instrument and said into the microphone, "Listen, I need all security staff to report to central control immediately. Don't worry about surveillance, this'll be quick. Hurry up." He sat down the device with a look that announced, how did I do?

Willie and Lora took their places on the side of the door as Camila pulled the two remaining man out of the view of the men who would enter any moment.

When the two men entered, Lora came up behind one of them with her weapons poked in his back and whispered, "Keep walking towards the back with your hands in the air." She saw him nervously look back at her. "Don't play superman."

The man complied, and within minutes, six of the armed bouncers were secured inside the control station. There was one more bouncer, who hadn't arrived yet, and Lora was itching to go find him, but Willie instructed her to be patient.

The lone bouncer, Big Mike, was standing near the dance floor when Critter's voice crackled through his earpiece communication device; this was extremely unusual since Critter wasn't in charge of Central Control, and ever since he heard this transmission his gut had been bubbling with a bad vibration. As he bobbed his head to Tupac Shakur's, Hail Mary, Big Mike realized that all night he'd been feeling jittery as though his instincts were trying to warn him of some type of impending doom. He had watched the others rush to

Central Control, but decided he was going to drag ass this trip, since technically speaking he didn't have to follow the command, because Critter wasn't authorized to give the order. He was going to let him call for him again.

Inside the control station, Willie, Lora, and Camila were growing more and more nervous by the seconds; they had disarmed all the bouncers, and now had them all lying face down. They had also activated the exit and entrance shut down systems, had deactivated all surveillance cameras, and had destroyed all surveillance recordings. Without having to utter a word, their facial and bodily gestures broadcast that this last bouncer, who still hadn't shown up, was about to fuck up this run in a vicious way.

Willie pulled the plastic handcuff stripes from his back pocket and began securing each of the bouncers' arms and legs, while Camila kept her gun trained on them. Lora remained at the entrance with her gun in the ready, wishing this last gun-toting bouncer would hurry up and enter.

When all the bouncers were secured, and their mouths gagged, Willie pulled Lora and Camila towards the door and whispered. "This loose arrow is about to fuck this thing up some type of crazy. Rah's about ready to come up any minute." His nervousness was pronounced, and it made him look like he was definitely in the wrong line of work.

Lora had a deep thought expression on her face that lasted for only a few seconds. She began nodding her head as though the ultimate light switch was suddenly turned on inside of her head. "It's only one way to handle this. I'll go out and get him."

"Hold up!" Camila said, as she grabbed at Lora, who was already in motion. "Rah specifically said there can't be no gunplay up here until he's on the set. I say we lay low until just before he comes up, and then we spread out. We can—"

"What if this dude starts lickin' off shots!?" Lora's tone was stepped up a notch. "And what if he goes in before we get situated? If we don't lock this shit down, Rasheen and them could walk right into a fuckin' ambush."

There was a moment of silence as the two women waited for Willie to give the final call, since Rasheen made him the captain of the up top team.

Willie saw this shit wasn't what he was put on the planet to do. He shook his head indecisively as his jumbled thoughts rambled around in his head. He was a salesman of universal stature but a stick-up kid he apparently was not. He didn't fully understand the unique tactical approaches required of the job under such circumstances, but he did know for certain that this situation obviously called for some kind of immediate action; he had to do something, and real fast.

When his ego flared up as the two women started becoming impatient, Willie poked out his chest, and said firmly. "Yeah, we gotta do something." He peered at his synchronized watch. "We got five minutes til they come up here. Here's the plan. Lora, you go out and find this cat. Lock on to him, but don't take him down until Rasheen comes up on the elevator. By then me and Camila'll put the rest of the plan into motion from there."

Lora stepped straight to the business, and was out of the door within seconds

* *** *

Eugene cruised the blue rental car pass the front of the elegant Night Club that had a sign overhead that read, Ramon's Rendezvous. Aaron was in the passenger seat hawk-eyeing the two huge bouncers dressed in tuxedos; one was ushering a suited down, stylishly dressed couple inside the club.

Aaron pulled his cell phone, hit the call button, and said into the device. "This establishment looks real expensive, Clark."

Clark was inside a black Laredo 4x4, sitting in the passenger seat; this vehicle was two cars behind the blue rental. "Yeah, I know." He said into his cellular phone as the Laredo slid pass the club. "Is this a problem? I thought we were focusing on underground gambling joints with big money?"

"Yeah, we are," Aaron said as Eugene made a turn at the corner, looking for a parking space. He was about to inform him that this place looked like it was going to be a dud, but decided to hold back the comment. "Let's check it out."

Eugene parked in front of a fire hydrant.

As Aaron got out of the car, he decided if this club produced no results he was going to come up with a new plan.

After the other vehicles found parking spaces, and one person from each car exited, they followed Aaron towards the club. The five of them entered, covertly searched the entire premises and were heading back towards their vehicles around the corner within twenty minutes.

Aaron put his back up against the gate of a dress shop as the high potency stress ran high and his anger ran even higher. The late night Streets within this commercial district were completely desolated except for a stray cat, and a brown paper bag flapping in the wind. He waved for the others to get out of the car and to join them.

When the entire team was huddled up, Aaron said. "We need to revise this plan a little. I think we can cover more ground if we split up. This is the second place we checked out and it took us an hour to do it; we're wasting too much time." He inwardly scolded himself for assuming the first two clubs on the list would produce instant results. "We have four teams, and thirteen locations to check out. Each team takes three establishments and whoever finds them first contact the rest of us."

It took three minutes to assign the four teams to the various clubs throughout the entire city, from one end to the other. The team assigned to Shooties was Big Gains, Frukwan, and Jackhammer Jones; it was the second establishment on their list.

* ** *

"Keep your eyes down!" Rasheen shouted when he saw several individuals trying to sneak a few peeks; his two weapons were ready to rock and roll as he watched Ja-King, Tania, and Rashango stripping each gambler and croupiers of all their valuables, ranging from wallets, and expensive jewelry to watches and anything that looked like it might be worth something.

Rasheen's heart pounded with an excitement that was mind numbing, since the four backpacks sitting next to him were filled with two nights' worth of proceeds from the main vault inside the hidden room, and it had to be at least 15 million in cash (all big bills). Sharon wasn't lying when she said this was the best time to hit this place, since tomorrow was the day the owners intended to divvy out the weekly profits amongst themselves, and she definitely wasn't lying when she said this was the mother-load!

As Rasheen shifted his weight onto his other foot, he calculated the probable amount of the side takings they were going to get from everyone down here, and realized there was no question when they finished cleaning out everything, they would easily walk out of this place with an additional couple of million dollars that would all go to him and his team.

When Rasheen saw Ja-King, Tania and Rashango searching the last cluster of people, he looked at his watch and saw everything was unfolding according to plan, even down to the timing, and that pessimistic voice was telling him to watch out, because this was too good to be true, which meant something was bound to go wrong.

Rasheen felt a wave of anxiety stirring in the pit of his stomach, because he'd long since convinced himself there was no such thing as a perfect plan when engaging in this sort of livelihood, and right now his mind, and especially his eyes, were wide open for any signs of disaster.

Then, suddenly, previous instances of robberies gone terribly bad emerged in Rasheen's mind as though to give him an affirmative head nod; the time when Dirty Ricky was killed and he was shot and subsequently arrested appeared; the time Jack-Mack was murdered and Candy got arrested danced around inside his dome. With a mental brush, Rasheen swept these invading thoughts under a cognitive rug, and locked them away as tightly as he could.

He saw Ja-King approaching and knew it was time to take this mission to the next level; Rasheen tucked his .50 caliber handgun in his waist, retrieved the communications device and activated the signal to Willie and the others.

Without saying a word, Rasheen snatched up a backpack, gave the others the other backpacks, wiggled the straps onto his shoulders, and realized this fuckin' bag was extremely heavy as he headed towards the elevator and the others followed.

They entered the elevator.

Meanwhile, upstairs on the main floor, Willie and Camila were in motion. They rushed out of the control station and began looking for Lora.

Camila headed for the door in accordance with her instructions, and as she approached, she saw three men standing out front as if they were trying to get inside. *Didn't these fools see the fuckin' sign that clearly said the club was closed!?* On the heels of this thought, Camila she saw one of their faces and nearly fainted, because this dude looked like one of Killer Kato's henchmen. She dipped to the side and merged with a group of guys having drinks at a table.

"I'm sorry, big fella," Camila smiled brilliantly at the brother with a scruffy looking beard as she sat in the empty chair, keeping her eyes glued on the three guys at the entrance. Then, she saw the three men suddenly started walking away. She was momentarily dazed with deep confusion as she tried to figure out was her eyes playing tricks on her.

When Camila saw the bearded brother gaping at her as though she had three heads, she snapped out of her perplexed dazed, and took her position by the door; after peering outside and examining the empty streets while noticing the three had disappeared, she had by now convinced herself that it couldn't have been Big Gains.

When the elevator door slid open, and Lora saw Rasheen and the others getting off the elevator, she inconspicuously pulled her 9-mm as she watched the lone bouncer closely. When she saw his startled facial response, she rapidly crept closer to him. She saw him reaching. Just when she took aim, a hysterical woman screamed upon seeing the gun and the whole place went crazy.

Lora fired a shot that missed the bouncer.

Big Mike felt the bullet zipped pass his face and saw a man dressed in a brown suit was knocked off his feet just as the loud explosion boomed over the music. He instantly knew it was a bullet that struck him, and in an instant, Big Mike moved with the grace and speed of a ballerina, despite the fact he weighed nearly 220 pounds.

Big Mike dove for cover. By the time Big Mike's shoulder touched the floor and the rest of his body went into a roll, he had his gun in the ready. He couldn't determine who fired the shot, because people were running and screaming frantically. His attention was pulled back to the group that just gotten off the elevator and he knew this was a code red. Just as the old tune by Black Box came to a stop, the circumstances registered clearly. They were apparently being robbed! *But how!? How the fuck is this possible!?* Big Mike got up and was moving in a crouching position, heading towards a section near the dance floor where he could get off a shot at one of the guys wearing a backpack, who was kneeling beside the bar.

Lora weaved through the stampeding crowd of people, keeping her eye on Big Mike. When she saw the bouncer heading towards Rasheen who was now shouting for everyone to get down to the floor while the others were taking places in their designated positions, so as to box everyone in, she increased her speed.

Just as the big bouncer took aim, Lora unleashed several rapid shots.

Big Mike felt the fiery hot lead missiles ripping through his back, and as he went down to the floor, he spun around and fired at Lora who was still coming up behind him.

Lora felt a tremendous blow to her chest, and the power of the impact knocked her clean off her feet. She impacted with the hard marble floor, slamming the back of her head as twinkling stars appeared before her eyes.

Willie saw what happened and was galvanized into motion, and just as the big bouncer fired at Lora, he took aim and pumped off three rounds that caused the bouncer's body to recoil violently. When he took his finger off the trigger, Willie was certain the huge man was dead and was mesmerized by what he had just done. He not only busted his gun but bodied this dude in the process!? Then, he turned and saw Lora lying on the floor clutching her chest and he raced over to her as he heard Rasheen screaming, "Get the fuck down! Now!"

When Willie reached Lora, he saw she was holding her shoulder. "Is it bad!? Can you move!?"

"Help me up!" Lora said through clenched teeth with her hand extended. "I'll make it. It didn't go through; I think the bullet broke something." As Willie pulled her onto her feet, she was inwardly glad this bulletproof fabric was working correctly because if that bullet had cut into her body she would've been out of commission. She tried to move her arm and the searing pain told her something was definitely broken. With one arm dangling lifelessly, she picked up her 9-mm, and joined the others as the crowd of about forty or more partygoers were lying face down, waiting to have all their valuables removed from their possession.

Moments earlier, just before the shots rang out, Big Gains, Frukwan and Jackhammer Jones were about two blocks away debating whether they should go on to the next club on their list or should they force their way inside Shooties.

When the muffled gunshots came from inside the club, they received the answers to their questions as they each made eye contact with each other.

As Big Gains raced down the street, running behind Frukwan and Jackhammer Jones, he pulled his cell phone, and hit the re-dial button. When he heard Aaron's voice on the other end, he spoke excitedly. "We got some shots bustin' off at Shooties! When we tried to get in they had a sign on the door that said they were closed, even though the joint got mad people inside. I think this is it. . ."

CHAPTER # 18

Aaron sat in the passenger seat screaming in the cell phone. "I think Big Gains' crew found them." The blue rental was moving at NASCAR racecar speeds. "He said shots were fired inside Shooties."

Donald was on the other end of the phone. "Did he confirm these shots are connected to Rasheen? What if we—"

"Believe me, it's them! Gains said he saw a female inside he knew from Brooklyn. Some chick that used to run with Rasheen. Get over there as fast as you can. I'll call the others and pull their coats. Later!" He disconnected the call and hit another dial.

As Aaron waited for Clark to pick up, he felt his rage roaring at a rate that was making his head hurt. It suddenly felt like Eugene wasn't moving fast enough and his anxiety got the best of him. "Man, move this mufucka, Eugene! Shooties's on the other side of town for Christ sakes!"

Eugene cut his eyes at Aaron while he slammed down on the gas pedal, catapulting the car to 85 miles per hour, despite the fact they were on a residential street with a 40 miles per hour speed limit.

"Listen, Clark," Aaron said into the cell phone. "Meet us at Shooties. Gains found them. From what he said this thing is in full swing. I told Gains to hold them inside if possible, so hurry up over there. "

Aaron disconnected the line, and saw Eugene was now pushing the rental car the right way. Then, his runaway mental faculties started assessing everything surrounding this situation and for some unknown reason, he felt a strong sense of optimism, for a change.

* ** *

Rasheen stood near the bar watching the others putting the final and finishing touches on this perfect run. Ja-King and the others

165

were confiscating wallets, gold and diamond studded jewelry, and so on, from the patrons lying sprawled out on the floor. Suddenly, he saw Camila rushing away from the front door as though someone was approaching. An electrical bolt of lightning rippled through his body; the first thought that came to mind was the police.

As Rasheen watched Camila conceal herself behind the nearby manometer, he saw two men appear in front of the club, excitedly peering inside, which caused another lightning bolt to strike his Central Nervous System. *What the fuck is Big Gains and Frukwan doing out here!?*

With his eyes wide with a mixture of terror and confusion, Rasheen knelled as he swiftly moved towards Ja-King, while keeping his eyes on the two.

Just as Rasheen reached Ja-King he noticed a third man had arrived, said something to Big Gains and Frukwan, and the three disappeared, but he was certain they hadn't gone very far; their highly agitated bodily gestures announced they were here to stay, and were drawing close to the blood trail they apparently were pursuing. Then, he saw Camila waving to get his attention, and he waved for her to come over to him.

As Camila approached, Rasheen distraughtly waved to Rashango and Willie. When the whole team as huddled up, he said hastily, "We got a problem. Them dudes at the door are peeps from my hood and they was movin' with Killer Kato. I don't know how the fuck this happened, or what this shit is about, but I can promise you for sure, they ain't here to do any talkin'"

Tania smiled jubilantly, "This is wonderful! That means more fun!" She pulled the compact Uzi tucked in the back waist of her black denim jeans and ejected a bullet into the chamber. "Now we get two treats for one."

"Sorry, Tania," Rasheen continued. "If we can avoid a bang out that's what we're gonna do. Here's the plan; we're all going out through the back, since that's the closest route to the van." He wondered if this was wise, but right now his mind was telling him to move quickly; with so many questions surging through his mind it was only logical to make a decision and roll with it. "Is all this shit in order?"

"Everything's good to go." Willie confirmed. "Everybody's tied up. There's about ten more people we didn't check."

"Fuck 'em," Rasheen lead the way. "Gotta leave it behind. We out."

The others followed Rasheen with their weapons ready and their money-filled packs secured to their backs.

When Rasheen reached the backdoor, he put his ear close to the door, heard nothing, and activated the small electrical box he got from Sharon. The lock buzzed open, and he gently pushed open the door while standing on the side of the threshold.

Rasheen peeked outside, looked in both directions, saw the coast was clear and exited in a crouching position with the heavy backpack killing his shoulders where the straps were damn near cutting into his skin. The 9-mm was in one hand while the other was free. The green van was twenty yards away as they had left it.

As the last of the team stepped out of the club, rapidly heading down the alley towards their getaway ride, Big Gains turned the corner and saw the group heading towards the other end, and frantically took aim just as two of the people at the back of the group saw him.

Lora and Willie were covering the group's rear, and both saw Big Gains turn the corner.

"In back of us!" Willie shouted as he fired two rapid shots just as Big Gains opened fired.

Big Gains pulled back around the corner after firing three rapid shots and the return fire whizzed by him.

Rasheen and the others had taken cover and additional gunfire came from in front of them. It was obvious they were boxed in, and the thought of getting bogged down in this fashion was far more than terrifying. He immediately realized it was time for provocative action.

Rasheen took a deep breath, checked out the path in front of him, saw there were several dumpsters that he could dip and weave in and out of. He quickly slid the backpack off, gave it to Ja-King and his feet were in motion.

Moments earlier, Frukwan was peering around a white Land Rover 4x4, and when he saw Rasheen and the others moving towards him, he fired off several shots but was instantly forced to pull back when a barrage of bullets ate at the Land Rover. He was forced to stay put until there was a pause in the gunfire

Rasheen was elated with glee upon noticing his team knew to open fire at the precise moment he was in motion, which gave him enough time to get closer to the shooter hiding behind the Land Rover. He zipped to the other side, where the shooter was positioned, and rushed towards him as the others continued firing.

When Rasheen was at the back of the Rover, he slowed his pace, tip toeing towards the front of the vehicle. Rasheen raised his hand and waved to signal to the others to stop shooting.

When the bullets stopped, Rasheen rushed around the front end of the Rover just as the shooter fired two shots down the alley.

BOW! BOW!

Rasheen's two 9-mm bullets pounded Frukwan in the back, causing him to fall flat on his face.

Rasheen smiled when he noticed it was Frukwan; the promise he made to him over a decade ago when he had shot Frukwan's cousin Snoop for trying to get some cats from Bushwick to rob him caressed his memory bank. The inward smile was about to creep upon his face, but it disappeared when he saw Frukwan twitching as though he was trying to get in position to get off a shot; he planted a bullet into the back of his head while spurts of gunfire resumed ringing out from the shooter at the other end of the alley.

Rasheen bolted towards the green van, leaped behind the wheel and ignited the ignition. He frantically slid open the side door, got back behind the wheel, and backed the van down the alley with screaming tires.

As the van drew closer to his team, Rasheen crouched down as far as possible, since stray bullets were hitting the van; one bullet had gone straight through the back window and came out the windshield.

The van's tires screamed as Rasheen brought the van to a vicious head-jolting stop.

The gunfire suddenly increased significantly as Ja-King, Lora, Willie, Rashango and then Tania piled inside.

Once they were inside, Rasheen slammed the accelerator down until it touched the floorboard, and the van jerked into action as the burning rubber left behind a white cloud of smoke.

The bullets continued pulverizing the van.

Then, suddenly, Lora rushed to the back window with a fresh clip in her mini-Mac 11 and unleashed a heavy sheet of Uzi bullets, even though their pursuers were still firing shots.

Big Gains and Jackhammer Jones were running after the van while firing their weapons; both of Jackhammer's 9-mms were spitting strips of flames.

Suddenly, Big Gains was violently swept off his feet just as the Uzi gunfire sounded off. The shot to the forehead killed him instantly.

Jackhammer went down in belly whopping fashion and kept licking off shots, despite the bullet wound to the hip.

Inside the van, Lora was knocked backwards from the bullet that tore through the thin metal and lunged itself into her neck. As her warm blood splattered onto the others, Lora fell on top of Rashango.

"Lora, no!" Willie cried in deep agony. "She's shot!" He went to her and held onto her despite the violent turns, bumps and bounces caused by the van tearing away from the scene. Willie clamped his hands around her neck wound, praying this wasn't the end for the only true partner he'd had since third grade. "We gotta get her to a hospital!" His voice was saturated with total grief and despair as he forgot all about what they all agreed to. "Please, Rah, we gotta get her to—"

"If you fall!" Tania shouted, "You forfeit! We all agreed no hosp—"

"We supposed to let her die!?" Willie shrilled, realizing he wasn't ready to deal this shit. "We can't let her die! This shit ain't right—"

"You shouldn't have agreed to it then!" Tania shot back as her envious dislike for Lora had reached a festering level. "She said she was built like that, so now she gotta—"

"Be easy, y'all!" Rasheen shouted as he abruptly turned the steering wheel, sending everyone into a vicious tumble. When all four wheels were back on the freeway, Rasheen slowed down the van to a sensible speed. "Ain't gone be no fightin' among ourselves while we still in the jungle. Willie, if you want us to drop you off at a hospital, you got it, but it won't be in this county. I hope baby-girl can hold on."

"Yeah, we can do that, man!" Willie's voice was laced with genuine relief and hope. "I'll ride with her. I'ma hold her down." He then spoke softly to Lora while increasing the pressure on the neck injury. "Hold on, boo. We gonna get you some help, alright? Please hang on, Lora." When he felt her head nod, he sighed with partial relief.

Rasheen brooded inwardly, since he had undermined his position as the team's leader and General by not keeping his word, and by making a major final call without the others' input. There was no question they adamantly agreed there would be no hospitals, and especially that if a member of the team fell while in the midst of the mission, he or she forfeited their cut. He sighed, noticing his heart wasn't like it used to be, but truthfully, he honestly didn't give a fuck what the others felt or thought about the call, since he was seriously considering a new way of making money. Plus, Lora was good peoples, and he owed her for taking care of him when he was in Cali recuperating from his bullet wound, and for the excellent work she put in with the Phil Henderson run. Leaving her for dead didn't sit well with him at all, and even though he meant what he said earlier about hospitals and forfeiting the cut, now that he was looking at the consequences head on, he realized he couldn't do it, not to Lora.

The more Rasheen thought about it, the more he realized he couldn't leave anyone in this team for dead.

Rasheen peeked through the rearview mirror and saw Tania and Rashango staring at him with vengeful screw faces. He also noticed there was something about these grimaces that made him feel squeamish since their expressions possessed something that harbored a whole lot more than just anger induced by a failure to honor an agreement.

* * * *

Twenty minutes later, the blue rental car came to a tire yelling stop and as Aaron got out of the passenger side of the vehicle, he saw the numerous police cars coming to a screeching stop in front of Shooties across the Street. He nervously noticed two undercover and three marked police vehicles were already on the scene, and he even noticed a fleet of other marked police cars were appearing down the Street but were making sharp turns as though they were heading for the back of the club.

As Aaron strutted towards the club, Eugene came up alongside of him.

The two uniformed officers, standing on each side of the entrance like military sentry, held up a hand when they saw Aaron and Eugene approaching.

Both Aaron and Eugene pulled their wallets, showed their badges, while Aaron uttered the statement, "FBI."

The two cops checked out the badges, stepped aside and allowed the Aaron and Eugene to enter.

Aaron saw the huge crowd of partygoers being uncuffed while excitedly explaining what happened to the several plainclothes Detectives, and uniformed cops, and he also noticed there was apparently a secondary crime scene in the back of the club, since cops were milling into the club from the back entrance.

Aaron's eyes were darting across the area, searching for that familiar face, and something assured him that he wasn't going to find it. When he was upon a bulky built Detective with an olive complexion dressed in a black suit, Aaron displayed his badge and said. "I'm special agent Wilson. This is special agent Lee."

"Detective Jim Moore," He stuck out his hand, and Aaron and Eugene shook it.

Aaron continued, "We have reason to believe one of our perps might be involved in this altercation. What'd we got here?"

"It was a full-scale robbery," Detective Moore gestured towards the scene. "We got a few homicides as well; up here, down in the basement and in the back. There was some heavy black-market gambling going on in this place; some of it was legit, but most of it was totally illicit, and had actually evaded our radar."

Eugene said, "What happened in the back?"

"It was a shootout," Detective Moore said. "We got two bodies back there; someone else was apparently shot but got away. With the amount of blood loss, he won't get too far."

Aaron's mind was working overtime as his eyes were examining all the distraught looking faces. Then, he saw Norman and Donald enter; they instantly spotted him and Eugene and the two approached. After Aaron spoke briefly to Norman and Donald, he made eye contact with Detective Moore and said, "I need to take a look at those bodies in the back." He and Detective Moore exchanged head nods as he followed the Detective towards the back. Detective Moore gestured towards the back entrance and went to another Detective as Aaron and Norman exited the backdoor, and Eugene and Donald went to check out the basement.

When Aaron stepped outside and saw the parade of cops moving about, he was still hoping Rasheen was amongst the dead, even though the unfolding events were telling him this was very unlikely. His infuriation with the spy he had inside Rasheen's crew had long since reached a boiling point, and now with the likelihood that this was a failed attempt to get rid of a major loose end, his rage was beyond blinding. He saw a white cop with an inherently racist demeanor grilling him, and to spite him, Aaron walked right pass him and spoke to the black officer. "FBI." He flipped his badge. "We need to take a peek at these stiffs."

"Be my guest," the cop smiled, realizing what had just happened.

It took Aaron and Norman ten minutes to determine Rasheen wasn't here, and that Big Gains and Frukwan had caught a bad one. There was a trail of blood droplets, which they could obviously surmise was Jackhammer Jones'.

As Aaron stood staring at the trail of blood, struggling to keep from blowing a gasket, his cell phone rumbled in his jacket coat and he retrieved it. "Talk to me."

"Yo—yo, Aaron," Jackhammer Jones stammered in pain. "I'm hit! Real bad, man. I'm hold up in an apartment b-building—" He pressed down hard on the hip wound as he sat on the bottom stair. "I'm a c—couple blocks from Shooties! I need somebody—"

"Hold it together, bro," Aaron said as Eugene and Donald arrived and gave him the signal indicating the basement produced nothing. "We'll come get you. Tell us exactly where you're at." The thought of leaving Jackhammer was very tempting, but reality told him this would only create more of the wrong kind of tension; in any event, Jackhammer was way too loyal, and especially far too dangerous to mistreat by turning your back on.

Jackhammer struggled to his feet, limped towards the door, and peered out of the plate glass window. "I—I'm—I remember the Street I'm on is 54th, but I can't—" He abruptly pulled from the window when he saw the two uniform cops coming from the other end of the Street. "Shit!"

"What's up!?" Aaron sensed there was more bad news.

"Fuckin' cops! I think they f—following my blood." Jackhammer allowed his shoulder to hold the phone to his ear, pulled both 9-mms with fresh 16 shot clips, and began screwing on the silencers as he spoke while preparing for combat. "Listen, Aaron, you gotta get over here real fast, man." The excitement of the moment made the pain miraculously vanish. "You know I don't pull punches, especially when I'm cornered by po-po."

"Try to be easy. I'm on the way," Aaron disconnected the call as he moved with an obvious urgency. His team followed with similar energy.

Meanwhile, Jackhammer Jones stood on the side of the door cringing in pain with both 9-mms ready; he could feel himself becoming dizzy as the warm blood trickled down his leg, forming a small puddle of his body's life sustaining crimson liquid.

How the fuck was he going to get out of this fucked up bind!? He asked himself for the first time. With all this biological evidence he was leaving behind escaping unscathed was a trick nobody could pull off, his subconscious inner voice of rationale assured him.

Pondering these facts on the table, Jackhammer noticed a spectrum of all sorts of variables was surging through his mind. And to his sudden surprise he started praying he didn't have to slay these cops, since Philadelphia had no problem murdering cop killers. Indeed, there were more than enough capital cases on the TV and in the newspapers to confirm this fact; it was even considered common knowledge amongst the hitters' circle that Philly should be avoided, and if it couldn't be avoided to charge very high rates, since it was second only to Texas in State sponsored executions, which meant a hitter had to do everything within his power not to get caught, even if it meant killing cops.

The thought of getting caught crossed his mind and his three grand babies (Damilla, Marc & Shameeka) came into full focus. He'd been putting away large sums of money to help with their schooling in the future, and realized he needed at least thirty grand more to add to their college trust funds, and this run here could've done it.

When he started telling himself he was going to stop if he somehow got around this situation, he sighed because he knew he couldn't. It wasn't that he was addicted to killing, or that he killed for the thrill of it all, like so many of his fellow contract killers, but he did what he did as a genuine means of maintaining a livelihood. He literally kept food on the table and a roof over his and his family's head by picking up contracts. Plus, he hated working a nine to five with an utter compassion and vowed after his injury during a construction site accident (a crane tipped over, fell crashing to the ground and hurled a piece a metal at him that broke his arm) he'd find a way to become self-employed.

That's when his past military experiences came into play, and since he'd done a lot of killing in the Vietnam War, and did such a wonderful job, he figured why not take this talent and use it accordingly. Since he vowed to kill only bad guys, he had no problem going to sleep at nights.

His reverie was brought to a screeching end when he heard the noise. As if bad luck had a monstrous hold on him, Jackhammer heard the cops had stopped right out front of the building he was hiding inside. The sound of their walkie-talkies commingled with their cop like comments were loud and clear. Then, in accordance with Murphy's Law, he heard them approaching; he took several deep breaths and braced himself for the fireworks.

CHAPTER # 19

"Dadda!" Little Rasheen toddled rapidly towards his father with his hands extended when he saw Rasheen and Camila enter the house.

Rasheen's heart was instantly filled with something that sealed his decision to stop all of this madness he seemed to be locked in; with a beaming smile he scooped up his son and embraced him with a loving hug.

"Oh, so you don't see nobody else, huh?" Camila said with an attitude and a smile as she gave her son a huge, playful kiss on the cheek. "What about momma!?" She tickled his tummy, and then said to Rosa who was standing at the entrance leading to the dining room area. "So, how'd it go? My baby boy gave you a hard time or what?"

"No, no, Camila, he was a real nice child," Rosa said smilingly with her strong Mexican accent. "He was very, very good, and he listened to me." She couldn't fix her mouth to tell her that Rasheen was a natural born terror, climbing on everything in sight, throwing anything he touched, spitting his food everywhere while making playful sounds, and in essence, nearly drove her insane and ran her ragged. "He was just wonderful!"

Rasheen sat the black duffel bag of money down and Camila immediately scooped it up and headed for the basement.

As Rasheen headed to the living room to play with his son, his mind reflected on all the drama of the past couple of days. He was glad to be home with his son since it gave his heart a break from all the pain bombarding it. After Lora had died just as they approached the hospital, the whole team was hurled into a state of despair and disbelief. He could still hear Willie's sobbing moans as he held on to Lora's lifeless corpse. Even Tania nearly shredded a tear since the reality was that it could've been her lying there dead.

"Dadda, TB, TB" Little Rasheen pointed at the Television, and his father turned it on.

"Yeah, we gonna watch some TV, but we gone make sure you don't get too crazy with it. This idiot box is responsible for so much disempowerment in our community; you gotta learn how to use this thing in moderation."

As Rasheen held his son in his arms, his mind flashed back to the intricacies of this last run. There was no doubt it was a successful robbery, even though they lost a comrade; in total they came off with about 1.3 million each (after Lora's cut was re-circulated back into the pool). Sharon got the most (almost 4 million) since the agreement was that she would automatically get a third of the house money, which was about 13 million, while the rest and anything else went to the team in the field.

At first everybody was beefing when they realized how much of the proceeds Sharon was receiving, but after Rasheen pointed out that none of this would've been remotely possible without her, and that they had all agreed to this, they all calmed down some; at least outwardly they stopped bitching and complaining. When they tried to figure out how Big Gains and Frukwan (well-known Killer Kato cronies) had found them, while they were in the middle of a heist, no one came up with a logical explanation, which caused even more bitching and complaining.

Reflecting back on all the beefing they'd done with these issues, Rasheen instantly realized he hadn't gotten around to telling everybody that he was officially out of the game. Although at the moment he saw Lora's life fizz out of her body his decision was made, it wasn't until it dawned on him that Little Rasheen could be messed up for life if anything happened to both him and Camila that his decision was confirmed.

Another factor that influenced his decision was the long sit down he had with himself, at which time he looked at his situation under a microscope. He couldn't deny the fact he was making excuses, procrastinating, and was subliminally afraid of change. But, every time he thought about those little children playing in the playground, and how that image had brought him back to this world of the living, he knew he had to come to grips with reality. He genuinely wanted to be free of all the inner turmoil.

He also wanted to give his son the best, make sure he grew up to be someone important like a doctor, lawyer, a judge, a legit businessman, or even an astronaut. After thoroughly re-evaluating and then re-ingesting all of his countless struggles, trials, tribulations, conflicts, disappointments, and the never-ending turmoil that seemed to fully saturate his entire being, as well as the countless jewels tucked away in the archives of his memory bank, Rasheen's decision was clearly written in stone. He was out of the game!

But, how was he gonna break the news to everybody?

Rasheen sighed when he imaged how each of his team members was going to react. He couldn't even fathom how Sharon was going to take the news; she already had four additional hits lined up and was currently counting dollars as though the stolen cash was already in the bank. As he sat enjoying the quality time with his son, no easy way to break the news came to mind.

He started re-evaluating what he was about to do, looking at it from all angles and perspectives once again, and he still concluded that it was now or never; he had to get out of the country with his family. Maybe to Cuba or one of those Caribbean places where the U.S. didn't have a lot of pull and influence. The dude he had helping him, known as The Judge, had proven beyond all doubts that he was more of a miracle maker than even Sharon Walker, and he was banking on the fact he could make it happen. He'd been keeping his dealings with the Judge completely concealed from everyone, even Camila, and this was what he'd termed his ultimate ace in the hole. So far, the Judge helped him with the identity change, the purchase of this Somerset County house they were living in, and was making arrangements to re-channel Lameek's riches into the appropriate hands it belonged. He had even asked the Judge to do a background check on Sharon Walker, and she was basically a ghost; he was still searching and promised to get back to Rasheen when he found something solid. It wasn't that he didn't trust Sharon, it was only that he was all too aware of the crazy, foul effects money had on people, and in light of the reality that their relationship evolved around big money, he was making it his business to be on top of any and everything that involved his interests.

Suddenly, a commercial popped on the TV screen, and Little Rasheen screamed excitedly. "Cer! Cer! Want! Want!" He pointed while bouncing vibrantly as the colorful cartoon bird spoke. "Cer! Cer!"

"Easy, man," Rasheen saw his son wanted some breakfast cereal. The Fruit loop bird on the tube was starting some stuff, and he yelled towards the kitchen. "Rosa, come in here for a minute, please."

Ten seconds later, Rosa appeared, wearing a cooking apron. "Yes, Rasheen."

"Bring us two bowls of cereal. Make sure it's Fruit loops. Thanks."

Rosa did an about face and returned four minutes later with the bowls of cereal on a silver serving tray.

After they ate this late afternoon snack, Rasheen decided it was time to burn Little Rasheen out, so he could tend to other business. He took his son out to the backyard and played football with him, running him back and forth until he saw his little Shorty was tired.

As Rasheen washed his son in the bathtub, he saw the trick worked as unusual; Little Rasheen was nodding sleepily in the tub, and once he dried him off, he was tucked into bed.

After Rasheen made a few calls on his secured cell phone, and talked for about two hours, he decided to have a talk with Camila. She was the first to be blessed with the new developments.

As the two lay in bed, dressed for sleep, while watching a late-night talk show, Rasheen said, "You ever wondered how it would be to live in Cuba?"

Camila's bewildered reaction was far from subtle. "Cuba!? Why would I wanna live in Cuba?"

"You never thought about spending time on one of those Caribbean Islands, laid back soaking up all that sun and shit, all year around?"

She thought about the question. "Yeah, I thought about going over there on a vacation. But, Cuba, seems like it ain't even a part of that vacation place. The way they make Cuba sound, it's like Russia, Communist and all that shit. Naw, I ain't never thought about moving there." She held onto a long moment of silence. "Rasheen, don't tell me you're thinking about going over there and dragging us with you!?"

"Why not! Cuba got made black people over there, and from what I can tell Castro be showing mad love to black folks. Look at how he holdin' down Assata Shakur. She slid up out of this country back in the day after they lied on her about killing some cops, and this country couldn't touch her."

"Assata Shakur? Who the hell is that?"

Rasheen was about to spazz out on Camila for not knowing something as basic as this piece of black history until he realized he wouldn't have heard of her if it wasn't for the extensive reading he had done while in prison. Then, a de ja vu moment caressed his thought waves when he realized he had done exactly what Camila had just done when Rondu, Born Master, and Divine Supreme had mentioned names like Cheikh Anta Diop, Josef Ben-Jochanan, Dr. Jawanza Kunjufu, John Henrik Clarke, Ivan Van Sertima, J.A. Rogers, George GM. James, Anna Mellisa Graves, and Dr. Naim Akbar to him. "She was a sister who was down with the Black Panthers back in the early 70s, and since she was fighting for the liberation of Black folks, the FBI's cointel program went on a vicious rampage to frame her and some other panthers, accusing them of killing cops, and tried to kill and throw them in jail, but they wiggled out of that shit."

"Word!? I know about the Black Panthers." She held the moment of silence, fearing that Rasheen was going to start making moves to leave the country. "I thought you said your peeps had mad Casinos lined up for the taking? If all them joints are holding like this last piece we just rocked, we gonna be set for life—"

"We already set for life, Camila!" Rasheen laid on his back and cupped his hands behind his head. "I been planning to get the fuck out of the game ever since I caught that slug out there in Cali, and now I'm dead ass serious."

Camila felt a dark sheet of terror growing; it was gaining speed and momentum like a tidal wave in a savage storm. This was her big chance to finally get right, and she wasn't trying to hear anything Rasheen was shooting at her. "Rasheen, boo, pulling out now is like hustling backwards. I know you got mad cheddar stashed and everything, and I believe you when you say it's more than enough to keep us straight, but you know how money works. The more you got, the faster it goes, and the more you need it. Let's just do these last few Casino hits, and then—"

"No! Fuck that! This last run was the last! I'm off this mufuckin' merry-go-round. All this shit is straight madness. We got millions, and for us to keep going out in the jungle, risking our lives, and putting our son in a possible fucked up situation, is stupid. If we didn't have Little Rasheen in the picture then maybe shit might be different. We gotta start looking out for him; the things we do have to be done with him in mind." He paused a moment as he could feel the tension pulsating from Camila. "What happened to Lora could've happened to any one of us."

"Naw, Rasheen, we was bulletproof down. It was just her time to go, that all it was."

"And I guess we all catching amnesia! Since nobody's asking the fuckin' question, I will! How the fuck did Frukwan and Big Gains tracked us to that spot, and did it while we was in the middle of that run?"

Camila shook her head to that one because that dilemma had her completely stumped. "I don't know how it happened, but you can bet it ain't coming from inside our team. When you took everybody's' cell phones, and then flipped the planning locations at the last minute that threw a crazy monkey wrench in any cut throat tricks; if anybody on the team had a hidden agenda."

"That don't mean that, Camila," Rasheen said with disgust. He couldn't believe she was closing her mind to the reality that nobody could be trusted in this business. "Once the area was locked down, all type of shit could get put in the game."

"So, what you saying!? One of the reasons you're throwing the towel in is because you don't trust somebody down with our team?"

Rasheen was about to blow up on her but held his frustration in check. "We pullin' outta this shit; the bottom line is we got enough cheddar! We got a seed to look after! I'm running from the police, the feds, and all type of other motherfuckers that wanna murder my black ass and the people I love. For me to keep at this game, Camila, would mean I'm on a suicide mission. It would mean I'm not looking at the reality of my situation. And between you and me, my heart ain't in this shit no more. All the killing, shooting, robbing, the bloodshed. I'm sick of it all! And, actually, I don't give a fuck what people think no more. The Hood would say I'm gettin' soft, since I'm not busting my gun to the bitter end, but that type of shit is straight insanity! Only a dumb ass nigga—" He caught himself. "Only a stupid ass cat would keep down a path that's bound to consume him, Camila. Sooner or later, our luck will run out if we don't pull back." He saw even the time she was shot and had to do a bid hadn't slowed her down in the least. "The way I'm going to prevent us from catching that bad decision is to take what we got and get the fuck out of this country."

Camila sighed realizing his mind was made up. The deep passion in his voice was scary, since she'd never heard that much sincerity before, but she couldn't bow down just that easy. She had her own aspirations and had no intentions of letting Rasheen bully her into getting on some soft shit cause he suddenly wanted to get religious; there was no way she was going to let him control her life. "So all this boils down to is, I gotta take my dream of gettin' really right and throw them in the garbage because you want out of—"

"Don't go there, Camila. Now, you letting that little greedy ass monster inside you get off its leash. The 1 million you got out of this last run is enough to hold you for at least 15 years if you spend it right, and once I show you how to invest it, you could live damn good off the interest. When we merge our shit together, boo, believe me we holdin'."

Camila saw trying to change his mind wasn't going to work, so she simply played her position. "Alright, alright. I think we got a few more runs in us, but you always been the shot caller, and I've always rolled with you, right or wrong, and I guess ain't shit changed."

As Rasheen moved on to another topic, Camila was so caught up in her own thoughts she didn't even know what Rasheen was saying, since she was plotting on how she was going to start making her own moves. This was the first time she ever had this much money of her own, and there was no way she was going to blow an opportunity to find out if the saying, you gotta have money to make money, was true.

* ** *

Aaron knocked lightly on the door, and on the other side he heard Klingaman say, "Come in; it's open."

Aaron stepped inside and saw Klingaman sitting behind his desk with an expression that announced he was enmeshed in a totally heart-rending moment. His bulldog cheeks had a reddish glow as if he was recently embarrassed. Although he was unusually clean-shaven, Aaron could see a shadow forming which meant he was too stressed out to shave. The smell of his Irish Spring soap was lingering on his body as though he failed to properly rinse. This was very serious.

As Aaron sat in the hot seat in front of Klingaman's desk, he was searching his blue eyes for any signs of why he was summoned to his office.

"So how's it going, Mr. Klingaman?" Aaron said in ice breaking fashion. "I got your note and came right over."

Klingaman sighed theatrically. "Wilson, Wilson, WILSON!" His crescendo comment rose as he fought not to start cursing, shouting, ranting and raving. "I thought I made myself clear that you were not to get involved in any matters outside of this office's jurisdiction!"

Ah Shit. Aaron saw the cat was out of the bag. The Philly run about bite him in the ass. He'd sensed this was coming when he had intervened in order to save Jackhammer Jones from being arrested. Donald had warned against snatching Jackhammer just as the police were about to enter the apartment building Jackhammer was held up in but he was certain he did the right thing. In fact, he was convinced he had saved those two cops lives.

As Klingaman stared at him with the pit bull screw face, Aaron reflected back on the moment he sprung from the blue rental car after it came to a screaming halt just as the cops were approaching the apartment building while following Jackhammer's blood droppings. "FBI!" Aaron had shouted as he displayed his badge. "I need you two to stand down!" He rushed towards the door and whispered. "Jackhammer, it's me, come on out. You alright, you good."

Jackhammer came out limping and Norman and Eugene helped him to the car as Aaron told the two cops. "Listen officers, this man is a part of a special opts mission. I need you to turn—"

"He may have been at the crime scene—"

"This is a classified matter! If you interfere, in any way, you will be prosecuted for obstruction of justice and for interfering with an ongoing federal undercover operation." Aaron headed for the car and said over his shoulder. "Speak to your superiors. They'll give you the rundown." He jumped in the rental car and sped away.

Klingaman pulled him back to the here and now when he said, "This time I can't slap you on the wrist, Agent Wilson." He allowed the silence to shake him up a little.

Aaron's heart responded accordingly, pounding with a fast pace rhythm, since it was clear he was getting the axe. He held firm to his cool demeanor as he nodded his head.

"I probably shouldn't be doing this, but everybody knows you're one of our gifted field agents. And because of all the good you have done over the years, I'm gonna give you a heads up. In fact, I'm gonna throw you a bone. But, you didn't hear it from me, and I advise you to keep it to yourself. An internal affairs probe has been launched against you. This last incident in Philadelphia did it. Now, they're going into your jacket, looking at anything that even hints at impropriety. But, the Victorville altercation seems to be of the greatest importance to the investigators, and I'm hearing they're also looking for this Rasheen Smith individual you were looking for prior to the Victorville fiasco."

Klingaman leaned back in his chair while sighing and shaking his head disbelievingly. "I'm going to cut straight to the chase here, Wilson. Whatever you're doing stop it. Stop it right this fuckin' minute, because this shit is starting to fall in my god damn lap."

The silence returned and Aaron didn't give into the temptation to proffer an explanation.

Klingaman continued. "As a way to protect you from yourself, and for your own good, I'm pulling you out of the field—"

"Wait a minute, Klingaman! I haven't been found guilty of anything—"

"It's either that or you're suspended without pay pending the outcome of the investigation. This is coming straight from Washington, and I had to fight to get you this desk assignment."

Desk assignment!? Aaron threw up both hands in total dismay, but he knew not to utter another word of protest, since he was smart enough to know when a supervisor was trying to throw him a life raft.

Later that evening, Aaron and his entire team sat in the living room of Keith's Peachtree Street Condo, discussing the cataclysmic news.

"Klingaman said nothing about you guys!" Aaron said energetically; the tone of his voice had a strong touch of desperation. "They're focusing on me because I was the Chief agent in charge of the Victorville incident. Cutting and running at a time like this don't make—"

"Let's be realistic, Aaron," Donald's voice boomed. "It's no longer possible for us to maneuver, in any way, with our moonlighting activities!"

Eugene said seriously, "Everything is dead. We gotta put everything on hold until this probe dies down some."

"Sorry, Aaron," Norman spoke sympathetically. "But, we'll be playing Russian roulette if we don't stop all activities. If we slip up, in the slightest way, it could mean major consequences."

Aaron looked over at Keith for help, and when he saw even Keith was at a loss for words, he knew they were fucked up royally. But there was one last shot he had up his sleeve and it was time to fire it off. "Okay, I hear you loud and clear. I got one more point to toss at y'all and then we can move on. What'd you think is going to happen if these internal affairs investigators get hold of Rasheen, and he identifies us all? What if he mentions y'all as well?"

The room was deadly silent.

Aaron continued, "What that says to me, is that none of us can pull back until this dude is dead. The spy I got inside his crew said he's alive, and during that robbery they lost only one person; a female, and from what I was told, they got a couple of more places they're casing."

Keith finally spoke. "This fuckin' spy of yours, what the fuck is he worth when he can't get us the information we need to bring this god dam mess to an end!"

Donald said sarcastically. "I'm glad somebody else sees this CI situation as I do."

"You know," Aaron said with a twisted smirk. "You guy are truly amazing. Here it is I'm in a room full of agents with decades of experience in universal undercover procedure, including drug and mob infiltration, and you've all forgotten the first basic rule of dealing with confidential informants." He paused and then shouted. "Patience!" He shook his head disgustedly. "This fuckin' guy Rasheen is no imbecile! And he's not like the common criminal! He's taking every precaution in the fuckin' book! We can't blame the CI because Rasheen was smart enough to confiscate all electronic devices, and to also change all locations in mid-range of planning the robbery. This is a case that'll produce results, if we stay the course!"

"I can't do it," Eugene said. "I'll take my chances on the possibility that the investigators won't snatch Rasheen."

"I agree," Norman chimed in.

"So do I," Donald said as he downed the remainder of his beer, finding it hard to believe Aaron was seriously trying to convince them to keep cutting corner and gambling with their jobs and their freedom to clean up a loose end that might not materialize into a problem.

Keith turned to Aaron and said, "Looks like it's me and you against the world."

Aaron sucked his teeth as he sat back in the chair with an attitude, realizing he couldn't blame the others for pulling back. In fact, if he was thinking correctly, and wasn't scared of this guy coming to kill him, he would be doing exactly what they were doing. But, he had a series of major aces in the hole, some were up his sleeve, others were tucked in his pants, a few were cupped behind his hands, and until he expended each and every one of them, he would not only stay the course, but in light of the loss of most of his manpower, he had every intention of taking his actions to a level that he'd never taken them to before.

CHAPTER # 20

Rasheen wanted to scream with delight as he felt his seed ejaculating from his body with the force of a volcanic eruption; his pumping motion was at a level of urgency and was in perfect synch with the upward thrusting motion of Sharon's hips. Once the high point of the release was gradually subsiding, he squeezed her soft, warm voluptuous body as the condom was filled with his steamy hot juices.

When the orgasm came to an end, Rasheen laid on top of Sharon savoring the sound of their hearts, pounding in unison. After he caught his breath, he rolled off of her and immediately locked her in a cuddling embrace. The sweet smell of her perfume like body aroma was truly tranquilizing. It wasn't hard to figure out she had bathed in a high-grade body ointment that apparently contained those sexual stimulating chemicals. The euphoria of this moment wouldn't last long, because he came here for the sole purpose of letting her know he was out of the game and was going overseas to live.

Sharon wiggled closer to Rasheen, feeling exceptionally energetic with joy. "Now we get down to the real business. This next spot is totally off the chain, Rasheen. It's in Kansas, and man, the take is bigger than the last job. I know that sounds impossible, and believe me, I'm not hyping it up. We talkin' at least 30 million in the vault alone. And the owners don't believe in banks, so we talking about cash on hand from weeks' worth of cash flow. You might even need a few extra—"

"I can't do it, Sharon."

Sharon blinked her eyes as though what she had just heard was more shocking than a slap to the face. She eased away in order to gaze fully into his eyes. When she saw his serious facial expression, she knew he wasn't joking. "What's the matter, Rasheen? These upcoming jobs are worth major millions. And they're not as complicated as the Philly job." She lied, but knew it didn't matter, because once Rasheen was determined to get the job done, it would get done. "Is it the death of Lora that's giving you cold feet?"

Rasheen sighed with an attitude; he was sick and tired of explaining to people the reason he was getting out of the game! What he did with his life as his fuckin' business! He was about to let his anger show, but held it in deep check, since Sharon did have a right to know. "It's a whole lot of shit, Sharon. We talked about this before, but now, I'm dead ass serious. I'm taking what I got, and I'm gettin' the fuck out of this country. I'm just tired of all the drama; the killing; the tit for tat."

He reflected back on the song he heard a few hours ago while he was on the plane listening to a CD, and it seemed to fit what he was currently feeling and going through. It almost felt like the words to the song provided an answer to Sharon's inquiry, but he thought better than to share this with her. The lyrics were so profound that it almost brought a tear to his eyes, and he didn't know why, but all throughout the song his son's face, and all the beautiful memories of the times he'd been blessed to spend with him were glued inside his third eye.

As he went into a silent cocoon, the lyrics spiraled to life and they were again inside his head. "The greatest love of all is happening to me . . . I found the greatest love of all inside of me . . . The greatest love of all is easy to see . . . Learning to love yourself is the greatest love of all. . . . . I decided long ago, never to walk in anyone's shadow, if I fail, if I succeed, at least I'll live as I believe; no matter what they take from me, they can't take away my dignity . . ."

Rasheen shifted and brought himself back to the here and now, realizing that besides these lyrics from the Movie the Greatest, a story about the famous boxer Muhammad Ali, he noticed all the Afrocentric material he was reading, had been reading to his son, and had read while in prison were suddenly starting to have some relevancy in his life. His conscience was kicking him square in the ass, because what he was doing made him the enemy of his people. There was no question most of the people who fell victim to his over ambitious quest to become rich and to quench his thirst for revenge were black folks, Latinos, people of color who were all caught up in a vicious cycle of oppression, ignorance, and self-hatred, and all he was doing was making the problem worse. Why his feelings were freaking out like this was a mystery to him, but they were real enough and powerful enough to make him acknowledge them and attempt to alter his behavior. The bottom line was that he was out of the game and wasn't going let anybody alter this decision. "Basically, Sharon, my mind is made up; I'm out."

"Rasheen," she sighed with clear impatience. "Once we finish these last three jobs, we'll have enough money to shut it down for good." The despair in her voice was growing. "We talked about this, Rah, and you promised we'd complete these Casino runs. I've been kicking out crazy cash, straight out of my pocket to get all the ducks lined up for these jobs, and now you talking—"

"I'll pay you for your out-of-pocket expenses. If it means that much to you, I'll pay it, but you gotta understand, I'm out of this shit, Sharon." He felt her pull away from him with an attitude. "I know this sudden change in the Program is fuckin' things up, but I got a son to look after." He shook his head as his emotions were stirred. "I can't help believing my luck is gonna run out. I can almost feel something telling me if I go out in the jungle after this voice inside of me is telling me to pull back, this might be the one I won't come out of alive. I'm not gonna play myself by getting greedy when I got enough loot to live the rest of my life alright. And I got a mean hook up with this cat my brother Lameek plugged me in to. He's hooking shit up to where I'll be touching all of Lameek's paper. I know we were going to rock that contract thing, but this dude here was already making moves with Lameek when he was alive, and his shit is thorough." He resisted the urge to go in depth and establish to her that the Judge was the real deal, since this wasn't her business anyway.

Rasheen sighed tiredly. "I'm telling you, I can feel my luck is running out, and my son's well being is enough to make me wake the fuck up and smell the coffee. Not only that, I don't feel the energy and the urge like I used to. This shit is making me feel empty. Spike Lee once said, 'A whole lot of people have money, but they're not happy, they're spiritually bankrupt'. That's how I feel, spiritually bankrupt, and getting out of the game is my cure."

"That sounds good, but I bet you one thing, you or Spike Lee won't change places with one of those bums living on the Bowery, eating shit out of the garbage can. You can talk all this spiritual stuff all you want, you and I both know without money you will be socially bankrupted. If you or Spike Lee had to pick one, we know which one we all will choose."

"Maybe you're right. But, I'm out of this shit."

Sharon felt her whole world crumbling down around her; the way Rasheen was talking it was clear he wasn't going to bend. Since she knew no one else capable of pulling off such a complex robbery, this shit was more than fucked up! She had detected he was moving away from all this robbing and stealing during their last discussion, but she had honestly thought she had him fully onboard; at least until after he finished the Casino jobs.

As the terror mounted, Sharon began grappling for a new strategy to get him back on deck; it took seconds to conclude there were no new ideas left in her mental reserves, and she instantly realized she needed some time to concoct something that would turn him around, and get him back on track, even if it meant getting down and dirty.

* ** *

At about the moment Rasheen was getting his groove on with Sharon, Camila was doing her thing with Rashango.

Rashango had Camila in a doggy style position and was long dicking her down, trying his hardest to make the tip of his rod touch her tonsils to the beat of Jaheim's song, I choose you, that oozed softly from the nearby CD Player.

"Harder!" Camila screamed, "Hit it harder, daddy! Harder!" She was throwing her full weight into the stride, handling everything Rashango was dishing out like a hardcore porn star.

The only difference between Rasheen's and Camila's sexual excursions was that Rasheen had sense enough to use protection, while Camila relied solely on Rashango's adamant insistence that he took an AIDS test, and it came back negative. But little did Camila know Rashango had well over a dozen episodes of unprotected sex since his release from prison and hadn't had a recent HIV test after these numerous sexual encounters.

Camila felt Rashango's wood pulsating as though he was about to explode and she stopped completely; she could hear him breathing deliriously with delight and knew she almost had him where she wanted. When she felt his nut had gone back, she resumed her motioning and Rashango followed her lead.

Camila's thoughts started bouncing around in her head and she felt good about the status of her plan; it was moving along beautifully and if everything went right with the meeting with her home girl, Lisa, and a crew of money thirsty hood rats that knew how to bust their guns, her mission would be complete. She wasn't surprised all she had to do was give Rashango a piece of this ass and he was ready to follow her into the pits of hell if she ordered him to. He wasn't a Rasheen by a long shot, but he was a loyal soldier and once there was something real serious hanging over his head, she could puppeteer his ass like a TV set under the grips of a remote-control device.

Now that he made the fatal mistake of laying pipe to his man's girl, Camila knew she had that one piece of information that she could use to daggle over his head; info that he knew if disclosed would cost him his life. She was nervous just imaging how Rasheen would react when he found out about this. Despite knowing Rasheen would do more than just break fool, and knowing she was playing a very dangerous game, she was sure she could convince him that it was Rashango who initiated this. Because she also knew Rasheen loved his son so much, she sensed if she manipulated that love correctly she could probably get away with anything.

When she felt Rashango pumping as though the fire started back up again, Camila decided to put this to an end. She tightened her grippers in vice grip fashion while increasing her rhythm. She felt his warm juices exploded inside of her. His pussy whipped grunts and moans made her blast off as well because it was synonymous with the sound of big dollars.

Two hours later, Camila was in the passenger seat of her Black Escalade with Rashango doing the chauffeuring. They were cruising down Atlantic Avenue, a main vein Street within Brooklyn, and were on their way to meet Lisa at her crib on Gates between Nostrand and Bedford Avenues. Another ten minutes later, Rashango had parked the Escalade, and he and Camila got out and approached. Unbeknownst, a car was following them, and just as they entered the tenement building, the dark tinted brown Cherokee Jeep cruised by with the four occupants checking them out very closely.

It took an hour for Camila, Rashango, Lisa, and three dusty looking chicks with thirsty grills to come up with a plan; in two days they were going to hit a spot over in Crown Heights; it was a steel gate drug spot, and according to Lisa, they were holding major paper. Rashango would be their main muscle, the gun man; Camila, Lisa and two of the hood rats would have his back, while one of the hood rats would be in charge of the getaway ride. Since Rasheen said his trip would take a week and half, Camila saw she had plenty of time to pull this hit off before he got back. After the meeting they immediate drove pass the spot, casing out the joint, mapping out the routes they would use to flee, and getting a feel of the amount of security they were working with. All the while the brown Cherokee was following them.

Even after Rashango dropped Lisa and her crew off, and headed back to New Jersey, they still had no idea the Cherokee was still following them, since Camila and Rashango were treed out of their minds, their senses were way off, and mostly because of their cockiness, they never thought anyone was bold enough to try them.

When the Escalade pulled up in front of Rasheen's New Jersey house, Camila saw Rosa approaching, and the look on her face told her that it was time to put some major straightened on this chick's attitude. She was responding this way because she had brought someone to the house, explicitly in violation of Rasheen's instructions.

As Rashango got out of the Escalade, he said, "God damn, my man, Rasheen got mad taste." He examined the house with jealous eyes. He knew he could have everything this nigga had if he could just find a way to get these fools off his back.

As Camila walked pass Rosa, she said. "I know I ain't gotta to tell you to keep this between us." She knew Rasheen made it a universal rule that no one was to come to this house, not even family or friends. "This is my family, Rosa; he's my cousin, Rashango. Rashango this is Rosa."

Rashango gave her a hard stare, and saw she wasn't too bad looking for a maid.

Camila continued. "And if you tell him anything, your ass will be out of a job, or better yet I'll put a fuckin' bullet in your head." She felt in the mood to get rowdy from all the weed she smoked; she pulled the 9-mm from the back of her waist and aimed it at Rosa's forehead. Camila was surprised when Rosa gave her an unflinching stare as if she wasn't fazed by this senseless act of aggression. In fact, Rosa's response made her nervous because it told something about this woman and it didn't signify that there was any fear or weaknesses roaming around in her bloodstream. Intuition was telling her that Rosa had a twinkle of dangerousness inside of her, and now that she had pulled the gun, she had better use it, but Camila was too headstrong to correctly read this inner voice.

Two hours later, it was 10 o'clock, Little Rasheen was asleep, and Camila and Rashango were at it again.

As the bed squeaked, and Rashango struggled to keep his sex talk to a minimum, Rosa was eavesdropping with a brilliant smile on her face. She was elated with a genuine joy. She couldn't believe her luck was this good.

* ** *

Phil Henderson sat behind the state-of-the-art recording studio consol next to Karl "Breakmaster" Jones, with a set of headphones on, rocking rhythmically to the beat while watching Karl do his magic; his fingers were tap-dancing across dials, levers and switches as if he was a professional keyboardist playing a foreign instrument.

Several feet away, behind the Plexiglas window of the soundproof recording booth, Clay Ripper was spewing gangsta rap lyrics of a caliber that could easily embarrass any of the industry's rowdiest gangsta rappers in view of the roguish, unruly and almost ranting nature of this rap song. When combined with Clay Ripper's thugged out hand waving and showboating bodily gesture, he represented the epitome of hardcore hip-hop; he was a towering force from which those to come will be measured by. In fact, that was what an editor at Source Magazine wrote about Clay Ripper and for anyone that saw him in high-strung mode would have to agree.

Phil started clapping his hands to the beat while taping his foot, already feeling the heavy cash flow that was destined to start rolling in once the public feasted their eyes and ears upon this blazing hot cut. He truly welcomed this feel-good moment, since it took his mind off of all the other drama that seemed to be escalating with every breath of air he drew.

When the track ended, and Clay Ripper took off the headphones, Phil said into the microphone in front of him, "Hold up! Hold up, Clay. Run it one more time." He saw Clay started beefing but was popping shit while putting the headphones back on, which was cool with Phil.

As Phil watched Clay getting himself back into his thug mode, he realized there was one thing he had learned from Killer Kato that he would always keep with him, and that was, the art of always pushing artists beyond the extra mile. Twice he had pushed Clay Ripper to take another crack at a track, and that particular cut turned out to be the best of all the others. Another lesson he learned from Killer was that certain Hoodaroma personnel had to be held onto at any and all cost, thus, Karl was with Killer and stayed with him when he took over, even though he had Karl thinking he was paying him enough money to easily hire five musical engineers/producers/directors with as much experience as Karl.

After they completed the recording of this untitled track, the three sat in the studio, eating, drinking and talking.

Clay spoke with a mouthful of the last of his turkey and cheese hero. "Yo' son, I ain't feelin' that shit that happened with Big Gains. Mufuckas gotta pay for that shit! He was fam for real, Phil."

Karl tapped the ashes from his Newport into the ashtray. "What the hell was he doing out there in Philly anyway? I thought that was part of Cowboy's stomping grounds. He had Baltimore and Philly for years, and was possessive over his shit, too. I hope this ain't no internal beef."

"Damn Karl," Clay said playfully. "You don't know what time it is?"

"What you talking about?" Karl pulled on the Newport.

Phil interjected. "Big Gains and some of his associates went out there to handle that problem with Rasheen. They must've found out Rasheen was robbing Shooties, and tried to step to him. I guess things didn't go Big Gains' way."

Karl shook his head as he took a long drag and snuffed out the cigarette. "That nigga Rasheen is wreaking havoc on Hoodaroma. He wreakin' us like crack did to the Hood in the mid-1980s. Another funeral and it ain't even been a hot year. Why you ain't get them mob motherfuckers to step to him? They in our pockets deep enough. You need to put them grease balls to work."

Phil instantly felt a blinding rage forming in the pit of his stomach just being reminded of Sammy, and of the fact he had produced no results. In fact, from the way shit was looking, he wasn't even looking for Rasheen. "They are involved. They put a track on him. The last time I talked to Sammy, he said they were still working on it." Phil instantly lost his appetite and shoved his Pastrami and rye Hero aside. It was obvious Sammy had taken the upfront money with no intentions of fulfilling the contract. *Low-life, cutthroat motherfucker!* During damn near every conversation he had with this scrum bag, it became clear he was playing the old carrot on the stick trick on him, and since Sammy was unable to tell him what his hitters had done so far or what they were planning to do, even though he had Derek and Troy feeding them clues on Rasheen's possible whereabouts, it was obvious Sammy was basically fucking him over.

"I know we gonna have to do something with this dude," Clay Ripper said as he leaned back in his chair with a can of ginger ale in his hand. "I dam sho' don't want this nigga steppin' to us the same way he did just before we got all that love from Vibe Magazine. I'm telling you, Phil, I know some peeps that will take a track and will guarantee you results no matter who, where, what or when, but they want a quarter million."

"I told you, Clay, that's too much money," Phil said. "We can hire five hitters with that kind of money. It's a waste."

"Word up," Karl chimed in. "For an eighth of that amount I could find you a top notch hitter that'll murder up a whole Street corner full of folks."

Clay sighed frustratedly. "We gettin' ready to pop off this Movie project, and I know we don't want him fuckin' that up."

"Yeah," Karl nodded vibrantly. "That Movie project is gonna put Hoodaroma back in the game like it was when—"

"Back in the game!?" Phillip clearly took offense to the remark. "What the fuck are you talkin' about? We never went anywhere. We got two singles in the top five list. One in the third slot, and the other in the fifth slot. Money is pouring in like water!"

"Okay, okay," Karl said humbly. "Don't tear my head off, Phil." He saw Phil wanted to believe that because he was the captain of the ship, everything was gravy, but the true of the matter was that it wasn't. This corny ass nigga could never run this operation the way Killer Kato had it popping. "All I'm saying is when Killer Kato was rocking this thing, we held the number one spot like that shit was a spot that God made just for us. Yeah, the money's still good, but I do what I do cause I like being number one." He suddenly felt in the mood to mess with Phil's mind a little. "Them cats over at Visa Records been stepping to me with offers. I turned them down, but we gotta make sure we all want the same thing; cause if we don't, I can find another home that wants what I want." He couldn't imagine saying no shit like that to Killer Kato, but fortunate, Phil was no Killer Kato kinda guy. "We all gotta know that anything we touch that ain't number one ain't good enough . . ."

As Phil listened to Karl basically telling him that he wanted to be number one or nothing else discussion, he saw this remark instantly reminded him of the shocking news he'd just received from Lionel Rollack, an associate he went to law school with at UCLA and who was now working for Barclay's law firm; Lionel had informed him of the secret attorney/client relationships Lameek and Ja-King had with a high-powered lawyer when they were working for Hoodaroma. This had him trembling in his boots. There were simply too many dirty dealings going on to have anyone snooping around behind the scenes of those relationships.

Phil shifted uncomfortable in his seat as Clay Ripper joined in their number one or nothing else discussion; Phil noticed his anger was about to reach a fuming level. *How could both Lameek and Ja-King be making moves behind our backs?* The sneaky bastards were involved in some kind of backdoor arrangement in an effort to undo years of maneuvering he and Killer Kato had instituted. When he tried to ascertain the name of this Big time lawyer, Lionel Rollack claimed he was still trying to obtain it.

As he listened to Karl stroking his ego, while making sure everybody understood that he was the man, Phil wondered was Clay and Karl engaged in similar backdoor dealings. This scared him deeply because he didn't discriminate when he dealt with folks; if they started looking, they were definitely going to find some things they weren't going to like.

Phil leaned back in his chair realizing with this Rasheen dilemma growing daily (Lionel also indicated he heard there was talk going around about the Lameek Smith issue was going to take Hoodaroma through some heavy changes at the top), the last thing he needed was to start losing his most valuable resources (his crew). He wondered should he shift gears, and stop what he was doing to Clay, Karl and half the Hoodaroma staff?

DIVINE G

It took only a few seconds for him to realize he couldn't stop even if he wanted to, since he was forever locked in the grim clutches of money-grip.

CHAPTER # 21

Aaron paced back and forth in front of the desk Keith sat behind. Aaron's remarkably handsome features no longer held that vibrant glow of youthfulness and stately firmness. His persona seemed haggard and uneasy. He stopped pacing and said, "If I could answer that question, I wouldn't be standing here twisting my mind with that question, while stopping you from doing your work. Like I said, Alberto and his boys promised me they would look into it. You of all people know how notorious these Colombians are for dragging their feet when it comes time to reciprocate. Now that I'm on desk detail, I can't pull the same strings like I used to, so now they dragging ass."

"What the fuck is so complicated about finding out whether or not they saw this guy in Brooklyn or not? They either seen him or they didn't. Rasheen stole enough of their money for them to know his face if he crossed their path."

"Keith, you're not listening to me," Aaron sat down. "I didn't say they saw Rasheen, I said they believed one of their soldiers saw the woman who had his kid. Since they saw her with some other guy, they at first assumed it was him. After they followed them around and got a good look at the two, they were sure it was her and not Rasheen. They followed them around some more and when they got on the New Jersey Turnpike, heading South, they got flagged by State Troopers and lost them. A couple days later a drug spot ran by some Jamaicans was hit, and Alberto's peoples think it was her behind it. They believe this because when they were following them, they noticed they were scoping out the spot that was hit. He's supposed to get in contact with me and let me know if it's confirmed; he's also supposed to give me the address to the tenement building they entered. Once I get the green light, I'm going out there personally to Brooklyn—"

"Wow! I don't think you should go to that extreme, not right now, Aaron. I know this thing is driving you to the point of desperation, but this isn't the time to start getting too active. We still got foot soldiers to do that kind of work you're talking about. It would be different if this was a confirmed location where we could definitely find Rasheen; then we could go in full force. Even I would come out of retirement and put some work in."

"I thought when I got the news of this internal affairs probe, you were officially out of retirement? Since this company of ours," He gestured with his hands as though indicating everything around him, "Was built on money stolen from this cat, what'd you think'll happen if these investigators get hold of him, and possibly start offering him benefits to turn state evidence? You think he'll forget you rob his ass blind? Think he might say, naw Keith Ramsey wasn't somehow down with the murders in Victorville?" He screwed up his face as if he was thinking deeply. "With that said, and with our team out of the equation, you better wipe off the dust on that trigger finger of yours."

Keith laughed genuinely. "I hope you remember what you just said, cause the last time I let my trigger finger get loose, you were cryin' and bitchin' about I was taking shit overboard. How that saying goes, be careful what you ask for . . . "

"Right now, with all the damage and turmoil this one motherfucker has caused, if we gotta give ruthlessness a whole new fuckin' name, I'm for it."

"What's up with that CI of yours? Maybe you gotta find a way to create a better incentive. We strictly need results, and none seems to be coming our way. Not to mention, you might have to find a way to assess the reliability of this CI, since you're telling me that Rasheen is throwing the towel in, and giving up his lucrative career of robbing million dollar establishments, even though he's got a team of thugs begging him to keep the program going, and he's even got an inside man feeding him enough information to pull off an easy insider job is simply unbelievable. That whole scenario is not clicking correctly in my mind."

Aaron crossed one leg over the other. "Yeah, it sounds crazy don't it? But, the CI wasn't playing head games when he told me this."

* ** *

Rasheen sat at the table eating a Steak and Lobster combo dinner with various salads and an expensive bottle of wine on the side. Camila sat across from him eating a similar meal, while Little Rasheen sat next to his father eating a Soya bean burger, fries, and a milk shake. At three years old, Rasheen Junior had no problem putting in work on the meal in front of him, and today he was more interested in putting the food in his stomach than on the tabletop and the floor. This Disney World restaurant was top of the line, and the prices of the food, the blue blooded looking customers, the clean carpeted floors, the neatly dressed waiters, and the soft elevator music in the background were unquestionable proof of this place's elegance.

With a fake smile, Rasheen said, "Now that you done dragged us in this silly ass restaurant, wasting good money on food they over charging us twenty times the legal prices, are we rich in the eyes of these people looking at us like we out of our rabbit ass minds?"

The customers dressed in suits and expensive gowns were staring at Rasheen and his family since they were dressed in casual urban attire.

"We got a right to eat here, Rasheen," Camila shot back in whisper like fashion with a mouthful of food. After she swallowed the masticated Lobster meat, Camila said, "With all this money we holding we need to start acting like we got cheddar."

Rasheen didn't respond, since if he could have he would've of unleashed his anger. He looked over at little Rasheen and knew it was his son's presence that was the cause for his case of the mums. Just laying eyes on his son, and realizing his little man was having a good time brought a genuine smile to his face. The last thing he wanted to do was spoil it for him. His son was now making a complete mess as he ate the burger, and Rasheen was compelled to take a picture. He grabbed the small camera dangling from his neck and flicked off several shots. They had been here in Disney World for a week so far and Rasheen must've taken a thousand pictures and had enough microchips to take another thousand.

After they completed their meal, paid the bill, and gave the waiter a hundred-dollar tip (Camila was compelled to showoff), they were back on the track, making sure they visited every amusement ride this place had to offer. As Rasheen followed Little Rah and Camila into this place, and to that place, his mind was on other matters. Everything was going perfectly, which scared him immensely. However, because he was batting a 100 when it came to things blowing up in his face once things started going good for him, he was trembling at the thought of something undermining his move to Cuba. The Judge said in another month, he, Camila and Little Rasheen would have passports, a house waiting for them in Havana, and most of his money would be at their disposal. With the amount of money they had, the Judge said they would live like elites for at least a decade and a half, and would have to readjust their spending during their latter years. Little Rasheen's schooling would consist of a private tutor, and his current higher education Trust Fund was already at an amount that would allow him to attend any University on the planet (if his grades enabled him to get in), but as far as money, that aspect of their lives would not pose as a barrier.

Despite the good news, there was some bad news lurking about. As Rasheen took pictures of Little Rasheen trying to pull off Daffy Duck's costume, he reflected back on Camila's suspicious behavior. He'd been with her long enough to know she was doing something she wasn't supposed to be doing; her insane defensiveness was an issue that told on her every time.

After he returned from his visit with Sharon, Rasheen instantly knew something was wrong. Camila seemed unusually jittery, and when he inquired about her sensitiveness, she reacted hostile, trying to flip the whole thing on him, and even went so far as to start accusing him of going out to Florida to fuck his connect (he had slipped up and referred to his robbery connect as a she, and Camila had never forgot it). If he was into abusing women, he would've slapped the shit out of her for getting real fly out of the mouth, but he had vowed years ago that he would never mistreat women, mainly because his mother was brutally beatin' by her boyfriend Black Bob. Not to mention, he committed his first homicide because of his desire to stop the abuse Black Bob was inflicting on his mom and other women in his hood, and couldn't see himself perpetuating something he totally despised.

But, the thought of Camila trying to play him was seriously making him reconsider his principles. When he heard Little Rasheen saying, "Uncle Ra, see momma!" while pointing at their bedroom, and then right on the heels of this comment he noticed Rosa's nervous reaction to this remark, he knew something was up. He'd been around long enough to know children told everything they saw, and because of their inherent innocence, they knew only how to tell the truth. He was about to sit Little Rasheen and Rosa down and get to the bottom of whatever it was that caused his son to refer to an "Uncle Ra", while pointing to the bedroom, but his better side told him it wasn't the right time for that. In any event, he'd detected Camila wasn't happy with his decision to move to Cuba and was ready for her attempt to sabotage that whole endeavor. He was just hoping and praying she wasn't stupid enough to violate in such a way that would be impossible to embrace her as his woman.

When they finished with Daffy Duck, Little Rasheen went to Bugsy Bunny, and the pictures started flicking again. When he saw Camila was having as much fun as his son, he suddenly was compelled to look at his relationship with Camila once again, and hated the idea he was basically locked in a relationship against his will. If he didn't have a son by her things would've been different, if he wasn't on the run from corrupt feds, state police in Connecticut, Colombian drug lords, Killer Kato's honchos, and many other dangerous people, he wouldn't be with Camila. There was no question he didn't see her as wifey material. Of course, she was the perfect ride or die chick, she held him down when he was on lock down, she had a crazy body, and wasn't bad looking grill wise, but she was a hood rat; although she wasn't as loose as other hood rats, but nonetheless she was a fast chick, and any dude with sense knew fast chicks did fast things.

Reflecting back on how he got her pregnant he realized he needed a swift kick in his ass for running up inside Camila raw head, solely because her HIV test results came back negative. His being deprived of a woman for years, and his being released from prison while Camila was waiting for him with open arms (and plenty of hardware), it was natural for him to get with her on an intimate level.

When Rasheen saw his emotions were becoming negative as he realized he would've preferred to be with Sharon instead of Camila, and realizing that was unlikely since he couldn't dump Camila in light of the fact she was his son's mother, he forced the whole issue to the back of his mind.

Two days later, they were back at their New Jersey home, and Rasheen had resumed his daily reading to his son. The main books he used were those by Dr. Jawanza Kunjufu, since his style was raw and very uplifting. His books "Children are the Reward of Life" and Developing Positive Self Images" were the ones he read to his son out loud constantly, even though half the time Rasheen's three year old mind wasn't paying him any attention. But, none of that matter because he'd heard that reading to a toddler on a daily basis had a priming effect on the child's mind, which in turn gave the child a learning boost upon involvement in an academic setting; whether this was true or not, really didn't matter, since this whole ritual seemed more therapeutic for Rasheen; it made him feel he was guaranteeing his child would be someone great and that he was laying the groundwork to this path to greatness.

After this vacation, Rasheen saw his and Camila's relationship was taking a downward spiral. When he approached her about the new car she had purchased against his instructions, the fight almost escalated into blows being thrown.

"Why would you go buy a fuckin' Benz!?" Rasheen said with clenched teeth. "We about to cash in all this shit, and here you are buying an expensive ass car!?"

"I do I want with my money! I don't tell you how to spend your cheddar, so you should do the same."

"What you do affects me, so I can step to you, Camila. We agreed no flashy cars, no wild and excessive spending, and don't catch amnesia, either, cause we talked about this shit constantly." He felt the fury growing; he sighed as he tightened the lid on his emotions. "We ain't out of woods yet. Until we out of this country, all this shit could end in a matter of seconds. The motherfuckers we been stepping to, taking they shit don't forget easy, Camila. That means we don't draw attention to ourselves. This is 101 shit when you in the game."

"This fuckin' house is way up in the damn boondocks. Ain't nobody coming out here. And if they do, they ain't comin' to see us on that level." She was praying Rasheen didn't find out about the run she, Rashango, and Lisa pulled off. Although they came off with a descent piece of change (20 grand each), it was peanuts in comparison to the jobs Rasheen was setting up. "On the real to real, Rah, I don't see the logic in having money and not spending it."

Rasheen gritted his teeth. "All that's gonna come, Camila. You gotta work with me. Once our feet touch safe grounds, then we can live it up. Right now, we gotta stay focus. We gotta discipline ourselves. If we slip in the slightest way, all this shit can end, and when I say end, I'm talking permanent. Lights out. The nail in the coffin."

Camila was growing frustrated. She'd been holding back, but now she decided she was going to speak her mind, even though she knew she would live to regret it. "Yeah, shit can get funky, but if we keep it real with ourselves, and don't start gettin' soft, everything will work itself out. All this shit about going to Cuba, running, and hiding and shit! I ain't feelin' it, Rasheen. I know you hot and shit, and I'm riding with you, but—but I can't get with not stepping to the beef and throwing away all this easy money out here—"

"Ain't no such thing as easy money, Camila. When we go in the jungle, ain't no fuckin' guarantee we comin' back alive." He saw where this was going, since it was evident the money had a vicious grip on her, and it couldn't be shook loose. "You still don't get it, do you? You wanna keep doing these runs. We sitting on millions and you still want more?" He shook his head in sheer disbelief; her greed was about as appalling as his was a few years back. "I tell you what. You stay the fuck here. I'm taking my son and we'll—"

"Hell no!" Camila sprung to her feet. "I'm never leaving my baby—"

"If you loved him, you would cool your fuckin' heels, and start thinking about him!" He was about to point out the fact she very rarely spent any real time with him, but didn't want to start throwing shots below the belt. In any event, everybody knew she wasn't ready to be a mother. "We got the opportunity of a lifetime floating right before our eyes. The paper we got right now has opened doors for opportunities; now the challenge is to be smart enough not to get greedy."

"Greedy!?" Camila couldn't believe Rasheen was actually taking it there. "Rasheen, you acting like we got Donald Trump money or some shit! This is the shit that pisses me the hell off! The minute we get close to doing something big, we start getting scared of su—"

"We got enough cheddar to hold us for decades! We made it through the game without getting killed, and we got us a seed. You been shot, I been shot twice; what is it gonna take to convince you it's time to pull out of this shit? The next time around, we could be like Jack Mack, Dirty Ricky, Lameek, Lora! I got a hook up where we can leave this country, and not have to look over our shoulders every day—"

"Not true," Camila vibrantly shook her head no. "Those Colombians, Dominicans, and even those corrupt fed dudes can come right over to Cuba and bring the noise. If we running from them, we might as well just buckle the fuck down, keep the heaters close by, and live life for all it's worth. Ain't no different between here and Cuba, if we running from folks from the underworld, and you know it. When we stepped to them, we knew upfront there was really no real place to hide or run to."

Rasheen was seconds from exploding because Camila was fucking up his emotional rhythm. He would never admit she was right about this issue, even though subconsciously that voice of rationale was talking to him. "Listen, Camila, we out of this motherfucker! I'm taking my son away from this shit! If you wanna roll with us, the door is open. If you don't, then do you!"

He stomped towards the bedroom and Camila ran up behind him.

"Rah, Rah," she said softly as she gently grabbed his arm. "I'm sorry. I ain't mean to get you upset. Fuck it, I'm with you, boo.

We gonna do this together." She kissed him. He resisted the act of affection, but she insisted, and he gave in. "You know what we need?"

"What?" Rasheen said as he grabbed her meaty behind.

"We need to go out, have a few drinks, have us a good time, clear our minds, come back home, and fuck like horny Junior High School kids."

Rasheen thought about it and began nodding his head as a smile crept on his face. "You know something, boo, that sounds like a plan."

An hour later, Rasheen and Camila were nicely dressed up, and exited the house.

"Rosa," Rasheen said as he was about to get inside the Escalade. "We'll be back in a couple of hours. Call if you need us."

"Enjoy yourselves." Rosa smiled deviously. "Don't worry, everything's okay. Everything is just fine."

* ** *

Little Rasheen awoke when he heard someone entering the house. In crescendo fashion the noise grew into a state of crisis. Although his infantile mind wasn't familiar with this sort of dangerous situation, the instinctual component of his brain could tell something was out of the norm, since the loud crashing noises were very disturbing, and clearly could pose a threat to his physical wellbeing.

He heaved a deep breath of air and unleashed a lung-bursting cry that could've awakened life on Mars, "Mamma! I want mamma! Dadda! Dadda!"

Rosa was hurled out of a semi-deep sleep and rushed out of bed and towards the source of the sudden commotion. When she entered the living room section of the house and saw the three men, she was about to retreat back to her room until she saw the familiar face. She sighed, wondering why he entered in this manner. "What is wrong with you, Leo? Why are you messing up this pretty house!?"

"Who gives a shit about this house," Leo said with a heavy Latino accent as he approached Rosa and noticed the child's cries slowly subsiding. "What matters is, is this kid the right kid Mario is looking for."

Rosa immediately got on the defensive. "I told you, I'm certain this is the man. I told you I got audio tapes of them saying they are the ones."

"Hey, I guess there's only one way to find out," Leo headed towards Little Rasheen's bedroom.

Rosa held up her hands, "Let me do that. I'll get him."

Leo stopped and watched Rosa sashayed towards the room.

Five minutes later, Rasheen exited and was dressed in an expensive brown sweat suit with baby Timberland boots on, and a matching leather baseball hat that made him look like the typical baller on any urban street corner in any hood in the country.

The three Dominican men laughed when they saw Little Rasheen.

Leo said through his snickers, "Now that's cradle to the grave thuggin', my friend!"

The laughter ignited again.

A Dominican man standing next to Leo, dressed in a black leather jacket and matching gloves said, "This gotta to be the right one; how they say, like father like son." He nodded his head smilingly.

Leo took a step forward, kneeled and said to Little Rasheen, "Hey, little buddy; it's time to come with us. Your daddy did some bad things to some of my friends, and you better hope he loves you very very much because your life is going to depend on it." He smiled, savoring the terrified look on the child's face as he roughly grabbed Rasheen into his uncaring arms, and headed towards the door. "Make sure you put the ransom note where he can't miss it."

Rosa sat the note in the center of the coffee table and followed the three members of the Dominican Mafia out of the house as she fought the rapidly growing guilt that was telling her this was so wrong. How could she do this to an innocent child, that voice of reason spoke from within, but she wasn't trying to hear it; with a small effort she was able to tuck her feelings away and place them in suspended animation. In fact, she could quench, neutralize or even disintegrate any emotion that flared up inside of her just by thinking about the money.

CHAPTER # 22

Rasheen was behind the wheel of Camila's black Escalade. He was feeling tipsy from the four drinks of Hennessey he'd consumed, and his mood was in a tranquil state. Camila sat next to him rocking to one of Lameek's rap songs on his third CD entitled Grand Narratives. It was a little after 3 o'clock in the morning and the New Jersey roads were empty.

As Rasheen turned onto the Road leading to his house, he ritualistically began looking for anything out of the norm. Everything looked good until the house came into view, and he saw the living room lights were still on. This was the signal Rosa was instructed to use to let them know there was a problem.

Camila snapped into attention when she saw the lights and Rasheen's abrupt reaction. She turned off the CD player and immediately retrieved her two 9-mms and the three extra clips stashed in the high-tech hiding place under the leather seats.

"This is not a good look at all!" Rasheen's heart began pounding lively as he hit the headlight switch and brought the Escalade to a slow-paced crawl. His mind went instantly into combat mode. The adrenaline chemicals within his bloodstream rose so high they reached a toxic level; the thought of his son being in danger put him in a place that had instantly transformed him into something far deadlier than the venom of fifty cobra snakes combine.

Without taking his eyes off the house, Rasheen parked the vehicle within a thick batch of underbrush a few yards off the road, and retrieved his two 9-mms, and two clips from the secret compartment under the seat. "Let's do it."

They quickly got out the Escalade on tiptoes, scanning their surroundings for any signs of intruders, and saw there apparently was no one on the outskirts of their home. Rasheen had instructed

Camila on how to approach such a situation and he saw she had digested his instructions well.

When Rasheen reached the front yard of the house, his eyes searched feverishly for any trip wires or anything else that would tell him what was going on. After concluding everything was safe, he cautiously headed towards the front door with both 9-mms ready to spit fire. Camila was on his heels making sure his back was covered in accordance with his explicit instructions.

Upon arriving at the front door, Rasheen wasn't surprised when he found it was not only unlocked, but there was also evidence of a forced entry. With the barrel of the gun he pushed open the jarred door, shattering all hope that maybe this could be a false alarm, or an inadvertent mistake on Rosa's part.

In military fashion, Rasheen entered with both weapons pointing while the aim swept across the area; Camila was behind him with both arms extended in spread eagle fashion.

It took two minutes of rushing through the rooms of the house for them to conclude it was empty.

With each room Rasheen searched, and found empty, the tears in his eyes grew exponentially. By the time he found the ransom note the tears were dripping. Although he tried desperately not to breakdown in front of Camila, the pain of losing his son was so overwhelming that he was powerless to stop the release of the tears.

Camila's tears were flowing, but they were nowhere near the amount Rasheen was unleashing.

Rasheen read the note, read it again, and again, as he refused to believe they had stolen the only person he literally loved more than himself. When Camila tried to take the note from him, he selfishly snatched it out of her reach as though releasing it would somehow cause the loss of the one thing that he had that could bring his son back.

Rasheen sat down on the sofa, and read the typewritten note out loud:

"If you want your son back in two weeks, come to the junkyard on Ditmas

Avenue and East 91st Street, East Flatbush Brooklyn, with 25 million dollars

in big bills. Since you're on the wrong side of the law, we assume you know

not to go to the police. If you do the right thing your son will be traded for the

money. Rasheen, if you love your son do not miss this date!"

As his son's face appeared in his third eye, Rasheen felt the debilitating wave of depression shoving him into a state of sheer recklessness. The compulsive urge to kill those responsible for this outlandish act of utter disrespect was blinding! Images of a river of blood rolling down the gutters of the Hood, initiated by his own trigger finger, were stuck inside his third eye. The first thing he wanted to do was go out and bring forth a wrath on anybody he even thought was behind this shit.

Suddenly, his raging thoughts stopped like skidding tires on a car. *Who could it be!? Who had the audacity to try some shit like this!?* The terror grew in leaps in bounds because he honestly didn't know who was behind this! It could be any of the people he had drama with. Then, he started back tracking, and the culprit at the top of the list came to his mind. *It had to be that motherfucker, Aaron! He did the same thing to Lameek and now he's doing the same thing to my him son!*

But how the fuck did he find him!? His tracks were covered so thoroughly, the Judge assured him, no underworld forces would find him unless—- He instantly remembered the Judge had told him as long as he stayed out of any public arenas he would be safe. After pondering all their contacts with the public, he was certain his trips to the store, and other minor activities couldn't be the root of their hide-out being blown. Even their little hang out tonight at a club in Cambridge couldn't have caused this because the place catered to straight cornballs. He instantly started wondering did Camila disobey his instructions. After a moment, he immediately scrapped these invading thoughts in order to begin the process of getting this situation underway.

"Rasheen," Camila cried out as she wiped away her runaway tears. "We can't stay here. Whoever did this know where we live." The thought of laying her head down to rest in a house where the enemy knew where they were was too horrifying to even fathom. She was also scared shitless because she was wondering if this was the blowback from the last run she did without telling Rasheen!? The thought even crossed her mind that Rashango might have had his hands in this shit. The game was so foul, so cutthroat and so heartless, nobody could be excluded as the potential source of this ultimate violation. There was no way she would share this with Rasheen, and it was already tormenting her conscience, because this was information that might be able to help them maneuver. She felt herself growing weak. "Oh, god, Rasheen, they took our baby!" Her pleas were almost pitiful sounding. "We gotta get him back!"

With a struggle Rasheen internally slapped himself out of his traumatized state. If he were going to save his son, he would have to get focused. He felt himself relaxing and the critical thinking part of his mind started to take control. The first thing that jumped out at him was he didn't even have 25 million, which meant he had to find the rest of the money. The acquisition of 5 million dollars was no small feat and getting it within two weeks looked to be even more impossible. But one thing that was absolutely certain was that he would get the money, and he would do everything in his powers to bring his son back to him safely.

His mind started searching for a way to find the rest of the money, and his tension eased up; Camila had a stash of close to a million, Rashango had about that much, and Ja-King and Willie would come through for him. But the rage returned with full force, because although he would give up the money, heads would roll. Indeed, he wanted desperately to stop all the violence, but with this violation in activation the people responsible for this had officially created a monster.

Two days later, Rasheen sat at the head of the table inside a New Jersey Hotel; Camila sat on his right; Ja-King and Tania sat across from him; Rashango sit on Rasheen's left while Willie sat next to Ja-King.

"The motherfuckers took my son," Rasheen said with a calm fury. He was pleased by the shocked expressions on his comrades' faces. "And they want 25 mills." The what goes around comes around realization was taunting his long range memory cells, since now he knew how the Colombian Cartel, Emanuel Gomez, felt when he snatched his family back in 2003. "I'm gonna do everything it takes to bring my baby boy out of this shit alive, including giving up the money they want."

"You holdin' like that, Rah!?" Tania said with her bubbly persona and bodily gestures. "25 mill ain't no lightweight cash." Her smile was not only flirtatious, but it was as bold as it could be. She gave Camila a stern smirk that said, bitch you better not play yourself, and when Camila looked away, she was glad everybody on this team understood she was the Queen bee of flying bullets. "Rasheen, I talk for myself when I do things. I'm with you, no matter how you wanna do this. Ja-King and me with you to the end!"

Ja-King gave Tania an impatient smirk and said, "Tania, would you please shut the fuck up, baby!" He looked at Rasheen and said, "Ain't no doubt we with you, son. We ready to ride whenever you ready."

In domino fashion everybody inside the room agreed with head nods and affirmative mutters.

Rasheen knew what he now was about to ask of them was the real proving ground as to whether he could trust them, and whether or not they were a family in reality, as opposed to one only on the basis of words, and what each individual could personally exploit from the strengths of group. He was about to ask them to back him on the 5 million. This even include Camila, since he'd didn't tell her he was short 5 mill, and he also wanted to put her right on the spot like everybody else.

Rasheen sighed as he stared into the eyes of each person in the room, making sure he was able to see their initial responses at the moment he sprung this news on them. He cleared his voice for theatrical emphasis. "It's a beautiful thing to know our team got made love for each other. And for the record, I would never let any of y'all down." His eyes bounced about. "But, there's a major issue up in the air. . . . I'm short 5 million dollars."

The silence was momentarily thick.

"I got 500 gees for yah," Willie said. "It probably ain't much when we look at 5 mill, but anything more than that, and I'm back in the dog house."

Tania didn't put any cut on her discomfort. "Damn, Rah, 5 million ain't the kind of cash folks like us just be flinging around free heartedly. I mean—I don't mind shooting motherfuckers for you, but kicking out cash in that amount is very, very serious!"

Rasheen couldn't help cracking a smile at Tania's uncut attitude. He wanted to tell her as long as she dropped a few bodies for him he would be satisfied with her services but knew that would give the others an easy way to duck out of helping with this financial obstacle.

Ja-King sighed. "Fuck it!" He locked eyes with Rasheen and saw this was the perfect opportunity to get him back into the game. It was indeed a bittersweet situation. "I'll put up whatever's left after everybody contributes to this cause," He still had his proceeds from all his record deals and was technically a millionaire legally. "But I got one stipulation."

The silence grew, and Ja-King let it simmer in the air, until he was positive everybody was uncomfortable.

"Rasheen," Ja-King said as he allowed his stare to bounce around. "I'll kick out as long as when this shit becomes water under the bridge, we start back getting paper. All those Casinos waiting to get gotten, gots to get got."

Rasheen had suddenly come to the realization that all the debates he had with cats in prison, when the cynical cats argued that the people you think will hold you down will usually turn out to be the ones who will disappoint you was the hardcore truth. He was shattered when he didn't hear Camila and Rashango utter a single word. He sincerely wanted them to do whatever they could on their own volition, without him doing what he was about to do.

"So what's it gonna be, Camila and Rashango?" Rasheen gave the two a look that said clearly, I'll kill you right here if you even think about playing yourself!

"I'll put it all on the table, Rah," Camila said with a shock expression. "You should know you ain't gotta ask me no shit like that. That's my child, and I want him back just as much as you do!"

"Whatever I got is yours, Rah," Rashango said sincerely. "I got 500 K I can kick out. I agree with Ja-King; after this we gotta go back in the jungle."

"Just so you know," Rasheen said. "The only concern is my son's safety. I don't want no urban cowboy shit put in the game." He stared at Tania, and then Ja-King. "But, if they slip up, and I think we can get my son back without giving up the loot, then I'll be the only that will make that call."

The following day Rasheen sat at Sharon's dining room table in her Florida mansion; Sharon sat across from him eating a plate of scrambled eggs with cheddar cheese, toast, turkey sausages, and orange juice. It was obvious she had just been awakened not too long ago and was still dressed in her night coat. The maid could be heard in the kitchen rambling with pots and pans.

"Damn, Rasheen," Sharon swallowed her food. "I'm sorry about this. I can image what you're going through." She took a sip of her glass of orange juice. "The minute you called me I got right on it. It ain't Aaron or Keith. I know they're a bunch of foul, heartless sons of bitches, but Keith would never allow kids to get tossed in the mix. They both got children of their own, and I'm assuming they're operating from a mutual unspoken understanding that the children are to be kept out of it. I'm still tossing around a few favors. Give me a minute, and hopefully, I'll have something for you real soon." She scooped up a folk full of eggs and savored the cheesy taste.

Rasheen sat staring off into the oblivion. He was marinating in anger, rage and fear.

After Sharon swallowed, she said, "You straight with that ransom money? 25 million is a lot of doe."

"My team came through." Rasheen went back into his silent trance.

Sharon sighed, feeling extremely good, and had to fight not to show her happiness. "I'm assuming with the lost of this much money, I should start re-lining up those ducks for those Casino jobs?"

Rasheen stared into her eyes, and although he sensed Sharon was still down for him, he also detected that she was enjoying this current unfortunate situation, since it was evident he was back in the game whether he liked it or not.

* ** *

"They kidnapped his kid!?" Aaron said while rubbing the palms of his hands together as if he was about to dig into a nice hefty meal.

"This is the key to ending this shit! I told you my CI would come through with something soon."

"We still don't know where the son of bitch lives," Keith shot back from behind his desk. "That's the kind of information that'll make this CI worth all of these headaches."

Aaron held back the urge to respond, since he vowed last week, he wasn't going to debate that issue anymore. "I got the Colombians looking into this—"

"Looking into what!? We already know when and where Rasheen's supposed to drop off the money! I say we step to these Dominicans with a deal, get them to back away—"

"Hear me out first! I can already see we're saying the same thing. And stop cutting me off for once in your life, Keith. You're right about the deal, but we should do it through the Colombians. They got the coke, and we got them in the pocket. The Dominican Mafia is into the drug trade, and there's not many underworld groups that are not interested in high-grade Colombian coke. The plan is simple, we pay the Dominicans to stand down; we get the kid—"

"Come on, Aaron. Stop it, please. We don't deal like that. A kid!? You wanna start throwing children into this shit!? I thought we agreed no kids. We got kids of our own; imagine if the what goes around comes around monster comes back and bits us on the ass!?"

Aaron sighed with impatience. "Yeah, we agreed no kids." He nodded his head for emphasis. "But I'm gonna be blunt about this. The kid card is a guaranteed way to end this. According to the CI, Rasheen will sacrifice himself to save his son."

"What real man wouldn't!? All I'm saying is this is gonna fuck up with my ability to sleep at night. I'm not into the business for that kinda shit!"

"Well, if we blow this, we can get ready for prison. The investigators finished scouring Victorville, they found nothing, and decided Rasheen Smith is their number one witness. If they snatch him, they'll offer him something he won't turn down. You and I both know they'll look the other way with Rasheen's criminal transgressions to win a trophy like you and I."

The silence was ear shattering.

Keith's face was twisted with disgust, but he knew he had no choice but to bend. "Okay, let's get down and dirty. But, that 25 million is ours. Before or after we kill this clown, we gotta get that money. In fact, promise both those scrum bags the world; whatever you gotta promise them to get them to ride with us on this, do it. Just as long as we keep that money everything's fine. With the crew on ice, and our surplus cash dwindling every day we need every dollar we can touch. I'm also planning to expand the security company. I talked to Steve, and he said it's the perfect moment for expansion, since there's a huge spike in the market."

"No problem," Aaron smiled. "Our Colombians are more concerned about staying out of American prisons, and no amount of money is worth even a day in prison for most of them. Believe me; they'll do whatever we ask them to do."

CHAPTER # 23

"What's happenin', Judge," Rasheen said into the cell phone as he sat behind the wheel of his Lincoln Navigator. He was waiting for the light to turn green. "Tell me something good."

"I checked out everything you asked for." The judge's deep voice boomed with a Barry White bass tone. "And I got some crazy surprises. The Dominicans took your son. I ain't trying to get in your business, but whatever you did or didn't do seems to be the root of this kidnapping."

"Yeah, it's all starting to make sense now that you mention them." Rasheen's mind was now running rampage like a rabid dog with scrambled brains. He hit the gas pedal when the light changed. *How the fuck did the Dominicans find me!?* He sighed more so out of utter bewilderment than anything else. "How about Rosa Rodriguez? Did you get the photos I e-mailed you?"

"Yeah, I got 'em. This was a simple track; it was so simple I'm advising you to move with caution, since it might be a trap. Then again, since she's a Mexican immigrant she might be ignorant of the efficiency levels of this country's tracking apparatuses, or she's a throw away. She's currently living in the Bronx, 674 Walton Avenue, apartment 2C."

Rasheen wrote down the address as he handled the steering wheel and kept the phone to his ear with the help of the top of his shoulder blade. "You's a show-nuff lifesaver, Judge. About that move to Cuba—"

"I know what time it is, bro. Please don't insult my intelligence. No sane person could possibly believe a major move like going to Cuba would still be in effect with a kidnapped kid up in the air. Like I said before, I got your back, man."

Rasheen wished he could give the Judge a huge hug to let him know he was forever grateful for all the support. "How's the test results coming along?"

"That's still up in the air. Getting the body exhumed was a lot harder than I thought, but with some persistency the job'll get done. Rest assured, I'm on it Rasheen."

"I know you are. Believe me; I know what time it is."

"I got some more news. I don't know if it's good or bad, but I guess the only way to find out is to lay it on you. I hope you're sitting down."

Rasheen's heart flickered as the silence mounted.

"I'm hearing the Colombians are trying to make a swop with the Dominicans. They want your son and are willing to give the Dominican mafia a series of discounts on drug shipments. The last I heard, it was all talk, however, I'm almost certain the exchange is going to go down. I'll say this much, Rasheen, I see why your holdin' the way you are. I commend any man smart enough to step to folks with real money. Unfortunately, these are the headaches that come with the territory."

"Did they say the ransom will stay the same? Will I be able to get my son back if I cough up the 25 mills?"

"That's something I'll have to get back to you on. Give me a few days, and I'll have something solid. In the meantime, I'm assuming they may contact you on the cell number Rosa had. I hope you didn't discard the phone."

"I still got it."

"Good. That's the likely way they'll let you know about the change in the plans."

"One more issue; I want the addresses of all the Dominican Big Wigs. Whatever it cost I got you."

The Judge sighed. "I got you. But a hit on a top cat right now, could put your son at risk, even after the Colombians take possession."

"Let me deal with that. You just get me those addresses."

* ** *

Rosa Rodriguez strutted down the earlier evening Bronx Streets, with a grocery bag tucked close to her bosom. Ever since the Dominicans gave her the 30 thousand dollars for assisting them with the kidnapping, she'd been nervously peeking over her shoulders as if she was a paranoid schizophrenic on heavy psychotropic medication.

Dressed in a makeshift disguise (she dyed her hair blonde and wore sexy clothing), Rosa now had serious second thoughts about what she had done. For the pass four days, she'd been having nightmares of what Leo and his sadistic friends might be doing to that poor child. Little Rasheen dream world screams were driving her insane with a guilt that was very toxic to her mental well-being.

Suddenly, a stray black cat shot across her path.

Rosa nearly dropped her grocery bag as she recoiled in terror. She sighed with relief when she noticed it was just a cat. As her nerves rebalanced themselves, she realized she couldn't wait any longer for her cousin, Isabella, to call her back with the information on how she could buy a home in New Mexico with a white picket fence with the money she received from the Dominicans. As her heart rate went back to normal, she made a mental note to call Isabella in the morning, and demand that she speed up the process. If it was going to take longer than another week she was going to catch a bus ride out to New Mexico and stay with Isabella and her family even if she had to sleep on the floor, since Isabella's home was already jammed packed with friends and relatives, some newly arrived from Mexico.

When she arrived at the vestibule door of her apartment building, Rosa finally took note of the fact the Streets were empty, which was a good thing since it was 9 o'clock in the evening and she hated crowds. Then, suddenly, it dawned on her that this was the first time in four days this Street was this empty. Or was it!? It took minutes to conclude that the previous days weren't like this. She wondered was this an omen of some sort? Then it dawned on her that the black cat crossed her path and this meant bad luck.

After a moment she scolded herself as an inward giggle escaped her lips; she was allowing her mind to get the best of her, and she compelled herself to hurry up and get inside the safety of her apartment. She also swept the superstitious non-sense regarding black cats to the side. Once the door was open, she scurried inside, closed the door behind her, stopped, looked and listened for anything out of the unusual.

Before climbing the stairs, she repositioned her 32 automatic in the front of her pants. She hated guns, but she'd learned many years ago that there was no such thing as being over-prepared for anything, especially when she had done some things that could lead to consequences.

Upon reaching her second-floor apartment, Rosa placed her ear to the door, heard nothing, and unfastened the locks. After she had heard what Rasheen had done to the Dominicans, she decided to take every precaution possible, and again, she asked herself why did she do it!? And again, that voice told her it was the money. She needed it, she wanted it, and she definitely had to have it.

She sat the bag on the small table next to the door, took off her jacket, hung it on the coat hook by the door, retrieved the bag, and headed to the small kitchen table. She sat the bag down, and began taking the items out. As she was sitting the groceries on the table, she heard movement.

BLAAM!

The blow to the side of her head stopped her hand as it went for the 32 automatic; she felt herself stumbling to the floor.

Rasheen held the silencer equipped 9-mm in his right hand and was surprised he was able to floor Rosa with his weaker hand. He was right-handed by nature, and normally a TKO punch could never be pulled off with the left. When he saw Rosa reaching for her weapon, Rasheen fired a shot at her shoulder.

Rosa screamed as her hand shifted gears and shot up to the shoulder wound.

Rasheen stepped to her, confiscated the 32 automatic, dunked it in his pocket, and stood staring down at her cringing in pain.

"Please Rasheen," Rosa pleaded. "They forced me! They made me do it! I swear to God, I didn't want to do it." She cried explosively. The fear of death galvanized her into a state of terror; her mind raced for a way to prevent him from killing her.

Rasheen reached down, grabbed a head full of blonde hair and dragged Rosa out of the kitchen area and into the small living room. He needed a lot of room for what he was about to do. There were too many unanswered questions, and he had every intention of getting every one of them answered before this evening was over. He tossed her into the DVD player component set and took a seat on the raggedy sofa.

The silence grew as the two stared at each other.

Rasheen was still trying to figure out how did he let Camila talk him into letting this suspicious looking bitch into the comfort and sanctity of his home. He must have been out of his fuckin' mind to let this bitch get that close to him. His first instinct was that she was Mexican, and because of that, she was too similar to the people he was giving hell. But he now realized this was simply one of those situations where he could say he lived to regret. "Listen, Rosa, if you wanna live I want clear, specific and straightforward answers." His sounding professional and remarkably calm had nothing to do with an attempt to be nice but had everything to do with preventing himself from impulsively killing this bitch. "How did the Dominicans find me?"

Rosa thought rapidly and suddenly realized she had information that could be used to knock Rasheen off balance; this could fuck with his emotions in such a way that she might be able to wiggle around this predicament. It was a long shot, but anything right now was worth a try. She spoke through her tears and sniffles, "Camila and Rashango talked about it. They were at the house talking about it, and they said you all robbed the Dominicans, and killed one of them in prison."

Rasheen was jolted by the comment; it felt almost as violent as a slap to the face. *Camila and Rashango talked about it!?* "What the fuck you talkin' about, Rosa?" His voice became venomous. "I'm telling you; if you playing mind games with me, I'll lay some torture tactics on your mufuckin' ass that'll put the Spanish Inquisition to shame!"

"No! No, Rasheen, I no play head games! It is true! She and him were at the house, and they said they robbed the Dominicans some years ago. I even got them on tape. I recorded them. I even videotaped Camila and Rashango fucking!" She held back the smile when she saw Rasheen's stunned response. "I'll give you this stuff, if you let me live. I'll give you everything, names and addresses to the men who forced me into this. Everything! But you have to let me leave here. You let me live. I'll go away for good. I'll disappear . . ."

As Rosa rattled on and on with her pleas, Rasheen was brain locked on one particular statement she made. *Rashango was fuckin' Camila!?* He almost lost control of his emotions. He cut into Rosa's gibberish. "Where's the tapes? You said you got videotapes?" He toyed with the 9-mm in his hand as he stared menacingly at Rosa. "I want 'em, Rosa. All of them."

"Yes, I'll give them to you; I'll give you everything. But, please, you have to let me live, Rasheen," Her weeping sounds increased as the thought of never seeing her daughter again broke her down into a mesh of heart wrenching emotions. "I'll give them to you if you let me live!" Her tearful eyes locked with his squinted eyes.

Rasheen wanted those tapes and didn't have time to play games with this bitch. If he didn't agree to let her live it was obvious he'd have to tear up the apartment looking for those tapes, and in the end, he might not find them. "Okay, Rosa," He spoke softly. "I'll let you live if he give me those tapes and the names and addresses of the dudes who made you do this." He nodded his head humbly. "Don't worry, I'm a man of my word. I'll let you live. My right hand to God." He held up his hand for dramatic emphasis. "I wanna know everything, who's who, the when, where and everything else in between."

Rosa smiled inwardly, and hoped and prayed he would keep his word. In any event, she had nothing to lose. She struggled to her feet. "I'll go get the stuff." She wobbled as she headed towards the back of the apartment while clasping her wounded arm. She saw Rasheen was dead on her back.

As Rosa crept towards the bedroom, she wondered if she gave Rasheen some pussy would that help guarantee her survival. She decided to use every tactic up her sleeve to save her live.

Rosa opened her closest, reached up for the plastic bag, and pulled it down from the shelf. The bag crashed down to the floor and CDs, DVDs and micro-cassette tapes spilled from the bag.

Rasheen instantly realized this broad was probably secretly recording all of his and Camila's conversations.

Rosa stood staring at Rasheen as if to say, there it is. "This is everything." She then gave him a seductive stare as she licked her lips. "You like?" She unfastened her blouse, showcasing her breasts.

231

Rasheen pushed her away, reached down, swept the tapes, CDs and DVDs back in the bag and scooped it up. "Come on, get in front of me. Go back to the living room." He remembered seeing a CD player in there. As he watched Rosa moving slowly, he shook his head disbelievingly at the thought of this crazy broad thinking she could simply throw some skins at him, and all would be forgotten.

As Rosa took a seat in the armchair, Rasheen inserted the CD labeled Camila and Rashango, and hit play. As Rasheen listened to the shocking information, he watched Rosa squirm in her seat. He noticed the blood was pouring from her shoulder wound and was now soaking her blouse. He had told Camila and Rashango that everything; and he specifically said everything they did involving all their moneymaking activities were to never be discussed ever again. When the hit ended and the money was divvied off, it no longer existed. It died and disappeared the minute they started working on the next mission.

". . . And that time I murdered that nigga Dario Montero for y'all," Rashango's voice slid from the speakers of the CD player. "And you telling me that bitch ass nigga, Rasheen was playin' me when he gave me them fuckin' crumbs!?"

Rasheen felt the rage marinating. He had helped Rashango when he got out of prison. Gave that nigga thousands of dollars, got him a crib, a car, and didn't ask for a fuckin' penny back! He sighed as he realized he was going to enjoy stepping to his business.

After the first set of recordings finished, the CD player flipped to the next set, and when he heard his son's voice, apparently on the other side of the bedroom, he nearly screamed with sheer rage as he heard the sexual moans and groans. When Camila told Little Rasheen to go back to his room and he apparently obeyed, and then she heard Rashango instructing Camila to get on her knees, so he "could hit it from the backside", he noticed he couldn't hear any more. The thought of what he was going to do to Camila was making him very uncomfortable; he was going to make his son a motherless child.

Rasheen sprung to his feet and turned off the CD player. He knew there were also two videotapes, but his stomach and emotions couldn't bear to see his main man, digging his girl's back out. He'd intended to watch it later, but right now he had too much business to take care of to be sitting around watching porno tapes. "Lemme get those names and addresses."

Rosa retrieved her address book and gave it to Rasheen.

Rasheen flipped through the pages, realizing Rosa was really efficient with writing things down. "This is excellent."

Rosa stared at Rasheen with hopeful eyes, "I'll leave, Rasheen, you'll never hear from me again. I'll leave here right now. I'll get on the plane, the bus, the train, whatever and leave for good."

"Yes, you can leave, Rosa," Rasheen said with a smoothness that had a strong ring of affection.

There was a moment of silence.

Rosa sensed this meant she could go. She stepped away and stared into Rasheen's eyes as she thought she detected he was holding back the tears. She also saw his pain was pronounced, and finally realized some hope was really at the end of the tunnel as she savored his words "you can leave."

"And, you will be leaving for good." Rasheen said softly as he hastily squeezed off two shots to her chest. When she hit the floor, he fired two more shots to her forehead.

CHAPTER # 24

Several hours later, Rasheen was exiting the private jet Sharon apparently had unlimited access to. When he saw Sharon Walker standing in between her two bodyguards, he was glad to see she was taking this thing serious.

After taking care of Rosa, he had talked to the Judge, and it was confirmed; the Colombians had his son, and they wanted him to meet them in two weeks at a warehouse in the State of Georgia. They also wanted the 25 million dollars. He then called Sharon and told her he needed to see her face-to-face and that it was an emergency, and without hesitation she was on her job. She told him to go to a private airstrip in Suffolk Long Island, and low and behold, the jet was waiting for him when he arrived.

Rasheen moved swiftly towards Sharon, and twenty minutes later, the two sat in an elegant restaurant with steamy hot meals in front of them. Rasheen had shoved his meal aside; his appetite was shot.

Sharon spoke after she took a sip of her wine. "I found out some very disturbing news. I'm a bit confused by it all, and it's definitely a surprise." She felt awkward talking about this, because it made her appear incompetent regarding matters of accurate intelligence gathering.

Rasheen saw she was toying with the old silent treatment head game once again, and he absolutely was not in the mood for this shit today. "Listen, Sharon, this ain't the time for the games. I wanna hear it. Right now, as we sittin' here bullshittin', my son is somewhere being tortured—"

"Okay, okay," Sharon said with a guilty tone. "I found out that Aaron and Keith are behind the Colombians taking your son. I think their gonna use it to pull you to them, and—"

"So this is how they play!? You were confident that they would never throw kids into this shit." Rasheen stared out the window as pedestrians went about their daily routines. His heart couldn't take it anymore! He wanted his son back, and any motherfucker who laid hands on his son was going to feel it! He fought back the misty eyed sensation. *Every one of them mufuckas is gonna pay with their lives for fucking my son!* "You know something, Sharon. This shit don't surprise me at all. All I'm asking from you is that you give me both of their addresses. I already got the SSS address, but I need their home—"

"Rasheen, their children and wives have no to do with any of their—"

"What about my son!? They're fuckin' with my son, and now you think it's wrong for me to fuck with their loved ones!?" Rasheen felt steam seething from his ears. After a moment he realized he was talking strictly from raw emotions. Punishing innocent folks wasn't something he was into. "You know what?" He stopped his emotions from running wild and tucked them into his pocket. "Believe it or not, Sharon, even though these chumps are fuckin' with my son, I'm not gonna do anything foul to their families. I'm a career stick up kid, a murderer, and a Hood hitter, baller, and hustler of grand proportions, but a person that hurts or do bad things to children and innocent people I'm not. And I ain't too egoistical to say that either. I've been raising hell my entire life. And I can brag about never being one of those dudes that did foul shit to weak, innocent folks." He flashed back to the time when he was in Elmira State Prison and had straggled a booty bandit to death for raping a dude. "It ain't my style to do wicked shit like hurt little kids, and innocent women who just happen to be involved in a relationship with a cat in the game."

There was a moment of wordless stares.

Rasheen continued, "You give me their addresses, and I promise I won't touch their families. In fact, I won't even touch Keith or

Aaron; not right now. I'm gonna hurt them where it'll really hurt the most."

Sharon saw her little emotional bit worked. She didn't give a flying fuck about Keith or Aaron in anyway. True, she would hate to see their families hurt or killed, but if it happened it would be something they would simply have to deal with, since it would be collateral damage. Aaron and Keith had committed an unforgivable violation when they even entertained the thought of using Rasheen's son as bait. She could understand their desperation, but touching his kid was way over the top. "Listen, Rasheen, you know I got your back. After hearing you out, I can already see where you're going with this. I'm not only gonna give you their addresses, but I'm gonna give you something else that'll help us lace it up to where we can throw them both into the hell fire and they won't know what hit 'em, or where it came from."

Rasheen saw Sharon's smile and couldn't help but feel a ping of apprehensive anxiety, because that smile had something in it that was very conniving.

* ** *

The following evening Aaron was in his BMW racing to his home. He'd just received a call from Geraldine; she was hysterical as she informed him of the fire that broke out in the mansion and had done major damage. He was grateful no one was hurt, since the fire broke out while Armena and Aaron Junior were in school, and Geraldine was at a Community Council meeting.

Suddenly, his cell phone buzzed, and he answered the call. "Aaron speaking."

"I got a situation!" Keith said excitedly; he stood watching the Fire Department spraying water on his once beautiful home as his wife, Wanda and his daughter Kimberly stood several yards away staring at their destroyed place of residence with traumatized eyes. "You ain't gonna fuckin' believe this! A fire broke out in my house! Of all the god damn times in my life—-"

"A fire!?" Aaron shouted with a blend of shock and terror saturating his tone. "Geraldine just called me and told me our house is on fire. I'm on my way home right now."

They both were hurled into a state of silence as the realization began to set in.

"This ain't a coincidence," Keith whispered as the overload of raw emotions assaulted his mind; staring at the blazing smoke swirling into the sunset-laden skies, he realized the self-imposed leash he had put on was now off.

"You motherfuckin' right this is no coincidence," Aaron's foot instantly got heavier on the accelerator. The car jerked and was now doing 85 miles per hour in a 55 miles per hour zone. "After you get things on your side under control we need to talk immediately. This could be emanating from anywhere, so we're now official in plan D. I'll see if Norman, Donald and Eugene will come out and at least put some security of our families."

"Plan D," Keith muttered emotionlessly as his rage became much more dominating than his fear. He looked around at the on-lookers hoping he saw a suspicious face, because what he was currently feeling, he could shoot something on GP (general principle). He spoke in a trance like fashion. "I'll call you soon."

Keith disconnected the call and approached a man who fitted the description of a "suspicious face."

Several hours later, Aaron and Keith sat on a park bench, taking. The half-moon hovered overhead, the late night air was crisp and clean, and the crickets and other night creatures and insects were letting their presence be known.

"All three fires," Aaron said in deep thought. "All set at approximately the same time tells me this is no ordinary enemy."

"The Albanians are no ordinary enemy."

Aaron shook his head in total disagreement. "It wasn't them."

"The notes left behind specifically said it was the Albanian brotherhood!" Keith was officially in his crazy zone. His whole world was turned upside down; his home was destroyed; his family was staying at the Hewitt Hotel, and he was ready to unleash a complete savage like violence on anyone responsible for this. Earlier, he had approached a strange man watching the fire, and just before he opened his mouth, his inner voice reminded him that this might be the internal affairs investigator the Bureau had tracking Aaron (and probably him as well). He walked pass the clean-shaved, average looking white man as he kept his hand close to his weapon. "We should've hunted down them son of a bitches and killed every one of those cock suckers!"

"We need to slow down," Aaron crossed his leg over the other. "This ain't how the Albanians operate. They knew nothing about your Peachtree Street Condo. In fact, almost nobody knows about that Condo, except certain people working at SSS. Had they hit only our homes, I might believe it was them."

"Come on, Aaron," Keith was about to blow up on him. "We took 3 million dollars from these guys during a money laundering scheme we entrapped them into; we had Colombian hit men kill half of their mob, sent five of them to prison with life sentences, and we made the reckless mistake of allowing a dozen or more of them to escape back to Albania. The ones that got away may have been the weaker of the bunch, but cowards can become lions if nurtured correctly. The bottom line is, you can complicate this shit if you want to, but the fact is, this is a clear case of chickens coming home to fuckin' roost!"

"Yeah, I agree this is blowback. But it ain't the Albanians." He wanted badly to inform him of the results of his covert activities involving watching Sharon Walker closely. He'd learned hours ago that Sharon was a secret investor and a silent partner with a nameless syndicate that financed and backed a series of underground Casinos, and Shooties just happened to be one of the Casinos this group sponsored and operated. It was the smoking gun he needed to link Sharon to Rasheen, but he was smart enough to know Keith wasn't ready for this news, at least not at the moment. He wondered if Keith would ever by ready to hear that Sharon was the one undermining them; she had access to all SSS files, she knew almost all sensitive information about Keith and him, and she had a previous relationship with Rasheen. Although Keith had no knowledge of their creeping adventures, and Aaron never saw them together in an intimate way, he spoke with several employees at the company who confirmed they had done some heavy hanging out. "Keith, let's keep it real with ourselves. What group in their right state of mind is going to take responsibility for transgressing against a force that nearly obliterated them in the past, and could now stomped them out of existence with the snap of a finger? Now, let's look at this on the flip side. Wouldn't it be wise for an enemy to get at us while making us think it was someone else? Smart enemies are only concerned with results, not getting the credit for being the next candidate to see if we can still reach out and touch anybody stupid enough to fuck with us. The Albanians? I can't digest this one."

"Who do you think it is?"

Aaron turned his head and made firm eye contact. Did he feel like arguing? Maybe a little argument wouldn't hurt. "You want my honest opinion?"

"No, I want you to lie in my fuckin' face!" Keith spatted sarcastically. "Of course I want your honest opinion! What else would I want?"

"I think its Rasheen."

Keith thought hard and long about that answer before jumping to any conclusions. He tried to force his mind to grasp this possibility, but it wasn't clicking; there were just too many holes and unlikely circumstances. "I don't see it, Aaron. This cat Rasheen is a killer. He wouldn't bust any girly shots at us if he knew where we lived. He'd come shooting shit up."

"Don't forget, we got his kid."

"He don't know we got his kid! And even if he suspects we got dealings with the Colombians, Rasheen has had major beef with the Colombians for so many years, he's gotta think it's a head on fight between them and him."

Aaron sighed awkwardly; if Keith knew Sharon and Rasheen had a relationship, and she was involved with Shooties on the down low, he knew it would change his views. "I'm telling you it's Rasheen, and I think Sharon's helping him. I know you're not trying to hear me, but before you get defensive just think about it." The urge to share his recent findings with Keith was strong, but he couldn't do it; he didn't want anything to interfere with the plan he was about to put into activation, at least not until after it was a success.

* ** *

About two hundred miles away, Rasheen laid on his stomach with an M 21 7.62 mm sniper rifle in his grasp. The thick forest like area he was hiding within was several hundred yards from a multi-million-dollar mansion in the suburbs of Danville Virginia. He was located on the Northeastern flank of the mansion and could see all movement coming from the front and the side, both areas where he noticed the target had utilized quite frequently. According to the Judge, Alberto Morales was the top man in the Dominican Mafia, and this was his comfortable kingdom he thought was hidden from his foes, and the law. Alberto controlled all east coast activities from Florida to Maine and had chosen Virginia as his headquarters.

Dressed in black army fatigue like clothing and a black knit hat, Rasheen noticed his emotions seemed like they were never going to stop tormenting him. He flipped the rifle into its ready position, peered through the scope again, and saw there was still no movement in the courtyard of the mansion. He relaxed his aim, shifted his body weight to a more comfortable position, and allowed his mind to wander once again.

Securing Little Rasheen's well-being was the strongest issue of them all and it stayed on his mind. Thoughts of what they might be doing to his son were driving him to the brinks of madness. He couldn't sleep, could barely eat, and at times he couldn't think straight unless the cognitive activity involved constructing a plot based on punishing those who'd done this to his son. He was thankful his mind seemed to function above optimum level when he engaged in activity geared towards either undoing this nightmare or balancing the scales of justice.

He had another week until he had to go to Georgia and get his son in exchange for the 25 million dollars. After a lifetime spent going toe to toe with forces several times more powerful than him, he was aware this kidnapping had nothing to do with the money. They wanted him dead. The Judge had also mentioned that Aaron had been suspended and some kind of investigator was going behind the scenes of the Victorville incident where three federal agents were murdered. From what the Judge was eluding to Rasheen still couldn't understand why this investigator was currently looking for him. He had nothing to offer this guy even if he could give him the world. He would go out with a blazing gun, before he would cooperate with any cop, investigator or law enforcement official. Certainly he didn't need the Judge to inform him that this was the reason Aaron and Keith wanted him dead.

Rasheen sighed as he peeked through the scope again, saw nothing and resumed his inward mental discourse. There was no question if he had known about this Investigator situation before he had set those fires in Aaron and Keith's cribs, he might have settled for just killing them, and getting this shit over with. He was seriously contemplating making a deadly move on them before this exchange, but something was telling him such an extreme action might cause the instant death of his son in retaliation. *Fuck it! It's too risky!* He'd have to ride it out the safest way. Nothing was worth gambling with his son's life. Not even his own life.

Then, suddenly, he wondered did they already kill his son? This thought was too much for him to even consider and immediately shoved it to the back of his mind.

The Camila and Rashango drama crossed his mind, and he welcomed it because it was an event that compelled him to become a solo artist. After experiencing this level of betrayal, it was evident that trust, loyalty, and honor were sacred commodities within his surroundings. Now, he had to decide what to do with them. There was no question they had to pay with their lives for what they had done. But the question was when should he do the deed? Should he kill them before he picked up his son? Or should he do it during the job? Or afterwards?

He sighed loudly and instantly decided it would have to be before. Since there was no guarantee he would come out of this ordeal alive, it went without saying he had to clear the air and make sure all debts were paid in full, before this run to get his son back. Camila and Rashango were destined to pay a heavy penalty when they chose to take his kindness, fairness, generosity, and good-natured way of treating anyone he perceived as family for weakness.

Rasheen saw movement from his peripheral vision and snapped into action. After he planted his eye to the scope, he moved the M 21 sniper rifle to the right and saw a group of men dressed in sleek suits.

When he saw Alberto along with another man, who looked like a big wig of equal status as Alberto, he smiled excitedly.

As the men dressed in military attire swarmed around the two big wigs, Rasheen knew for certain today was going to be a wonderful day. Images of Little Rasheen began flashing inside his mind and he felt a crippling sensation forming inside his heart. The mental image of Little Rasheen toddling around in his New Jersey home twirled around inside his mind; Rasheen steadied his aim and began firing the silenced armor piercing 7.62 mm bullets, promising there would be no survivors when he was through.

CHAPTER # 25

Sharon Walker sat in the back of the fast-moving limousine while hastily loading her two Beretta 9-mms. Her facial expression and the urgency in her handling of the weapons was a tell-tale sign that things had taken a turn for the worse. "Bobby, call Jerome and tell him I'm gonna be late."

From the front passenger seat, Bobby turned and said to his boss in an uneasy tone. "You think that'll be a good idea?"

"Yeah, Sharon," Carlos added his two cents from behind the wheel. His tone was equally filled with anxiety. "They said it was an extreme emergency. They made it very clear that we had to show up."

"Listen, you two," Sharon sat the two 9-mms on the seat on each side of her. "I pulled some strings after I heard the Syndicate wanted to see me. I was informed they wanna talk to me about the Shooties robbery."

Both Carlos and Bobby turned and looked at her with shocked eyes to make sure they were hearing her correctly.

Carlos faced forward, to keep his eyes on the partially crowded freeway. "Did they give any hints that they believe we were involved?"

"It ain't got shit to do with hints," Sharon said as she continued looking out the window and especially the back windshield to see if they were being followed. "Somebody blew the fuckin' spot up! They know I arranged this inside robbery." She also found out from a very close associate within the Syndicate that a friend of a friend of Aaron Wilson was the root of this leak. "There are multi-thousand-dollar tracks on all three of our heads."

"Fuckin' shit!" Bobby pounded his fist on the dashboard. "Who ratted us out!? I know your associates are well connected; they know who did it. If they know Shooties was an inside job, they gotta know who's feeding them this shit."

Sharon sighed and said, "That low-life motherfucker Aaron Wilson did it."

There was a moment of silence.

"Aaron Wilson!?" Carlos muttered. "So is Keith Ramsey involved as well?"

"Actually," Bobby's eyes were now looking at every car that came close to them; his weapons were no longer in their holsters. "This doesn't surprise me. When I was with the agency, Aaron's name was floating around with just about every underhanded activity that went down. I see the beef between you two has finally reached that life and death level."

"The question I need to know," Carlos said. "Is what you wanna do, boss?"

Sharon went into an indecisive silent cocoon. That was indeed the ten-million-dollar question. What was she going to do? She was still trying to formulate an answer to this question even though she knew of this current disaster hours ago. *What am I going to do!?* The good thing was that she had a good head start; at least she hoped she did. She was very nervous because the Syndicate was very powerful; they had the best killers in the world working for them, including the infamous Black-river Mercenaries, and collectively had a multi-billion dollar war chest, which enabled them to put almost anybody in their pockets, including Judges, Politicians, Police Commissioners, State and Federal Prosecutors, secret agents, military personnel, and so on, and make them dance to any tune their ruthless hearts desired. How she became a part of this Syndicate was like most of its members. She worked for a government agency, had acquired a series of skills, lost that job, and they presented her with a proposition to become a part of their group. Once they started talking major money, she was not only all ears, but was all action. She'd been with the Syndicate for close to four years and had made millions just playing by the Syndicate's rules.

Now, she wondered were all her secondary moneymaking tactics, in the form of setting up Syndicate sponsored establishments (among other things) worth it. When she realized the Shooties job was actually a complete success, she concluded it was obviously worth it. She made a cool 4 million for a couple hours of planning and didn't have to fire a single shot. That's why she went to great lengths to get Rasheen's nose open; thank goodness it worked.

Sharon saw her two bodyguards and personal friends were waiting for an answer, but she still hadn't formulated one, and so she held firm to the silent thought process she was locked in. The desire to initiate an all-out strike on Aaron was very tempting. After this slimy, cutthroat shit he'd just done, it was clear she could neutralize him with remarkable ease. If it weren't for Rasheen's predicament with his son, she would've commenced a full fledge hit on his ass. But, under the circumstances, she couldn't do that. If Aaron was to receive any kind of hostile attack, he might react by killing Rasheen's son.

She didn't want that type of blood on her hands and knew all she had to do was duck and weave the hitters the Syndicate would send at her, until she could pull some strings and get out of the country. She had a little over a hundred million dollars in various scattered offshore accounts, and she could technically throw in the towel and still be victorious and live the rest of her life rich and wealth.

For the first time Sharon realized she had enough money to leave the game. In fact, she had had enough money to pull out about two years ago, but still couldn't find the discipline to leave the game. The only conclusion to be drawn was that she was addicted to the ritual of accumulating money and the thrill of knowing she was living on the edge, winking her eye at danger, and literally disgracing the grim reaper.

About twenty minutes later, Sharon saw they were on a strip of highway with a mountainous area flanking both lanes. Sharon caught a flash back of the time when she had taken down a target in a moving car in a similar situation and a stabbing nervousness erupted. As she closely scanned the mountainous areas, she recalled it was in Turkey when she had instituted this hit to save her fellow agent from imminent death as hit men in an inconspicuous car followed him.

Just when she was about to instruct Carlos to increase his speed, havoc struck.

A sniper's bullet cut through the windshield and splattered Carlos's blood all over the interior of the limousine. Carlos's head exploded, the limousine went into a savage spin with tires screaming. Sharon took cover while Bobby did the same. Bobby tried desperately to take control of the steering wheel. Since Bobby couldn't see the road in front of him (he had ducked under the dashboard), he was forced to maneuver in the blind while trying to find the brake pedal with his other hand. When he found both pedals, his military experiences told him to hit the gas pedal until they were out of the sniper's firing range.

BANG!——SSHHHRRKKK!

The Limousine struck the guard railing and began scrapping it.

SZK! SZK!

Two more sniper bullets cut through the hood of the limo, the projectiles just missing Sharon.

The Limo veered violently off the highway into a forest like area. The violent bouncing motion had Sharon and Bobby taking a vicious beating as they held onto their weapons.

BLAAM! BLAAM!

The limo's right fender violently brushed against the side of a tree, tearing that particular part of the vehicle away. The limo then slammed into a tree head on, bringing the Limo to a gruesomely violent stop.

Both Sharon and Bobby were temporarily dazed.

Sharon was the first to stir. "Bobby, you alright?" She inquired as she rushed to the window to see where they were located.

"Yeah, I'm still here." His voice was saturated with a searing pain from the arm injury. The dashboard was shoved at him upon impact and had struck his arm. He felt the blood trickling out of his wound as he tried to open the passenger door.

Sharon kicked open the back driver side door, saw the trees were providing them with a blanket of cover from the snipers in the nearby mountains, and she moved quickly. With both 9-mms in her hands, she zipped out of the Limo and raced over to the passenger side of the vehicle while scanning everything within her vicinity.

When Sharon reached the other side of the Limo, she saw the door was sealed shut from the impact of the crash. "Climb over the seat and get out from the backdoor, hurry!" Sharon kneeled as she continued scoping out the immediate area for their attacks who she knew were on their way to this location, or maybe there was another hit team already down here and were moving in as she waited for Bobby.

When Bobby was out of the Limo, Sharon led the way. She and Bobby ran at top speed deeper into the forest, both looking around frantically for any movement.

Suddenly, a loud shot rang out, and Sharon both heard and saw Bobby go into a vicious spin as he collapsed to the ground. Her speed increased as she began running in a zig zagging fashion as the loud shots continued ringing out. The bullets viciously cutting pass her sounded like armor plated bees savagely buzzing all around her.

When she finally figured out where the shots were coming from, Sharon squeezed off a volley of bullets while still in full sprint.

She heard a grunt and saw the men running towards her on her left side had fallen. Just when she thought she was out of immediate danger, another shot zipped pass her. Since this one was silenced, she knew whoever was shooting at her wasn't going to be taken down as easy as the last group of men.

* ** *

"Mr. Phillip Henderson," Federal Internal Affairs Agent Steven Merenstein said, stopping Phil as he pulled open the door of his powder blue Aston Martin DB9. "Could we please have a moment of your time?" He flashed his badge, and so did his partner, Internal Affairs Agent Jessica Dorsette.

Phil's trembling eyes scrolled across their faces. "In relation to . . .?"

"Your dealings with Aaron Wilson," Jessica said, her freckled face and cold blue eyes zeroed in on Phillip's attempt to appear unnerved and confident.

Steven added immediately. "And before you commit a crime; you should know we have several videotape recordings of you, Mr. Gibson and Agent Wilson talking, as well as numerous phone records of calls made to and from your business number to Mr. Wilson."

Phil spoke as though he was bored out of his mind. "I didn't catch your names."

"I'm Special Agent Steven Merenstein."

"Special Agent Jessica Dorsette."

Phil politely slammed the car door. "I guess we can talk inside my office." He gave them a smile and led the two back towards the building, as his mind, heart and sweat glands raced.

Forty-five minutes later, after the federal agents left the building, Phil sat staring at the platinum records hanging on the wall in a trance like fashion. His brain was numb; his nerves were even more paralyzed, and his inner emotional workings had gone somewhere even he couldn't describe. He saw everything he'd worked so hard to attain rapidly unraveling before his eyes. If he didn't do something it was clear all of this would disappear.

Phil jarred himself out of this trance, and reached over and activated the intercom. "Denise, tell Clay Ripper I need to see him. It's an emergency." He let go of the intercom button and leaned back in the seat, reflecting back on this interrogation he'd just endured.

The Victorville murders, as these agents had called it, were heavy on their minds and seemed to be their main agenda. That issue took up more than half of the interrogation, and they apparently suspected Aaron Wilson was behind it.

It was also obvious Agents Merenstein and Dorsette had somehow found out Rasheen was at that scene and had even hinted that they knew it was because Lameek was kidnapped by Aaron Wilson and other agents, and Rasheen had went to that location to get him. Both agents even knew that immediately after the Victorville incident, the shootout at Killer Kato's Lakeside mansion was directly related. This made him very nervous, since it was clear and convincing evidence that they had someone that was doing some serious talking.

But, what terrified him most was that they wanted to question Rasheen.

Both agents explicitly stated that he was the key to this investigation, and when he told them he had no way of getting in touch with Rasheen, they clearly were very disappointed. Since they also knew about the five million dollars he'd recent transferred to Rasheen, Phil sensed they thought he was pulling their legs. Based on their responses, he knew it was just a matter of time after they questioned Rasheen, they would turn their full focus on him, and the way Hoodaroma's ownership was turned over to him would come under heavy scrutiny.

Indeed, Phil saw the writing on the wall, and it was telling him as clear as day that to sit around waiting for them to get hold of

Rasheen would add up to a death sentence. Agent Dorsette had made it very clear that they were coming for him if and when they find the dirt they were looking for when she said, "It strikes me as odd that the lawyer of a multi-million-dollar Entertainment company would miraculously become the CEO after the owner and founder suddenly turns up dead. I think that is something that can definitely make you go, hummm."

As Phil waited for Clay Ripper, while staring off into the oblivion, he decided the first order of business would be to contact Aaron and put him on point to this visit from these Investigators. Aaron had mentioned that he was being investigated and was put on a desk detail, but he honestly didn't thing they were going to go at him with this level of relentlessness.

The next order of business would be to get Clay Ripper on his job with these quarter million-dollar killers. With his life and career rapidly slipping from his grasp, Phil knew it was officially time to hire a team that could provide 100% guaranteed results or your money back.

CHAPTER # 26

Camila and Rashango sat in the dining room of Rashango's ranch style home in Wilmington Delaware, counting crazy paper, getting high and chit chatting.

"This shit is gonna turn out to be peanuts," Camila said after she retrieved the batch of bills from the money-counter (it was a thousand-dollar stack of bills); she sat it next to the other stacks; so far this was her fourth completed stack, and there still was a huge pile of bills waiting to be counted. "We gotta find us some richer ballers to bag up." She scooped up more uncounted bills and began feeding them into the machine.

"My model is slow motion is better than no motion," Rashango sat in a Tiger skin covered chair, drinking a glass of Hennessey, while smoking a blunt. "These little peanuts can add up to big doe if we stay on top of our game. Maybe after we get your little crumb snatcher back, and Rasheen's ass focused, we'll be back touching major paper."

Camila was about to pick up another batch of bills when the doorbell rang. "It's about fuckin' time! These Pizza delivery people in this town are slow as hell." She rose to her feet as she looked at her watch. "It took this motherfucker a whole hour to get his ass over here." She headed for the door. "He killed his tip."

Camila peeked through the peek hole, saw the Domino's pizza man dressed in the standard white, orange and light blue uniform with a matching cap; his face was concealed by the beak of the cap, and she opened the door. "What kinda racket y'all running in this town?" She stepped aside as she said, "Come on in." As the Pizza man stepped in with two pizzas in his hand, Camila continued. "And my pizza better be piping hot like y'all be poppin' shit on the TV."

Once the Pizza man was clearly in the house, the boxes of pizza dropped to the floor, and Rasheen pulled the silencer equipped 9-mm from his waist.

Camila nearly pissed in her pants when she saw it was Rasheen. When she saw the 9-mm with a silencer on it, she almost shitted in her pants, because this told her he was coming to do some serious work. She was getting ready to mutter his name, but Rasheen touched her mouth with his free hand while shaking his head "no."

Rasheen roughly collared her by the blouse and pulled her close to him. "Where's that nigga at?"

Camila hesitated, wondering should she start lying, but the level of Rasheen's aggressiveness caused her to point with a trembling finger towards the dining room.

Rasheen shoved her towards the dining as Camila stepped lightly as she moved.

Camila's mind was drenched with a mixture of fear, confusion and desperation. That inner voice was telling her this was the end of the line. She was now living her last minutes on this planet.

Rasheen entered and saw the back of Rashango's head as he sat in a tiger skin chair. The smell of the weed he was smoking had the room lit up from corner to corner.

With a firm grip on Camila's blouse, Rasheen shoved her towards the sofa.

"Let's get them slices movin'" Rashango said when he saw Camila; he started coughing from the weed. "Let's get our belly's full so we can get the next part of this show rollin'!"

Rasheen pointed at the chair next to Rashango and Camila sat down as he sat on the sofa across from the two.

When Rashango saw Rasheen had suddenly appeared, his eyes grew wide like a cartoon character. His mouth hung open in an equally comedic manner as if his jawbone had ceased functioning. His utter jackass look could've won an international competition on the world's silliest facial expressions.

"What's the next scene in the show, Homie?" Rasheen stared at Rashango unblinkingly. "Is that the part where you two creepers get butt ass naked and fuck up a storm?"

Rashango looked at the blunt as if it was causing this situation and stuffed it out in the ashtray on the coffee table. "Rasheen, it ain't what you think, bro." His mind was frantically grabbing at straws, and the weed and alcohol was interfering with his ability to think quickly.

Rasheen took careful aim at Rashango's chest, and said, "Before you say another word, I need you to slowly take that burner out of your waist and lay it on this table." He watched Rashango follow his instructions. Once it was on the table, he retrieved the weapon, tucked it in his waist and then said with comedic flare. "You may now proceed."

"We gonna come clean, Rasheen," Camila said, realizing he would know only what she allowed him to know. "We hit a drug spot over in Patterson." She gestured to the money on the coffee table. "Since we damn near on E and ain't got no hard cash, I felt we should go out and hit a few places. I would've pulled your coat, but I know you was out there handling the business with us getting back Little Rah, and I didn't want to start distracting you with this type of shit. You always said I need to stop sitting around waiting for you to tell me when to tie my shoe, how to shit straight, and when to set up runs, I figured this would be a good time to start doing that."

"And what's your story, homie?" He said to Rashango with a clear nasty attitude merged with a fake smile.

Camila cut straight in. "I asked him to hold me down."

Rasheen's head turned in slow motion and his dagger-laden eyes locked on hers. "Did I ask you!? He got a fuckin' mouth!"

"Sorry, Rasheen," Camila bowed her head.

"Why the fuck is y'all out here making moves when Little Rah is fucked up!?" Rasheen felt his rage involving his son's predicament was being projected on Camila and Rashango, and the urge to started shooting was strong. "We should be somewhere making plans on how we gonna step to these cats next week."

"They hit us for 25 mill, Rah," Camila whined, sensing she and Rashango were almost in the safe zone by the tone and texture of his remarks. "We need money to survive. The whole team kicked out crazy doe, and I figured it couldn't hurt to go out and snatch up some easy money."

"Yeah, Rah," Rashango said. "We just making moves for the team. After we get your Shorty back we going in hard and heavy, and since cash is gonna be tight we figured we could help out by puttin' in some side work for the team." He gestured at the money. "All this here is for the team."

Rasheen was toying with the silencer equipped 9-mm, realizing these fuckin' fools thought he was dumb as a rock. "What's up, this y'all first run or what?"

"Yeah, Rah," Camila blurred out the comment, knowing Rashango was probably stupid enough to tell him the truth. "After they took Rasheen, and now we gotta kick out all that doe, I decided it was time for me to start steppin' up a little more."

Rasheen nodded his head, but it wasn't because he approved of anything she had said. It was done because he received the confirmation he was looking for; Camila was going to lie about this whole shit to the bitter end, and he couldn't blame her, actually. "Y'all fuckin' or what?"

A deep silence clutched the room as the two tried to put on their best attempt at being surprised.

"Fuckin'!?" Rashango and Camila said almost at the same time. The response seemed almost rehearsed.

"Hell no!" Rashango said firmly. "I don't move like that, Rah! Me and you like family, man."

"Now you know," Camila added. "I wouldn't do no shit like that, and especially not to somebody close to you like Rashango. Just cause the two of us are in here counting cheddar don't mean we fuckin', Rasheen."

Rasheen was still nodding his head as he looked around the room for a CD player. When he saw the DVD player, he smiled. He decided to let them dig themselves deeper into their bullshit before he sprung the smoking gun evidence on them. "Yo', Rashango, you hatin' on a nigga or what?" After listening to all the tapes he'd gotten from Rosa, it was evident by the tone and texture of Rashango's words he had a deep-set hatred for him. Why he hated him so much could only be attributed to jealous and envy. "You wish you could be me, right!? I'm a humble, kind, freehearted brother, yet at the same time I can be as dangerous as a nuclear bomb. Helleva combination, right!"

There was a moment of silence as Rashango squinted his eyes in order to express the mind-numbing confusion.

Rasheen continued. "Maybe it's because I stopped snatchin' hams and crumbs since I was ten years old; I plan shit with military expertise; I'm relatively grounded in black history, and most of all, I'm a million-dollar nigga that could lose it all in a snap of a finger and gain it all back just as fast." He titled his head theatrically. "Could this be the reason you got so much mufuckin' hate in your heart against me!? Cause you's a jealous, envious, weak, mentally crippled ass mufucka, with high-octane hate in your blood, who wish he could be me!"

"Hold up, Rah," Rashango threw up both hands, realizing the rage in his voice was of a deadly nature. "Where you going with all this? I love you like a brother, man, and I ain't never gave off no negative energy that would even hint that I'm jealous of you, Rah. Man, in prison we was fam, we fought side by side. When them Rat Hunters stepped to you, I held you down. I took hits for you and everything. I even risked catching a life bid when I cut that nigga's Dario Montero's throat when you needed me to put that work in. I was always there for you. Always was and always will be, man."

Rasheen's stare now landed on Camila. His head started nodding again. "Haven't I always taken care of business with you, Camila?"

Camila was stumped; she didn't know where he was going with all this, but she was certain he was up to something. Whenever he engaged in vague questioning, he was always setting traps. She decided to play her cards wisely by proffering the least amount of info as possible. "Yes, you have Rasheen."

"So why is it that you can't trust me when I tell you everything's gonna be alright when we pull out of the game?" Rasheen felt the compulsion to put a few hot ones in her conniving ass, since her over-ambitious desire to stay in the game could be linked to all the hell they were now going through. "I wanted to get out the game before this shit swallowed us all up, but you didn't want that! That was too good for you, huh? Now the fuckin' game got us all by the balls."

"What're you talkin' about!?" She was genuinely confused, since he was talking in riddles. "I told you I'd go with you to Cuba or anywhere else. I—"

"That's what this shit is all about! This shit with you and this nigga! You can't leave the game! The greed got your silly ass all fucked out!"

"Where you going with this, Rah?" Camila saw him reach in his back pocket and pulled out a plastic bag containing a CD and mini-cassette tapes.

Camila and Rashango look at the items in Rasheen's hand as if it was a bomb about to explode.

"That DVD player working!?" Rasheen shouted and nearly gave them both a heart attack.

"Yeah, it's working!" Camila blurred out.

"Camila, take the CD in this bag and play it." Rasheen tossed the bag on the table. "And if I have to repeat myself one mo' mufuckin' time, shit is gonna get real crazy up in this piece."

Camila sprung to her feet, snatched up the bag, rushed to the DVD player, inserted the disk, activated all appropriate dials and wondered where the fuck was Rasheen going with this.

When Camila and Rashango saw images of themselves popped on the TV screen, fucking up a storm, both of their eyes nearly rolled from their sockets.

Camila sat down as she literally saw her life flashed before her eyes. She started crying. Her weeping rose in crescendo fashion.

Rashango started nervously rocking back and forth; he bowed his head in shame, fear and anger. He was grabbing at any and all ideas of how he could wiggle out of this predicament, but everything that came to mind made absolutely no sense at all. There was no way around this one that voice in the back of his mind told him.

"Look at the fuckin' TV!" Rasheen shouted. "We gonna sit here and watch the whole motherfuckin' tape. After that we're gonna listen to all the cassette tapes. I thought y'all wasn't fuckin'? That looks like a whole lot of fuckin' going on to me!"

When the tape ended, the silence was penetrating.

After they listened to the cassette tapes the same silence was still present.

Rasheen sat staring at the two; they couldn't look him in the eyes and rightfully so. He compelled his mind to look at the broader aspects of this situation; the reality of life in the hood, and the warped mentality that it bred, started becoming clearer to him. He suddenly felt like philosophizing and went with the feeling. "You know something, I'm finally startin' to understand this shit."

Rasheen scratched his chin with the hand holding the gun. "I always used to hear people say the most dangerous thing to black folk is other black folk. You probably heard mad people say that shit before, didn't you? They would say shit like, 'the most dangerous thing to us is us', but you know how it is when you hear shit and think you understand it, but you really don't, because your experiences are way too limited to truly grasp the essence of such a profound quote. You know what I'm talking about, don't you?"

Rashango wiped away the river of sweat from his forehead. "Yeah, son. I know what you talkin' 'bout."

"Another thing I used to hear, and used to agree with, actually, was how we would beef, bitch, and complain about how most black folk would make it out of the Hood and never come back to the Hood to help the unfortunate ones trapped in that hell. During that time, I never even looked at the fact that we was laying in the cut waiting to get at one of them when they had something we didn't have, and wanted. It never even dawned on me; we was the ones running them peoples away from us."

The silence grew and Rasheen banged on the table when he noticed Camila was too deep in her trance. The gesture nearly scared the two out of their minds.

Rasheen continued. "Finally, I'm startin' to see why a sane person would get the fuck outta the hood and not look back. It's sad to say this shit, but it's a fuckin' realty. Until we as a people find a cure to our crab in the barrel syndrome, a disease that's destined to keep us in this perpetual state of self-imposed hell, we gonna continue fuckin' over each other, killing each other, robbing each other, keeping each other down, and basically enslaving ourselves. The fucked-up thing is that this shit ain't a new phenomenon. You can bet yo' ass we didn't get here without the hand of a fellow black man, cause you can also bet yo' black ass them crackers didn't go inside the interior of Africa to catch slaves."

The silence returned and everyone rode it like rodeo cowboys on a broken stallion.

Rasheen sighed, "Rashango, you remember when we used to go to those NAACP Cultural Awareness Classes in Sing Sing on Saturday mornings, and how we used to talk about this crab in the barrel shit and how black folks had to first learn how to develop trust and love for one another? You remember them classes?"

Rashango looked up with trembling eyes.

"You remember that!? Rasheen said sternly and saw this little mind-torturing tactic was working just fine. "Tell me some of things you used to say about this topic?" He paused ever so slightly, and then said with pure venom. "Don't make me ask twice."

Rashango swallowed hard. "I—-I used to say we gotta stop fuckin' over other black folk that are tryin' to help."

"That's right! And you used to always say we should stop blaming this self-hatred and this compulsion to keep each other down on slavery. I even remember that time when you and Brother Blood argued for three classes about this issue. Blood was saying our crab mentality was effects of slavery and white supremacist tactics designed to keep us economical deprived, and at each other throats, while you held the position that it was improper upbringing, misguided morals and principles, and a lack of identity. You remember that, don't you?"

Rashango nodded, wondering why he was bringing up all this shit. He was about to wig out on Rasheen and tell him to do whatever the fuck he was going to do, but he was afraid of dying. Instead, he buckled down his emotions and decided to ride out the wave.

"What would you call what you just did to me?"

There was a heavy silence.

Rasheen continued. "When you stepped foot out of prison, I clothed you, put money in your pocket, put a roof over your head, put you down with my team, and gave you the chance to make million-dollar money, and didn't ask for a single penny in return.

And not to my surprise, you didn't even have the decency to even offer to repay me, not that I would've taken it, but the gesture on your part would've said a whole lot about keeping it real. You about as crabby as a crab in the barrel can get, you know that, Rashango."

Rashango suddenly felt his throat was dry and reached for the glass of Hennessey, causing Rasheen to take aim. "Pardon me, Rasheen. I need a drink." He sipped the drink, realizing even if he had a backup gun, it wouldn't have matter, since Rasheen was definitely on point.

"You's a fuckin' King Crab!" He held the moment of silence, and after a moment he decided it was time to shift gears. "And you Camila, what would you call what you just did?"

She couldn't answer it and wasn't even going to attempt to try.

"Now," Rasheen sighed. "This is the big question." He looked back and forth at the two. "What would be an appropriate punishment?" He nonchalantly took aim at Rashango's left kneecap. "If the shoe was on the other foot, what would you do, Rashango?"

"I would look at all the loyal stuff the person did, and then I would probably—"

SZK! -—URGGHH!

The silence bullet tore at the intended target, causing Rashango to scream explosively as he clutched the kneecap wound.

"You's a god damn liar!" Rasheen said with clenched teeth. He rose slowly with squinted eyes. Through his peripheral vision, he saw Camila was moments from having a coronary. He took aim at Rashango's head.

"Rasheen! Please, man! Don't kill me! I fucked up. I'm sorry, I admit, I got weak! Camila came onto me and I got weak when she—"

"You lying motherfucker!" Camila shouted in terror. "You stepped to me! I would've never got it on with you if you—"

"Shut the fuck up!" Rasheen shouted. "Both of you, don't say another fuckin' word!" His stare hardened as he readjusted his aim; he saw Rashango cowering as he anticipated the blazing hot missiles shredding him to pieces. When he saw Rashango breakdown as the tears leaked from his eyes, he fired a shot to his thigh.

Rashango screamed as Camila's terror grew in leaps and bounds.

Another shot tore at his manhood, which knocked Rashango into a state of speechlessness as he slithered from the chair, breathing hard as the pain numbed his brain. He clutched at his groin with crawled fingers.

Rasheen saw there was no more torture he could squeeze out of this cutthroat creep, and ended it with two shots to Rashango's forehead.

Camila was now on her knees, crying profusely. "Please, Rasheen, don't kill me!" Her boo whooing was full of theatrics. "You know I love you. I've loved you since we was kids, and I will always love you, and you know that, Rasheen. When everybody flipped on you when you did your bid, I was the only one there for you. That's gotta count for something, I gave up seven years of my life holding you down. That's love, Rasheen! Real love!. . ."

As Camila pleaded for her life Rasheen was in deep thought. There was no debating the fact he was furious enough to kill her, but the reality was that he couldn't do that, since he needed her. She loved her son, maybe not as much as he loved Little Rasheen, but she loved him nonetheless. The power of a mother's love was what he needed when he went to get his son back. She could be very useful and therefore this usefulness earned her trifling ass a stay of execution. He suddenly concluded that whether he would kill her would be decided if they survived this effort to rescue their son. Now, it was time to get her psychologically re-balanced. He spoke softly. "Come on, Camila, get up, boo." He gently pulled her up.

When she stood on trembling legs, Rasheen cuddled her in his strong embrace. It was time to get her focused and back on track, and the best way to do that was with love (the same kind of love she transmitted to him: fake love). "I know it was him, Camila. Don't worry, boo, I forgive you."

He pulled her from the embrace, held her at arm's length, and stared into her eyes with an affectionate gaze. "Get yourself together, Camila. It's all right. Don't worry, boo, its okay. I know he was on some cutthroat shit. Pack up all this cheddar; we gotta get our son back."

As Rasheen headed for the DVD player, Camila gave him an evil stare as she wiped away her tears. After years of being with Rasheen, she detected his inner mental workings in the way his eyes locked with hers; the body vibration he gave off was telling her that he was going to kill her after they got their son back, and common sense was telling her she would have to hurry up and find a way to kill him first.

CHAPTER # 27

"Why the hell would you do that without talking to me, first?" Keith said to Aaron as the two sat at a conference table within the Supremetech Security Services (SSS). "We could've used her involvement with these folks to put us in a better position all across the board. I've been trying to get my fuckin' foot in that group for years, and I would've loved to talk to someone who had firsthand knowledge of what goes on behind closed doors with them."

"These people pick and choose who they want in their little click," Aaron said. "I guess we don't fit the criteria, since they never felt compelled to approach any one of us."

Keith was still trying to grasp how Sharon became a part of this secret group that was known to make millions for almost all of its secret members; she was right amongst his ranks, probably spying for them, and that made him wonder. He shook his head, wondering was she a part of this group, simply known as the Syndicate or the Machine, when he was having an affair with her. But what really shocked him was that according to Aaron they were now trying to kill her because she had double crossed them when she orchestrated an inside robbery of one of their clandestine establishments, a robbery that the man they had been hunting for over a year was responsibility for committing. "If you would've come to me, we could've used this information to find a way to get access to Rasheen."

"That's bullshit! In hindsight you're just saying all this." Aaron had reached his feed up level with Keith's bullshit. "You still got feelings for Sharon. Your judgment will always be compromised whenever hard decisions have to be made involving her."

"With this type of evidence proving her hands were involved in the Shooties robbery, I would've never went against you. Let's not forget, you got a personal beef with Sharon. Your hatred towards the woman is a matter of public record, and you've acted on that grudge quite a few times. So basically, anything you say has to be looked at closely. You keep saying I need to let go of the feelings I got for her, but you need to let go of the fact she didn't mean to cause you to lose that supervisor position when she uncovered that evidence while she was working for CIA as a support officer. She was doing her fuckin' job and didn't know you were the source of that information. You need to wipe it on your chest and stop harboring animosity, Aaron. You really need to move on."

"I don't like that woman because she's a fuckin' manipulating bitch! It ain't got shit to do with that rinky-dink hit I took. The bottom line here is, don't flip this thing on me like I made a bad call by not telling you about her involvement with this Machine group before taking action, especially when you know you would've protected her. I bet right now, you're trying to figure out how you can save her ass, if she's not already dead."

Keith felt offended but held his head. "Yeah, Sharon was close to me. But if she's trying to undermine me and putting me in a compromising position or helping an enemy do harm to me, she will be dealt with like anybody else engaged in that type of transgression. But you better watch your back; you threw to the wolves an ex-CIA support agent, highly experienced in watching field agents' backs, who's a master at cleaning up behind these agents, which means she's done a lot of truly dirty work." He sighed almost as if he felt sorry for his partner. "She's not the type you can step to in that way and then turn your back on."

"Well, I'll be more than happy to lock horns with her. Since these people she was in bed with sent their best hitters at her, I doubt I'll ever get the honors of seeing if she's all that they say she is. I should get word tomorrow on her status."

Keith shifted the topic abruptly, realizing they'd be here all night debating this topic back and forth and wouldn't get anywhere. "What's up with that 25 mill?"

"He's gonna kick out every dime of it."

"Beautiful! I do know we better get to him before those Internal Affairs folks do. Phil said one of those agents who visited him was named Dorsette?"

"Yeah. Jessica Dorsette."

"I know her." Keith nodded his head for emphasis, as his memory bank pulled up instances of his contact with this woman. "I was in the academy with this board. She's a bulldog for sure. When this bitch smells blood, she don't let up for nothing, and she can't be bought. I guess it's all good, since this Rasheen thing is finally coming to an end. This exchange is in two days, and I know you got all our troops in place."

"Everything is everything," Aaron smiled. "I got the Colombians ready, the Dominicans also want in, and we're gonna oblige them. Somebody sniped two Dominican bosses in Virginia, and they're assuming it was Rasheen, and they say even if it's not, they're sending some soldiers for the hell of it. Jackhammer Jones is gonna be there too. And most of all, our spy is ready and on standby in case things get too crazy, and if we can't bring him down like we want, our plant will pop him from the blindside. . ."

* ** *

Rasheen sat at the kitchen table in a hotel room in Atlanta Georgia, staring catatonically at the cell phone sitting in the middle of the table. Tomorrow was the big day; he was going to pick up his son and today was the day he would receive the call from the Colombians with instructions on where and when they would meet to make the exchange.

The only thing he knew for certain so far was it would take place in Georgia, which was why he made it his business to be in this State beforehand, so he would have a chance to at least steal a peek at the location in advance.

Camila was in the bedroom taking a nap while the other members of his crew (Willie, Ja-King and Tania) were in unspecified locations that were kept secret at the behest of Rasheen; he decided that after he received the location of the exchange, he would contact the others, and they would meet up at a designated area to be announced. Ever since the last time he was shot, Rasheen noticed he'd been making very good on his vow to always take special precautions, and to put in place all sorts of safety approaches that would make it very difficult for an insider to pull off a successful hit. Since he was the master of inside jobs, he didn't need to be stung to know it was better to be safe than sorry. In any event, 25 million dollars was simply too much money for Rasheen to even trust his own crew, and since this money could save the life of his son, even more substantial precautions had to be taken.

Rasheen went to the refrigerator, retrieved a Vanilla health drink, returned to the kitchen, took a seat, sipped on his drink and allowed his mind to resume its activities. There were so many issues bombarding his mind all at once that Rasheen hoped his brain didn't undergo a massive burnout before he got his son back. He was forcing himself to believe that the only outcome would be him getting his son back, but reality was constantly reminding him that this could end really bad; he and his entire crew could be stomped out at the onset, and Little Rasheen murdered along with them. Every time this truly disturbing possibility crossed his mind it shook him deeply, so deeply it rattled his bone marrow all throughout his body.

Rasheen also felt that cringing sensation of dread formulating in the pit of his stomach as he re-evaluated the fact that they were working against David and Goliath odds. His five-man squad was obviously no match for a Colombian hit mob along with Aaron and Keith and whomever else they were bringing along. If his love for his son wasn't beyond the realm of being strong and impenetrable, he would've opted to simply let him go, turn his back, make plans to make another son, and keep it moving.

He even saw the twinkle in Tania's eyes that clearly said it would probably be wise to let them have Little Rasheen, keep the money, break out, save their own lives, and make another child some other day. It sounded like a sensible plan to some extent, but the thought of turning his back on an innocent child that wouldn't have been in this situation, if he didn't have parents living on the wild side of life, touched him way down in places that made it impossible for him to cut and run from a problem that he created. He would be something far less than a man; he would be something that didn't have a word in any dictionary, in view of its indescribable foulness. It was something he would never become, and he was willing to give his life to avoid becoming this indescribable thing.

He instantly stopped this negative thought process by shouting inwardly, *I'm gonna be victorious! There is no other way!* The thought of Little Rasheen not coming out of this in one piece was too much to even fathom.

But the hard and painful realty was that victory was not guaranteed. His nervous anxiety was at a mind crippling level for both good and bad reasons. The most stressful good reason was that this was the phone call they promised to finally let him talk to his son and hear his baby talk. It wasn't much his three-year-old son could say to him but as long as he could talk to him and hear any response it would be enough to at least give him the surge of energy and motivation he needed to catapult him to the doorstep of victory.

Another issue on his mind was the crazy call he got from Sharon. She was in trouble, and sounded as though she was injured. He wanted to come to her aide, but she refused to allow him, claiming she'd meet up with him soon. She insisted she'd call again, so he was waiting for that phone call as well.

Rasheen chugged down his drink and was about to go get another one when the phone rang.

To his surprise, Rasheen noticed he suddenly started trembling with an uncontrollable nervousness. He turned his head in the direction of the bedroom, "Camila! We got the call."

Within seconds Camila was standing before him with hopeful eyes.

Rasheen reached for the phone in slow motion with a slightly trembling hand, grabbed it, and flipped it open. He listened and could hear a child's voice in the background. A joy engulfed him. "Yeah, Rasheen speaking."

"Here are the instructions." A deep Latino male voice said. "You will meet us in Cascade Heights tomorrow night at 2 o clock in the morning. Find a hotel in that county, and we'll contact you again."

"Hold up, man," Rasheen saw disaster coming his way. "Where's the drop off and pick up. I got your money, man. Where's the exact location?"

"You no need exact location yet. You will get tomorrow. Tomorrow, one hour before 2 o'clock you will be told of the exact place."

Rasheen instantly saw they were playing some serious hardball. This was a smooth tactic, because it prevented him from going to the drop off and pick up site beforehand. He wasn't in a position to demand anything and so he moved on to the next phase. "Where's my son? Put him on the phone."

On the other end, the fat Colombian scooped Little Rasheen up, who was sitting next to him, and put the phone to the child's ear and mouth. "Talk my little friend."

Rasheen heard the man's voice in the background and said. "Rasheen, that you?"

"Ah, bee! Who you be. They was me."

When Rasheen heard his son's baby talk, a tear exploded from his eyes. "Hey, what's happening, man!?" He lit up with glee and had to fight Camila back by waving off her reaching hands. He held the receiver out of reaching distance and said to Camila. "Give me a minute, damn it!" He flipped the phone back to his ear and heard Rasheen was still talking. "Hey, Rasheen, how they treating you over there?"

"Dadda! Want go home! Dadda!" Little Rasheen said as he remembered his father's voice clearly. "Cer! Cer! They no give cer!"

Rasheen laughed; he saw his son loved his cereal. "You'll get some cereal soon. We gonna get you as much cereal as you wanna eat. I'm coming to get you, buddy. Don't worry; daddy's coming for you. I'ma put your mother on the phone now, okay."

Camila snatched the phone with teary eyes. "Rasheen, baby, it's me, momma! You alright baby!?" She listened to him talk and she broke down completely when she noticed he remembered her voice.

"Momma!" Little Rasheen shrieked happily. "Momma, I want Momma! Where you, momma! They give me hot water!" He suddenly remembered drinking some of Camila's alcohol and let her know these new people were giving him the same hot water. "Hurt tummy, momma!"

Camila nearly freaked out. "They gave you hot water!?" She remembered that was what he called alcohol. The time she caught him sneaking a sip of her drink, she recalled he named it "hot water". "When they gave you hot water, Rasheen?" As Little Rasheen talked, she cupped the phone to her chest and said to Rasheen. "They giving him alcohol!" She spoke back into the phone. "Rasheen, baby, tell—"

"Put man back on phone." The Columbian said.

"Listen, you motherfucker!" Camila said furiously. "Y'all niggas better not be giving my son no fuckin' liquor! What kinda of people are you—"

"He so bad, he needed stiff drink to stop him driving us crazy!" He laughed, causing a cacophony of laughter from the other men in the room.

Rasheen snatched the phone from Camila. "The deal was you take care of my son, and you'll get your money." He knew they had to be easy, since these creeps still had the upper hand, and Camila was bound to let her emotions create more problems. "Please, man, take care of my son—"

"You'll be hearing from us tomorrow." The Colombian hung up the phone.

Rasheen sat the phone down as the gravity of the situation sunk in completely. He gave Camila the look that said, he needed to be left alone, and she headed back to the bedroom.

Rasheen sat down with a lethargic energy that said he was sick and tired of being sick and tired. How was he going to plan an effective approach around this dilemma!? Without knowing beforehand how the area looked, it would be impossible to devise an effective plan that would enable him to maneuver successfully.

It took only minutes for Rasheen to realize that he was, in essence, walking into a death trap.

CHAPTER # 28

Aaron got out of the driver side of the black GMC step van as Keith exited the passenger side and Jackhammer Jones got out from the back with Little Rasheen in his arms. The van was parked on the northern side of a recently shut down food processing plant that had two huge tanks on its grounds; one of the tanks was located on the eastern section and the other on the western section. From miles away the shadowy moonlight glistening off these two giant tanks made these monolithic edifices look like two steel plated monsters watching over the entire complex.

As Aaron led the way towards the outer fence of the compound, a few dozen yards way, he pulled his cell phone and flipped it open. Keith, Jackhammer and Little Rasheen followed him as he spoke. "I'm on my way inside. I need everybody on deck for last minute talks . . ."

On all four corners of the compound men were approaching the factory like buildings after receiving Aaron's call. On the eastern side, near a tank, eight heavily armed Columbians approached the compound. On the western side, nine Dominicans dressed in casual attire with military weaponry approached. In the southern section, six more Columbians headed towards the abandoned food processing plant.

On the outskirts of all four sections a sniper with the best sharpshooter rifles money could buy were covertly positioned within the woodland area that encased the entire compound.

Aaron entered the warehouse section and saw everything was as it was when he had visited this place four days ago to determine if it would be a suitable place to deal with the pain in his ass that had turned into the worse headache of his entire career. He would've never image one single thug from the heart of Bedstuy could've cause so much havoc, the utilization of so much time and so much money.

After Aaron hit the main power switch only to the interior lights, he said to Keith. "How we looking? Good ain't it?" He smiled as he saw Jackhammer Jones walking around the place inspecting the infrastructure as though he was a military man preparing for an invasion. He was also surprised how well he was handling Little Rasheen. Prior to Jackhammer Jones taking responsibility for keeping an eye of him, Rasheen was crying, screaming and spitting on everybody that came near him. Once Jackhammer took him, they hadn't heard a peep from him since.

Keith examined the place. "I thought you said we were going to address this down in the lower level?"

"Yeah, that's where we're gonna deal with this." Aaron said. "I'm talking about this whole set up. Look at it. It's secluded, out of the way of prying eyes, and once we get them down into the bowels of this place, we can kill them all and nobody will know the difference." He really wanted to point out what happened after the Victorville disaster, where he made the fatal mistake of designating the ransom location in an area that wasn't confined, which allowed for too many unpredictable circumstances, was the main reason he chose this location, but that was self-explanatory. "With them having to go down inside this place, it prevents them from bringing in back up, and possibly catching us off guard."

"Like what happened at Victorville?" Keith reminded him. "Yeah, I like the idea of confining them. It gives us total control."

"That's right," Aaron said. "And as long as we control the physical environment, we control the outcome. There's five of them in total. He asked to bring four people along with him; he claims he needed them to help carry all the money, and I obviously saw that as no problem at all."

"I guess they're coming with small to medium size bills," Keith nodded in agreement. "25 million would definitely take four people to carry that much—"

Raul entered with his seven other Columbian comrades; he oversaw the east side team. "Aaron, my friend," His Latino accent was very heavy, almost incomprehensible. "More last-minute talks, we see, no?"

"In this country, there's no such thing as being over-prepared, Raul." Aaron added with a smile.

Teofilo entered with his eight casually dressed honchos on his heels. He was from the western section, and his Dominican accent was not very different from the Columbians, as far as Aaron was concerned. "We are ready to go. We must say it again; the only thing we ask is that one of us," He gestured at his men, "Must take part in killing this man, who killed our boss. This is non-negotiable, and—"

"I know, I know," Aaron said almost irritated, since they asked this same shit about ten times already as if he didn't hear him the first nine times he asked. "I told you; you don't have to worry about that. Your men can stay close to me. All I ask is that you do nothing until I say so. Once I give the word, you can do whatever you choose, and whatever you like; are we clear?"

"Yes, yes," Teofilo smiled. "We are very clear." He gave him that stare because he decided if things didn't feel right, he was going to let his heart and gut instincts guide the way he responded. No Yankee boy was going to tell him what to do and how to handle Dominican business.

After the six Colombians from the southern section entered Aaron and Keith gave their final instructions to the groups. Upon completion of this five-minute talk, they all headed to their designated hiding places.

As Aaron proceeded down a dark, moldy, smelly staircase that had rats and all sorts of other rodents running around rampantly, he looked at his watch and realized there were fifteen minutes to go before they were scheduled to make the call to Rasheen. Aaron decided to disregard this minor time difference; once he, Keith,

Jackhammer, Little Rasheen and the Dominicans reached the bottom of the staircase, Aaron called Raul and told him to make the call to Rasheen, and let him know they were ready for him to come to this food processing plant to pick up his son in exchange for the money (and a long awaited death sentence).

* ** *

Rasheen was in the passenger seat of the black Dodge van watching the huge tanks draw closer. Willie was behind the steering wheel cruising towards the old food processing plant as Ja-King, Camila and Tania were in the back compartment, listening to 50 cent's rap song, Get Rich or Die Trying humming softly through the van's speakers. Everyone except Rasheen and Willie were rocking their heads and bodies ever so lightly to the hard-hitting beat, and if Rasheen had it his way he would've played Lameek's rap songs all night; they had been playing Lameek's rap songs so long, back to back that everybody agreed it was time to change it up some. With the exception of Willie all four of them were wearing backpacks that were stuffed with money, adding up to 25 million, give or take a few thousand short.

Ja-King was smoking a Newport cigarette and had everyone (except Tania) ready to jump down his throat in light of the irritating secondhand smoke they were being forced to breath.

"I still don't like this shit, Rasheen." Willie said nervously. "They want us to enter from the front and park right there in the front. This shit is crazy, man. They asking us to turn ourselves into sitting ducks—"

"Yeah, it's crazy," Rasheen agreed. "And like I said, I don't want no bullshit out of nobody, until I get hold of my son. We follow the instructions down to the last letter."

Ja-King overheard the exchange and decided to add his two-cent. "I was thinking a few of us could bale out before we get there, and come up—"

"What part y'all don't understand?" Rasheen said, restraining the hostile and angry energy bursting at the seams. "They said if we don't follow their instructions, they'd kill Little Rah. We can't step to it like that anyway; each one of us is carrying a part of the money; so, we gotta stick together."

Rasheen gazed at the compound that was now only a few minutes away, and his mind went into combat mode. Everything had to be played by ear and split-second decisions would be the nature of everything they did. The only thing that gave Rasheen some sense of comfort was the fact he required everyone on the team to wear double layers of body-armored clothing. Even the black hoodies they wore were bulletproofed, which meant the upper part of their bodies was covered with triple layered protection. Although an armor-piercing bullet would render all this bullet-proof attire a complete waste, he convinced himself that any protection was better than none.

He also found some degree of comfort in the fact that they each had two handguns, a mini-Uzi, over a dozen extra clips, and all their bullets were armor-plated. In fact, they were so heavily weighted down it took a lot of energy just moving with these materials on their backs and in their possession. Then, the odds they were up against circulated in his mind once again, and that voice of pessimism reassured him that he was walking into a situation where he was about to confront an army of mass murderers. He had to keep forcing himself to think positive. *Think positive! Think victory! If I conceive it I will achieve it!* But there was something else he was feeling that was making him very nervous. It was some sort of innate voice that was trying to tell him something, but he couldn't or didn't know how to comprehend it.

When the van reached the front, and slowly approached a warehouse looking building, they saw the entire compound looked dark, ugly and foreboding. The place reminded Rasheen of that old scary movie where a psychotic child killer with knives for fingernails, would visit these helpless children in their dreams and kill them. Just looking at this place gave Rasheen and the others the willies as they exited the van.

Rasheen did a rapid scan of the immediate surroundings and didn't like what he was seeing and feeling. That sensation one gets when they were certain they were being watch was creeping all over Rasheen's intuition. He went to the driver side of the van and said to Willie, whose job on this run was to stay behind the wheel, "Keep the engine running, we'll be in and out here, bet that."

Rasheen stared at the trees circling the perimeter of this huge factory, looking for the snipers he knew were somewhere out there. He wasn't worried about them picking them off at the moment, since they still had the money, but common sense told him it was a bad idea to have Willie sitting here when they exited. It took seconds to decide what had to be done.

Rasheen whispered to Willie. "Yo' check this out, in 15 minutes move over there." He nodded his head westward. "You right, man, we can't allow ourselves to be sitting ducks. Fuck it, we gotta chance it."

Willie smiled; the relief on his face was unquestionable. "I gotcha!"

Rasheen reached through the window and squeezed his friend's shoulder, hoping they would see each other again, and that they both made it out of this alive. "Once again, thanks for holdin' me down, Willie. See you soon, big Papa."

With weapons in the full ready position, Rasheen led his crew inside the warehouse area. Once inside they noticed the dimly lit lights emitted a dreary glow that was consistent with the gloomy outer structure. Even the mildew mixed with other rotting smells in the air broadcast the dilapidated nature of this once flourishing food factory.

The sounds of squealing rats could be heard nearby, which had Camila on edge; she was terrified of rats.

Rasheen remembered the instructions the Latino man told, once he entered this building, and Rasheen stepped straight to business.

Camila had both 9-mms in her hands and her eyes seemed more peeled for the rats than anything else.

Ja-King's nervousness was so clear it resonated through the air. In one hand he had a mini-Uzi with a long clip (two clips were taped together for swift reloading purposes); in the other hand he had a standard 9-mm.

Tania was smiling crazily as though she was having a good time. She was still just as bubbly as she wanted to be even though she understood she was walking to a very deadly situation. With two 9-mms in her hands, she was the last person in the line and allowed her eyes to stay in constant motion for anything that would get this show started.

* ** *

Aaron stood near a rusty vat, while the others were scattered about, when his cell phone buzzed, and he answered it. "Yeah, what's up?"

Co-Co, the sniper positioned in the western section, said with a Latino accent. "The guy in the van is driving away." He was in a tree looking through a set of binocular as he watched the van moving slowly. "What'd you want me to do?"

Aaron screwed up his face infuriately. *These hardheaded ass niggers don't know how to follow instructions? Apparent they think this shit is a game.* "Kill him. Didn't we say if they disobeyed our instructions, we would kill them?"

"You said to call you before we do anything," Co-Co said with an attitude as he started repositioning his sniper rifle. He hated the arrogant way most Americans talked to people from his country. "I'm about to take him down. Talk to you later."

Co-Co closed the flip phone, pocketed it, planted his eye to the scope and saw the van had parked near a parking lot. He wondered why he moved there. What the hell was this guy up to? As he placed Willie's head in his sights, Co-Co heard a noise behind him and frantically turned his head to see the source of the noise. Squinting his eyes he could've sworn he saw a dark shadow move in a hasty fashion about ten yards away. He continued examining the area he thought he saw movement.

A moment later, Co-Co explained away the noise as a deer or other wild animal, scurrying about, and took aim again. He smiled when he saw this was going to be one of his best shots ever, and if the Rifle's Association could document this one, he was certain he would win a sharpshooter's award. With this thought in mind, Co-Co pulled the trigger.

About three hundred yards away, Willie's head snapped violently as the bullet cut through the window on the driver's side. Blood and gray brain matter was spattered all over the interior of the van. Luckily for Willie he didn't know what hit him, since his death was instantaneous.

The last thought going through Willie's mind upon impact was how was he going to finally take a much-needed vacation. He was thinking, maybe somewhere in the Caribbean Islands or Hawaii.

About a minute after C-Co fired the bullseye shot, another shot rang out.

The last thing Co-Co remembered was the awesome blow to the back of his head, and the sudden falling sensation as he tumbled lifelessly from the high tree branch. By the time he hit the ground, his heart was still beating, but his brain had stopped functioning due to the gruesome head wound in the form of a small entry hole in the back of his skull, while the exit hole had disintegrated 50% of Co-Co's face. Just like Willie he died instantaneously.

CHAPTER # 29

Rasheen and the others moved down the same staircase Aaron and his team had descended about an hour ago.

Rasheen felt the air was becoming cold, stale and almost unbreathable; the rotting odors along with the airborne molds did much more than make matters worse. With the nervousness and fear of failure adding to the problem, Rasheen saw it was a miracle he was able to appear completely decisive and confident. He was moving strictly off of raw emotions and an iron will to save his son.

After they slid across an empty hall that used to be the Administrative Department, Rasheen led the way inside another stairwell leading further down into the bowels of the building. When they completed the first flight, they slowed their pace considerably as they eased down the next flight; this was the final flight before entering the section where the exchange would occur, and it apparently would mark the beginning of the drama of all dramas.

Suddenly, a noise came from upstairs.

Rasheen and the others stopped in mid-stride while everyone took aim in an upward fashion with flinching speed. Standing in the middle of the flight of stairs, they listened closely, heard the muffled footsteps, and knew they were being boxed in.

After a moment Rasheen continued, and when he reached the bottom of the stairs, he peeked around the corner and saw a huge room with all sorts of industrial machinery scattered in various places, while on the side of the walls that went two flights upwards there were catwalks that were apparently connected to the upper levels they had just came from. The sight instantly reminded Rasheen of a prison cellblock, but the only difference between the two was that the tiers in this place were circular instead of straight.

Rasheen saw movement and pull away from the corner.

"How it looks out there?" Camila whispered as Rasheen moved to the side and allowed her to look for herself.

When Camila was finished, Ja-King and Tania got a look at the area.

Rasheen stepped back to the corner and knew what was to come next. He shouted. "Yo! I'm here! I got your fuckin' money!"

His voice reverberated across the hall, the sound echoing as it bounced off the dust and spider web covered walls and machinery.

"Rasheen," Aaron shouted back from the other end of the hall, his voice echoing in the same fashion. "We got your son. We got another surprise for you. You remember my voice?"

Rasheen wanted to tell him, he wasn't born yesterday, and that he'd suspected his grimy ass was behind this the moment the Columbians' name came up. But, instead, he played alone. "No, I don't remember the voice. Who the fuck is that?"

"The person you embarrassed during that incident in Victorville. The guy who has your son; the same guy who did the same thing to your brother, Lameek. Should I continue?"

"No, you don't. I know who the fuck you are! I don't remember your name, but what you did is enough for me to know who you are."

"The names Aaron Wilson. Special Agent Aaron Wilson."

"Now that we got the intros out of the way, can we get on with this?"

Aaron waved Keith over. "Not yet, we got one more intro." He gestured for Keith to speak.

"What's up, Rasheen?" Keith said. "I heard what happened to our homie Jack-Mack. That was very unfortunate, huh?"

"That you, Keith?" Rasheen knew this clown would be here, of course, but for the sake of maintaining Sharon's cover, he continued to pretend. "What the fuck is all this sap-rap about? What y'all two slim bucket motherfuckers doing together? By the way, Keith, whatever happened to the Security Company? You took me and

Jack-Mack's money, and we ain't hear from you since. I still want my share of the profits you promised."

Keith laughed vibrantly. "If you haven't figured it out by now, then you're not the person I thought you were."

Rasheen continued. "Where's the Colombians? I thought this was a beef between me and them. Why y'all coming at me like this anyway?"

Aaron and Keith looked at each other with surprised expressions. His tone genuinely indicated that Sharon hadn't put him on point about them.

Keith whispered, "You think he really don't know? Sounds like Sharon wasn't feeding him information after all."

Aaron gave him a twisted facial expression that said he wasn't buying it. He shrugged his shoulders, realizing it didn't matter anyway, since he was going to die no matter what happened. "You got the money, Rasheen?"

"You got my son?"

There was a moment of silence as Aaron waved to Jackhammer, who brought Little Rasheen to him. When Jackhammer tried to give him to Aaron, Little Rasheen started crying while belligerently refusing to go to him.

When Rasheen and Camila heard his cries, they became very agitated; their responses displayed a mixture of glee, fear and anxiousness.

Rasheen shouted. "Let's get this shit over with, Aaron!"

Aaron roughly grabbed Little Rasheen by his collar, and Jackhammer grabbed his hand. Aaron looked into Jackhammer's eyes and saw something that made him realize he had better find a quick way to kill this man, because he had apparently become emotionally attached to this kid.

Jackhammer said in a deathly tone, "Let me handle the kid. Ain't no need to get abusive." He scooped Rasheen in his arms, and he instantly stopped crying.

Aaron sighed as he forced himself to pull away from the staring match with Jackhammer Jones. He waved to Teofilo, informing him it was time to start the show. Just before he was about to shout to Rasheen, he realized this situation with Jackhammer was much more serious than he initially thought it would be. He was planning to make the exchange and turn these Columbians and Dominicans loose. With Jackhammer letting it be known he didn't want to see the kid hurt, this meant there was a serious problem hovering on the horizon. He figured if he gave himself a few more seconds to think about the issue a solution would come to mind.

* ** *

Meanwhile, Tito, the sniper on eastern side of the complex, was becoming agitated by the fact Co-Co, who was on the west side of the compound, didn't respond when he called him to find out what those shots coming from his area were all about. Tito had also called the other snipers and none of them knew what was going on. They were about to called Raul, but Jose and Eduardo suggested that they go check it out first, remembering how violently Raul reacted to false alarms, and they assigned Tito to leave his position to do a visual check.

Tito climbed down from his hiding place in the tree and moved covertly towards the west side of the complex. His eyes and ears were on full alert and so far he neither saw, nor heard anything unusual. When he turned the corner, he saw the van the targets arrived in and headed towards it. A few minutes later he was upon the van and peered inside; he saw a dead black man with his brains blown all over the insides, and knew something had gone wrong. Co-Co wasn't supposed to start shooting until after the others exited or if they had brought in a covert crew.

Tito started looking around nervously, and then locked his eyes on the area where Co-Co was supposed to be. Just as he rose his hand as though to get Co-Co's attention, a bullet fired from a silenced weapon struck him square in the chest. A crimson cloud exploded into the atmosphere. The impact of the bullet spun him in a circle as he collapsed to the pavement.

When he was down two more shots pounded his body. One of the bullets entered his jaw and came out the back of his head just below the ear; the bullet lodged itself in the concrete, while the other bullet struck him in the neck.

* *** *

Aaron realized there was no simple, swift solution to this potential problem with Jackhammer. When he realized the Dominicans were now in place and were fidgeting impatiently, Aaron forced himself to keep the ball rolling. "Rasheen, this is how we're gonna do this. You and someone else will bring the money to the center of the room, and me, Keith, and two other men will bring your son to this section. If you look closely there's an aluminum desk right in the center. After we check the bags, we make the exchange; we take the money, you take your son."

"And what happens after that?" Rasheen shouted back. "How do we start the next chapter of this drama?"

Aaron laughed. "Hey, all I can say is once we complete our transaction my part in this show is over."

Rasheen grinned inwardly; he was going love hitting them with his contingency tactic. "Okay, let's do this," Rasheen waved for Camila to come along, and she stepped forth ready to go.

Ja-King and Tania flipped their backpacks off their backs and Rasheen and Camila snatched them up.

Aaron waved to Jackhammer, who whispered in Little Rasheen's ear, and put the child down.

Keith gently grabbed the toddler's hand as he headed towards Aaron.

Aaron waved to Raul, who stepped up along with one of his soldiers.

Aaron approached the center of the hall as the others followed. He reflected on the Jackhammer issue and was hurled into a state of discomfort by Jackhammer's magical handling of the child. He caressed the handle of his 9-mm tucked in his waist, wondering if he pulled the weapon in gunslinger's fashion, spun around and shot Jackhammer would this undermine the success of this mission. When he realized the Dominicans were already itching to start shooting, he knew if he took this course of action this whole thing would end badly. He decided to wait until he had the money in his hands and was out of Rasheen's shooting zone.

Aaron was walking along side of Keith, who was holding Rasheen's hand, as the two Dominicans were behind them. The group weaved around the machinery, heading towards the table.

With a backpack in his hand, Rasheen saw the desk and then Aaron, Keith and his son, and two Latino men. A burst of mixed emotions almost unhinged him, but he held them in check. He saw Camila didn't put any shade on her emotions as her pace increased; she was about to run to Little Rasheen, but he gestured to her to stay focused.

Moments later, Rasheen and Camila arrived at the table and sat the two packs in their hands on the table. As Rasheen took off the pack on his back, he saw through his peripheral vision Camila was doing the same.

Rasheen and Camila both had their eyes glued on their son, who was now standing several feet behind Aaron, flanked by the two Latino men.

"So far so good," Aaron said as he moved slowly towards the desk while checking the tiers overhead. When he reached the desk, he started inspecting the bags with a smile.

When little Rasheen noticed the familiar faces, he went wild. "Dadda! Mamma!" He tried to run to them, but Keith and Raul held him in place. "Momma! I want momma!"

Rasheen saw things were about to spiral out of control as Camila pulled her gun, causing Aaron and the others to pull theirs. "Easy! Everybody maintain!" He spoke softly to his son. "Rasheen, take it easy. Relax, little man, relax. It's gonna be alright, daddy's here."

Little Rasheen stopped thrashing but was still making it known that he wanted his parents.

Aaron spoke calmly. "Let's put the weapons away slowly." He tucked his weapon when Camila tucked hers. "Open the bags. Unzip all the bags, and step away."

Rasheen nodded to Camila to unzip the bags, and she obeyed. His eyes were locked on the men and saw Keith and the others were getting very loose with the way they were grandstanding with their weapons they didn't put away as Aaron had instructed. He instantly saw it was now time to unveil his contingency tactic. He pulled a remote control from his pocket and held it high for all to see. "I think you oughta know I'm walking out of here alive, or nobody else will." He unzipped his black hoodie displaying a belt filled with huge sticks of C4. "Since you's a fed, I'm sure you know what this is."

Aaron couldn't control how his terrified eyes and bodily gestures reacted.

Keith almost lost it totally, while Raul and his sidekick were even more terrified than Camila.

Rasheen savored the fear pulsating from everyone. "If me, my son, and the people who came here with me, don't make it out of here, I'll give you my word is bond, nobody else will. This is enough plastic explosive to blow up at least two buildings the size of this one, so I promise you, you can't outrun the blast. Now, go on and check your money. When you finish, I'll get my son and go about my business."

As Rasheen watched Aaron and Keith searching through the backpacks with trembling hands, he was literally praying to God no one called his bluff, because if they did they would discover that the C4 strapped to him was about as explosive as a carton of orange juice opened after being shaken thoroughly.

* ** *

On the Southside outskirts of the food processing plant, Jose was on his cell phone talking to Eduardo on the northern region. His adrenaline was boiling. "Something's wrong. It's got to be!" Jose was looking around the immediate area; he was no longer in his sniper's hiding place and stood at the base of the tree he'd just climbed down from. "Tito would never ignore his phone. He's not answering because he is down!" He nodded his head as Eduardo made a suggestion. "Good! That's a good plan!" He continued nodding while looking in all directions at the darkness surrounding him. The only source of light seemed to be the moon, which didn't do much when it came to seeing objects at a distance. "Yes, we'll meet in that area. That is where the problems began."

Jose closed his cell phone and moved silently towards the chain link fence with his rifle ready. Common sense was telling him to call Raul about this communication problem, but he was determined to find out what was the cause of Co-Co and Tito's failure to respond, even if he had to first find the person responsible for killing his comrades. He was certain no one but them were on or around the grounds, and this is what totally had him mentally twisted by all of these unexplained issues.

As Jose stepped onto the blacktop road that circled the complex, he saw a shadow and it looked like it was a person. He took aim but whoever it was had disappeared inside the trees.

Jose flipped open his phone as he moved hastily towards the area he saw the fleeing figure and hit the speed dial button. "Eduardo! I saw someone; somebody's—"

The silenced bullet struck Jose smack dab in the forehead, knocking him off his feet as though he was the victim of a cloth-line wrestling maneuver.

When Jose and the cell phone crashed to the blacktop pavement, Eduardo's voice coming from the cell phone could still be heard as the blood oozed from Jose's grotesque head wound. "Jose! You there, Jose! Say something..."

CHAPTER # 30

"This is the part," Rasheen said sternly. "You send my son to us. You take your money and you tell all the hitters you got all over this piece that if we don't walk out of here alive, this whole motherfucker is going up in flames."

Aaron stared at Rasheen as something much stronger than rage and despair tap-danced on his central nervous system. He couldn't let this motherfucker do this to him. The thought of allowing him to walk out of here after all the hell he went through to kill this one hood dweller was beyond his conceptual reality.

"Let's go!" Rasheen shouted, jarring Aaron out of his daydream and into a state of action.

"Give him the kid!" Aaron said as Raul and his soldier let Little Rasheen go, and the child toddled frantically to Camila. "Everybody grab a bag—"

"Make that call right here and now!" Rasheen said as the bags were being snatched up. "In front of me! Lemme hear it." He waved the remote as a reminder as he saw Camila wisely retreated with Rasheen towards a huge iron cabinet.

Aaron critically examined this situation and suddenly detected something in Rasheen's voice. Even his eyes were wavering. Also, common sense should've told Rasheen that if they wanted to live to spend these 25 million dollars, which obviously was the case, they would make sure those explosives were not detonated. In any event, why did he need to hear and see him send out the order to stand down!?

Something was wrong here. Aaron could feel it in his bones. Then, he looked at this situation on the flip side, and realized he could be seeing what he wanted to see because he wanted to believe this couldn't be happening. But something was genuinely telling him Rasheen was not only not suicidal, but he also wouldn't kill his son, and therefore was probably playing a head game. Those blocks of material on that belt looked like C4, no doubt about it, but there were lots of other materials that could be made to look like plastic explosives.

Before Aaron could monopolize on this possibility, the frantic sound from up above within the tiers told everyone the situation was no longer stable.

Seconds after this noise, a stream of machine gunfire rained down from up above, completely unleashing a powder keg of explosive pandemonium and gunfire-laden chaos. Everyone within the confines of this abandon food-processing plant went into def-con mode in response to the gunfire of the Columbian man who was fed up with all the talking and was unaware of the allege plastic explosives.

At the moment the noise was heard, Rasheen and Camila reached for their weapons just as Aaron, Keith and Raul impulsively reacted to their response. By the time the shots rang out from the tier, Rasheen was in motion heading towards a vat. When the machine gunfire rang out the bullets ricocheted off the vat as Rasheen held down on the trigger of his 9-mm aimed at Aaron and Keith. When he saw a wave of his bullets tear into Keith, a sensation of unadulterated happiness touched his being.

Rasheen felt a sigh of relief when he saw Camila cowering behind an iron box, firing at the man on top of the tier while Little Rasheen was behind her. Since Camila was smart enough to know to take cover the moment Little Rasheen came to her, he knew they were relatively safe from the onslaught of bullets.

At the moment the Columbian man on the tier initiated this explosion of chaos, Jackhammer Jones pulled both of his weapons and began plucking off Dominicans as he raced for cover behind a pile of old machinery parts.

Moments before this pandemonium ignited, Jackhammer Jones' mind was pulling up images of his grandbabies and how Little Rasheen reminded him so much of them. Ever since he came on this job, he'd been pissed off by the fact Aaron didn't tell him he was paying him to get involved in a mission that could result in hurting an innocent child. Then, when he overheard the Dominican men bragging about how they were going to kill them all (including Little Rasheen), something literally snapped inside his mind. His first mind told him to start killing them right then and there, but after taking a few deep breaths, and allowing the rational side of his mind to take control, he knew it would be more advantageous to wait for the right moment. When he heard the gunfire that was all he needed to open the curtain to the first act of this show.

By the time Jackhammer Jones reached the four-foot-tall mountain of junk, he had cut down four of the Dominicans with carefully aimed head shots, but the three remaining men forced him to retreat for cover; he leaped over the pile as they opened fire. The savage blitz of bullets tore at the pile of materials as Jackhammer got in position to return more gunfire.

On the other side of the hall, Ja-King and Tania reacted no different from anyone else when the first wave of machine gunfire rang out. Ja-King rushed inside with his mini-Uzi and a 9-mm spitting fire at the men on the tiers.

Tania, on the other hand, shouted to Ja-King, "I'll cover the stairs." She quickly crept up the stairs they entered; she correctly assumed that the men up there would eventually approach from this location. On tiptoes she eased upward, and within seconds, a door slammed open and rapid footsteps were heard. She couched down, took aim, and the moment she saw the first Columbians, both of her weapons roared like a stirred-up hornet's nest as the bullet ripped, tore and pulverized the four men who were unable to stop their downward descent. They tumbled down the flight of stairs, and when they came to a stop, Tania blessed all four of them with headshots, just in case they wore body armor. Plus, she had a serious faddish for headshots; her infatuation with these sort of gunshot wounds were so overwhelming she often got moist between the legs when she inflicted them.

Tania rushed up the stairs to the next floor, and just when she was about to step through the door, she heard commotion coming from the next flight up. Before she was able to turn, she heard and felt the bullets. Despite the searing pain she spun around with her fingers on both triggers as she hurled herself away from the spot she was positioned. She saw she had dropped one of the two men, while the other was untouched. The pain to her back was hurting with blistering agony. She could tell the bullets hadn't penetrated because of the triple layer bulletproofed fabric, but the pain was out of this world. She just knew one of her ribs was either fractured or a bone was chipped.

Inside the hall, Rasheen saw his bullets had knocked Keith out of the picture and had severely wounded Raul's sidekick.

Aaron had made it to cover and was returning fire. Raul was across from Aaron firing at him, while taking periodic pot shot behind him at something that was going on at the other end of the hall. Who was he shooting at, Rasheen asked inwardly?

Aaron saw this whole situation had spiraled completely out of control. At first he cringed as he expected the whole place to go up in a C4 induced blaze. When that didn't happen, he knew Rasheen was bluffing. As Aaron took shots at Rasheen and Camila, he realized it was time to put his spy to work. He pulled his cell phone and punched in the number.

Rasheen stopped firing and waved to Camila to do the same.

Suddenly, the sound of a cell phone buzzed, and Rasheen heard it was coming from someone in back of him.

Aaron shouted excitedly. "Do it now! Do it right this minute!"

Rasheen peeked around the corner and saw Ja-King approaching with a cell phone to his ear. When he heard Ja-King say, "Alright, alright, I got it! Be easy, man, I'm on it!" and then he disconnected the call, Rasheen instantly made the connection. The realization almost crippled him mentally, emotionally and psychologically.

Just as Rasheen was about to ponder this matter more closely, he heard a sudden frantic movement coming from the tiers up above, and on his far right he saw the men appear. Just as the three men opened fire, so did he. Terror gripped him because he saw the men's location gave them an unobstructed aim at Camila and Rasheen.

As Rasheen fired his 9-mm, he heard Camila scream while returning fire and all the facts and circumstances told him the three-man machine gun attack was inevitably fatal. Rasheen saw he dropped one of the men with a headshot and forced the other two back.

"Camila!" Rasheen screamed in terror. "Rasheen!"

Little Rasheen started crying, but Camila didn't response. Rasheen stole a frantic peek and saw Camila's feet sticking out from behind the cabinet. They were clearly in a position that said she was immobilized; she was laying on her back, down permanently for the count.

"Stay where you're at Rasheen!" Rasheen shouted to his son. "Don't move!"

"Mamma!" Little Rasheen continued crying. "Get up, momma!" He shook his mother as her blood poured from the several bullet wounds. He cried even harder.

Rasheen noticed gunfire was going off all around him, and even noticed Ja-King was firing at the two men on the upper tier the moment they came back into view, about to squeeze off another round of gunfire. He even managed to drop one of them. Rasheen fired at Aaron when he stuck his head out; his shock and confusion with regard to Ja-King and Aaron had him moving in a perplexed and hesitant fashion; he started doubting whether or not he heard the exchange correctly. Maybe it was a coincidence; he subconsciously tried to convince himself.

Several yards away, Jackhammer saw he was locked in a quagmire. They shot at him, he shot back, and they both knew whoever attempted to leave their position of protection from the bullets would become the victim of deadly gunfire.

Suddenly, Rasheen saw his son crawling out from behind the hiding place. His eyes grew wide as he fired at both the upper tier and then at Aaron and Raul. He continued firing as he ran towards his son; a wave of bullets from the upper tier cut Rasheen down, just as Ja-King mowed down the shooter.

Rasheen hit the ground still firing at Aaron as he slid to his son and pulled him back behind the cabinet. He instantly saw Camila had died from a series of armor-piercing bullets to the chest and other fatal wounds to her center mass. He immediately noticed he was bleeding from a bullet wound to the thigh.

Moments earlier, Tania was on the second floor, where the second level tier was located, and she was following the sound of the gunfire. When she reached a corridor like room that lead to the tier overlooking the hall, she looked in and saw the four Columbians. She made certain her min-Uzi and 9-mm were fully loaded, and entered with both weapons spitting armor piercing bullets; all four Colombians dropped, and when Tania was upon their fallen bodies, they each received a carefully planted headshot. She instantly saw she had a bird's eye view of the entire hall below.

When Tania saw Aaron, Raul, and the three Dominicans, she saw she had to select which one she would open fire upon first. She quickly chose Raul, since he was the easiest target and her bullets instantly rained upon him; he was instantly knocked out of the game. Her aim shot to the three Dominicans, and as her bullets gnawed at them, she noticed someone else was apparently shooting at them as well, since the moment the two of them tried to scramble away from her assault, she was certain it wasn't her bullets that had cut them down. By the time she was finished picking off these individuals, she saw Aaron was gone.

Suddenly, she heard the noise behind her and knew she was too late as she spun around with her weapons about to spit fire

BOW! BOW! BOW! BOW! . . .

The two Uzi totting Columbians opened fire on Tania. The vicious power of both weapons combined lifted her up and off her feet and then hurled her over the railing. She hit the floor below with a sickening, bone-shattering force.

Ja-King saw what had happened and was about to open fire but the two men started firing at anything and anybody below. It was almost as if they started shooting well before they reached the railing.

After Rasheen saw Tania fall from the railing, he saw what time it was, and he had to make a very quick decision. He could try to fire at the men up there and risk exposing his son to a fatal bullet wound or he could cover his son with his body and definitely prevent him from being hit. Just as the gunfire started, he made his decision, and threw his body over his son like a huge blanket. The bullets came and Rasheen saw his life flashing before him as the armor piercing bullets sliced through his bulletproofed clothing. When he felt the boiling hot bullets cutting through his body, he knew this time he struck out. This was the third time he was shot, and based on the number of bullets he was currently taking and their locations he knew it was his last.

Jackhammer ran to a huge machine, saw the two firing, took aim and picked both men off with brilliantly instituted chest and headshots.

Jackhammer Jones heard the noise behind him and took off running as he spun and fired, but Aaron clearly had the advantage as he was pumping off shots.

Jackhammer stumbled and fell.

When the brief exchange ended Aaron was clutching his stomach. He raised his hand from the wound and saw he was bleeding. "Shit! Fuckin' armor covered bullets! Ain't this about a bitch!"

Meanwhile, Ja-King walked towards Rasheen in a trance. When he saw the huge pool of blood, and heard a muffled cry coming from underneath Rasheen, Ja-King realized Rasheen had sacrificed himself to save his son. He reached over and rolled Rasheen's bullet-ridden body off his son. The kid's cries became extremely loud as though the door to a soundproof room had suddenly opened; he saw Rasheen Junior was covered in blood and started scrambling to his feet. Ja-King couldn't hold back his tears. *I fucked up! Shit! This was a major fuck up!* He wanted to go into a vicious rant, realizing what he had done had caused this!

Aaron heard Little Rasheen crying and the screams brought him out of his mini-trance, and he limped in the direction of the cries. He saw Ja-King staring down at Rasheen, while the kid was crying over his father's dead body. Aaron sighed with relief as he looked around at the carnage; bodies were all over the place and the scene looked almost as bad as the aftermath of the Victorville fiasco. When he saw Keith's dead body, he couldn't help but feel the pain of this devastating loss. How he was going to explain this to his wife and children was beyond him. His eyes became misty.

After a moment, Aaron pulled himself together and limped over to Ja-King. "Damn, man! You did a damn good job!" He patted him playfully on the shoulder and was a bit disturbed by Ja-King's saddened expression. It seemed as if he was genuinely grieving over Rasheen's death. When he saw the kid was bleeding, he assumed this was the source of all this distress because it would mean they would have to take the kid out of his misery. "That's a shame, the kid is wounded. Since the kid is suffering, and we can't take him to a hospital, we might as well take him out of his misery." He looked over at Ja-King who continued staring at Rasheen.

"Be my guest." Ja-King took a step back, completely out of Aaron's sight.

The moment Aaron raised his arm Ja-King took aim and fired a shot into Aaron's head at pointblank range. The warm blood sprayed the area as Aaron stumbled to the floor like a lifeless rag doll. Ja-King took aim and fire two more times into his head as the tears dripped freely.

Ja-King walked over to Rasheen's corpse, and he noticed Little Rasheen had crawling over to Camila and started shouting, "Get up! Up! Up!" He was shaking her frustratedly.

Ja-King couldn't believe what he had just done. This whole shit didn't work the way he thought it would. His tears burst from his eyes, "Rasheen, man, I'm sorry, I—I—I. . . ." he stuttered tearfully. "I had a plan that could've got us all around this shit—"

A noise stirred from behind him.

Ja-King spun with the 9-mm aimed.

"Easy bro!" Jackhammer Jones had both hands up in the air. "I'm a friend, and I knows you's a friend of mine, if you shot that son of a bitch right there." He pointed to Aaron as he admired the way the headshots had damn near decapitated him. He also admired his good luck since his bulletproof vest easily withstood Aaron's non-armor covered bullets.

Ja-King instantly remembered this guy was responsible for shooting the two men that opened fire on Rasheen from the tier. Where this guy fitted into all this drama was a complete mystery, but he sounded like he could be trusted, and there wasn't no need to make enemies with a fellow last man standing that had beef with the same foe.

"The names Jackhammer Jones," He extended his hand for a shake, and Ja-King took it.

"They call me Ja-King," He saw Jackhammer screwed up his face as though the name rang a bell.

"Oh, shit, you that rapper dude that was on the run!?" Jackhammer moved in closer and began smiling. "It is you. My daughters got posters and shit of you all over their bedrooms. I knew there was something about yo' face, man." He turned his head and saw Little Rasheen who had suddenly started screaming again, and the mood was plunge into a bone chilling sadness.

"I want my dadda!" Little Rasheen wobbled back to his father's body. "Dadda! Up dad! Up dad!"

Jackhammer saw the kid was covered in a lot of blood. "I hope he ain't hit." His concern was at a terror-stricken level.

"No, he's cool. The blood is from his father."

Jackhammer sighed. "Good. It's time we get outta here, Ja-King, don't you think?"

"Yeah, it's time to go," Ja-King looked around at the devastation and realized this was an event that was bound to haunt him for the rest of his life, since he'd constructed a plan that backfired in every sense of the word.

"There's 25 million in them bags," Jackhammer Jones said as though he was testing the waters. "And I guess we can split it up two ways. Rule says last men standing cut the prize evenly."

"You agree to cut it three ways," Ja-King said as he reached down and scooped up Little Rasheen. "And you got yourself a deal."

Jackhammer smiled proudly. "Folks with some good ole fashion down home morals and principles!" He held his clenched fist up to the sky. "Yes! Three ways it is."

It took three minutes to find the four backpacks; Ja-King and Jackhammer Jones flipped on a pack each while Jackhammer carried the other two packs and Ja-King held Little Rasheen in his arms.

As they rushed out of the hall, Little Rasheen cried and screamed, "Momma! Dadda! Come! Come up! No go!"

On the other side of the food processing plant, two Colombians listened closely as they heard the cries and followed those sounds like bloodhounds locked on the scent of a wounded rabbit.

* ** *

Eduardo was a nervous wreck as he sat covertly in a tree in the front of the food plant. He was convinced there was someone else besides them out here, and whoever it was, was not friendly. This fellow sniper was picking them off with remarkable efficiency.

Earlier, he'd found Tito's dead body and the black guy in the van and had even seen a shadowy figure moving about through the lenses of his scope about ten minutes ago. When the slim person dressed in tight fitting dark clothing disappeared into the trees, he returned to the trees as well to follow this person but altered his plans when he received a call from Raul instructing him and the others to cover the front because things had gone wrong on the inside, and they would need some assistance when they exited. As he spoke to his leader, Eduardo could hear massive gunfire as if they were locked in a brutal gun battle.

Suddenly, he saw movement in the trees on his left and he shot his eye to his scope and adjusted his rifle in the direction the movement came from. Seconds later, yards away, in the front of the building, he heard the door slam open, and he swung his aim in that direction.

When he saw the two men, one carrying a kid, and were apparently heading for the van where the dead guy was inside,

Eduardo positioned his aim on the black guy with the bags in both hands. When he zeroed his sights in on the black man's center mass, he pulled the trigger.

A moment after he fired his rifle, a small noise rang out from the direction he saw the movement seconds ago, and almost simultaneously felt the silenced bullet strike him in the shoulder. The impact of the projectile knocked him off balance just enough to cause him to loss his footing and tumble downward. He hit the ground hard and was momentarily dazed.

Earlier, Ja-King had frantically crouched down the second he saw the flash, heard the shot, and saw Jackhammer recoil in pain. When his mind registered the reality that a sniper's bullet had taken Jackhammer down, Ja-King frantically ran for the van with Little Rasheen firmly in his embrace.

"Hurry!" Jackhammer cringed in pain as he held his arm. "Shit!" He couldn't understand why he stayed getting shot and was furious that this particular bullet had hit him in a part of the body not covered by bulletproofed fabric.

About a hundred yards within the confines of a tree, Sharon Walker peered through her sights, searching for the last sniper. Her infrared scope lenses had started malfunctioning right after she plucked off the third sniper, and she was forced to rely on this shooter revealing his whereabouts by firing his weapon. When he fired a shot at the two men exiting the warehouse, she'd finally found him. Although she knew she had hit him and noticed the shot had knocked him out of the tree, she wasn't certain the shot was fatal, and was peering through her scope for another opportunity to finish this guy off.

Suddenly, she saw action emitting from the front of the warehouse. She snapped her aim at the area as she noticed it was Ja-King along with a kid, apparently Little Rasheen, were frantically getting inside the van. Another man was behind them running towards the vehicle.

Suddenly, two Columbians crashed out of the front door, and started firing at the van.

In an instant, Sharon blew the top of one of the man's head clean off with dazzling ease, and swiftly repositioned her aim as the other man started running back towards the building, apparently realizing he was a sitting duck. Just as he was about to rush back inside the front door, the sniper bullet entered the back of his cranium and exited his nasal area, leaving an exit wound the size of an orange. In fact, it looked almost as if the front of his face was missing.

As Sharon watched the van screeched way, the gravity of the outcome became clear.

Rasheen didn't make it.

She noticed Ja-King was one of the survivors and apparently was able to save the kid, which was well worth a sigh of relief, but she was shocked to see one of Aaron's men had obviously flipped sides. She remembered seeing this black man enter the plant with Aaron and Keith when they arrived earlier.

It was also good to know they had that 25 mill in them bags. On the heels of this thought another outcome grew clearer as she saw no one else was leaving this plant.

Aaron and Keith didn't make it either.

Sharon looked in the direction where the last sniper was located and her mind took a stroll down memory lane. She recalled the first time she met Ja-King in person when Rasheen and Jack-Mack brought him to SSS. She could never understand what possessed Rasheen and Jack-Mack to roll on the wild side with a celebrity on the run from the police. She was now even more surprised Ja-King made it out of this thing alive, since he was no harden thug like Rasheen and Jack-Mack, and certainly didn't have that killer instinct. She guessed it wasn't his time.

She sighed as her mind shifted to another issue. With the loss of Rasheen, it was evident she had lost a true friend. She'd lost a very special friend, in fact, and fought back the tears. There was no question Rasheen was like no other thug the hood would ever know. He wasn't just a gifted organizer and a moneymaker of monolithic magnitude, but most of all, he was a man who was filled with love. He sincerely cared about other people, was wise enough to bring his wrath upon those who were technically enemies of the community (drug dealers), and wasn't afraid to step up for the weak, even when the odds were clearly against him. He was a hard lover, as loyal as they came and the most passionate man she'd ever known.

Sharon looked around at the starry skies and realized it was amazing how those who could be perceived as the worse of the worse could in reality be the best of the best. Although she didn't have the opportunity to live with Rasheen for an extended period, she knew men very well and had spent enough time with Rasheen to know the content and true nature of his heart. The way he loved his brother Lameek, his mother, his son, and the people he perceived as a part of his extended family was unique only to those truly in touch with their humanity.

As Sharon Walker climbed from the tree, and concluded her bittersweet mission, while gearing up for another tussle with the Syndicate, she allowed her tears to flow, since Rasheen Smith was going to be deeply missed.

CHAPTER # 31

A year later.

The Judge sat in a lounge chair in the backyard of his multi-million-dollar mansion, watching the seven children playing in the huge diamond shaped, in-ground pool. He was a sixty-seven year old black man with salt and pepper hair, a clean shaved face, a remarkable physique for a senior citizen, and transmitted an aura that told the world he was satisfied with where life had taken him. Dress in a Hawaii shirt and white shorts, the Judge was sipping on an alcohol-free Pina Colada, and was pondering his next move against Phillip Henderson. Things were finally taking a turn for the best, but it was far from over. It was way too early to start pulling out the champagne.

Arlene Whitfield exited the backdoor of the mansion and approached her husband with Ja-King on her heels. "Derrick. He's here." She was a slim, light chocolate complexion woman with a sparkling smile that never let up, who moved with a confidence and gracefulness that revealed her intellectual soundness.

Derrick "The Judge" Whitfield turned in his chair and saw the two approaching. He rose to his feet with a small struggle. "Ja-King! It's a pleasure to see you, man."

"Actually, it's my pleasure, Judge."

The two men shook and hugged each other.

"Thanks Arlene." The Judge said and gave his wife a kiss on the lips, taking full advantage of the opportunity to demonstrate his love for her. Indeed, he was grateful to have a woman fifteen years younger than him who cherished the institution of marriage as a union worthy of the utmost praise and respect. After twelve years of marriage, he wasn't surprised he and Arlene were still going strong, since she loved him for him and not because he was one of the richest and most powerful lawyers in the country with connections to various United States Presidents, Congressman, leaders of Countries all across the globe, and was virtually worshipped by corporate giants. An ex-Federal District Court Judge for the Eastern District of Illinois, Derrick "the Judge" Whitfield could boast of being a man of worldly stature.

The Judge led Ja-King towards the patio section while Arlene returned to the mansion, after instructing the kids to "play nice" when she saw them arguing over who would play with the plastic toy first. As the grandmother of four of the children, and the adopted grandparents of the other three (Rasheen being the newest addition), Arlene prided herself on her expert ability to rear children that eventually became very successful; her and the Judge's son (David) and daughter (Aeisha) were the best evidence of this fact.

Ja-King looked over at the group of kids and saw Little Rasheen. He smiled upon realizing the kid was looking more and more like his father as time ticked on.

The two men took seats and went straight to business.

"I called you over because some things have come up," The Judge said. "I know you're aware Phil is about to be arrested for fraud." He saw Ja-King nod his head. "But what you might not know is, Hoodaroma is going to be up for grabs."

"Up for grabs!? I thought since Little Rasheen is directly related to Lameek, and since Lameek is the son of Killer Kato, and Killer Kato is the true owner of Hoodaroma, and since that contract Phil produced to get ownership of Hoodaroma was a fraud, wouldn't everything automatically go to Rasheen? How is Hoodaroma up for grabs when the only heir to the company is still alive?"

"Phil is no fool, Ja-King." The Judge shifted in his seat. "He's not going to roll over easy. One of the tactics he's now engaged in is instigating litigation to keep us off balance and distracted. I just received notice that Camila Nelson's family has brought a lawsuit, and so has one of Killer Kato's daughters. They're all contesting whether or not Rasheen is the rightfully heir, and they're challenging all the sworn statements of all deceased parties."

Ja-King realized this bad news felt as uncomfortable as a huge slap in the face. His anger was explicit and couldn't be concealed. "So, you're basically telling me, we don't get Hoodaroma?"

"Not right now."

Ja-King's shoulders sagged defeatedly. "All this long-range maneuvering, my risking life, limb and liberty, just to be told that after waiting a whole year this thing could go on for another—what, year or more!?"

"It won't be that long," The Judge said almost with a jolly tone.

"Come one, Judge, you said that last year!" Ja-King felt a wave of stress chemicals pouring into his bloodstream. "All the years of hard work and sacrifice I've put in building Hoodaroma; it's long overdue for us to start reaping some of the fruits of our labor. Without me and Lameek, there was no Hoodaroma, and we never got our just due from Killer Kato and Phil." He was about to go into his usual rant about his stolen royalties, but the Judge had heard it a hundred times already. "Hoodaroma is ours!"

"You're right about that! And those happy days are coming. This time I'm going deep into my treasure chest of strings and other instruments of favor facilitation. And, believe it or not, we're well leveraged; before Rasheen died we videotaped him and Camila giving me custody of Rasheen if something happened to them, we have Lameek's sworn statements, his mother Barbara Smith's affidavits, we got the matching DNA tests proving Lameek, Rasheen and Little Rasheen are family, and most of all, our ultimate secret weapon, Colin Gibson's last will and testament, signed the very night he was killed, confirming that his entire empire would go to Lameek, his son, if anything should happen to him. Hoodaroma will inevitably be in Little Rasheen's control. These little stall tactics are not worth getting your blood pressure up, Ja-King," He smiled, but really wanted to add the remark, not just yet. "You'll never make it to my age, if you continue allowing things like this to get too deeply under your skin."

After hearing the Judge's finally remarks about their secret weapon, Ja-King realized he was overreacting. "You never told me you had Killer Kato's last will and testament giving Lameek control of Hoodaroma. I mean, I knew about Lameek's situation, since when we were both cutting records for Hoodaroma, he told me all about how he had gotten with you and hooked it up to where if something happened to him his money and everything else would go to his family, but this." He whistled rhythmically. "This is off the chain!"

"That's why it's called a secret weapon, AKA the ace in the hole." He wondered should he hit him with the bad news now. After a moment he decided to hold off a bit longer.

Ja-King went into a moment of silence as his mind rewind to his major fuck up. "I just wish I had moved a little quicker when I was at that Food plant. I—I keep asking myself over and over, if I didn't wait so long, and if I had—"

"Stop beatin' yourself up, Ja-King," The Judge said is a fatherly tone. "I told you, trust in the fact that your intentions were good. You were clearing your name and trying to save a friend. Aaron and Keith would've never stopped trying to kill Rasheen. We both know that. And if you had allowed the system to run its course with those murder charges hovering over you at the time, without Aaron's intervention, there's a damn good chance you wouldn't be sitting here today. Yes, things went wrong, it cost Rasheen his life, but it would be grossly unfair to say you, per say, caused his death."

Ja-King looked into the Judge's eyes, and realized this reminder, once again, began to extinguish the pain in his heart.

The Judge continued, "Unless you had a crystal ball, you would've never known they were going to kidnap Rasheen's son, nor could you have anticipated that whole situation spiraling that far out of control. And who's to say, even if you had pulled Rasheen's coat to what you were up to, Aaron and his well-equipped hit team wouldn't have succeeded in killing Rasheen anyway?" He really wanted to point out that he could've approached it a little better, but now wasn't the time to alienate him, since he was going to need him to complete what was started. "Actually, you should consider yourself lucky. You made it out of that scrap alive, you saved Rasheen's son, and you got the money. Believe me, Rasheen would've been proud of you for doing all of that. Believe me."

Ja-King tried to crack a smile, but nothing the Judge said would change the way he felt about his hesitancy regarding this issue. "Yeah, you right, Judge."

"You dag gone right, I'm right," He saw the time was almost ripe to hit him with the bad news, but first he had to soften him up just a tad bit more. "Do you remember the quote I presented to you when I first met you? When you came to me for help when you figured out Killer Kato was scamming you?"

Ja-King went into a deep thought process, but nothing immediately clicked. The Judge had quite a few quotes he used quite frequently. "Man, you got a whole lotta quotes."

"It's the same quote I presented to Lameek when you introduced him to me for the same problems you were experiencing."

It instantly registered. "Oh, yeah, I remember. I don't remember it word for word. You said ah . . . It's up to us to create our own future, or something like that."

"Exactly. Now look at that adage while examining your decision to play on Aaron's warped desire to kill Rasheen."

Ja-King allowed his mind to make the comparison. After a moment, he realized he completely missed the point, and had no problem letting it be known. "No disrespect, but I don't see it."

"It's up to you to create your own future, is the quote. You took charge of your life, came up with a plan, thought it through, took affirmative action, stuck with it, and the end results were bittersweet. Now, let's move on to the next chapter of this drama. The milk is spilled, and there's no need to continue crying over it. I hope you can finally put it away for good."

Ja-King noticed it still didn't make any sense to him, but the part about moving on did make a very lot of sense. "You called me over here to tell me Phil Henderson is about to be arrested, and he's putting batteries in peoples' backs, getting them to file lawsuits. You told me it was a matter of life and death; it was dealing with Little Rasheen." He took a glance at the pool and saw Rasheen hogging the toy from the other kids. *Strong and aggressive, just like his daddy.* "He looks all right to me; these issues don't call for me carrying this around." He flipped open his jacket displaying the Browning 9-mm.

"I'm glad to see you're taking the appropriate precautions." The Judge said, admiring his decision to arm himself. "That's very good. Actually, I like to save bad news for last. I've received word that Phil and his associates have put out a contract on Rasheen."

"What!?"

"That's right. They believe if he disappeared, it could keep Hoodaroma in their hands, and technically they're right. They got key family members in the pocket, so this is about as serious as this thing can get."

"How much is the hit for? The amount always determines the quality of folks we're gonna be up against."

"Yes, money is the master of all motivators. The awesome grip that money has on the human mind is absolutely phenomenal." The Judge felt a ping of anxiety because the price tag on this track was one of the biggest, he'd seen in years. He sighed and said. "We're gonna be up against the best of the best. They're dishing out a half million dollars."

"Jesus Christ!" Ja-King blurred in shock. After the initial shock waves subsided, he immediately began searching the archives of his memory bank for the best ways to protect Rasheen, as well as for offensive tactics that could kill the contract before certain over-qualified professional killers got wind of it.

THE END

About the Author

Divine G is the real person Colman Domingo portrays in the movie Sing Sing. He was also an executive producer, co-writer, and made a cameo appearance in this Hollywood feature film. John "Divine G" Whitfield is the founder and owner of Divine G Entertainment and a founding member of Rehabilitation Through the Arts (RTA). He is a four-time PEN American Center award winning writer and the winner of the 2008 Tacenda Literary award for best play. Divine G has written over a dozen novels and screenplays, performed in countless plays, appeared as an extra in the Hollywood movie *Analyze This*, hosted his own internet radio show (*The Divine G Show*), produced, directed and starred in his debut short film (*Enigma of Love*), worked with Lil Wayne as a supervisory carpenter on his 2013 America's Most Wanted (AMW) tour, and has been quoted by the United Nations in its UN Report of the Special Rapporteur on the right of education of persons in detention (A/HRC/11/8 - 2 April 2009).

Upcoming Novels from Divine G
THE TRIALS AND TRIBULATIONS OF BISHME CARLSON

Under the pseudonym John Whitfield (In bookstores Fall 202?)

The story of Bishme Carlson is one that epitomizes a tale of a man on a noble mission. After accidentally killing his family, Bishme vows to save as many lives as he can, especially young lives from the ravaging onslaught of HIV/AIDS. He pledges to start his own AIDS Prevention Organization, but there are many unresolved matters still haunting and hindering him; the most serious of them all is he's being followed by a stalker, a mysterious man who makes clear that his intentions are malevolent. Receiving his drive, energy and iron will to succeed from a statement his four-year-old daughter bestowed upon him before dying, Bishme confronts the life-threatening trials and tribulations while a tantalizing question looms omnipotently; will he survive and accomplish his mission, or will he lose his life to a heartless foe?

FOLLOW THE SIGNS. . .

The Sequel To TGONG (In bookstores Fall 202?)

"Follow the Signs, they are everywhere" was the recurring dream world command Rayhiem Jones had been receiving all his life. In this sequel to TGONG, Rayhiem finally discovers the reason he's been experiencing the strange, recurring dreams. He was being groomed for a divine mission to save all life on the planet from a

celestial virus lodged inside a meteorite sent to Earth by the Setphian Deities.

The Ausarian Deities (the Setphian's archrivals) reveals to Rayhiem during one of his mystifying dreams that he must find the two people on the planet who has the cure within their bodies and get them to Phoenix Arizona within 13 days to make a celestial exchange or the entire planet will perish. But, Samuel Griener, the

Setphian's General on the planet, and his very powerful and wealthy subordinates have no intentions of allowing Rayhiem to succeed.